LORD OF THE CLOUDS

G.S. Lewis

FIRST EDITION

This book is a work of fiction. Names, characters, places, and incidents are either products of the author's imagination or are used fictiously. Any resemblence to actual events, locales or persons, living or dead, is entirely coincindental.

ISBN: 978-0-578-72098-2

For my mom and dad

PART I

HOTEL CALIFORNIA

1

GOLGOTHA

Albus Cake sat in his brown leather-bound office chair; the plump, familiar armrests of which were beginning to deteriorate from innumerable years of use, nylon stitching splitting apart at the seams. Creamy cottony batting imprisoned within the upholstery sent wispy white feelers shooting up through the cracks, attempting to escape back out into the wild.

Mr. Cake absently flexed and flicked his fingers through the fleeing fibers, his eyes closed. Dimpled at regular intervals into the aged leather of his chair were a number of tarnished brass tacks, serving some purpose that escaped him, decoration perhaps; most had fallen out over time.

Albus could easily afford a new chair; he just happened to really like this one. It could rock back and forth, its springs squeaking and creaking at just the right frequencies when he got anxious or needed to think deeply about something. *Can a new office chair do that?* he mused, *No, definitely not.*

There he sat in welcome solitude on the highest floor of his one-thousand story tall obsidian monolith; the back of his chair pivoted towards the entryway to his chambers. He turned to face the plate-glass windows that stretched from floor to ceiling, windows that came together at a right angle, orthogonally forming the corner of his office. Albus was overseeing the operations below; his eyes remained closed.

It really didn't matter to Albus if it was the thousandth floor or the millionth floor; to him—it was all the same. Thousandth just had a particularly commanding ring to it. If he were to tell an associate at a cocktail party that he worked in an office on the *one-millionth* floor of a monolith he had designed and built himself, they might accuse him of fibbing or hyperbole. But, if he said the thousandth floor, while that still seemed highly unbelievable—one could imagine it.

He rocked and he rocked, occasionally stopping to twist from side to side, then back to rocking. The *squeak squeak squeak* of his chair provided a rhythmic and repetitive droning to his otherwise gravely silent chamber. Albus Cake was thinking.

"Sire, your appointment…" chimed Victoria, his personal assistant, interrupting his reverie in her thick accent that was from *somewhere other than here*. Victoria was tall, very tall, as tall as she wanted to be. It was part of her contract. She had black skin, not dark brown skin. Pitch-black skin, skin so dark not even *light* could escape its gravitational pull if it made the mistake of getting too close to her. The striking darkness of her skin was incongruous with her perfectly blue eyes, no whites, no pupils, just blue, but strangely pleasant.

Albus turned slowly round in his chair to face her; each tip of his fingers pressed in tension against its opposing digit, like the cables of a suspension bridge. "Everything okay, sire…I mean, Mr. Cake?" Victoria asked in her unplaceable accent.

Long ago, Albus had abandoned his attempts to enlighten Victoria that she needn't refer to him as *sire*. He could only assume that she must just enjoy saying the word at this point. Albus leaned forward resting his elbows on his desk. His desk, like his chair, was ancient.

"Yes, Victoria. Just thinking," replied Albus. Victoria had known Mr. Cake for eons, just long enough to know when her boss was itching to pontificate on some obscure notion, but was waiting for the invitation. In some sense, it was the purpose of her existence.

"What about?" she asked.

"Just wondering if I made the right choices."

"Right? Choices?" The words were totally foreign to her. She laughed, "You crack me up, sire...err—Mr. Cake. Did you ever think about becoming a comedian?"

"No."

Victoria laughed even harder, "See!" She composed herself, shuffling the papers needlessly on her clipboard. "Your appointment, sire?"

"Send them in."

Albus leaned back in his chair clasping his hands together behind his head; he greatly admired the transcendent job his wife had done in decorating his office shortly after he had completed construction of the monolithic edifice. An interior decorator by trade, his wife spared no expense embellishing the quarters.

Dark granite walls formed the boundaries of the chamber; walls which grew upwards beyond visible recognition, fading away into a starry sky-field. Swirling celestial players drifted endlessly in the vaults. Flocks of cherub-like beings flitted about the upper echelons, occasionally breaking into song. They weren't very good at singing, because they were babies. Mr. Cake appreciated their efforts anyway.

Hung from the many stone cross beams, held aloft by massive iron chains, were enormous bowl-shaped censers smelted from precious metals like rhodium, iridium, and osmium. The hanging censers slowly burned coils of roasting frankincense and other unusual compounds, wafting electrically charged tufts of blue and pink smoke that would pirouette out of their metallic bowls like cotton candy. Occasionally, the crackling billows of galvanized, bubblegum-scented haze would converge into rainclouds dawdling about the upper reaches of the office chamber, puncturing open with little showers that would lightly sprinkle on Albus, dampening whatever he happened to be working on, though usually nothing of major importance.

Cut into the dark granite wall furthest from his desk, a

huge fireplace with an eternally roaring inferno cast its runs of yellow, orange, and red tongues, expertly bouncing the rays at right angles off the highly reflective surface of the office's black marble floor. Unfortunately, to maintain its elegant sheen, the marble floor had to be polished nightly to remove the smoldering embers expelled by the never-ending blaze, that would drift through the air helplessly turning to splats of dust on impact with the cold black marble.

Albus' desk was positioned too far away from the sputtering fireplace to garner any of its warmth-giving energy; he often found himself quite cold. His wife insisted he wear the wool sweater his mother-in-law had knitted him to combat the problem, though it never seemed to do him any good.

....

Mr. Cake glanced over at the ever-ticking clock hanging from one of the dark walls; his appointment was taking their sweet time. He could hear a loud voice flirting with Victoria right outside the door. Looking back towards the entryway, Albus thought, *This can't be good,* as a large man, with an even larger belly, and the head of an elephant sauntered into his office, in no particular rush at all. Golgotha hadn't paid Mr. Cake a visit—in the flesh—in centuries.

The mammoth man with the head of an elephant half-heartedly picked up the various baubles, curios, and idols from the shelves around Albus' office. He examined the objects, poorly feigning that they held some interest to him, setting them back down in slightly different orientations and positions from which he found them, leaving the tchotchke's dusty footprint naked and exposed.

As Golgotha turned, one of his long ivory tusks snagged on a porcelain figurine of a grieving woman holding a dying man in her arms, lopping the delicate head of the porcelain woman clean off, offering no apology. Albus cringed, but knew better than to call attention to the now decapitated figurine; he'd get Victoria to sweep up the shattered pieces later. It wasn't that the ham-fisted man ignored the incident, Golgotha was completely unaware that he had done it, as if it never happened.

Cake rose from his leather chair situated behind his desk to greet his guest. "Don't get up! Don't get up!" proclaimed Golgotha. Mr. Cake halted his upward motion in a half-standing half-crouching position, leaned over his desk, and extended his arm to shake his visitor's meaty palm. The large man enveloped the smaller man's hand tightly with both palms and squeezed; his pointed nails slathered in bright-yellow polish dug into Cake's wrist, though not intentionally, nor maliciously.

Golgotha's neon-pink skin radiated in stark contrast to the dark tones of the surrounding office. Like some jellyfish discovered on a deep-sea dive, beads of electricity and multi-hued light shot about his veins. A terrifyingly complex crystal, said to possess a truly infinite number of facets, sat between the eyes of his elephant head. Steadying himself, he wedged his portly frame into a wicker chair in front of Cake's desk that buckled some under the immense load. The two sat opposite each other. Golgotha reclined, folding his hands together on his exposed belly and extended his trunk, resting it lazily on Mr. Cake's desk with a dull thud.

"Peanut?" offered Albus.

Golgotha roared with laughter, flapping his ears, pounding his trunk against the inlaid ebony and ash finish of the desktop, with a little too much enthusiasm. Albus' 'World's Best Dad' coffee mug trembled and bounced, splashing droplets of cold coffee across the desk's checkered surface, becoming agitated to the point of diving off the edge towards the ground. In a bolt of lightning, a cherub-like being swooped down and rescued the mug moments before being dashed to pieces against the polished marble, setting it gently back in its rightful place.

"How the hell are you, Albus!?" trumpeted Golgotha.

"Oh, I'm sure you know, Golgotha, just *sublime*."

The portly elephant slowly wrapped his trunk against the ancient desktop studying the man's expression for any sign of sarcasm. Nuance and delicacy were not his greatest strengths. Over the eons he had come to realize he often missed a small inflection or evasive enunciation, failing to recognize when Albus was mocking him, which infuriated Golgotha beyond belief. However, he was experimenting at getting better. "You weren't at the Ascension Festival this year," said Golgotha with a shade of purple disappointment tinging his voice.

"Was feeling a bit under the weather for this one," replied Albus, adding a perfunctory, "your Grace."

Golgotha laughed again. "Oh Albus, you are a riot!" The elephant-headed man continued to yammer on about how utterly rapturous the Ascension Festival had been—a raucous, raging, and completely mandatory festival that he had commissioned in his own honor. Golgotha lauded the otherworldly, orgasmic lights, the supremely serene sounds, the floats, the pageantry, the endless celebrating. He divulged to Albus he had almost canceled the event one year, but people's heads would have literally exploded. He went on to claim that they enjoyed the celebration even more than he did, clamored for it, demanded it. "It's their absolute *favorite*," said Golgotha, pronouncing the word favorite with learned affect.

"My apologies," Albus genuflected. "It won't happen again."

Golgotha clicked his tongue. "No need to apologize, Albus, shit happens."

"Indeed, it does," said Cake.

The gaze of Golgotha's deeply set elephant-eyes focused out the window directly behind Albus. The gentle flapping of his ears eased then halted, hanging limply at the sides of his massive head. Absentmindedly, he picked at a fleck of gray lint from his gaping pink belly button and flicked it onto Albus' coffee-stained desk; he didn't enjoy his dependence on Albus.

Golgotha knew a great many things; for instance, he knew that he was quantifiably more omnipotent than Albus, and let's not forget more omniscient and exceedingly more omnipresent to boot. Still, there were things that Albus Cake could do that he could not; this apparent paradox irritated the elephant to no end.

Of course, Golgotha would never reveal his frustrations to

the man sitting across from him at the mundane desk in the crummy, brown leather chair. Although, he suspected Albus was aware of his ire, based on the man's less than deferential attitudes towards him, and Golgotha's ability to know everything, which only frustrated the elephant further. A pregnant pause gestated in the air. Albus decided to induce.

"Is that it then? Have you come all this way to chastise me about my truancy?"

Golgotha returned his attention away from the window to Albus, staring the man directly in the eye. Slowly, he unfolded his fat, pink fingers from his rotund, naked belly and placed his hands flat out, fingers spread wide, onto Albus' desk.

Every digit was adorned with a treasure trove of precious gemstones. Facets of quixotically cut lapis lazulis, rubies, emeralds, and ambers all glinted in the light radiating from the windows behind Albus. Straining to maintain their structural integrity against bloated fingers, the rings' platinum bands ballooned to their near breaking point. A preponderance of gold chains hung heavy around the elephant's neck, dangling with every sign, sigil, and symbol imaginable. The chains shuffled and clanged together as Golgotha leaned in, his pink belly jutting over the desk's edge. "Unfortunately...no," he said, his voice hushed to a low growl, "it seems we have a *small* problem."

Albus leaned away. The news of a problem was alarming, perhaps even morbidly exciting. Problems rarely, if ever, occurred. Golgotha ran a tight ship; there just weren't room for them anymore. Albus couldn't recall an *actual* problem occurring in ages, which only made this news that much more problematic. Golgotha continued, "We have discovered a child in the Low Place—"

"The Low Place?" spasmed Albus, interrupting. "A child!?" Doubly alarming. Albus had been under the impression that the Low Place had been vanquished; subdued for all intents and purposes. In fact, he was almost sure of it; he had been instrumental in its subjugation. The Low Place was something that they rarely spoke of these days, choosing instead to ignore the fact that it had ever existed to begin with.

Golgotha, not used to being spoken over, cleared his throat, shifted his trunk slightly to his right and continued, "—A child that will lead to the destruction of our world. Our eternal utopia that we have labored so heroically to birth."

Albus scoffed. He took no credit for their world's existence; moreover, he was no longer so certain it was the paradise he was promised. Golgotha, already running late for his afternoon tee time, had grown weary of the man and ignored the slight. "Anyway...you will descend to the Low Place and kill the little punk before it becomes a *big* problem," demanded the tyrant with the flippant sympathy of a mosh pit.

Albus' mind raced. Two toy cars, one red and one green, with friction engines went round and round on a slotted piezo-electric track, sometimes flying off at the hairpin turns. Albus knew, rather intimately, what the Low Place was like and despised it. *There has to be some way out of this*, he thought as he wracked his brain, *Why not ask one of the others, Dr. Blue? Or even that dirty rat Mr. Molehill?* They were far more qualified for this type of thing.

"Why me?"

"Because I said so."

It was hard to argue with that. Once the stubborn bull elephant had made up his mind on a matter, there was little use trying to dissuade him. Mr. Cake stalled for more time.

"And how do you know of this? This child? The destruction of our world?"

"A prophecy."

Here it comes, thought Albus. He restrained himself from rolling his eyes; his efforts were of little use. The thought had already percolated up to Golgotha's all-knowing awareness. "It is coming," riposted the elephant. "My magi have foretold it," adding with assurance, "and they are never wrong."

Golgotha employed a vast legion of seers, soothsayers, and fortune tellers to advise him; their abilities had been critical in his rise to power and the elephant trusted them without question. It wasn't that Albus doubted the providence of the magi's eerily predictive algorithms. No, he had witnessed them work first hand; it was just that after the Ascension, the future was already known. It was just *this*—for the rest of eternity. Albus eyed the fortunes and prognostications of the magi with a great deal of skepticism, wondering if they might not invent quandaries just to keep themselves gainfully employed.

Albus continued to contemplate the elephant's unsavory wishes. The request was absolutely ludicrous in a sense. There was no way (that he knew of) back to the Low Place. And even if there were some way back, it would most surely be a suicide mission. Besides, the murderous demand was far outside his purview; nowhere in his contract did it state that he had to be Golgotha's axeman, his executioner. *I'm not some heartless, cold-blooded killer.* This wasn't what he signed up for—callously murdering a hitherto innocent child. *No way.*

"I won't do it."

"So be it." Golgotha extended his pink, chunky arms for emphasis, the fat jiggling and swaying, bronze bangles jangling together. The beads of electricity pulsating just beneath his skin quickened. As he turned his head away, the horrifically complex, prismatic jewel in the middle of Golgotha's forehead grabbed hold of the singular white light-beam emanating from the window behind Albus; the crystal sprayed the beam back out in a mutilated rainbow splayed across the reflective marble floor.

The self-styled deva placed his hands on his knees and slowly rose from his seat, his lumbering frame playing catch-up. As he pivoted towards the door, he cocked his preposterous elephant head and said, "Look what I have become." With that, he turned his back on Albus and left.

Squeak squeak squeak. Mr. Cake rocked in his chair. *Shit.*

Victoria popped her head back into the office. "Everything okay, sire?" The cherub-like beings began softly cooing a song that sounded something like a funeral dirge.

"No Victoria, nothing is okay."

2

ELIXABETH

Albus Cake, being who he was, was entitled to a certain number of privileges that not all beings in his realm shared—free will being among them. He was more than allowed to refuse Golgotha's bidding and had, in fact, defied the all-powerful elephant's wishes many times throughout their complicated, eons-long relationship. It was almost a running joke between the two at this point. Although, that did not necessarily shield Albus from Golgotha's wrath.

Once again though, Albus being who he was, there was not a whole lot Golgotha could really do to punish Mr. Cake for his insubordination. Golgotha would often resort to minor annoyances to express his displeasure with the man that he relied so heavily upon. He would do things such as order gremlins to fill Albus' shoes with sand, or replace all the complimentary Oranginas in the break-room of Albus' precious monolith—with more sand. Golgotha's pranks, for some inexplicable reason, always seemed to involve sand. Albus had given up long ago on trying to pierce the inner workings of the elephantine tyrant's mind.

Albus mulled over Golgotha's cryptic last words to him: 'look what I have become.' It was true that the already powerful pink pachyderm had become even more powerful since the Ascension, standing now unopposed. Regardless, Golgotha could not violate his own rules, the rules of their world; it was demonstrably and empirically impossible. Still, Albus felt it might be wise to finish his work early for the day and head home to his beloved wife, Elixabeth, and the cloyingly bucolic cottage that they blissfully shared. As he shuffled some papers, he looked at the clock ticking away on the wall, trying to recall when he had arrived at the office; the time escaped him.

During his commute, without the distraction of his work, Albus' mind jumped from branch to branch like a monkey, chattering with distracting and unlikely scenarios. Perhaps, Golgotha would inundate his cottage with dump trucks full of sand, or fill in his cherished lake—with sand. Not the worst things in the world, Albus could remove the sand just as easily as Golgotha had placed it. Or perhaps, more likely than not, the elephant would do nothing. Distracted by other matters, he no longer seemed interested in vexing Albus these days.

Albus stepped on it, accelerating. It took him thirteen minutes and forty-eight seconds to travel from his monolithic office on Mars back to his cozy cottage. It felt like an eternity; even when moving at the speed of light, there was still a speed limit.

As he decelerated from light-speed over his cottage, he was relieved to spot his gorgeous wife below, standing at the threshold to their home, awaiting his arrival—no sand in sight. Albus touched down at the base of the rolling green hill atop which their cottage was situated.

Above him, the sky was somewhere between twilight and dusk. It was always somewhere between twilight and dusk when he arrived home; he liked it that way. The orchestra of glittering stars and violet comets had begun tuning up in the firmament, preparing for their nightly performance, while the vibrant orange and purple stains of the setting sun could still be detected reflecting off the ripples of the lake.

Licking off the face of the waters, a cool breeze rustled the overgrown cattails, pickerel weeds, and tall grasses in a shushing rattle that reassured you that everything was going to be okay in the end. Mockingbirds, robins, and thrushes that had been lovingly tweeting their songs throughout the day, bequeathed their cherished melodies to the chirping of brown crickets (*scientific name: Acheta Domesticus*), as they retired for the evening. The first stanza of the bioluminescent, binary pulse of the fireflies, *(scientific name: Photuris)*, began right on cue.

Albus bolted up mottled, moss-covered slate steps that were unevenly spaced so that he always had to pay a little more attention to not slip or stumble on them, running along the curving path cut into the hillside that snaked back and forth leading up towards the red ochre door of his modest three-bedroom cottage that was painted eggshell white, with a thatched roof of tightly bundled twigs and sticks. Poking out of the thick tresses of the roof, sprouted a beige brick chimney that often pooted out lazy, grey clouds in winter.

Safely surrounding the home, a white picket fence ensconced all manner of sunflowers, lavenders, bee balms, and toad lilies. Resting amongst the overgrown floral clumps sat a cement birdbath painted robins egg blue, inviting fowl creatures to bathe, converse, and chirp amongst themselves. The cottage was nestled deep in the deepest woods, woods that reminded Albus of his childhood in rural Maine; it sat squarely on top of a hill, the backside of which sloped down to a crystal lake of the clearest, coldest water anyone had ever encountered. It was his own little slice of heaven.

He rounded the last bend in the serpentine stone path towards his awaiting Elixabeth whose long, luxurious blonde hair, every strand accounted for, was blowing ebulliently in the breeze. She hadn't aged a day, quite literally, since relocating. Her impish smile, that went up a little higher on one side of her mouth than the other, though still every bit as beautiful, showed no cracks, no fissures, no vagaries of the passage of time.

As Albus came around the bend, the red ochre door now in sight, curiously, Elixabeth was no longer there. No sign of his wife anywhere, he would have sworn she was standing there only moments before. Confused, he assumed that perhaps she had gone back inside to start on supper. He reached out his hand and wiggled the brass doorknob back and forth. The door was locked. The door had never been locked; he didn't even own a key. Albus banged against the wooden red door and peered through the unlit windows, shouting for Elixabeth to come let him in. There was no response. His wife was *just gone*.

3

CHEAT CODES

In the long, long ago, even long before the Ascension, there existed (for a brief time) a man named Albus B. Cake. Named after his mother's favorite wizard from a beloved and classic children's book and his father's—love of cake. Albus had been employed as a chief architect at the internet technology company Google. He was the first architect to pioneer a dubious process he dubbed relocation; the unprovable, potentially unethical, and arguably supernatural process in which a person's essence—their immortal soul—was uploaded to a bank of computer servers connected to the internet, or the Cloud, as it later came to be known. With the hope or intent of the process being that one could exist in the coalescing, nebulous ether forever.

Albus had become obsessed with his research, unflinching in his belief that he was on the verge of besting humanity's oldest and most ancient nemesis: death. After a slew of failed attempts on lab rats and unwitting test subjects from within his clandestine lab, his superiors at Google began pressuring him to show results or they would pull the plug, terminating the project.

Most of his colleagues derided him as a crack-pot or dismissed the idea as utter lunacy; there was no such thing as souls, they spouted with absolute certainty. Undeterred, Albus began to postulate that for the process to be fully successful, one's physical body had to first perish, had to die.

His wife begged him to turn away from his feverish dreams, to give up on such foolishness; it was becoming unhealthy—consuming him. Only further inflamed by the naysayers and those who doubted his genius, one late night in his lab, Mr. Cake had a major breakthrough. Surrounded by snuffed cigarette butts and empty liquor bottles—in an effort to prove his point—Albus placed the cold barrel of a gun in his mouth. Without much hesitation, he pulled the trigger, and blew his brains out, splattering his gray matter across silent, brightly-lit computer monitors and open reams of notebooks.

Following the media circus surrounding Albus' untimely and highly publicized death, the Alphabet Corporation (Google's parent company) issued a press release; they promised the public they had put a halt to Mr. Cake's controversial and downright silly research project. Again and again, the mammoth conglomerate assured the public that there were no such things as souls—and even if there were—there was certainly no such way to upload them to the Cloud.

Alphabet further advised the public, warning should they receive any emails from someone claiming to be Mr. Cake, asking for their social security number so they could join him on his ethereal cloud, or begging to send him money to release him from his approximate purgatory, to delete the communications immediately. The communiques were merely scammers or Nigerian royalty attempting to exploit the man's bizarre death for their own personal gain, Alphabet claimed. Albus' suicide even became something of a meme, with hacked together images flippantly mocking the man's death replicating across the inter-webs. Google dismantled Albus' lab, ingested his esoteric research, and hermetically sealed away his reams of notebooks and equipment deep in the annals of their facilities.

However, much to his credit—Albus Cake was able to exist fully within a non-material realm...

....

Back at the scene of his cottage, entering through the screened-in backdoor, Albus searched—endlessly—for his absent wife. His mind could not accept that she could be gone. That she could evaporate into nothingness so suddenly and so thoroughly, without even a word or explanation. Not even a dramatic puff of smoke or pillar of salt left in her wake.

People weren't supposed to be able to leave, disappear, or be forgotten here. That would have defeated the whole point. Briefly, he wondered if Golgotha had something to do with it. He immediately dismissed the notion; it wasn't possible. Golgotha was incapable of making people vanish. Albus knew this beyond the shadow of a doubt; nor would the power-hungry elephant ever have allowed it.

Convincing himself that she must only be playing a game of hide-and-seek, Albus meandered between the three tiny bedrooms over and over again; he got down on hands and knees checking under the beds. Lifting the beds' ruffled skirts, hoping they didn't mind the intrusion, he glanced about amongst the poorly lit, long-forgotten detritus: a single tube sock, a bible, a child's top—no sign of his wife.

Yanking on a cord dangling from the hallway ceiling, a wooden ladder creaking forth, he ascended the ladder's rungs and scoured over the stuffy, dusty attic. An overstuffed attic that he knew Elixabeth detested and had been begging him to clean out forever, which he always balked at; he would defend himself, claiming how valuable his useless mounds of knick-knacks and memorabilia would be one day.

Wedged snuggly in their kitchen, their reproduction 1960's style refrigerator shellacked in seafoam green industrial paint, with just the right number of dings and scratches distributed about its exterior to give it character, hummed audibly as it diligently cooled a whole lotta nothing. Albus opened the door to the empty fridge, peered in at the non-existent contents, and closed it—repeatedly.

Snapping back under the force of its stiff spring, the screen door would shudder with a loud *CLAP*, as he walked out the backdoor and back in from the outdoors, so many times he lost count; expecting her to just be sitting there, her silk robe draped loosely around her body. Sitting there at the rough, round wooden table of their cozy breakfast nook, the yellowed morning light filtering in through the sluggish and uneven glass panes of their cottage's windows exposing the motes of dust attending their own private ballroom dance, a dance that he had not been invited to, a piece of undercooked toast in her hand, a bowl of steel-cut oats getting cold in front of her as the butter from grass-fed Irish cows melted into a greasy pool on top.

....

At a loss, Albus sat on the stone bench in the gardens of their cottage for several days, grasping at the bench's cold hard edge with his hands, his shoulders slumped; absently he watched the colorful birds chirp and peep as they ruffled their feathers in the shallow bath, preening themselves. He recalled Elixabeth had bought that birdbath as a crafts project and painted it robin's egg blue in their woodshed. Albus called his wife many times, but the call wouldn't go to voicemail, it wouldn't even ring; he would just hear the same three robotic tones, *bee boo beep,* indicating the call didn't go anywhere, as though the number had never existed in the first place.

His wife vanishing into thin air was inexplicable, this wasn't some errand that ran overlong or weekend girl's trip she had somehow forgotten to mention. She wasn't going to show back up in a few days' time with some wild story about her absence. She certainly hadn't been kidnapped or attacked. Crime was impossible under Golgotha's regime. Additionally, Elixabeth possessed a formidable number of powers, just like her husband—free will being among them.

A frigid sinking feeling grew within him as he wrestled with the notion that she was *just gone* and never coming back, some titanic glitch in the fabric of reality perhaps, and there was nothing he could do about it. Cumbersome clouds coalesced in the heavens above; it began to rain, heavy drops assaulting Albus. He didn't care; he sat there a while longer, catching a chill as the leaden raindrops soaked through him.

Elixabeth had been his anchor, his root, his mooring. When Albus drifted too far into the madness of this world, she always tugged him back to shore. Mr. Cake walked to the lake. Wading into the shallows, the icy water stirred all around to greet him. "Hello," whispered dampness. "Welcome," wafted wetness. Floating on his back out to the middle of the vast pool, aimlessly adrift, he let himself sink into the engulfing abyss; eventually reaching the bottom, he plopped his backside down onto the sediment-rich lakebed.

....

Exhaling his last breath, the carbon dioxide-enriched air bubbles escaped Albus' mouth, competing with one another in a race back to the surface. The bubbles zipped around and past one another in their mad dash to rejoin the atmosphere above. Bubble number three, affectionately named Carla, won. Deeply sucking in his first breath of water, some vestigial panic circled his head like a shark. Albus already knew his plan wasn't going to work; one of the burdens of immortality was being unable to die. Utterly freezing fluid permeated his being as he opened his eyes to the aqueous underworld. A school of fish swam by. *Red fish, blue fish, one fish, two fish*, he thought, as he tried to recall where he had learned that koan.

"20th Century teller of children's tales, Dr. Goose," chimed the voice of a disembodied and (supposedly) omniscient Golgotha, denying Albus the pleasure of coming up with the answer on his own, adding, "and it's One Fish, Two Fish, Red Fish—"

"Go away!" yelled Albus cutting Golgotha off. "You did this!"

"You did this," replied the pink pachyderm, mockingly.

"You're bullshit!"

"You're bullshit."

"Shut up! Just shut up!!" shouted Albus in an uncharacteristic outburst of anger that sent sonic shockwaves undulating and echoing through the water; Golgotha leered and was quiet once more. Scattering skittishly, a school of minnows darted in every direction at the unexpected commotion.

As he watched the incredible abundance of aquatic organisms passing through his vision like a watery slide show, Albus adjusted to his new life on the bottom of the lake, thinking that he may just stay there forever in self-centered exile. Mundanely minding their own business, oblivious to their new visitor's sorrow, the plethora of marine creatures went about their days: tiny fish were eaten by small fish, small fish eaten by big fish, big fish eaten by even bigger fish, and so on and so on. At some point, an opportunistic clan of zebra mussels moved into the lake and began colonizing Albus, along with algae, and various kelps using him for anchoring, while hordes of red and blue crabs dug into the silty muck beneath him, utilizing the immobile man as shelter.

Bobbing into view, *A flock? A school?* of impossibly tiny, translucent jellyfish *boing – boing – boinged* their way past the man. Albus cracked a smile, a few zebra mussels crusting off him as he did. A dim memory of the jellyfish, like flipping open a high school yearbook rotting away in an attic, flickered in his mind. He had seen them before, on a class field trip to some aquarium. He had tried to hold Anna Potato's hand on that trip; she promptly pulled it away. *Clione limacina. Sea Angels,* thought Albus, recalling the scientific name of the jellyfish.

The sea angels had cutesy little wings on each side of their translucent bodies that fluttered as they swam. Their luminous, internal organs were visible to the outside world; as to what role the glowing organelles played in keeping the jellyfish alive, Albus had no idea, but they resembled pulsating fuchsia hearts cribbed off the cover of a sappy Valentine's Day card.

The overwhelming permutations of purpose, form, and color of the lifeforms moving through the waters, was at the very least *impressive*, thought Albus. Leaning in a little closer, crabs scuttling out from under him, Albus could hear the flock of sea angels gloriously singing as they swam; their teensy voices raised up a chorus praising all of creation.

....

Around this time, another curious creature was floating across the aqueous membrane of the lake. The orange and black speck-led cheetah-man, Cheshire Cheato, (or just Chet for short), decked out in nothing but jet-black shades, lazily backstroked across the water's surface. Much to his own amusement, Chet would siphon gulps of cool, microbe-rich water into his mouth; pursing his lips together, he would then spurt the water out spraying little fountains into the air. As Chet ejaculated another fountain, he happened to spot a mollusk-encrusted man sitting cross-legged on the lakebed beneath him. Seizing on the op-portunity, Chet hollered a piercing *AAA-OOOWWGA* like a submarine announcing its descent, as he leapt into the air with a swan dive, plunging beneath the surface, cheetah paddling his way towards Albus.

"My radical bro-man dude!" exclaimed Cheshire Cheato, appearing in front of Albus. Chet's voice took on the timbre of Macho Man Randy Savage, crowing, "Have a little *taste* of my gnarly Scaldin' Hot, Chicken Nugget Cheese-Os bursting with Ranch Sprinkles, Chipotle Flavor Nards, and Signature Honey Smoked Semen Sauce™!" Chet offered, popping a few of the Cheese-Os into his own mouth, tilting the open sack of snacks towards Albus.

Albus had never met Chet in-person; however, he knew who he was. The cheetah-man was another one of Golgotha's lackeys, his Archduke of Advertising, his Herald of Hype, that ruled over the vast marketing and sales dominion of the almighty elephant's ever-growing empire. The cheetah prided himself on two things: crafting tantalizing treats and always sealing the deal.

Shaking his head as zebra mussels clacked together, Albus politely declined Chet's cheesy offer. Flustered by the refusal of this barnacle-bedecked chump before him, the cheetah-man growled, "These Cheese-Os are lit!" baring his formidable in-cisors one by one as his lips curled upwards into a supine smile.

Determined to get his slightly curved snack inside this bi-valve bro's mouth, Chet pressed his crinkled foil bag into Albus' chest, as water-logged Cheese-Os floated freely into the abyss.

Even snack foods obeyed the rules. Ranch sprinkles studded about the Cheese-O sparkled unnaturally in the dim light as the signature semen sauce dissolved into a milky-white aura surrounding the snack.

Whereas others might have felt compelled by the cheetah's domineering persistence, Albus knew the twat was nothing more than a puffed-up nuisance. Again, Albus politely declined.

Chet slowly raised his jet-black sunglasses in disbelief, as they floated away off his head. No one had ever turned him down in all his existence. The brittle foundation of the cheetah-man's solitudinous fortress of hyper-inflated, alpha-machismo, constructed entirely on his ability to always seal the deal, was crumbling down all around him. He was shaken to his very core by how flippantly this clam-covered freak had declined his divinely beguiling cheesy ambrosia. Chet hightailed it out of there, his tail between his legs; he motorboated his way across the lake to seek out Golgotha and tattle.

Snapped back to the scene around him by the off-putting encounter with the overly pushy cheetah creature, Albus looked down at his clammy hands; it dawned on him how quite ridiculous it all was, really.

....

The gloomy clouds hanging oppressively over the body of water started to dissipate, as the clear sanitizing light of acceptance began to filter its way down to the dim, murky lakebed, willfully pressing itself in upon Albus. The Elixabeth he had known was gone and never coming back. The love of his life had disappeared, vanished, dematerialized without a word. *She's just gone.* His only choice was to accept it. His lovingly preserved and carefully maintained world had changed.

Albus frowned, shaking his head; he found himself wondering again if he had made the right choices. Wallowing in exile on the bottom of a lake wasn't going to answer that question. Standing, he shook and plucked the invasive mussels off of him, ripping and grasping at the kelp affixed to him, yanking it off; he kicked towards the surface and swam back to shore. Heading back towards his cottage he thought, perhaps, it was time he made some changes of his own.

Cleaning out the attic first, he stuffed stuffed animals bereft of love, Beanie Babies stripped of value, and souvenirs from locales he no longer recalled, into overflowing plastic garbage bags. In his den, Albus rummaged through antiquated filing cabinets that had been passed down from his father. Shaking out the contents of yellowed manila folders, graph-paper scrawled with incorrect calculations, crumpled love notes, belated birthday cards, and other parched pieces of parchment, flooded forth flapping to the ground, inundating the varnished wood floor in disarray.

Sifting through mounds of desiccated documents, newspaper clippings with their dates missing, receipts for items rotting away in a landfill, and take-out menus from restaurants that now sold shoes, attentively Albus procured rectangular index cards from the mess, collecting and sorting the cards into neat little stacks. The stiff, white cards were punched through with incomprehensible blocky symbols. Meticulously, Albus scanned through the hole-punched pieces of paper, compiling his timecards.

To his astonishment, he discovered that he had worked, in some form or fashion, every single day since relocating, even when lounging with Elixabeth at their cottage on weekends or taking his geriatric dog, Argus, for walks around the lake.

It should be noted that Albus Cake wasn't the type of man that worked for the money. In fact, money didn't exist here; well it did, but it was used mostly ironically, streets of gold, props in rap videos, that sort of thing. No, Albus Cake was a man that worked for the sheer pleasure of having something to do. The only real currencies left were time and space.

Maybe I need a vacation, he mused, clear his head, take his mind off of everything. Some time away would do him good, bring into focus the aforementioned nebulous changes he intended to make. His head knew that his wife was gone, though his heart still desperately longed for her, further deluding himself into believing that perhaps he would find some clue to her disappearance on his travels.

Riffling back over his timecards, he counted; he had accrued 3,141,592 days, six hours, five minutes, three seconds, five deciseconds, eight centiseconds, nine milliseconds, seven microseconds, nine nanoseconds, three picoseconds, two femtoseconds, three attoseconds, eight zeptoseconds, four yoctoseconds, and so on, and so on, of vacation time. *Not bad*, Albus thought, *I deserve this.*

Penning a hand-written note, should Elixabeth magically return in his absence (a note, that deep down, he knew his wife was never going to read), he pinned the missive to the door of their humming refrigerator held in place with a magnet of the Eiffel tower, a souvenir from their last trip to Paris together. The note read:

> *Lixa,*
>   *Love you to Mars and back.*
>   *Be home soon.*
>
>   *Eternally yours,*
>
>   *A.B.C.'*

....

In the cottage's master bedroom Albus clicked the strap of his stylish, tri-color fanny pack into place around his waist. He filled Argus' bowl with an indeterminate quantity of kibble as he scratched the ruddy, tired dog about his neck, saying his goodbyes to the nearly deaf hound. Argus forlornly lifted his exhausted head from his chewed-through pillow, beholding his master with cataract-caked puppy dog eyes one last time. As Albus made his way towards the backdoor of his idyllic haven, he took one last look over his right shoulder—and left.

4

GENJI

Sometime later, but really not that much later at all, Albus touched down in the disorienting, scathingly-bright mega-metropolis of Neo Tokyo. There is always a Neo Tokyo in these sorts of things. He spent the next several hours helplessly swept about the streets suffocated by soaring skyscrapers and towering high-rises on all sides, as he fought against drowning beneath the churning river of Neo Tokyo's citizens flooding through the metropolis.

On the surface, everything appeared exactly the same as when he had traveled to the island nation so long, long ago with Elixabeth; although, at the same time, so drastically different. He couldn't quite put his finger on it. Perhaps it was because, on this journey, he was completely alone.

As he grasped onto a railing to prevent himself from being carried away by the throng, he briefly wondered if his brilliant idea of taking a vacation had been a misguided folly. It had been longer than he could remember since he had ventured from his monolithic office or the safety of their cottage, all on his lonesome.

However, there was some shred of saving grace What they often fail to mention, is that there is always a Neo Kyoto (in these sorts of things), as well. Recalling this fact as he became increasingly lost to the crush of Neo Tokyo, Albus opted to set his sights on the quaint, laid-back city of Neo Kyoto, the city that at one time served as the neo historical capital of the island nation.

With a plan now in place, Albus let go of the railing and allowed himself to be carried along by the herd of hustle and bustle until he eventually washed up at a train station. At first, he intended to board the Neo Shinkansen, an absurdly high-speed bullet train, to his destination, when he spotted an offbeat passenger bus bounce into the depot advertising 'Neo Kyoto,' in bright letters scrolling across its marquee. Given that time was most certainly not of the essence, the infinitely slower and arguably more pedestrian coach, would do just fine.

He flopped his backside down into a worn-out seat, the frayed upholstery splitting some at the seams, vaguely reminiscent of his favorite chair. The bus chugged and slogged along the highways, at times rambling through the backroads of the neo countryside. It would make frequent stops, coming to a jarring halt to deposit decrepit passengers, only to refill itself with more decrepit passengers.

Albus didn't mind the excruciatingly slow pace one bit. He was more than happy to gaze out the greasy windows, getting lost in thought as he watched the spinning zoetrope of neo farmers and neo fishermen go about their livelihoods. Jostled from his pastoral daydreams, the voice of the anonymous bus driver crackled over the intercom. The coach had reached its final stop, coming to rest at Neo Kyoto Station.

....

He stretched his legs and arched his back some before disembarking. At first glance, Albus thought Neo Kyoto looked exactly like Paleo Kyoto, only brighter. The whole city seemed to glow with a certain otherworldly irradiance. Again, he felt that odd juxtaposition of alien familiarity creeping over him. He had memories of being in Kyoto from long, long ago, however, something was different this time, not in the buildings nor the people, something unplaceable, something was missing.

Relieved to find his new destination far less oppressive than Neo Tokyo, he quashed the strange feeling and made his way from the station, strolling down the uncrowded, luminous streets towards the Neo Kamo River.

Crossing over the enigmatically sublime river that cut through the center of the city, walking over a wood-slatted bridge, Albus halted in the middle for a moment; he looked on wistfully. As he rested his forearms on the railing watching the scene before him, a flock of noble ducks deigned to descend from the sky realm; slowing the beating of their wings, they crash-landed with a splash into the languidly flowing river. Tipping their tail feathers skyward, the noble ducks plunged their hungry beaks beneath the water to greedily devour prepubescent minnows and adolescent tadpoles too green around the gills to know better than to swim that close to the sun.

Not far in the distance, neo children played and hopped along the slick gray stones that crisscrossed the shallow, slow-moving river. Gripping pine-handled nets, they swung away wildly at all sorts of insects and critters. The children reveled in the nascent, unencumbered delights of youth, every catch netting discoveries the world had yet to see.

One boy, of five and a half, swung his net far too eagerly at a turquoise dragonfly, (*scientific name: Anisoptera*), in his efforts to befriend the insect. As he swung, the stiff edge of the net's wire-rim collided with the flying insect's neck, slicing the dragonfly's head clean from its torso like a guillotine—sending the elements cascading to the ground in two opposite directions: he was a murderer. The irreversible impermanence of the boy's own existence was laid bare at his feet in that moment. The boy cried. Albus moved on.

....

On the other side of the bridge, a street vendor pressed a folded brochure printed on high-gloss card stock into Albus' hand as he passed, lettering across the top read, "Dumb Tourist's Guide to Neo Kyoto." Albus nodded, exchanging a grab-bag's worth of silver and copper yen pieces from his fanny pack in a quantity he hoped was sufficient for the guide. The vendor grinned broadly, quickly heading off in the other direction.

Thumbing through the full-color images of various attractions, the sheen of the glossy paper shimmered some; he searched for the location of the Fushimi Inari Taisha Shrine, a well known religious site Albus had always longed to visit.

A sprawling collection of smaller shrines situated along the sides of a sacred mountain, networked together in a web of winding paths, the revered site was dedicated to foxes, *or is it rice? Or the ancestors?* Anyway, it was one of those things.

Somewhat troublingly, he could not locate the mountainous shrine complex listed anywhere on the brochure's map. In its place, he found a site called the Fukushima Inari Daiichi Shrine. The name was similar, though different enough to give him pause.

He contemplated querying Golgotha for the source of the discrepancy; they had not spoken since his outburst on the lake bottom. *No*, he had to do this on his own. *I must have just had the name wrong this entire time*, he concluded.

Hailing a taxi awash in a lambent aura, he pointed to the shrine, exaggeratedly tapping the location on his shiny map. The cabby courteously nodded in understanding. Arriving at his destination sometime later, he exited the cab and set out at the base of the sacred mountain.

....

Albus hiked up the trails of the impressive Fukushima Inari Daiichi Shrine. Large, ceremonial torii gates, twice as tall as a tall man, straddled the dirt paths. Made from two upright posts lacquered in bright neon-scarlet paint, the ritualist structures pulsed from within with the same unexplainable glow as the rest of Neo Kyoto; the two posts joined at the top by a flared, intricately carved headpiece.

The endless cavalcade of neon torii, like two mirrors forced up against one another, appeared to extend infinitely in equal but opposite directions. It was quite probable that they did.

Etched individually into each torii were a dizzying multitude of charcoal black symbols and lettering. Albus could have chosen to stop and read each and every one, but decided to leave it a mystery. It was a tale for another time. Instead, he grew a nice bushy fox tail and swished it back and forth. He had heard all the kids were doing it, *so why not?* Just as quickly as he had grown it, he felt embarrassed by his tail; he was a lot older than the kids, after all. As easily as he had sprouted it, he chopped his tail off. It wriggled helplessly on the ground before transforming into a frog, hopping away.

....

Along the winding web of trails, occasionally a small shrine would pop into view, branching off the main path, erected to honor some important ancestor or beseech the powers-that-be for wild riches. Albus strolled past most, casually taking them in. For reasons unknown to his conscious narrative (which had been playing on loop longing memories of his vanished wife), he halted his trek in front of a pavilion covering an innocuous altar. Perhaps he just needed a moment to rest.

Swaying white pines and omnipresent bamboo sprouting up in every direction, reaching for the stars, bordered the average-looking shrine located on the northern side of the mountain, nestled amongst upright cairns, trickles of water running down from an unknown source. Moss-covered stone lanterns dotted the shrine in some configuration impenetrable to Albus, but surely it had some meaning, some purpose. They did not get there by accident.

Four trunk-sized posts, lacquered with the same neon-scarlet paint of the torii gates, supported the swooping black-tiled roof of the shrine's pavilion giving cover to a small stone altar. Suspended in the rafters of the pavilion hung a trapezoidal bronze bell; a long red cord dangled down from its hinges.

An unexceptional chest made of kiri wood rested atop the plain altar; joined without nail or screw, lovingly crafted dovetail joints held the box together. Blotches of taupe wood-mold and mildew had begun to reclaim the exterior of the innocent chest.

Sitting in front of the altar, slotted coin containers solicited donations from Neo Shintoists and clueless tourists alike, taking in easy money.

Against his better judgment, Albus procured a yen piece from his stylish fanny pack and dropped it between the slots of one of the containers, the coin rattling as it fell, landing with a *kerplunk*. Observing the custom of the Neo Shintoists, after depositing his monetary offering, Albus rang the bronze bell by giving a tepid tug on the limply hanging cord. Examining the cord more closely in his hand, he observed it was more of a carnelian color, soft to the touch, braided together from an abundance of fine threads.

The bell tolled three times as the hammer oscillated against its bronze sides, the volume decaying with each ping or pong as the seesawing motion of the bell slowed on its hinges, returning to rest. The metallic chiming ran off, joining forces with the sublime whistling wind. Bringing his hands together, Albus did a small bow purely out of courtesy.

Without warning, the lid of the kiri wood chest sprang open with a loud *THWAP*. A dazzling array of laser-light shot out of the open box, sending brilliant beams of solid colors strafing through the air: reds, blues, and greens. The beams bounced off the interior of the pavilion and its supporting posts. As the atomic colors of the lasers intersected one another, more hues burst into existence at their junctions. A round puff of smoke billowed from the open box to better highlight the impressive laser light show.

What have I done now? Albus wondered. Appearing out of nowhere at the center of the lighted display a furled, blurry blob streaked with orange and white hues, spun rapidly in place. As the lasers homed in on the energetically gyrating orb, it began to slow, proceeding to unravel, popping out first a pair of arms, then legs, and finally its head, revealing a translucent fox-like creature with the hands of a human.

"TA-DA!" the fox said, levitating in the space above the stone altar. Albus stared hesitantly, unsure if the semitransparent fox expected him to applaud or not. "Hiya! I'm Genji," the float-ing fox-spirit yipped as it slowed, doing one final spin in place.

"Hello, Genji. I'm Albus," said Albus in a deflated tone. The two strangers continued to look at one another, while Genji bobbed in the air like a fishing lure on the surface of a choppy lake, performing backflips and overly exaggerated gestures, tossing up peace signs and karate chops to an invisible audience. Albus wondered if he deposited more money into the coin con-tainer, would the fox creature go away? *Can I force the lid to his box closed?*

Genji continued to emote as he defied gravity, pantomiming an electric slide. Albus pursed his lips together in a semi-frown. At a loss, "Alright, I'll be going then," he said, offering an awk-ward half-wave from the hip. Albus turned away from the pa-vilion and departed, continuing his trek along the mountainous path. Genji obediently followed. Albus, mid-stride, looked back over his shoulder and said, "Please stop following me."

"I can't!" replied Genji.

"And why not?"

"Because," said Genji, "I'm the plucky and lovable sidekick, silly! I'll be the Toto to your Dorothy, the Mushu to your Mulan, the Donkey to your Shrek!" squealed the fox excitedly, bringing his fur-covered hands together, squeezing and interlocking his fingers.

Albus did not understand any of these apropos and clever cultural references; they were from before his time. The mute expression on his face remained unchanged. He turned fully to face Genji. The persnickety and somewhat annoying fox-spirit was clearly not getting the message. Placing his hands firmly on his hips, he glanced towards the ground then back up again, exhaling an obvious and exasperated breath. "Look, you seem like a really nice fox-spirit," barked Albus, "but I don't need a sidekick, spirit guide, life debt, best friend, love interest, distant father figure, or any of that! I'm perfectly fine just being alone." He crossed his arms and huffed.

The harsh rebuttal knocked some of the wind out of Genji's

sails; however, his resolve to become a permanent fixture in this man's life (a man he had met not five minutes ago) remained no less abated. "Aw come on! Pwweeease mister. I don't want to go back in there," Genji begged, apprehensively pointing back at the coffin-like wooden box, adding with timid resignation, "it's dark in there." The fox-spirit tossed himself to his knees, dramatically clasping his hands together in prostration, throwing himself at the mercy of Albus.

"Sorry, kid. Tough," said Albus trying to come off like a gruff and tumble cowboy. "Maybe next time, pardner."

With Albus' rebuff, a coiling onyx vortex snaked out from the box, tendrils surrounding and engulfing Genji. Ethereal dark hands reached from the vortex grasping at the fox, pulling him away, back towards his unceasing confinement. Genji furiously paddled against the current with his adorable little hands in an effort to escape its gravitational pull. He paddled more and more frantically the closer he was dragged back to his wooden chest. It was no use; like Elixabeth he was gone, into nothingness, sucked back into the box atop the altar from whence he came.

At least, that's what Albus wished had happened. "Hah! Too bad," shrieked Genji maniacally, "them's the rules!" adding with some sense of self-satisfaction, "You're stuck with me forever! Like glitter or mental illness!!"

"Alright then," Albus deeply sighed, "just try to keep up."

"You're the boss! Where to?"

"Udon?"

"Yummy!" Genji did a backflip and made finger guns at the sky.

....

The newly acquainted pair meandered the luminous streets of Neo Kyoto, passing by phosphorescent electronics kiosks and neo elderly citizens flashing bright toothless grins, on a hunt for the best udon in town.

Genji bobbed along behind Albus' right shoulder, sometimes halting to sniff at the eternally blooming sakura blossoms, other times bounding ahead to yap after a hopping frog or scurrying bug, but always catching back up to Albus. The floating fox-spirit blabbered Albus' ear off about nothing in particular, spectacularly managing to never say anything of consequence, occasionally stopping to point out some of his favorite udon eateries. Albus would shake his head and they would continue their hunt.

They hooked a left down a shady path. Up ahead, partially obscured by a lustrous vending machine, Albus spotted the now familiar figure of an orange and black speckled cheetah-man. Thankfully, Cheshire Cheato was preoccupied, forcefully pressing a young man's head into a dirty trash can while he crammed artificially cheese-flavored mouthfuls of puffed-corn down the innocent victim's throat. Genji began to involuntarily growl at the figure. Chet looked up from his handiwork, spying Albus in the distance; the cheetah-man pointed two clawed fingers at his own sunglass-veiled eyes, then reversed the gesture pointing one finger in Albus' direction.

"Not this way," said Albus. Backtracking their steps, the man and fox hung a right, a right, then another right.

Genji's snout suddenly shot into the air as he became enslaved to animated scent lines wafting his way, forming a seductive come-hither motion. He began to drift in their direction, mesmerized. Albus grabbed the fox-spirit by the tail, yanking him out of his trance.

"I know this place!" Genji yapped excitedly. "They have the best udon in town!"

"If you say so."

....

They approached a ramshackle restaurant that looked as though it had been constructed from the remnants and scraps of other restaurants, plastered in the patina of a ridiculously oversized neon sign, twice the size of the eatery itself. The sign flashed "Best-Udon-In-Town," in bright red neon—on and off again.

Neon was seriously big business in Neo Kyoto. A large cartel, called the Neon Bandits, regulated and enforced all neon signage throughout the city. They imposed minimum size requirements for all signs, with no maximum, the bigger the better. In fact, the larger and more garish the neon sign one purchased for their establishment, ensured the less likelihood of the Neon Bandit's gang burning it to the ground.

Albus slid the wonky bamboo screen door along its tracks, requiring more effort than he had anticipated. Ducking slightly, he entered. Genji followed behind. Inside the cramped dining room, a table to the left was open; they made their way towards it. Other patrons politely pretended not to notice the outsiders and hid their disdain behind their menus. Before Albus could sit and get his legs fully crossed beneath the low table, an elderly woman with the face of a frog barreled through an irregularly stained curtain with a daisy floral print split down the middle. Swinging a broom wildly in Genji's direction, she shouted, "Shoo! Shoo!! He's not welcome here! He's a demon!"

Genji nimbly dodged the athletically arcing swings of her broom, darting, leaping to and fro; he paused for a moment, hovering in front of another diner's face. The froggy woman, singularly focused on the flying fox, swatted the unsuspecting diner square upside the head. The thundering strike sent the patron's thin-rimmed glasses sailing through the air tumbling tumultuously into his companion's soup bowl, ejecting noodles and broth that splashed against a wall with a wet sound, like guts hitting pavement. Genji couldn't help but snicker. The broom-struck diner apologized profusely to the matron for getting in her way.

As she continued to chase, indiscriminately swinging at the fox dancing about her dining room, she knocked over dozens of hand-thrown clay sake jugs, bowls, and china, sending plates and glassware clattering to the floor, sweeping entire tables clean. This nonsense had gone on long enough; it was left to Albus to take control of the chaos. He intercepted the broom's wooden handle mid-swing with his open palm held outright and explained, "Ma'am, he's not a demon. Just a giant pain."

"I don't care. I know him. Not allowed here," she croaked.

"Ma'am, he is my guest."

The matron narrowed her froggy eyes towards Albus and harrumphed, *play the guest card, will he?* Deflated but not defeated, she retreated back towards the stained daisy curtains guarding her kitchen. Parting them with her broom handle held in front of her, scowling, she disappeared.

The other patrons looked on in silence making a genuine effort to remain composed as they collected their cups and dining-ware from the floor as if nothing had happened. Re-setting their own tables, their bowls and glassware empty, they politely feigned as if they were still eating—scooping up spoonfuls of nothingness. Smiling, they continued their hushed conversations with their dining partners.

The frog matron had lived in Neo Kyoto all her life. In fact, she grew up right there in the waters of the Neo Kamo River, dodging greedy ducks and carnivorous fish until she got big enough to follow her dreams and open up her very own udon shop; she was a hometown girl through and through. She returned from the kitchen, backing through the threshold, the worn curtains swishing aside and draping off her shoulders. Turning in place, she revealed a tray set with two fresh bowls of udon soup. Graciously, she placed the bowls in front of the man and fox; she readjusted the ceramic vessels ever so gently, ensuring her new guests saw how preciously she was attending to them.

Bowing deeply—far more deeply than either of them ever deserved, not even if they had rescued a thousand orphans from a thousand burning orphanages—she practically folded herself in half. At the perigee of her bow, a devious smile crept across her frog lips; her revenge was at hand. She had bestowed the man and fox-spirit with her *ugliest* soup bowls, each marred with a noticeable crack in its lip: but not in a pleasing Wabi-sabi sort of way. When they caught sight of the fissured imperfection, the outsiders would surely be beside themselves; the shame and dishonor they had brought upon their own heads, at her doing, would haunt the echoes of their minds for all eternity.

Albus wasn't particularly hungry. Staring down into the

brown and yellow glazed bowl, failing to notice the cracked lip whatsoever, he got lost in the hypnotic perturbations of the milky broth. Particulate matter formed and reformed, swirling galaxies came together and dissipated just as quickly as they had coalesced. The soup was starting to look somewhat appetizing. A thin slice of a white saucer-shaped thing with spiked edges and wonky pink swirl in its center, (which Albus was pretty sure was called a fish-cake), cruised along through the broth on its own power, evading green scallion asteroids; it was the last surviving spaceship of a dying race desperately speeding to bring their seed-children to a new, verdant world.

Thick, round wheat noodles roiled over and around each other, forming the lattice structure giving shape to this otherwise unknowable and chaotic universe in his bowl. The noodles stared back up at him from their primeval broth: they begged to be taken to their final destination, to be released from the torture of their existence.

Maybe he could eat.

....

Albus armed himself with a spoon in his left-hand, chop-sticks in his right; like a drunken dock-worker, he craned the noodles into his mouth, relieving the latest barge to arrive in port of its overloaded cargo. The soup was already cold. However, Genji was right; this really was the best udon in town. It was nice to know those things for certain. When Albus looked up to let the fox know as much, the strange creature already had the bowl cupped to his snout, slurping away at the remnants of broth. Genji, also blissfully ignorant to the tiny crack, caught sight of Albus glaring at him over the lip of his chipped bowl.

"So. Fill me in," quipped Genji, draining the last drops of soup into his foxy mouth. "Where are we at on our quest?"

"I'm not on a quest," replied Albus, "I'm on vacation." Albus further explained that he had taken a sabbatical from work for personal reasons; he had been mulling over some changes he intended to make. Before he could elaborate on the details, Genji began to rapidly fire.

"A vacation?" the fox said, spraying bullets of broth onto the table. "What's on the ol' itinerary then? What's the plan, Kazakhstan? Visit the Shrieking Molehills of Marduk? Dip your toes in that puddle? Chase the World's Largest Prairie Dog off of that I-70 pit stop—"

"Figure first, I'll do a little sight-seeing," said Albus halting the barrage, noodles protruding from his churning maw, gleefully accepting their utter destruction; their purpose fulfilled they could reach noodle nirvana with zero karma. Following that, as casually as one might mention popping over to the corner bodega for a refreshing Orangina and an at-home pregnancy test, Albus added with aplomb, "Then kill Golgotha."

Coming from nowhere and everywhere, "Not possible!!" Golgotha's discarnate voice derisively boomed in response, brutally echoing off the dining room walls, violently shaking tables and chairs. Genji went pale as a ghost; had his mouth still been full of broth, he would have done a spit-take. His ugly udon bowl, equally shocked, escaped its master's grasp falling to the hard bamboo floor. The bowl landed with its vulnerable crack hitting the ground first, absorbing the brunt of the impact; shockwaves reverberated back through the porcelain structure emitting an inaudible *wom wom wom* frequency as it broke apart against the floor, fracturing into one thousand six hundred and eighteen pieces.

At the peal of Golgotha's thunderous bombardment, the remaining diners' craniums rapidly expanded like latex balloons in the hands of an overzealous clown; then burst, their heads exploded spectacularly, splattering brain bits and viscera across the dining room—coating the walls, floor, and ceiling. As if for dramatic effect, a loose eyeball streamed through the air and landed in Albus' soup with a dainty plop. As it bobbed to the surface of the broth the ocular orb rotated to look Albus right in the eye; its black pupil still fully dilated from its owner's last moments of inexplicable shock.

Albus had known Golgotha for a very long time and was not in the least perturbed by the diva deva's temper tantrum; he didn't even feel much remorse for the now headless patrons of the udon eatery; they had made their own choices to be here. Mucking about for his white linen napkin cowering somewhere underneath the entrails, as he lifted it, he saw that the virginal cloth had become a casualty of the outburst as well. It was a bright-red sopping mess, dripping with blood.

"Or die trying!" Albus defiantly shouted back, wiping the sticky gore and guts off his face with his bare hands.

The frog matron, that had been crouching behind a washtub at the far reaches of her kitchen, rocking herself back and forth, anxiously anticipating the moment her victims would discover the onerous crack in their unsightly bowls—mistook the commotion for the wails and shame-fueled laments of her two targets. Excitedly, she hurried through the stained curtains one final time, wooden broom in her clutches, to savor her glorious moment of triumph.

"Also not possible!!" thundered Golgotha's voice yet again, in response to Albus' blasphemous needling. The frog matron's head exploded.

"We should probably go," said Albus. Genji nodded mutely and followed after Albus out of the udon shop.

5

URUK

The pair left the udon shop and walked on, or floated on in Genji's case. They walked west for a long time, a very long time. There was probably an endless desert involved at some point, but it was hard to say for certain. It was difficult to tell if they were actually even moving at all, or if they were standing still and the scenery around them morphed and colluded against them, like the waxy, red blobs of a lava lamp.

They became an antique Motorola AM radio sitting on the living room dinette, its dials rotated and tuned to various frequencies. The music changed, they remained static. Backdrops of locales they passed devolved into the appearance of an early Flintstones cartoon with the same Bronto Burger, bubbling tar pit, and lumpy stone house, repeated on loop—with the hope that the audience would be paying more attention to the antics of the characters.

"Can we rest for a minute?" piped Genji, "I'm getting blisters!"

"You don't even walk!"

"I still get blisters though!"

Albus didn't get blisters; he could walk forever. Walking was one of the few joys left in his life; it was when he did some of his best thinking. Genji lucked out though and happened to catch the man at a moment when his mind was disconcertingly blank. Taking in his surroundings, Albus had no idea where he was and no idea where he was going. However, he was most certainly not lost. He had hoped that if he kept walking long enough, the pesky fox-spirit would grow bored and ditch him—no such luck. Lacking an arguably sound reason to deny Genji's request, Albus acquiesced and halted in his tracks.

In the near distance, a flat and dusty-looking walled city rose from the desert like unleavened bread; the shimmery haze of the sun's rays attempted to coax the city further along in its baking process, to no avail. Seeing nothing else of interest in sight, Albus changed headings and plotted a course for the squat settlement. As it came closer to greet them, Albus observed that the city was built from beige clay bricks bleached white by the sun, and roughly hewn stones, stacked unceremoniously one on top of the other. An unimpressive gate wide enough for two people to squeeze awkwardly through rubbing shoulder-to-shoulder was the only visible entrance. The gate's double wooden doors, composed of poorly lashed sticks, branches, and twigs, were sealed shut.

They approached cautiously. On one side of the gate, tacked into the beige brick wall, was a crudely painted sign consisting of a red circle with a slash cutting through a sophomoric image of a cheetah-man in sunglasses. "Good a place as any," said Albus, walking up to the gate, his fist clenched, poised to knock.

Before his knuckles could make contact with the gnarled wood, a man that had been watching their approach perched atop the rampart, leapt down, landing straight as a stick in front of Albus and Genji. The impact crater sent a plume of dust radiating outwardly from the man's shiny, shiny, shiny boots of leather. The travelers' path was blocked.

....

An emaciated black man with white skin, skin that had been bleached white to the bone, not unlike the bricks of the city he guarded, stood motionless before them, his head cocked towards the ground. Albus looked the ghoulish man up and down, getting the measure of him. A sable gambler-style cowboy hat with a broad, perfectly flat brim, rested atop the skeletal gatekeeper's crown, two round silver pieces tucked into the hat's black leather band. The black hat sat squarely on the skeleton-man's head, requiring no re-adjustment, despite his leap from the ramparts.

A tunic made of tanned black leather, buttoned to the neck with ivory buttons, covered his gaunt torso, an outline of ribs poking out from beneath. Black leather pants held up by a cobra-skin belt—clasped with a pewter belt buckle engraved with a confederate flag, kept the pants hugged tightly against an anorexic waist. The skeleton-man possessed a finely-made acoustic guitar slung across his narrow back, its neck pointing downwards. An aged strap made of (*you guessed it*) black leather supported the instrument.

Slowly, the black and white skeleton-man raised his head to look at them, joints moving as if animated from above, a marionette on a string not privy to its next movement. With an unspoken word, the guitar whooshed silently on its own accord under the crook of the man's arm, settling in front of him into its well-worn position.

Four underfed vultures circling overhead descended one by one, momentarily blotting out the sun with their flight path, straining out their clawed talons to find some foothold in the decaying beige bricks of the ramparts. They took turns stretching and retracting their haggard wings, revealing their impressive spans, as they settled in for their performance, not making a sound.

Five skeletal fingers of the gatekeeper found their place on the guitar as easily as one finds themselves at the end of their life with nothing to show for it; without hesitation his digits deftly plucked the instrument like a cosmic loom, weaving together vibrations into an aural tapestry.

Six superstrings undulated a melody with which the very fabric of spacetime coalesced around, demanding—with the authority of a judge—that order be brought forth from the din of primordial chaos. For a moment, the multi-colored braids of Indra's jewel-net were made visible. Lifting their voices, the vultures, which had remained silent up to this point, each cawed a singularly sustaining frequency in sequence:

440 Hz

523.5 Hz

629.25 Hz

783.99 Hz

The sonic display would have ruined most men, including Albus, if Albus had been paying attention. Between the screech of the second and third vulture, he had become distracted by a feather shed by one of the birds, languishing in the dust in front of him. Albus bent down to the ground to retrieve it. Crouching, he examined it closely, running his fingers along the vanes.

His performance concluded, "Password," rasped the skeleton-man in a hollow voice.

Jamming the tip of his thumb against the pointy end of the feather's quill, *Ouch*, Albus was still distracted by the feather, it was sharper than he thought. Microscopic six-legged bugs, that Albus would never know the names of, crawled up and down the barbs of the vanes living out the entire drama of their lives on this one feather; he couldn't help but wonder what kinds of bugs lived on the backs of those bugs. From his peripheral vision, he became aware that Genji was glowering at him. *Did someone just ask a question?* replaying the tape in his mind, *Ah, password.* He stashed the black and white vulture feather in his fanny pack and stood slowly.

Looking over at Genji, Albus shrugged and said, "I don't think we've got one," his mind still occupied by that damn feather. The skeletal gatekeeper remained firmly planted while the vultures jostled and shuffled against each other in anticipation of their next meal.

Genji threw up his arms and exclaimed in exasperation, "I guess I've gotta do everything around here!" Getting down on all fours, the fox-spirit hoovered in a deep breath, huffing and puffing his white, furry chest hair out. When it looked as though he would surely pop like a pufferfish or frog matron's head—Genji loosed a furious salvo of, "Yips," "Yaps," and "Yeeps," barring his pointy teeth, pouncing up and down as he did; his hackles raised to a full salute, no relenting in sight.

Like screeching audio-feedback injected directly into the cerebellum, the skeleton man instinctually plastered his hands to the sides of his head, pressing in tightly against his ears; he winced and grimaced. The first of the vultures took flight almost immediately. Smart bird, knew when it was beat. Intent on weathering this cruel and unusual auditory onslaught, the skeleton-man dug his shiny leather boot heels into the dry sandy soil. Flapping their carrion wings carrying them back into the sky realm, the second and third vulture took off. Genji was still going full tilt. Straining even harder, beads of salty liquid formed on the gatekeeper's brow like a sweaty tiara. There were easier meals than these back out in the endless desert, decided the fourth vulture; it too abandoned the skeleton-man.

With his last ally taking flight, he broke. "Alright! Chill out! You can enter, just stop barking at me, *man*," said the skeleton-man in surrender. Stepping aside, he cordially extended a leather-clad arm, "Welcome to Uruk, the first city."

....

The interior of Uruk was not much different from its exterior. The buildings were constructed of the same bleached-bone beige bricks and lopsided rocks of the city walls, none higher than two to three stories, some with square empty windows and squat, square door frames. All the buildings were square with the exception of being square to each other, butting up against one another at acute or obtuse angles. Little to no planning went into a building's placement in Uruk making for an incomprehensible branching network of alleyways, tributaries feeding into the main road, which bisected the settlement in two from end-to-end. A banner strung across the main dusty causeway from the previous year's Ascension festival had come untethered on one side; it flagged limply in the non-existent wind.

All Albus knew of Uruk was that the city was the final

resting place for all the world's dust: where dust went to die. Thick layers of it accumulated on every flat surface, under every bed, and in every corner. Hopping and darting between the warren-like alleyways, were sentient dust bunnies made up of all sorts of detritus: dead skin, loose hairs, unidentifiable grey matter, clipped toenails; held together by sinews of black-tar and brittle bones of twigs. Dust rats scurried in and out of the holes and cracks in the mortar between the bricks, while dust lizards basked in the never-ending sun, their tarry black sinews oozing from their bodies.

Albus and this fox-spirit that had become attached to him (for better or worse) strolled along the main drag kicking up dust devils of grime; if there were people in Uruk, they certainly weren't making their presence known to these newcomers. That was, until they heard indistinct shouts echoing towards them off the crooked walls of an alleyway. Albus hung a right; he followed the bouncing sound of the chatter, zig-zagging through the entangled streets until they emerged at what must have been the city's marketplace. A slate slab hanging from a nearby post read: **PLA+EA ⊕SSIBUS**, in thickly chiseled letters. A street that looked like all the other streets in Uruk, except for the fact that this one was irregularly peppered with tents and vendor stalls, sprawled out before them.

Native Urukians, squat people, which would explain the squat doors, with slightly sloping brows, browsed up and down the market street purchasing their daily goods. They caught up on the Uruk goings-on with neighbors: "How are you handling your allergies?" "Had the exterminator gotten rid of that dust rat infestation?" and so on. A few raised a heavy brow to the newcomers before returning to ignoring them completely. Merchants manning booths hawked their wares; their loud shouts the source of the echo that had drawn Albus and Genji to the Platea Ossibus.

"Beige bricks for sale! Get yur beige bricks!" one man shouted. "Rocks, all types of rocks!" came another. "Twigs, stems, and sticks, every size!!" shouted a third. Commerce wasn't Uruk's strong suit. Seeing the bustle of industry with men and women hard at work reminded Albus it had been a while, a long while, since he had contacted his office back on Mars. He began to worry everything might be falling apart without him.

"I better check in with work," Albus said to Genji, "wait here." Ducking down one of the many anonymous streets that split off the market, he hunted for a strong signal and a place quite enough to make a call. He managed to find some privacy in the alcove of a restaurant's entryway advertising "Teeth Soup." Albus didn't know what teeth soup was, but he could guess. The owner of the establishment peered at Albus suspiciously through the pane-less square window of the eatery, then emphatically shut the blinds on him in a puff of dust. Maybe word had gotten out about the incident at the udon shop. *It was a real udon it.*

....

Back on the Platea Ossibus, Genji tried to sit still, that mysterious tail of his, swishing back and forth, provided him a brief stay from the all-consuming boredom. Until it dawned on him, this was the longest he and Albus had been apart since they met. The two had been pretty much joined at the shoulder since Neo Kyoto. *Have I been ditched in this dust bowl?*

Popping his head up, he frantically glanced up and down the street for any sign of the man, when something else piqued the spirit's interests, a Urukian merchant shouting, "Dust bunnies! Dust rats! All kinds of dust rodents!" All his fears of abandonment abated instantaneously by the barkers call, replaced with something else entirely: Genji—had a lust for dust. The peckish fox crept closer to the stall doling out the delicious, dusty flanks. Strung by ropes across the stall's window hung a menagerie of dust critters, hypnotically swaying, frothing the fox into a frenzy.

Standing in the alcove of the Teeth Soup eatery Albus dialed his office, it rang once then nine minutes later he heard his assistant's voice say, "Mr. Cake's office, this is Victoria speaking. How may I direct your call?"

"Hello Victoria, it's Albus."

Nine minutes later, "Oh! Hello, sire! I mean Mr. Cake. Is

today your day off?" came the reply.

Fidgeting on the Platea Ossibus, Genji found himself in a real pickle. The critter vendor's rhythmic chant became a siren's song inflaming his desire for detritus, only he didn't have any money, or sticks, or stones, or whatever item an Urukian might accept as tender; he didn't even have any pockets or a fanny pack to keep that stuff in. Albus might have been able to help him out, but the man had clearly ditched him; no, this was a pickle he'd have to solve all on his lonesome. Luckily, Genji considered himself something of a world-class trickster, a trait gleaned from his grandfather; he began devising an elaborate and foolproof plan.

Albus became quickly irritated by the tedious nine-minute delay in communication between his location and his assistant's, back on Mars. He explained to Victoria that he was going to batch all of his questions into one statement and say "over" when he was done speaking, then she could reply, answering all his questions in the order in which they were received. He began his batched inquiry, interrupting him nine minutes later he heard, "Okay, Mr. Cake."

Ugh.

Albus quizzed her about the operations on Mars: "Is everything running smoothly?" "Has Golgotha stopped by again?" "Do the cherub-like beings miss me?" "Has Dr. Blue or Mr. Molehill left any messages?" "Over." Nine minutes later he learned that his assistant hadn't even realized Albus was away on holiday. A serious blow to his ego, which Albus later rationalized by telling himself that he ran such a well-organized outfit that he needn't be there to oversee it, *and that's a good thing?* Things were running smoothly. The cherub-like beings seemed fine though she didn't think they had been singing as much lately. That concerned Albus a great deal. Golgotha had not been back to the office. Not a single message from Dr. Blue or Mr. Molehill.

Knowing it was useless, he couldn't help but wonder. He almost disconnected before asking his real question, the hidden intent behind his call, which he played off as nonchalantly as possible. "Thanks, Victoria, oh and I almost forgot..." he said, pacing and wagging his finger even though she couldn't see it, "has my wife tried to get in touch with you by any chance?" The countdown for the return response began, *eight minutes fifty-nine seconds...eight minutes fifty-eight seconds*, and so on.

....

Now a mere arms-length away from the critter stall, Genji—trickster extraordinaire—put the gears of his elaborate plan into motion, the byzantine machinations of which were known only to him. His keen fox eyes darted left, then right, then left again: no interlopers in sight. Confidently, he strode up to the stall window, arms relaxed swinging at his sides, shoulders back, whistling an old and alluring tune his mother used to hum to him at night in their fox den. Making sure to establish strong eye contact with the merchant, Genji backflipped onto the vendor's stone counter and stuck the landing. Hit 'em with the ol' *razzle-dazzle* his grampy used to say—like, way too often.

Flayed critter carcasses dangled dangerously close to the spirit's hungering grasp. He could almost taste success; the next moments of his ploy would be crucial. Genji bowed politely before the stout man gripping a butcher's cleaver in his clenched fist, a cleaver which now looked much larger from his new vantage point. Reestablishing his assertive eye contact, he locked his amber eyes with that of the dust bunny butcher's.

Genji reached down into his metaphorical grifter's bag of tricks and pulled out his empty hand, dramatically pointing and shouting in the opposite direction, "Hey! What's that over there?!"

The Urukian butcher did not flinch, not a single muscle fiber. His large cleaver swung down in an all too intimidating thunk, as an unlucky dust bunny squealed, its body relieved of its head. He eyed the flabbergasted, translucent fox, who was far too slick for its own good, and said in a gravelly voice, "Stone, brick, or stick," turning back to his task of butchering the bunny.

Genji was utterly perplexed, his plan was foolproof. Still standing on the counter, tapping his foot and scratching his fuzzy chin, Genji mentally reviewed every aspect of the ploy, *Old and alluring tune. Check. Backflip. Razzle dazzle. Check. Assertive eye contact. Check. How did this not work?* Dumbfounded, he came to the only logical conclusion—it was the doltish butcher's fault for his failure. Therefore, he was still owed the juiciest most delicious dust bunny available for his efforts. In a nimble, twinkle-toed leap, the wily (and for the most part, law-abiding) fox, propelled himself upwards and snagged the plumpest carcass he could get his mitts on. Landing back on the stone slab, prize in hand, Genji tucked and rolled off the countertop, then took off sprinting down the Platea Ossibus.

....

Nineteen...eighteen. Albus anxiously counted down the seconds until the response would reach him over the waves. He was certain her answer would be no. Though he hadn't been able to completely banish these nagging thoughts, wondering if his vanished love still existed somewhere out in the ether, perhaps trying to call out from beyond the void...*seventeen.*

As Albus counted, he watched with some confusion. An orange and white blur sprinted towards him, a revolting carcass shedding reams of muck tucked tightly in its arms. An extremely aggravated, squat man shouting Urukian curses, waving a butcher's cleaver, chased after the fleeing blur, not that far behind. "Run!!" hollered Genji as he careened past Albus, tossing the sticky bunny carcass like a stolen football into the man's surprised arms, skidding around the next corner, disappearing out of sight.

A thunderous rumble growing behind him, Albus looked back in the direction from which Genji came, the pilfered goods now clutched in his arms. An angry mob of Urukians, brandishing sticks and stones, intent on breaking bones, barreled down the street, a gargantuan gray cloud of dust dragging in their wake. *Shit...eleven seconds.* The mob was upon him: no choice. Albus ran, losing his signal with Mars, and scrambled after his idiot fox.

6

THE TWO-TONE
TOMB TOME

"Phew!" panted Genji.

"What was that all about?" asked Albus, with a mixture of agitation and bemusement as he freed himself of the sticky carcass, handing it back to the fox who was making a frantic *gimme gimme* motion with his flailing arms. Genji proudly hoisted the ragged hunk of butchered dust bunny into the air. He beamed from ear to ear showing off his prize, as though he had just won the King of the Universe trophy. Albus sucked in a short breath through gritted teeth and shook his head. Had he been hungry, he thought 'teeth soup' might have been a more palatable option than what Genji was about to willingly chow down on.

With reckless abandon, the fox sank his sharp, pointy teeth into the critter's repugnant flesh, tearing and lacerating huge mouthfuls of dry twig and tar-laced chunks. Genji spat profusely. "PFFt—pfft pllbt. PBBTTHH. This is…pplb…terrible!" he managed to choke out through a snout that was now glued with oozing strands of resinous tar, his lower jaw combating the sticky, viscous substance to open and close, spewing dusty globules. Albus couldn't help but laugh a little. Maybe donating that coin back at the Fukushima shrine wasn't the worst thing he had ever done. Genji, still recovering from his ill-fated meal, looked around and asked, "Where…PBbTh," a tar coated twig spat from his mouth, "are we?"

It was damp and cool, subterranean. A few petering torches around a bend in the corridor miserly tossed dismal scraps of light their way, but it was still very dark. Albus recalled, that in their frantic dash to evade the angered Urukians, he had kicked in some boards nailed over an opening in a wall and dove into the cavity, spelunking into the darkened maw, grabbing Genji by the scruff as he did. The maw had led them down a set of slicked stone stairs; however, when he retraced his steps, the stairs were nowhere to be found. The sound of dripping water could be heard faintly in the distance.

Pacing back in forth in search of the nonexistent stairs, Albus could barely see his hands in front of his face. *This darkness just won't do.* He steadied himself, extending his arms; as he held his arms outstretched in front of him, the pitch-black darkness engulfing his hands began to gnash, vibrate, and bend, begrudgingly kowtowing to Albus—then suddenly—light. Using some of the power vested in him, he brought forth light from darkness, illuminating the corridor.

Genji's jaw dropped; a few stringy strands of tar still swayed back and forth. His typically narrow eyes bugged out as he watched Albus manifest brilliant light out of the nothingness. Completely unaware that the man was capable of such a feat, Genji felt it was best to play it cool. *Just act like you knew he could do that all along.* Silently contemplating who this new friend of his really was, Genji said nothing and closed his gaping snout before Albus could catch sight of his astonished expression in the newly created brightness.

The narrow corridor they found themselves in, now bathed in light, revealed a dusty floor tessellated in a distinct pattern of hexagonal black and white tiles, a low hung ceiling imitating the same. Stacked floor to ceiling, the walls were mortared in skulls; the skulls painted in the same alternating black and white pattern. Vacuous eye sockets blankly stared through Albus and

Genji, oblivious to the intruders. Everything was completely coated in thick layers of dust and cobwebs; they were definitely somewhere beneath Uruk. Despite the multitude of eye sockets staring at them being patently empty, Albus couldn't shake the feeling of being watched. He glanced over his shoulder, nothing there. *Just my imagination.* "This must be the catacomb—" he began to say.

"You seek to defeat the Lord of the Clouds," came a voice from behind them. It was a mewling and teetering voice that sounded like thousands of other tiny voices whispering together in unison. Genji, who was floating behind Albus, jumped even higher into the air, releasing an involuntary "Yeep!" Albus spun in place searching for the source of the voice. There was still no one behind him.

"Yes," Albus shouted into the vacant corridor, hoping for a reply.

"Then come closer," came the rasping chorus again. This time, Albus was able to better zero in on its origin. He inspected the sides of the catacomb and noticed an unassuming portion of wall not entirely covered in skulls. The blank segment of the wall looked as though it might have been an arched doorway at one time, but had been sealed, bricked over with Uruk's signature beige bricks. Perhaps the voice originated from behind there.

....

He approached the bricks and wrapped his knuckles against them, a hollow echo rang out. Albus summoned the fox over and pointed. With Genji's help, the two picked and scratched away at the caked and perforated mortar. Albus pulled the feather from his fanny pack and used the pointy end like a scrawling instrument, further digging away at the binding until he was able to poke his finger into a gap between two bricks. He wiggled his finger loosening the brick, then tugged, freeing it from its prison.

The loose brick tumbled to the catacomb floor making a dampened plunk in the grimy mantle of dust coating the tiles. *Red brick, blue brick, one brick, two brick*, thought Albus. With one gone, they easily pulled out more bricks from the wall that clinked off their fallen brethren forming a small pile, creating a hole in the barricade large enough to peer through. The brilliant light Albus had created pitched-in as well, casting its rays through the peephole revealing an alcove not much larger than a closet.

Hunched inside the cell, a desiccated person cloaked in a threadbare black and white habit, sat huddled with knees pulled into their chest. The person's face, resting on their knees, was further obscured by a cowl pulled low. Genji and Albus doubled their efforts, pulling out brick after brick until they had created a gap large enough for the hunched creature to pass through. Crawling through the gap on hands and knees, the top of its cowl briefly caught on the corner of a brick jutting out from the improvised passageway in the wall; quickly it tugged the cowl back down.

Inching out from her imprisonment into the lighted, skull-lined corridor, an ancient woman rose with deliberate effort, bones and joints audibly popping as she stood; she straightened herself out as best she could and brushed her habit off, patting the clinging dust off with wrinkled hands. Exposed skin not cloaked by her habit was papery and insubstantial; a soft saffron cord was tied around her waist in a knot, keeping her habit tucked in close to her sagging body. Around her neck hung a thin gold chain with a symbol Albus did not recognize. The three stood flanked by the walls of skulls saying nothing. Albus waited for the decrepit woman to make the first move.

The ancient woman turned towards them and lowered her cowl, her eyes shut tight, revealing a lumpy and misshapen face blanketed with an appalling amalgam of imperfections: warts, moles, pimples, sties, and boils. Floating his way behind the hideous hag's back, Genji opened his snout and stuck a finger in his mouth, miming a barf. Albus glared sternly at the fox-spirit making a slicing motion with his hand across his throat.

"Come closer, Albus Cake," wheezed the crone, her voice resonating like pockets of air escaping from proofing bread dough. Albus leaned in as close as he felt comfortable; the hag grabbed him by the shoulder and pulled him in closer still. She opened her eyes. What Albus saw shocked him. The woman's face was not covered in boils and warts at all—but more faces: her face was a tiled mosaic of thousands of other smaller faces. When the crone had opened her eyes, every one of her tiny faces opened their eyes along with hers, eyelids popping open in an unsettling shuffle.

Intrigue replacing disgust, as it so often does when new evidence is admitted, Albus leaned in closer still. Sure enough, each individual face of her patchwork of faces was quilted from thousands of even tinier faces. In one face he thought he spotted the likeness of his grandmother, the crone turned away some before he could be certain.

Albus found himself wishing he had a magnifying lens or scanning electron microscope on hand to get a closer look, but was quite certain that it was likely just more faces; faces all the way down. When the woman spoke, each mouth of every face of her faces moved along in unison with hers. "If you seek to defeat the Lord of the Clouds," she began, the breath leaking through her orchestra of mouths like air traveling listlessly through cathedral organ pipes, "you will require three divine instruments not even Golgotha knows of."

Emanating from nowhere like an unanticipated thunderstorm, "Hello!?" interrupted Golgotha, "all-knowing deity here!" he sneered. The trio of man, fox, and crone standing in the catacomb's corridor glanced back and forth at one another; unanimously they chose to ignore the pink elephant metaphorically in the room. The multifaceted crone continued speaking, listing the three instruments Albus would need in the final confrontation.

"A needle," she held up her arthritic index finger and placed it to her sunken left breast, "to pierce the heart."

"A sword," she chopped with an open hand at the empty air in a downward strike, "to cut away the trunk."

"Whispered words," she cupped her palm up to the side of her mouth and hissed with a *pssh pssh psh* sound, made even more sibilant by her multitudinous mouths copy-catting one another, "that once heard cannot be unheard."

Albus listened with rapt attention, crouching at the old woman's height straining to hear every word as best he could; his right hand held to his chin. Genji was frolicking and toying with a dust rat he had spotted attempting to scurry away between the hollow sockets belonging to one of the skulls.

"Where can I find the instruments," Albus asked somberly of the wizened woman.

The crone replied, contorting her face, "The needle is at the end of a book." She extended her frail, twiggy arm gesturing further down the esophageal corridor. "That way you will find a tome. Read it from beginning—to end."

"And the sword—" started Albus. Before he could finish his query, the multifaceted woman fractured, breaking apart, crumbling; she dissolved into dust, rejoining the city all around her: her final resting place had been reached.

Albus stood in silence for a moment. Genji pounced, catching the dust rat he had been toying with, shredding it apart; in no time his mouth was a sticky mess again of crud and debris. *He never learns,* chuckled Albus to himself. The man snapped his fingers; Genji fell in line, bobbing behind his companion's right shoulder.

....

They followed along the winding corridor of the Uruk catacombs in search of the needle containing tome; the sound of dripping water was still detectable somewhere in the distance. As they walked, Albus tried to estimate if they were traveling higher or lower in elevation. It was hard to say for certain. At times it felt like the floors of the tunnel had a noticeable incline at others they were definitely sloping downward. Albus kept one hand in loose contact with the right-side wall grazing his fingertips over the barren skulls. Occasionally Genji pricked up his ears, thinking that he heard creatures skittering behind the bone-laden walls. *I'd sure like to get my paws on another dust rat,* he thought. Coming around a bend, the grade of the corridor declined dramatically and without warning. Suddenly, Albus found himself skidding down the tunnel on his backside at a quickening pace. *At least this is faster than walking,* he thought as he slid down the snaking tube. Genji hovered quickly behind trying to keep up.

Tumbling out of an elevated hole in a wall, they were fed into an abnormally shaped subterranean chamber not sparing a single accoutrement: cobwebs, unlit torches, chains, stacks of book-shelves, damp moldy walls. The floor and ceiling of the chamber matched that of the catacomb tunnels, with the same pattern of hexagonal black and white tiles, only these tiles were larger in size. Six gray stone columns supported the tons of dirt and dust that they could now only assume rested above their heads. At the back was a single exit. Standing in the center of the stomach-shaped chamber was a circular stone dais, the diameter of Golgotha's belly at its widest point. Resting on the dais was a book.

"This must be it," said Albus, in a hushed tone.

"This looks like bad news bears to me," said Genji, hoping to sound less afraid than he really was. "What if it's a trap?" Albus had a fleeting vision of an action-adventure flick he was going to watch in a mostly forgotten future life. This certainly looked like the kind of place that would be booby-trapped—it wasn't. Regardless, Albus gingerly tip-toed from tile to tile, in-specting each one of the hexagons for any sign of malfeasance, before making his next move. Genji held his breath. Anxiously, he spectated as his man-friend made it all the way to the dais without incident; he exhaled a heavy sigh of relief. Albus turned around and gave the fox-spirit a thumbs up.

Albus examined the tome resting on the elevated center of the stone circle. *More like an encyclopedia,* he thought. It was ponderously thick and older than he could ponder, bound in cracking brown leather; tarnished brass tacks were hammered into each corner of the cover. The exposed edges of the pages— stacked like the strata of sedimentary rock—were succumbing to the same anonymous green mold that crept unabashedly up the chamber walls.

As he examined the tome more closely, he failed to locate a title nor author attribution anywhere, not on the cover, nor the spine. Laying across the cracking cover like a fainted bride, rested a byzantine blue ribbon, one single strand of gold foil woven in amongst the braided threads: a bookmark Albus reasoned. One end of the ribbon jutted from the spine, attached to the tome's binding; on the ribbon's other end hung a round tin bell looped and knotted to the fraying ends. Albus knelt before the tome and reluctantly placed his fingertips on its edge. He wondered if it might disintegrate as the multifaceted crone had. Lifting carefully, he cracked open the aged cover; the blue ribbon shifting and sliding off, its tin bell faintly chiming as it fell.

....

Albus opened to page one. Carefully hand-written flowery script with a large illuminated 'A' began the text. He read:

'**A**lbus Bartholomew Cake was born to Maria and Jimmy Cake weighing seven pounds and seven ounces, on July 7th.'

Let's skip past the boring stuff, he thought, as he skimmed the text, turning the delicate parchment.

'Albus' parents divorced when he was seven.'

Blah blah blah. He thumbed the pages skipping further ahead. As he continued to read, curiously, the hand-written text began to fade from its pages, giving way to still images.

A birthday party, red balloons, crying children; there was his dad, Jimmy, gripping the sweaty neck of a cold beer bottle in his hand as he lorded a pinata over overstimulated children. The amount of foamy, amber liquid sloshing around inside the bottle inconsistently changed between each shot, three-quarters full, now full again, empty, a quarter full; it had to be a newly opened beer in each image.

Albus stared at himself standing beneath the carved wooden sign of a summer camp; he holds a walking stick, unflinching feathers tied to the top. In another image he stands motionless on a cement pier in front of a large cruise liner, the smoke from the ship's stack stuck in the air; his mom and her new boyfriend smile behind him.

There was the outside of his first college dorm; walking, frozen in time, towards the punitive looking building with a milk crate full of useless crap in his arms. An image of his best friend with a big Ziplock bag full of marijuana perpetually held up for the camera. College graduation, he looked stoned.

Wait stop—he came across an image of him and Elixabeth together.

They're on a beach, lounging in long recliners. They looked much younger; it was from a time when he and Elixabeth were newly dating. Elixabeth holds a passion-fruit Mai Tai in her hand resplendent with a veritable fruit cocktail wedged onto the rim: pineapples, cherries, mint leaves, and orange slices. He cups a coconut piña colada garnished with a red-striped swizzle straw; a festive crepe-paper umbrella (that was utterly useless should it actually start to rain) juts out over the rim. He supposed it must have been a virgin piña colada in his hand; he had tried to give up drinking around that time in his life.

Elixabeth has on her teal bikini with white stripes outlining the cups and edges. His arm around her shoulders squeezes her in tight towards him, never wanting to let go. Elixabeth beams radiantly, raising her Mai Tai towards the camera. Reflected in the round lenses of her mirrored aviator sunglasses, Albus could almost make out the face of whoever was taking the photo. *Thanks for the memories...stranger.* He lingered a little longer.

As he continued on, the images grew larger, consuming his entire field of vision. Some of the images started to stitch together in a moving sequence, like a flip-book revving up. Then came audio, he could hear the images. There was their wedding. 'Do you, Diana Elixabeth Fettuccini, take this man, to be your lawfully wedded husband?' Now it was their first apartment together after relocating to Boston. His first job at Google. He stands outside the blue, red, yellow, and green Google marquee of the building in Cambridge. A few more moving sequences of him and Elixabeth together.

It went abruptly dark, abysmally dark. All around, a velveteen darkness consumed Albus in every direction. He tried to bring light to the darkness, but couldn't. *This thing must be broken.* It seemed his only choice was to patiently wait it out. All things ended eventually *right?*

The darkness lasted for some time. A camera flashbulb went off. He saw Elixabeth again! Only now she was really there! Fully realized, she was some distance in front of him, standing at the threshold to their cottage.

Her long, blonde hair ebulliently blows in the cool breeze coming off the lake. Albus shouts; he calls out to her. She can't hear or see him; he can only watch. She cradles a child in her arms, wrapped in homespun indigo swaddling cloth, it's a girl. There he is now too! He watched himself bound up the slate stone steps to their thatched-roof cottage with a red-ochre door, a bouquet of twelve long-stem red and white roses wrapped in yellow and blue tissue paper in his arms. He just got that big promotion at work. She acts so excited for him. She cheers wildly; they embrace.

Albus discovered he could watch the unfolding events from any angle; like a phantom unconstrained by gravity, he could float and move freely in space. When he first realized this, the shock of it sent him rocketing into the atmosphere, straight through the clouds and into space, until he learned to control it and stay mostly grounded. After watching for a while longer, he figured out he could fast-forward and slow down time as well (though, for some reason, never rewind).

They're on a camping trip. Their daughter is two now. He skipped ahead a little. At night, like an incubus, he hovered above Elixabeth while she slept so that he could listen to himself laying next to her whisper into her ear how much he loves her. He watched her in the shower more than he cared to admit.

....

He knew what was coming next, here came that inevitable day where Elixabeth was *just gone.* He didn't want to relive that pain a second time. Albus fast-forwarded ahead, eventually reaching the point where he was at now.

'Albus Bartholomew Cake was born to Maria—' *Skip.* 'Albus' parents divorced when—' *Skip. There's our wedding again. Skip.* Then the darkness. *Skip.* It didn't work; he couldn't fast forward through the darkness. It lasted for some time again; he patiently waited it out. A bright flash, then he spotted himself and Elixabeth at their cottage again! He binge-watched the details of their life, replaying all the greatest hits in high fidelity.

He skipped over her vanishing again. Back to the where he was now, 'Albus Bartholomew Cake was born—' *Skip.* Their move to Boston. His first job at Google. The darkness again. This time Albus did an experiment; he meticulously counted out the seconds of the darkness. 3,484,800 seconds. The number didn't have any significance to him. It was mathematically irrelevant and uninteresting; he lost all interest in the number as soon as Elixabeth appeared again at their cottage.

He watched their life unfold again. Skipped ahead, back to where he was now. Skipping ahead, the darkness. This time as he floated in the darkness, he found that he could take slices of it. There was a quality to it, of sorts. Like fumbling and lifting at parts of a heavy stage curtain, he could hold it and fold it in his hands. There was something there in the darkness—waiting for him.

No.

Albus ripped his face away from the tome, his violent reaction sending it crashing off the elevated stone dais. As the pages of the book receded away from him—he saw it.

There it was—*the needle*—on the very last page of the book. He grabbed for it; it was too late. The moldy, old codex was fluttering to the black and white tiled floor.

....

His awareness returning to the dank, mildewed catacombs surrounding him, Albus was alarmed to find himself covered in crystalline cobwebs. That *drip, drip, drip,* noise was still present though audibly much closer now. *How long was I gone for?* he wondered, coming out of the fog. As the daze faded away, Albus became even more alarmed; what he mistook for interlacing threads of spider's silk, were actually numerous intravenous needles crisscrossing and piercing him, a web of copper wires and electrodes interwoven amongst the IVs.

As he craned his neck side-to-side, he spotted dozens of vermin-like kobolds and blathering gibberlings clustered around the chamber dressed in loose, poorly fitting scrubs and surgical masks, chatting casually with one another in guttural clicks and belching gases, carrying trays of medical equipment. Albus began to frantically tear at the networks of IVs and wires.

"He's awake!" came a shrieking, ominous voice from an unseen place. Albus had no intention of sticking around long enough to learn to whom the voice belonged. The aimlessly puttering horde of kobolds and gibberlings jumped in surprise, dropping their metallic trays, sending, syringes, scalpels, and nasty looking serrated instruments clanging loudly against the hard tiled floor, (they had been assured that the man wasn't supposed to be able to wake up). Thrashing and ripping now, Albus freed himself from the remaining IVs; he scrambled on hands and knees across the cold floor to the place where he had seen the book fall, disappearing from sight.

As he crawled around to the other side of the dais, he found himself face-to-face with one of the wretched kobold orderlies. The two stared each other down; the tome—an innocent bystander—betwixt them. Like a shoot-out at the O.K. Corral, they sized each other up; Albus narrowed his dominant eye.

The dungeon dweller happened to be positioned much closer to the object of their mutual desire. *Fuck it.* Albus took his shot, making a dive for the heavy tome. The kobold, having the initiative, scooped up the book denying the man his prize as Albus landed with a thud, arms outstretched; the creature ran surprisingly fast, sprinting out the anterior exit, the book in its clutches. Albus got his feet beneath him; he rocketed after the thieving kobold, bowling over two gibberlings who had decided to make their heroic last stand against him. "Stop him!" the voice of the unseen and malevolent overlord commanded. The cabal of unpleasant subterranean creatures gave chase.

The tunnel exiting the stomach-shaped chamber was much narrower and more rounded than the previous passageways, as if it had been burrowed through the hard-packed crust by an earthworm the diameter of a man. Presenting an additional challenge, the tunnel forked and branched significantly, creating a maze of potential routes.

Albus' pursuit of the thieving kobold went south almost immediately. The creature had home-field advantage; it knew these passageways far better than he. Nimbly, it dove through a hole in the tunnel's wall far too small for Albus to fit through. Hopelessly, he stuck his arms through the opening, grasping away at nothing. With the motley federation of nightmarish cavern dwellers and malcontents nipping at his heels, Albus had no choice but to keep moving.

Somewhere up ahead, he could hear the rattling of a metal chain mixed with pained, labored growls. *Genji!* thought Albus, *where is Genji?!* He hadn't seen his pesky fox-spirit since coming back from the tome. Staying ahead of the horde, following along with the rattling and growling noises as best he could, he kept his hand in loose contact with the wall as he ran, always taking a right turn at any fork in the tunnel. Locked in a dank cell of cold-rolled steel bars, carved into the earthen wall of the tunnel, was his fox friend. Albus actually felt something when he saw him, joy was too strong a word, but it was something.

Inside the dirty cell decorated with decaying carcasses of unrecognizable beasts, Genji, his hind-leg clenched in the jaws of a sharp-toothed bear trap, furiously gnawed away at his trapped leg. Grunting and howling in pain as he chewed through his own appendage, the fox was attempting a desperate, last-ditch effort at escape.

"You're a fox-spirit!" shouted Albus, "You're incorporeal!"

Genji lifted his head, overjoyed to see his man-friend, "Oh yeah!" he recalled. His ectoplasmic body floated free from the jaws of the jagged trap. Squeezing his body between the cold-rolled steel bars of the cell, the fluffy hedges of his orange tufts pressing in against his face as he did, he chased after Albus.

"The book, Genji!" Albus yelled at the fox as they sprinted down the intestinal tunnel, "find the book boy!" Genji perked his ears, picking up on the tinkle of the tin bell tied to the bookmark, jingling and jangling away as the kobold ran along behind the walls. "I can hear it!" yipped Genji. The fox chased the bell. Albus chased the fox. The monsters chased Albus.

Goblins, trolls, and imps joined up with the growing horde of catacomb crawlers. That ever-present sound of dripping water, that once seemed so distant, became less so. It continued to grow stronger from a drip, to a tinkle, to a stream, to a torrent. Albus and Genji came clattering out of a passageway into a wide-open cavernous space; they stuttered to a stop at the hairs-edge of a narrow, rocky ledge, sending pebbles scattering, tumbling into the source of that once distant dripping sound, now a full-on deafening roar.

....

Some distance below the ledge, a bestial whirlpool gnashed and snarled watery teeth, draining out the bottom of the underground cavern to God knows where. Their thief came bursting onto the ledge from a hole in the wall not far from them, clutching the book in its dirty and unworthy paws. At the sight of the man, the kobold chittered and farted unintelligibly, backing away. Genji disappeared and materialized behind the creature. Albus stepped closer. They had it surrounded. "Give me the book," said Albus crouching and beckoning towards the pathetic creature.

Pulling the stolen tome in tighter against its matted, hairy chest as it backed towards the edge, the moronic kobold didn't fully grasp why it even desired the book so badly. All it understood was that the object possessed some great value to the man chasing after him, so therefore, he had to have it; it was written somewhere in his contract.

His back to the precipice, no allies in sight, the crusty, flea-bitten kobold mulled over the choices of his life, contemplating if he had ever even made choices, or if he had just been a lackey following orders this entire time. Eyeing the eddy below, he had one choice left: he could give the stupid book back to the stupid man, or—go out in a blaze of glory, diving into oblivion taking the stupid book along with him; Dave the gibberling would think he was so cool.

"Don't make me do this," Albus tried bargaining with the creature. "I really don't want to hurt you," he pleaded again. Seeing what passed for consternation on the slack-jawed kobold's face as it looked over the ledge, Albus had no choice; he had to act. Sighing, reluctantly Albus took aim.

He closed one eye, bringing his fist towards his face, his finger and thumb held outstretched like he was about to pinch someone. Narrowing his gaze through the gap between thumb and index finger, he sighted the gap over the kobold's malformed and unfortunate head. Taking no pleasure in it, he brought his outstretched fingers together in a squishing motion, as if popping a pimple.

In a loud *POP*, Steven the kobold's head promptly exploded, an over-ripened grape that had just had enough of it all. The explosive report satisfyingly echoed off the cavern walls mixing with the din of the savage whirlpool.

Blowing off his fingers, Albus strode over to the limp, headless corpse of the cavern creature; retrieving the tome, the bookmark tinkled some as he lifted it from the deceased kobold's stiff grasp. Genji, staring at the decapitated creature, once again unaware that Albus was capable of such a feat, chose to play it cool.

The torches and pitchforks rapidly increased in size behind them, accelerating down the tunnel. Skeletons, mummies, and green-skinned swamp-things had now enlisted in the contorting mass of monsters barreling down on them. There wasn't enough time for Albus to pop every one of the monsters' heads before they were overwhelmed by the mob. They were stuck between a rock and a hard place. "Scylla or Charybdis?" Albus puckishly asked Genji.

"Uhhh…Charybdis," replied Genji.

Hurriedly, Albus wrapped the tome in a flimsy plastic poncho procured from his fanny pack; he tucked the wrapped book in tight against him, securing it with the elastic strap of his pack. Albus hoped the fox was as indifferent to drowning as he was. Taking one last look over his shoulder at the mob that was now upon them, he snagged hold of Genji and dove headfirst into the maelstrom. Fighting against the fiendish current, Genji managed to get one fuzzy hand above the rapids; making a fist, he extended his middle digit, as the pair were siphoned away to God knows where.

The angry, violent throng of smelly, underground things which no one particularly liked, packed onto the ledge, and wistfully watched the most exciting thing to happen in centuries in these catacombs—go right down the drain. This would be the talk of skulkings and monster mashes for years to come.

"Dang," said Dave the gibberling, tossing his pitchfork to the ground.

7

DUST TO DUST

Out of the shimmering waves of an endless desert, an upright pink elephant walked towards Uruk, the first city, from a distance, in no particular rush at all, a cheetah-man at his side. The cheetah-man swatted a fly from his butt with his tail. They approached the walled city, its lashed gate thrown open wide. This time, the four circling buzzards overhead merely landed on opposite sides of Golgotha's immense shoulders and rested. The thundering tyrant loomed over the gatekeeper. "You let them through but you will not allow my most loyal Cheshire through?!" A shade of purple disappointment tinged his voice. The skeleton-man groveled for his life.

"Are those the people that hurt your feelings?" Golgotha asked of his cheetah compatriot, pointing at the flat, walled city. He rested his overly plump pink hands with the yellow painted nails and sparkling gemstones of primary colors on the cheeky cheetah-man's shoulders. Chet nodded meekly. "Are they the ones that did the bad touch?" added Golgotha, his tone somewhere between mocking and genuine concern. Chet looked up at the large elephant-headed man and nodded again with opaline, watery eyes. Golgotha summoned from the sky a city-sized, skull-shaped meteor wreathed in flames. He clenched his fist bringing it down atop Uruk, leveling it. The city returned to dust.

8

WELCOME TO
THE JUNGLE

"We got it—the needle," Albus panted, spitting a tadpole from his mouth. Turning himself over from his stomach, he propped himself into a sitting position, the book held tightly against him. Albus and Genji had washed up on the muddy banks of a wide and quickly flowing river. Sitting in the mucky, turbid shallows of the river, he unwrapped the book and thumbed through it, flipping to the very last page. Nothing. He tried it again—still nothing—his agitation beginning to show. A third time, the preciously written ink was smudging and running down the pages, the letters spreading like stains in a coffee filter. The pages were clumping together, shedding from their binding like a man pulling out his hair in frustration. The book was a ruin.

Albus cursed, smashing his fists against the river banks, splashing a silty mixture into the air, sending future frog matrons dawdling in the mud close by fleeing for their lives. In a rare display, he stood, wound up like a discus thrower, and flung the book towards the river like a rectangular Frisbee. Its remaining pages scattered out, the jingling ribbon singing helplessly, as it skipped once off the water's surface before sinking beneath the rapids. Genji felt momentarily compelled to bound into the river after the book and retrieve it; he knew better. The man stood with his hands on his hips as his fox-spirit floated out of sight avoiding his ire. *What does it matter*, thought Albus, *we're all doomed anyway*. He felt like he needed a drink.

Flanking the wide river on both sides of its marshy banks grew impenetrable walls of dense, verdant jungle. A menagerie of vibrant green vegetation, which upon first inspection might have appeared rather homogenous, formed the barriers: palms, Ficus, gargantuan ferns, creeping vines as thick as a man's waist. Without a word, Albus turned and marched off into the jungle, using his hands to swat and part the claustrophobic leaves and branches brushing up against him, limbs simultaneously reaching for him while pushing him away: both repelling and welcoming his visit to their homeworld. Genji, not wanting to be left behind, quickly followed after, assuming his usual hovering position.

Contrasting sharply to the lifeless, muted hues of Uruk, the kaleidoscopic jungle took some adjustment to gaze upon without squinting. An ocean turned upside down, the fecundity and maddening variety of life contained within the rainforest ruptured from every pore. Still pouting over the loss of the needle, Albus refused to take in the splendor as he had during his time wallowing on the lakebed. Genji, on the other hand, could barely contain himself.

The fox-spirit felt overwhelmed by the innumerable new critters and creatures; things he had never seen before, things he could never imagine, to chase, sniff, stalk, growl, and yip at. Every nook and cranny crawled, slithered, or crept with an abundance of lifeforms springing forth from the fountainhead of an infinitely creative imagination.

Genji delightfully eyed a beetle roll a spherical turd diligently across the leaf-carpeted jungle floor; everyone's got to pay the bills somehow. *Poop Bug*, Genji named the beetle. The poop bug's turd ball looked appetizing; it was probably full of all sorts of tasty grubs and morsels. Before he could find out, he spotted an odd-looking animal coated in matted gray fur that looked like it just didn't give a fuck about anything; suspending itself from a thin branch with three long claws, the indolent animal moved with the speed of decaying uranium. *Three-toed Tanuki*, he named it. The fox gave the three-toed tanuki a few friendly barks: no response. *Rude*.

Something rustled the leaves beneath them. A fleshy, engorged tube that appeared to have no beginning and no end, plated in iridescent umber and olive scales (forming patterns not that dissimilar to the patterns in the floors and ceilings of the catacombs), slithered beneath their feet. *Daddy Long Tail*. Genji nipped and bit at the scaly tube, unaware that it possessed a vicious and hungering mouth somewhere farther along under the brush. Albus grabbed the intrepid yet foolhardy explorer by the tail and yanked him along before the daddy long tail could loop back around and attempt to consume them.

As the two trudged deeper into the morass, the light from the sun struggled valiantly to send its rays piercing to the ground, claiming small victories here and there at weak points in the canopies encompassing defenses. Genji wondered if Albus knew where he was going; he inhaled a deep breath of the steamy jungle air. It felt good to be free of those dusty, cramped catacombs that had felt slightly too reminiscent of his confinement within the kiri wood box.

The man stomping along in front of him contemplated the words the multifaceted crone had said: a needle to pierce the heart, a sword to cut away the trunk, whispered words once heard cannot be unheard. Cursing himself, he had lost the needle—he wondered if that book had possibly been a trap. *Will there be another needle?* Perhaps just the sword and the whispered words would be enough to put an end to Golgotha's reign.

Albus, resolving to at least try and locate the sword and the whispered words, jumped with a startle as a howler monkey crashed down on him, suspending itself from a branch overhead. Hanging by its prehensile tail, the monkey used its humanlike hands to aggressively grab Albus about the head; it whispered something into his ear before hoisting itself back up, disappearing into the canopy.

"What did it say?" asked Genji.

"Nothing. Just a damn dirty evolution denier."

Pushing their way through a mess of tangled vines, rather abruptly the jungle ended. The huge trees, waxy ferns, and stocky vines had been clear-cut revealing a vast, low-lying valley; at the center of which stood the most magnificent city either of them had ever laid eyes on. Seemingly out of nowhere, an enormous metropolis constructed entirely from gold sprawled out before them. Golden skyscrapers, that Albus imagined to be colossal termite mounds, grew towards the clouds like beanstalks, the windows of which were paned from emeralds the size of boulders, sheared to within a few molecules thickness.

Midway across the sprawling, golden city loomed an awe-inspiring tree of epic proportions. Cascading golden terraces, tufted with Elysium green fields and thundering waterfalls, radiated outwards from the tree's tremendous trunk. A monorail system that could have only been designed by Daedalus himself permeated the city; its tracks looped in wide clovers and dovetailed along optimal routes. As one of the trains sped past them, it appeared as though its carriages had been carved from singularly massive pearls.

Albus recognized the city immediately from Golgotha's endless tales of conquest: this was El Dorado, the legendary city of gold. He could hear the elephant-headed man now, trumpeting about his exploits in the city; how he had slept with this supermodel or raw-dogged that pornstar. He would quip things to Albus on the golf course, like, 'The trunk gets 'em in the bunk' or 'The pachyderm makes 'em squirm.' It would make Albus cringe on the inside (which Golgotha knew, and despised him for) yet Albus would laugh anyway out of deference. Albus and Genji shuffled down the slope of the valley side, knocking away a few loose rocks, but an otherwise uneventful descent; no gatekeepers or mobs of kobolds this time.

Words like cornucopia or abundance could only ever asymptotically approach describing the amount of wealth contained in El Dorado. The brilliant sunbeams reflecting off the gold streets and refracting through the skyscrapers' molecule-thin emerald windows were dazzling and all together disorienting. Albus sat himself down on a nearby golden park bench smelted from recycled gold soda cans, to get his bearings. The designers of the park bench were sure to include irregularly placed golden spikes on it—to discourage any undesirables from trying to lay down on the bench and sleep.

Whilst taking in the utter splendor of El Dorado, a statuesque woman strolled past them on the golden sidewalk; she towered head and shoulders above Albus, draped in animal skins and fine furs. Her arms were nicely defined and her pale skin looked as though it had been painted two shades darker than its natural color. Jet-black hair pulled back in a slicked tight ponytail, stretched and strained at the seams of the woman's forehead. Albus wondered if she might be some kind of tribal warrior.

The woman briefly glanced in Albus' direction, looking right through him. Her nose was attempting a very slow disappearing act off of her face. Pouty red lips were pinched together like inflamed baboon buttcheeks; while her breasts could only be described as two ginormous beach balls that didn't like each other very much, forced to sit next to one another at a charity gala. Fluttering by, lazily flapping its lavish wings, a monarch butterfly was overcome with wing-envy as it spotted the passing woman's eyelashes. The warrior woman's yoga pants were from LuluLemon.

Walking alongside her, overloaded with an assortment of shopping bags and boxes was the warrior woman's boyfriend—a real gorilla, no not in any derogatory sort of way. Her boyfriend was a literal silverback gorilla that had recently relocated from the surrounding misty mountains of the jungle to the city. He was new in town; his online dating profile read that he was looking for love and comically large boobs. Knuckling alongside his warrior princess looking up at her adoringly, it appeared he might have found the one. His woman wasn't quite as sure about her new beau; he was a great guy and all, but he was still a gorilla.

The amazonian woman and her silverback beau turned a corner, disappearing from view. Albus needed to focus; he needed to think. Sitting on the golden bench with his elbows resting on his knees, legs angled slightly apart he hung his head low, inspecting the green, superbly manicured grass beneath his feet.

He needed to find the sword but didn't know where to start, the multifaceted crone had really left him high and dry in that regard. As he gazed at the jade bilateral blades of grass, they grew upwards to meet him, consuming his vision. Albus couldn't help but notice long queues of brown ants, moving in lockstep—some towards the city, others away. Each ant carried snipped pieces of green leaves in their mandibles. *A. Cephalotes. Leafcutter Ants.* He recalled something about this type of ant having a caste system. He began counting them *one, two, three, four*—

Breaking Albus from his ant-induced amnesia Genji quipped, "Maybe they'll have a sword here?" Adding as a forgone afterthought, "Seems like they have everything here."

"Maybe," replied Albus, still thinking about the ants. He supposed that El Dorado was as good a place as any to search for the sword; some vacation this was turning out to be.

....

Albus stood from the park bench and followed the street signs, fox-spirit in tow, making his way to the nearest monorail station. At the station depot, as he studied the colorful, perplexing map of shifting lines and nodes, it took Albus some time to realize that the monorail system was capable of intelligently re-organizing its routes, ensuring that its trains hit all their required destinations in the absolute shortest distance possible, before returning to the depot.

A minor chill crept over him, momentarily he marveled at the deceptively complex feat, a problem he himself had once thought unsolvable within the confines of limited time and space. He called Genji over and tried to share in his eggheaded enthusiasm; the fox-spirit merely shrugged and pointed out an area on the map labeled "The Shopping District." Marginally deflated Albus agreed they should start there, perhaps they could purchase a sword with which to cut away the trunk.

The red LED signage above the track flashed that it would be exactly thirteen minutes and twenty-eight seconds for their train to arrive. Albus had a decent signal to Mars. *Maybe I should check back in with the office*, he thought. He told Genji to not go anywhere—for real this time—and ducked around the other side of the plastic placard.

Eight minutes and thirty-nine seconds later he heard Victoria's voice say,

"Hi."

"Hi Vict—"

"I'm not home right now," Victoria's voice continued, cutting Albus off, "but if you want to leave a message, just start talking at the sound of the tone," came the rest of his assistant's dulcet coo. It was her answering machine; Albus hadn't realized Victoria had an answering machine. Is that in her contract? *Beep*.

Caught off guard, he rambled, "Hi Victoria, it's Albus again…still on vacation. Just calling to check in on things. Has Golgotha come by? Are the cherub-like beings doing okay? Did I leave one of the osmium censers burning when I left?" he paused. "Oh and one last thing, has my wife…" his voice trailed off before completing the question. Albus disconnected.

Strolling back to the other side of the placard, he was glad to see that the mischievous fox-spirit had obeyed him this time and was sitting right where he left him; he patted Genji's ecto-plasmic head. The fox glanced up at his man-friend with some bewilderment. Albus looked left to one end of the platform then right to the other end. The station was eerily deserted; not another soul in sight. The sun hung overhead perpetually nearing its apex. It was mid to late-morning; Albus surmised that they must have just missed the rush-hour mass.

A pearlescent monorail, propelled by fairy dust and ground unicorn horn, arrived right on cue, coming to a genteel and silent stop. Double-wide doors opened with a satisfactory swoosh;

Albus and Genji boarded. Advertisements for Cheshire Cheato's Gnarly New Flamin' Hot Habanero Sweet-Chili Taquito Cheese-Os with Ground Placenta Dipping Sauce™ were copied and pasted along the interior length of the carriage, above the windows. Again, it did not escape Albus' notice that they were the sole passengers on the train.

"I call window!" barked Genji, which was perfectly fine with Albus. There were plenty of window seats to go around. The garish advertisements aside, the interior of the monorail carriage was in pristine condition; plush recliners of crushed red velvet sat two-by-two with an aisle down the middle. Long, oval windows, without a smudge to be found, provided an excellent view of the city. It was as if the monorail had been a shiny, new toy opened Christmas morning, only to be abandoned for a shinier, newer toy before the protective packaging had ever been removed. Albus planted himself into one of the recliners, taking window seat, 3D; Genji took the next window seat directly behind him, 4D.

....

With the same ease that it had come to a stop, the monorail glided forward. If Albus hadn't been absently gazing out the window, he may not have noticed they had started moving. Leaving the station behind, the train accelerated gracefully. The gentle swaying of the carriage as it quietly banked and turned at an absolutely ludicrous speed, lulled Albus into a daze. Reminding him of rocking back and forth in his office chair, he closed his eyes and zoned out. For the first time in forever, he had a dream.

The monorail hurtled them along its single-track suspended above the twenty-four lane highways and byways spiraling out beneath them, the roads jam-packed exclusively with the sexiest and all-around most titillating vehicles anyone had ever laid eyes on, Lamborghinis, Bugattis, Ferraris, McLarens, every type of super-car all capable of brain-melting speeds. Genji gawked out the window his mouth agape at the never-ending wonders of the golden city. Below the speeding train, horns blared and blasted in a cacophony of Sisyphean frustration, as the gridlocked drivers of said super-cars crept along at the speed of Zeno's paradoxical arrow.

In Albus' dream, he found himself in a derelict wooden boat, big enough for three people. He was moved by unseen forces across the surface of an ocean as blue as the sky, as flat and calm as glass. The white puffy clouds overhead meandered along without a care in the world, unaware that the man in the boat beneath was observing them. They whispered cloud secrets to one another and shared recipes for eleven different types of snow.

Without warning, the clouds turned on Albus, darkening. A dreadful storm filled the skies, tossing his small craft about in a deluge of rain and wind. His boat started taking on water: fast. For every bucket he dumped, two buckets came over the sides as replacements. Struggling to remind himself that he was incapable of drowning, that once abstract, appendix-like sense of panic felt visceral this time.

From the comfort of his recliner, Genji kicked at the back of Albus' seat attempting to get the man's attention; he wanted to point out a circus in town that advertised "The World's Smallest Horse." Genji had to see it for himself and was hoping they could go to the circus after they had purchased the sword.

Much to his chagrin, the man rudely ignored him; he floated up and over the back of his companion's seat, surprised to see that Albus' eyes were shut. His head lulled and lollygagged with the banking turns of the monorail. Genji couldn't recall ever seeing Albus' eyes closed; it was an unexpectedly off-putting sight. Quietly, he levitated back down into his own seat and was left to imagine just how small The World's Smallest Horse could possibly be, *like...how small?*

Back in Albus' dream world, the boat capsized. Albus clung to the hull by a single frayed rope as the overturned vessel descended beneath the dark waves. Overwhelmed by desperation for the first time in his life, he did something completely out of character; he cried out for help, for rescue, uncertain to whom exactly. Suddenly, there was someone coming for him. He was unable to make out the identity of the person, but it felt like someone that had known Albus from long, long ago. A hand reached out.

A loud, monotone *DING*, the sound of a hot-pocket indicating that it was ready to be eaten, deprived him of an answer. The dream dissolved into the ether. The loud ding was the monorail informing its first two passengers in history, that their lovely time together had concluded and they should exit *now*. Albus wearily looked around the carriage, blinking his eyes and flexing his fingers against the cushy armrests. The double-wide sliding doors of the carriage were already open and waiting. Anxiously hovering a few paces in front of Albus, Genji tapped his foot in the air. Albus stood and followed after his impatient fox-spirit.

9

DISTRICT TWELVE

The pearly monorail deposited them into an opulent and exasperatingly complex, complex of multi-floored stores, shops and walkways, a hundred stories high; suspension bridges, curly yellow slides, and zip-lines threaded the various floors together in a chaotic tangle. They were on the inside of the titanic tree that they had seen at the center of El Dorado from a distance. The builders of the city had hollowed out its trunk, transforming the mighty tree into a magnificent mega-mall, which Albus and Genji now stood on the ground floor of, looking about the palatial atrium, staring up in awe.

Fancy people scurried about in every direction, like the interior of an ant colony, some very important task known only to them (and Golgotha), in need of completion. The air inside the mega-mall felt perfectly conditioned. Jungle plants and vines had been brought in from the outside and quarantined to Carrara marble-encased fountains; the fountains gushed artificial waterfalls rushing between the dizzying number of floors.

Finding a sword in here would be like finding a needle in a library stack. They were in luck though, not far from where they were standing was a black marble kiosk with the word 'Directory' engraved across the top. Albus cocked his head in its direction and the two walked over, unawares that they had caught the attention of a very important woman since exiting the monorail. As Albus got close to the kiosk the marble illuminated from within, revealing a list of every store in the shopping district; thankfully it was in alphabetical order. He scrolled to 'S.' *Sword Shop. Sword Shop, Where's the Sword Shop?*

Scented Censers…hmm could maybe pick up a souvenir—add some more censers to the office.

Scented Centaurs. Nope.

A gracile woman with long thin features coolly eyed the man and scruffy looking creature-thing bobbing around him. She watched them walk from the monorail platform to the mega-mall directory, her delight only intensifying. Leaving her clucking cohort of like-minded individuals, she wafted over to Albus and Genji. From behind them, she proclaimed without introduction, "Did you *seriously* just get off the monorail?!" Banal amusement dripped off every word.

Interrupting his search, Albus turned towards the lilting voice to see a young-*ish* woman held aloft by an updraft of nobility. Her ears protruded to a point from beneath her platinum blonde hair that framed cheek-bones capable of cutting diamonds. Placed on the center of her face was a nose that turned decidedly up.

"That is…*hilarious*," the young-*ish* woman added, fluting air through her thin, upturned, nostrils. The way she said *hilarious* reminded Albus of the way Golgotha said *favorite.* The woman's violet eyes sparkled, belying an inner void as she introduced herself, "I'm Jezebel."

Draped by spindly limbs and lavish fabrics she extended a slender arm gracefully from beneath her flowing, white robes, at the end of which were long fingers capped with a painstakingly maintained French-dip manicure. She held her hand out elevated with an enervated level of energy awaiting Albus' courtesies, Pandora bracelet jingling softly on her wrist.

Albus didn't take the woman's hand in return. Instead, he said, "Hello, my name is Albus and this is my fox-spirit, Genji," making a thumb over his shoulder towards the translucent fox with the fuzzy human hands. "We're looking for a sword. Know where we can find one?"

Jezebel tersely retracted her hand into the safety of her robes; whereas normally she would have been bombastically offended by the snub, spending the rest of her energy utterly destroying this plebeian tourist in the El Dorado press—she instead found herself only further intrigued. This strange new man was nothing like the other El Doradans. *Oh, my...and is that a stylish tri-color fanny pack he is wearing? How daring!*

"A sword?" chortled Jezebel, "Why in the world would you want such a brutish and silly thing!?"

Albus began to reply, "We're on our way to kill Golga—"

"Gomer! Salome! Get over here!" commanded Jezebel, stamping her foot, cutting Albus off before he could tell her about his vacation plans. Her flock of attending descended on the recent arrivals. "You absolutely must meet my new friends, they are *hilarious*," added Jezebel, indicating towards the travelers. Jezebel's sycophants pecked and peppered Albus and Genji with a barrage of quotidian (as well as some very personal) questions: Where were they from? What brought them to El Dorado? What did they do? How much money did they make? How powerful were they? How big were their penises?

Albus was, without a doubt, the most powerful person in El Dorado, but it was something he would never brag about. Put off by the assault of unusually probing questions, he fielded them as best he could. With an air of finality only capable of being mustered by someone who had never experienced true tragedy, Jezebel aborted the small talk, abruptly declaring, "This has been absolutely *marvelous*." Rather surprisingly she added, "Albus, you must accompany me to the Red Letter Gala. Tonight. Nine PM sharp. *Kisses*!!" She didn't actually kiss him: she just said the words. Jezebel swooped away, her silky, gossamer garb twirling behind her. Gomer and Salome, caught flat-footed by Jezebel's hasty departure, juked around the new arrivals and clamored after their clique commander.

Albus watched Jezebel gallivant down the gold-plated, marble concourse longer than he had intended. Genji bobbed up and down in front of Albus' face and waved his hands.

"Earth to Albus! The sword?"

"Right."

Returning his focus to the directory slab the man picked up where he had left off.

Where was I? Scented Centaurs. Nope.

Scimitars, Sabers, and Lots of Other Things. That one sounds promising.

Scintillating Scabbards. Close, might be worth checking out.

Albus scrolled further.

Swag Swarthy Schwag.

Swanky Swine Swatches.

Swooning Swan Sweaters.

Swordfish (and other types of fish) Taxidermy Specialist

Sworn Blood Oaths.

He found himself longing for the simplicity of Uruk's economy. Scimitars, Sabers, and Lots of Other Things sounded like the closest thing to a sword shop and likely their best bet. They navigated their way through the tilt-a-whirl like commercial complex, only to be disappointed when the proprietor of Scimitars, Sabers, and Lots of Other Things regrettably informed them that they had stopped selling scimitars and sabers years ago. The shop had pivoted to focus solely on selling Lots of Other Things; they had not paid the fee yet to update their name in the district directory. The owner was profusely apologetic and offered them a racecar-print muumuu (thirty-five percent off) for their troubles.

The only other shop with a remotely sword related sobriquet was Scintillating Scabbards. It was a long shot, but certainly worth checking out. On their way towards the outlet, Genji stopped Albus, tugging on his arm. He begged Albus to let him throw a coin into one of the gushing fountains pouring from golden floor to golden floor. Albus still had some yen leftover from Neo Kyoto in his fanny pack and indulged the playful spirit.

He pulled out a copper coin stamped with a chrysanthemum, a round hole punched through its center, and placed it into Genji's outstretched paw. Albus took some small pleasure in the delight that radiated across Genji's face as the fox-spirit raptly stared, mesmerized by the copper coin tumbling and clattering off the marble, disappearing into the rushing waters below. Genji pumped his fist in the air.

As Albus suspected, Scintillating Scabbards trafficked solely in brilliantly decorated sheaths for bladed weapons, minus the blades. The brash owner of the kiosk berated them, mercilessly ripping at their very souls. Why would they *ever* come to him expecting such a silly thing as a sword? He clearly only sold scabbards; it was in the frickin' name. "Now scram!" He rudely chased them off. Deep down the owner knew he should probably sell swords too, but he was a scab man got' dammit.

Albus and Genji regrouped; they decided to split up to maximize their search effort and ask around of the various purveyors and shop owners, maybe someone knew someone who sold swords. Heading off in opposite directions, they popped into this shop and that shop, climbed up the inclined suspension bridges, and shot down zip-lines; it was at least a fun, albeit exhausting, shopping experience. Most merchants shook their heads. Others claimed that of course they had swords and invited the travelers in, only to try to sell them letter openers or really large daggers. Many laughed, asking with disdain, what would you ever need such a silly thing as a sword for in El Dorado? Genji and Albus crossed paths again on the 99th floor and shared a dejected look.

"No such luck?" asked Albus.

"I'm tired," complained Genji, slumping his shoulders, head hung towards the perfectly polished alabaster floor. Albus wasn't tired but he had, by this point, abandoned all hope that they would find a sword in the shopping district of El Dorado.

Weary from their fruitless errand the pair patronized an Orange Julius for a fruity refreshment. Their search was going nowhere. They sat and lamented at a laminated table with an image of an orange squeegeed into its surface; bright green leaves coiffed its stem. Chairs welded of thick metal wire dipped in gold plasti-coat supported their dejected frames in a heinously uncomfortable yet undeniably stylish fashion. Albus took notice of all of the carefully manicured plant-life restrained by the marble planters. *There's no way,* he thought, *that these plants are getting enough light to thrive.* Were the plants real or fake, he wondered. They certainly looked real enough and supposed that it didn't matter much.

While sipping and sucking away at the orange, icy-cold concoction, putting the plight of the plants out of his mind, Albus found his thoughts involuntarily turning towards Jezebel. He did have to admit that she was pretty and there was something aristocratic about her. *What about Elixabeth?* Elixabeth was *just gone* and never coming back. He had to accept that; move on. He knew that. His heart was torn; he still loved his wife. Albus looked down at his left-hand; he hadn't realized he was still wearing his wedding band on his ring-finger; he no longer felt it there. It had become a part of him like a wire wrapped around the trunk of a young sapling.

When he and Elixabeth were first married, he would constantly spin the ring with his thumb, slipping it forward and backward against his finger. Now the soft gold band was covered in nicks and dings from an eternity of absentmindedly knocking it against the edges of hard surfaces. The modest fourteen karat ring began to feel dull and unspecial against the overflowing brilliance of the El Doradan backdrop. Sorrowfully and with a twinge of shame, Albus slipped the ring off underneath the Orange Julius table and stashed it in his tri-color fanny pack. He wondered, *Does Jezebel like counting ants as much as I do?*

Genji slurped at his Orange Julius, struggling to make a solid seal with the end of the straw; his long snout made this a challenge. He didn't care much for frozen orange juice and found himself wishing it was a cup filled with the blood of a small mammal (or some more of that best-udon-in-town broth). Enjoying the reprieve from their search, he stretched his arms out to his sides and reflected again on how good it felt to be free of that dark wooden box back in Neo Kyoto. A pang of homesickness for the eternally blooming sakura trees and wild woods where he used to endlessly frolic, chasing after crickets and frogs, narrowly avoiding jagged toothed traps laid by hunters, gurgled loudly from his tummy. He thought about his fox mom and fox siblings back in the fox den. She had raised his six brothers and sisters all on her lonesome. He never knew his fox dad; his mom would never say what happened to him, only that he left before he was born.

Leafcutter ants marched deterministically up the legs of the table, up underneath the underside and over on top of the tabletop, frenetically scurrying all over the table's inlaid graphic of the faux orange and its artificial green leaves. Albus counted, *five, six, seven...* As he continued to count, he vowed that he would figure out what these ants were up to before leaving the jungles of El Dorado; he swore it. *One thousand two hundred and twenty-three, one thousand two hundred and twenty-four, one thousand two hundred and twenty-five.* The ants, growing wise to the table's ruse, lost interest and continued on their merry way; Albus was sad to see them go.

Genji glanced over at his peculiar new man-friend sitting across from him, sensing there was much more to Albus than he let on; not that Albus was the easiest person to get to know. He didn't talk about himself much, if ever, for that matter. At that moment, his man-friend wasn't contemplating anything of consequence; Albus wondered what the Red Letter Gala was all about. *Would I need new clothes for it?* He couldn't remember the last time he had bought new clothes. Jezebel was dressed so elegantly just for the shopping district.

"Hey, Genji, do you think—" he began, Genji perked his ears and looked over. "Never mind." The last slurps of their orange slushees dwindled, escaping the probing reaches of their straws; they had exhausted all their options in the shopping district and needed to search elsewhere. Tossing their used cups (each one a goblet of solid gold studded in precious gemstones worth a small medieval hamlet) into the overflowing trash can, they made their way towards the exit of the immense mega-mall. As they left the perfectly conditioned air behind, Albus paused, peering through a window display of sharply dressed mannequins decked out in nineteen-piece tuxedos; he lingered briefly.

10

THE RED LETTER GALA

It was difficult to state with absolute certainty where the boundaries of the shopping district ended, and other districts began in El Dorado. Gilded department stores, gem-studded boutiques, kiosks, stalls, and street-vendors erupted like an outbreak of hives from every corner, alcove, cranny, and nook of the overwhelmingly well-to-do city. All enthusiastically advertised their wares with garishly lit Jumbotron screens that would have compelled the neon signage from Neo Kyoto to commit seppuku in shame. The screens flashed with images of large breasted women seductively running their tongues along the latest pair of titanium scissors to hit the market; others displayed insanely ripped, chiseled men, bulges hardly restrained by banana hammocks, bouncing up and down on the newest innovation in pogo sticks.

As they roamed the golden sidewalks plotting their next move, ogling and gawking at the city's unmitigated wealth, Genji suggested a not so terrible idea; maybe they should rent a room in one of the many resplendent hotels. They could set up a base of operations while they continued their quest—err vacation scavenger hunt, for the elusive sword they sought.

Some six or seven blocks from the prodigious tree trunk, a

mega-resort skyscraper (unsurprisingly made of gold) displayed a living tableau on a balcony above its lobby entrance, composed of people and creatures contorting their bodies in unnatural positions, advertising the resort's name; Le Coq Hardi it spelled. It was French and meant The Daring Rooster. Genji and Albus shared a juvenile snicker over the hotel's moniker, deciding they would stay there.

The automated doors of the hotel, its frames carved from huge rubies, parted aside as Albus and Genji entered. The lobby of Le Coq Hardi, like everything in this damn city, was magnificent to the max. The non-stop, over-the-top flood of utmost luxury and riches, if it hadn't already, began to grate on Albus subconsciously. Rooms, the concierge informed them, cost ten billion dollars a night. That was no problem for Albus Cake.

They ascended in one of the crystalline elevators; a bellhop showed them to their new accommodations. Before the surly porter could tire of waiting for a tip that wasn't coming, Genji morphed into an orange and white blur (a phenomenon that Albus had grown accustomed to); the creamsicle blur rocketed about their new digs, eventually scuttling to a halt in the foyer. "Nineteen!! Nineteen solid gold toilets!" the fox-spirit proclaimed with a sense of personal accomplishment.

Albus sat down on the edge of the bed; picking up the golden remote, its buttons each a precious gemstone, he mindlessly surfed the channels. The allure of the mysterious Red Letter Gala still lingered in the air like fried chicken; of course, he would never attend something so stupid. He hoped Genji would bring it up, so he could tell his companion how stupid the thought of going was. A diffuse red glow from the digital clock resting on the golden nightstand declared that it was half-past six in the evening. As six became seven and seven ate nine, Genji still hadn't mentioned the gala.

"So about that gala? Stupid right?" Albus lead.

Genji snorted, "Yeah what was that about? Totally lame right?"

"Oh yeah, like totally lame..." Albus trailed off cooly, then came back in hot, "Although...there might be someone at the gala that would know about the sword?"

Unusual, unusual indeed, thought Genji, raising an eyebrow. He was supposed to be the trickster in this relationship. *What is Albus up to?* Skeptical that someone at the gala might be of assistance, Genji couldn't entirely rule it out either. After some back and forth, the fox-spirit accepted that it wasn't the absolute worst idea on the planet, perhaps they should check it out. Albus leapt up from the edge of the bed and splashed some cold water from the gold faucet onto his face, *Alright. Gala time.* He was ready to go.

....

It wasn't hard to find the soiree; every denizen of the golden metropolis was making their way there. All they had to do was follow the crowd. Albus pushed through the throng to get to the front, keeping an eye out for Jezebel as he did. With a honking noise that sounded like a swan song, an all-white stretch limo pulled by three white horses came around the bend. As it slowed to a stop, a man with the head of a goose opened the door. Out stepped Jezebel looking even more stunning than she had earlier in the day; her makeup was done-up so splendidly one could not tell where the roguish ruse ended and the aquiline woman's face began. Albus waved at her as she caught sight of them. Jezebel did not wave back; gliding in their direction she tried to conceal her irritation at the sight of the scruffy fox-thing hanging about Albus, which wasn't difficult considering her face did not move much. *Is he still wearing that stylish tri-color fanny-pack? Marvelous.*

Jezebel cheeped, "Albus, *darling*, you made it!" Her tone turning dour, "Unfortunately there is a strict no-pets policy; that *thing* will have to stay outside."

Momentarily befuddled Albus replied, "Oh, you mean Genji?" Not hesitating long enough for Genji's liking, Albus knelt to one knee and spoke in a soft, placating voice to his fox-spirit. "Listen buddy, you don't mind waiting outside right? I'll only be in there for two-maybe three hours tops." Arms crossed as he listened, the fox did not say a word. Genji did suppose they had been spending a lot of time together; perhaps it would be healthy to do his own thing for a little while. *What's the worst that could happen?* thought Genji as he agreed to wait outside. Albus barked, "Thanks bud! I owe you one!" Jezebel held out the crook of her arm waiting for her date to get the clue. They waltzed off together towards the entrance leaving Genji behind.

....

A parade of the most stupidly wealthy and well-dressed people in all existence led up to the gala threshold. A silk red carpet, spun on demand by a legion of silk-worms modified to bleed from their anuses, dying the carpet its signature sanguine color, sprawled out along the ground leading the way to the hall's entrance. Like the sheets of sanitary tissue paper used at doctor's offices, the silk carpet was torn off and discarded, a fresh red carpet spun in its place, for each guest to individually traipse down. Still, some in attendance insisted that the bespoke virginally spun red carpet was not worthy of their station and had their own red carpets crafted in equally quixotic and asinine fashions laid down for them to walk across, overlapping the one provided.

Anyone and everyone who was anyone and everyone was in attendance. As such, there were no photographers available to take photos, a fact which did not deter the attendees from halting in place and voguing at every possible opportunity. Much chatter about who wore it hot and who wore it not, chirped and tittered through the airwaves. Albus tried to keep up. Everyone's dress appeared pretty much identical—he thought—except with just radically different cuts, colors, patterns, shapes, and straps (or lack thereof).

Jezebel giddily explained to Albus that the Red Letter Gala was the biggest event of the season, second only to the Ascension Festival After-Party, which she also organized; excitedly adding that most years even Golgotha himself would attend and spray champagne all over everyone with his trunk. Albus unintentionally bristled at the mention of Golgotha's name. Jezebel, keenly detecting the repulsion, asked, "Do you know him?"

"Yeah, something like that."

....

The inside of the gala hall, a colossal domed atrium, contained more glitz and glamor than the entire known universe; it should have been mathematically impossible to fit it all, but somehow Jezebel had managed. Guests made their way from the entrance vestibule to the hall, crossing over a bridge (made of gold), beneath which flowed a river of rosacea hued lobster tails, split at the seams, their puffy innards forming the white tufts of the shellfish river's rapids; the chitinous shells clattered together with the sound of wooden wind chimes.

Thousands of round tables set in the finest finery were spread out across the venue floor, anxiously awaiting their insatiable diners to be. In one quadrant of the hall, a fondue lake spurted forth a fountain of molten chocolate high into the air; guests eagerly grabbed fishing poles, affixing tidbits of marshmallows or graham cracker to their lines, casting them into the cacao lake, reeling back in chocolate-coated morsels.

Albus followed Jezebel's lead, taking their seats at a reserved table towards the center. He took a few cursory sips of his wine as other guests filtered in, joining them at their table, shrilly kissing Jezebel on each cheek. A vast multitude of servers kept their glasses constantly filled; between sips of wine, magically a bottle would appear over Albus' shoulder pouring more of the intoxicating ambrosia into his glass to the point of overflowing.

Not wanting to appear rude, Albus chowed down on course after course with the rest of the gala attendees, despite his usual abstemiousness. The cornucopia of dishes and delicacies tasted extremely bland to him, and it was all quite cold; however, the other gala attendees didn't seem to notice or care. Forget seconds, they went straight for fourth and fifth helpings.

For the main course, chefs slaughtered an entire cow table-side for each guest, informing the diners that each bovine had been raised on its own private island (fed exclusively on a diet of Kobe beef sliders and craft IPA beer); removing only the choicest cuts of meat, the chefs discarded the rest. A part of Albus was mortified by the act; he quickly suppressed the revulsion, reminding himself that he was on vacation. *When in El Dorado.*

Jezebel prattled on with their adjacent table guests throughout the rest of the feast as Albus tried to follow along: who had slept with whose ex-nanny's gardener's pedicurist? Sufficiently gorged, the dinner service concluding, guests began rolling from their seats and started mingling. Throughout the entire dinner conversation, Albus had yet to ascertain what charity this gala was for, or what Jezebel even *did;* she just seemed to know everyone, and more importantly, everyone knew her.

....

As the mingling transformed to schmoozing, the emcee came over the PA system, introducing the first of the evening's entertainment. Hoisted into place by unseen hands, a magnificent champagne flute laser-cut from a single rocket-sized diamond emerged from beneath the venue floor. Filled to its brim, the bubbling champagne foamed and sloshed over its sides as the gigantic glass was brought into position. Three spotlights: one, two, three swiveled and focused in on the glass. Albus' *date?* left his side, perching herself in front of the diamond chalice; the bright lights only further washed out her pale skin. In her hand she held a laughably oversized silver spoon, like a pair of prop scissors a mayor might use to cut through a red-ribbon, only there was no sense of playfulness or whimsy in Jezebel's intention.

The party-goers gave her their attention adoringly as she *clang clang clanged* the jumbo spoon like a gong mallet against the side of the diamond-carved champagne flute. The last murmurs brutally assassinated, she smiled with self-satisfaction knowing that everyone was obediently admiring her. Jezebel began her speech first by profusely thanking everyone in attendance with utmost sincerity. She went on about their immense personal sacrifices, lauding everyone for all the terribly hard work they had done. Gratitudes and beatifications concluded, she did a stiff curtsey and exited stage left.

Over the PA system, the delightful hum of symphonic music began to leak into the air as the bubbles inside the champagne flute, which had been mingling as chaotically as the guests moments ago, fell into formation; each air-filled orb lined up in a crystalline lattice structure. Holding the pattern briefly, the bubbles then broke into a choreographed dance, zipping faster and ever faster about the gold-tinted fluid until they blurred together creating the illusion of nearly solid lines, forming rotating mandalas and all manner of interlocking geometries.

Albus could hardly believe his eyes, front and center of the dance was bubble number three, Carla! She was the star of the show! He tugged on Jezebel's arm. "I know her!" he said, pointing excitedly. Jezebel smiled and nodded politely. After the performance, Albus caught up with Carla backstage; it had been ages since they had seen each other so long ago at the lake bottom. He found out that winning the race to the surface had given her the courage to come out to her parents; she married her longtime partner, and with her wife's encouragement, had taken up choreographed champagne dancing. "That's wonderful!" Albus beamed, cheering Carla the bubble with his flat glass of bubbly.
....

Jezebel pulled Albus away, grabbing him by the strap of his fanny pack; she led him about the gala by his elbow, hobnobbing and constantly refilling their glasses as she traipsed about the hall. She introduced him to every person of importance, and in El Dorado, every person was important. Standing in a circle schmoozing with very important people, Albus casually sipped at his drink. Sensing a lull in the conversation, he thought now might be a good time to bring up the ants. He leaned into the circle asking Jezebel and company if they had ever noticed how many ants were crawling around El Dorado. "Do you ever wonder what the ants are up to?"

"Ants?! Darling, don't be so provincial," Jezebel responded with a dismissive laugh turning towards the circle of important and beautiful people. Her palm held flat to her chest, she added,

"Didn't I tell you he's *hilarious*." Albus sipped from his cocktail a little more quickly. *At least she laughed,* he thought.

As the drinks flowed like blood through cheesecloth, the schmoozing progressed to intense chit-chat, signaling the next phase of the evening. Guests (as if choreographed) parted from the middle of the venue; this wasn't their first gala. The floor slid further apart making for a hole the size of an American soccer pitch. From the gaping cavity a gargantuan, golden ziggurat was hoisted into place, to fanfare and much ado. Thirty-three tiers tall Albus counted. He had to admit he was impressed with its construction, etched with numerous intricate symbols, the ziggurat had steep stairs carved into each of its four sides leading to a flat stage on top.

Men and women with professionally sculpted bodies, their skin airbrushed about two shades darker than its natural color, populated every tier of the structure, kneeling patiently behind wooden drums stretched with calf skins, sticks in hand. Stationed among the ziggurat attendants, kneeling behind one of the drums on a lower tier, Albus spotted the statuesque warrior woman he had seen earlier from when he first arrived in the golden city. He waved towards her, realizing midway through the gesture she probably wouldn't recognize him, but it was too late to stop waving now. Standing close by, the woman's silverback beau snapped pics of her for the gram. They were still together and that made Albus feel good. Maybe love would conquer all in the end.

Responding to some signal that Albus didn't catch, the ziggurat attendants held up their drumsticks in unison; they began rhythmically drumming, slowly and softly at first in a *lento pianissimo* fashion. The drumming emanated a subtle energy into the ginormous space as conversations began to animate. Albus would lose track of Jezebel, only for her to reappear by his side, somehow finding him again in the throng of thousands, like a swallow returning to Capistrano, replenishing him with a fresh drink. Taking him by the elbow again, she carted him around, introducing Albus to a seemingly endless parade of important people.

....

Outside, Genji waited. The gold streets and sidewalks of the extravagant city were eerily empty, no critter vendors peddling enticing tidbits of grub or frog matrons to pester for bowls of soup. From the direction of the gala hall, he could hear the garbled clamor of the enormous party reverberating towards him as a hypnotic drum beat joined the fray. He imagined his man-friend inside, valiantly zeroing in on the whereabouts of the mythical sword they sought.

To keep himself entertained, he leapt along a row of golden park benches running adjacent to the sidewalk. Leaping across the gaps from bench to bench, sticking his landings, he would then turn around to hop back the other way. Thankfully, there were still plenty of bugs milling about in the vacant beams of streetlight to investigate.

A chartreuse jewel scarab, *Chrysina Gloriosa*, furiously flapped its yucky yellow wings as it buzzed past Genji's snout en route to its hot date at the local streetlamp. Genji gave chase, nipping at it half-heartedly; growing bored, he abandoned his hunt and curled into a ball. The lustrous beetle narrowly escaped its doom. *Phew!* thought the scarab; he'd hate to die a virgin.

....

Back inside the hall, the drumming intensified. The constant consumption of alcoholic beverages started to have an effect on Albus as the continuous and linear flow of the evening's events broke down, replaced with snippets and freeze frames, with large chunks missing from the middle. Chatting about how big everyone's penises were had grown a bit stale to Albus. Excusing himself from Jezebel's side, he went to look for the restroom.

An intense blast of arctic air hit him in the face as he opened the restroom door; there were no toilets, sinks, or anything re-motely bathroom-related in sight. An Alaskan tundra the size of a hockey rink filled the interior of the space. Men gleefully whizzed their names into the snow or used their streams to break apart thin ice sheets floating on the frozen creeks. Albus watched one man tip the restroom attendant to look the other way while he urinated on a baby seal's head, snapping selfies.

Piled up in the middle of the tundra sat a mountain of flakey, dandruff-like granules that could have been albino cousins to the gray dust from Uruk. Politicians and businessmen wearing red or blue ties, reflective ski-goggles obscuring their eyes, and nothing else, frolicked in the white dust with one another. Essentially nude, they sled down the mountain of white, rolling around in it, making snow angels; one hollered in Albus' general direction, "It's fresh pow pow brah!"

Albus didn't quite understand, but he got the gist. *What the hell, it's a party,* he thought as he joined in, doing a cannonball into the powdery white stuff, sending an ominous mushroom cloud above his head. Suddenly, Albus felt as though he could move at the speed of light plus one. Undergoing mitosis, he became a single-celled organism, dividing into a thousand copies of himself. He exited the restroom becoming a vector extending to infinity; conversing with every single person at the party at once, instantly an expert on any and every topic they could possibly be interested in. All the while every copy of himself knocked back any cocktail within his reach.

. . . .

The snippets and freeze frames of the evening deteriorated further into under-exposed Polaroids. Breakdancing in the middle of a large circle of partygoers, Albus spotted the frog matron from the udon shop! Having spent some time in the hospital recovering from her injuries, she was all healed up and down to get down. Doing a sick back-spin, she carried the maneuver into a windmill and then held for a freeze.

The crowd OOoo-ed and Aww-ed at the frog woman's impressive dance moves. Albus, excited to see she wasn't dead from Golgotha's outburst, broke into the dance circle and awkwardly offered her an apology for the events back in Neo Kyoto. "Shoo! Shoo!!" she leveled at him, acting as though she didn't remember him (it was quite possible that she didn't, with the head trauma and all). Albus was harshing her vibe and had to go; the partiers surrounding the dancing frog pushed Albus aside. The man gone, she went back to breakdancing, performing an up-rock into a hand hop, continuing to absolutely kill it.

The refined and sophisticated atmosphere that had kicked off the gala quickly drained away as guests began to let loose under the limitless deluge of alcohol and other substances. Burly men forming a security detail cleared a path through the crowd leading to the ziggurat steps. A loud commotion rose throughout the hall; the skeleton-man from the gates of Uruk had entered the building, backed by an entire legion of entertainers. In need of work since Uruk's destruction, the skeleton-man felt he was way too talented to be playing with this group of hacks, but he was contractually obligated to be there. His manager would murder him if he didn't show; he didn't really have a choice in the matter.

Taking the stage atop the tiered golden pyramid, any semblance of civility left the building as soon as the skeleton-man and his legions began to play. Not much of a dancer, in his intoxicated state Albus found himself unable to resist bumping and grinding with Jezebel's friend Salome, seductively gyrating together. Gomer latched onto them, flirting with Albus as her husband scowled from a dark corner against a wall.

In one Polaroid from the evening, Albus had his arm avuncularly slung around Cheshire Cheato's shoulders, the two of them feasting on Chet's Gnarly New Flamin' Hot Habanero Sweet-Chili Taquito Cheese-Os with Ground Placenta Dipping Sauce™, the bags plastered to their mouths like a horse's feedbag. Greedily Albus licked each cheese caked finger clean, including Chet's.

....

The under-exposed Polaroids of the night's shenanigans decayed even further into police sketches and watercolors made by a continuing education class from the local community college. 'Virgins' clawed and clamored their way to the top of the golden ziggurat begging to be sacrificed at the skeleton-man's feet, as the security detail pushed them back, attempting to maintain order. The frog matron, unaware that she was pregnant, gave birth to an armada of toads right in the middle of another sick back-spin, spewing the baby toads like a rotating machine-gun turret across the gala hall. Partygoers shrieked with delight and grabbed the toads by the forelegs. They spun them round and round to the rhythmic drum and bass, do-si-do-ing the toads as if at a hoe-down, letting them go, splattering the newborn amphibians against the walls with a plop.

With as much grace as a newborn giraffe, Albus eluded the security detail and stumbled his way up the ziggurat steps, struggling to keep his legs beneath him. Right in the middle of their big number he snatched the microphone away from the skeleton-man, emboldened to the point of annihilation by the copious amount of drugs and alcohol shorting out his circuits. Ducking and dodging the skeleton-man's attempts to wrest control of the mic back from him like some drunken jiu-jitsu savant, Albus shouted into the PA system, "Look what I can do!"

He demanded the emcee lower the house lights and shroud the venue in total darkness. The throng of partygoer's displeased murmurs escalated to a loud grumble. Doing the math in his head, the emcee decided it best to indulge this raving lunatic. If he lost control over the crowd, they would do what crowds do and start throwing things, possibly hitting one of the entertainers. Then he'd have a giant lawsuit on his hand (and El Dorado had no shortage of litigious-happy attorneys). At least if it was dark, they couldn't aim as well. Siding with the lesser of two evils, the emcee killed the house-lights, put the spotlights out of their misery, murdered the lasers, and bashed the LCDs to pieces with a hammer.

In the darkened, semi-hushed hall, Albus came to the edge of the ziggurat stage. Standing there momentarily, some part of his brain making a gallant effort to function under the avalanche of self-inflicted delirium, he questioned if this was a good idea or not. *Just kidding, this is a great idea.* Hesitation and inhibition laid to the wayside, Albus summoned his powers and in a magnificent display of grandeur and awe, brought forth light from the empty darkness.

Blinded by the light, the irritated murmurs of the crowd dispersed in an instant as total silence enveloped the venue in a dense fog, quiet enough to hear a needle drop. One second passed, then two seconds, two and a half seconds later, the crowd raptured like a supernova into raucous cheers and applause, beating their breasts and gnashing their teeth at the sheer impossibility of the spectacle. The amazon woman's silverback boyfriend went totally ape-shit. A number of people's heads exploded, but no one of importance. A self-satisfied smile rendezvoused with Jezebel's face; she knew this monorail man was *interesting* for a reason. She possessed an excellent eye for talent.

The debauchery continued to rage for a little while longer. Bodies merged and melted like butter into an inseparable mass. The rhythmic drum and bass thumped, substituting the need for any conscious thought. Imitation blood (or what Albus was pretty sure was imitation blood) sprayed from the emergency fire sprinklers suspended from the venue's domed ceiling, drenching the orgy of bodies in sanguine lubricant. It was the most fun Albus had ever had.

11

THE HANGOVER

The party ended. Guests, their clothing shred to tatters, makeup reduced to poorly imitated Picassos, in possession of half the footwear they had arrived with, filtered out into the streets to go wherever it was that they went. The fleeing partygoers avoided all eye contact with fellow attendees that, only moments earlier, they had been vowing to be "best friends forever" with. The sun hadn't just risen but was already well into its morning routine, enjoying a cup of joe, it beamed down on the scattering dilettantes with brightly lit disdain. Embracing him with her hands placed on his shoulders, half an arms-length away, Jezebel leaned in and air-kissed Albus on the cheek making an exaggerated smooch sound without any actual contact. She repeated the charade with Albus' other cheek, saying, "You were absolutely *brilliant*, darling! Green Letter Gala tomorrow night, nine o'clock!" and wilted away into her horse-drawn limousine disappearing around the corner.

Beneath a golden bench, a few paces from the venue's exit was an orange and white ball, its chest slowly rising and falling. *Oh shit*...thought Albus. *Genji*! He totally forgot he had left his friend outside the entirety of the night and felt slightly guilty; at the same time, he had had so much fun he couldn't wait to tell his sidekick all about it. He stroked the fox-spirit's scruff, waking him from his light slumber.

"Hey, buddy," Albus whispered. Genji unfurled, stretching out his arms and legs, opening his mouth wide to let a drawn-out yawn escape; his long pink tongue lolling out, flanked on either side by sharp pointy teeth. Blinking his amber eyes a few times to get his bearings, he was startled to see Albus standing over him donning the stupidest grin he had ever seen.

"Let's go back to the hotel." They walked down the early morning streets of El Dorado, the rays of the sun glinting off the golden buildings, filtering slabs of green light through emerald windows. Albus blabbered on about the very important people he had met; how he had danced and even flirted. Genji half-heartedly listened, hoping for any intel on the sword they were seeking. Instead, Albus went on and on about how the frog matron from Neo Kyoto was there; she had survived her head exploding and was even a new mom. "Can you believe it!?" Cheshire Cheato was there too, but it was totally cool—they were bros now; he even tried some of Chet's new Cheese-Os and liked them. On and on Albus went about the skeleton-man, the ziggurat…

"And the sword?" interrupted Genji.

His eyes glancing up to the right, "Oh yeah…A few people said they knew about it," Albus bold-faced lied, "but I need to gather more information." A watermelon-sized seed of concern for his friend germinated in Genji's tummy as he bobbed along; he had never seen this side of Albus.

At the door to their suite lay a copy of the *El Dorado Gazette* wrapped in a piece of gossamer twine. Plastered all over the Gazette's gala section (which made up ninety-nine percent of the paper's bulk) were images of Albus and Jezebel. Bold headlines read, 'Mystery Man Blows Minds' and 'Frog Matron Gives Birth: New Octingenti-Mom.' A small op-ed piece buried deep within the obituaries was titled, 'What About the Ants?' Albus didn't see it.

It's a well-known rule that for every action, there is an equal and opposite reaction. Yet most people tend to focus solely on the action, hoping the reaction will miss them or get lost in the mail. The grand culmination of Albus' actions from the previous night lagged, (he momentarily deluded himself that he had escaped their inevitability) and showed up all at once in one massive hangover. A hangover like none other tackled Albus around the waist banging his head against hard cement—*Stop hitting yourself, Stop hitting yourself.*

The energy and excitement drained out of him and in an instant, replaced with self-loathing and mumbled phrases. When Genji would speak, it began to sound like an annoying buzz of a gnat about his head. Mustering what little strength he had left, Albus strong-armed the fox-spirit into agreeing that their best course of action, for now, was to lay by the hotel pool and slowly sip Bloody Marys. A cabana boy approached Albus informing him that he had a phone call waiting at the pool-side Tiki hut. Stepping away from the lounge chairs he picked up the receiver; the call was from Jezebel. He 'mmm hmm-ed' and nodded while glancing back over at Genji. After hanging up the phone the thought occurred to him to check in with his office. *Fuck that. I'm on vacation.*

Later that evening back in the hotel room, Albus explained to Genji that he was going to the Green Letter Gala with Jezebel. Albus explained that there was some dumb rule that didn't allow fox-spirits. If it was up to him, he'd toss that silly rule out, but it wasn't up to him. He assured Genji he had tried again and again for them to make an exception. Besides, someone would have to stay back to hold down the fort. This would be the last one, he swore up and down; after this one, if he didn't get any intel on the sword they would leave El Dorado and continue looking elsewhere. Albus didn't come home that night, or the next night for that matter. Genji's seed of concern blossomed into a creeping strangle-vine.

The Green Letter Gala turned into the Blue Letter Gala which in turn became the Yellow Letter Gala. Like a stray cat Albus would intermittently return to the lavish hotel suite to splash some water on his face or sit in a chair with his eyes closed, then disappear again, off to the latest resort grand opening, yacht quinceañera, or golf course christening. On one of Albus' return visits, Genji had spread out an expansive map of the entire gilded city over the table. The fox had pushed red and green thumbtacks into the map and drawn circles around them with a compass in blue ball-point pen, connecting the circles with lines of yellow thread, plotting out potential locations to find the sword.

"Check it out. There's a street called the Alley of Blades!" said Genji. "Think they might have swords there?" Excitedly wagging his tail, proud of the hard work he had done.

"Maybe?" said Albus dismissively. "Might just be blender repair shops though," he added, shooting down the idea without much conscious effort as he vanished out the door again. The wagging of Genji's tail slowed then drooped. Albus hadn't even said goodbye this time.

Albus didn't return for many days; Genji's concern for his friend grew into an all-consuming kudzu patch. He couldn't stand idly by any longer. That night he left their ostentatious accommodations in search of his friend. Albus wasn't at all hard to find, not even a few paces from the exit of Le Coq Hardi's lobby, Genji caught sight of brilliant lights shooting into the air. He zipped along following the lights like rescue flairs.

. . . .

Turning a corner onto a wide avenue, Genji spotted Albus in a nineteen piece tuxedo, a top hat on his head, each piece of the tuxedo disheveled or undone in some way. Albus marched along at the head of a large procession of people, leading them raucously through the streets. In one hand he aimlessly waved a conductor's baton while using his free hand to blast his recognizable lights into the night sky. Jezebel marched alongside, grasping Albus about the shoulders. She egged Albus on, encouraging him to pop paparazzi's heads like pimples with a simple pinch of his fingers. Without a second thought he obeyed, causing Jezebel to cackle with laughter and hug him tight about the neck. The hanger-ons and groupies roared along at the unhinged abandon free of all consequence. It was far worse than Genji had feared.

"Albus!" shouted Genji. "Albus!!" Albus spun on one leg, kicking his other leg round in front of him to generate momentum: a pirouette by the world's worst ballerina. Steadying himself Albus caught sight of his fox-spirit that he hadn't seen in days, or had it been weeks? Or just a few minutes ago? He couldn't remember and it didn't matter, he was stoked to see him all the same.

"Hey, buddy!" Albus shouted back, smiling with crooked eyes. Telling the rest of the crowd to go on without him, Albus dismissed his coterie; he'd catch up with them at the after-party. Jezebel made a disgusted *bleh* that was quite audible, though Albus was far too intoxicated to register her displeasure. Swaying forwards and backwards Albus grabbed Genji by the scruff, ruffling the orange fur on top of his head a little too vigorously.

"Hey!" grrr-ed Genji peevishly.

Albus slurred "Wassa matta wit' you?" Losing his train of thought he added, "Oh Gemgee you gotta try these things, they're like... awesome."

Albus drunkenly fumbled, struggling to pull a crinkled red packet from the jacket pocket of his nineteen-piece tuxedo. A low, husky voice reverberated from the slickly designed packaging, seductively begging its bearer to savor its chromatic candies. Platonic solid, technicolor gemstones bounded out of the opened rip in the packet like bouncing balls to muted music homing in on Albus' mouth, each candy having a differing and exotic psychotropic effect on its consumer.

As he indiscriminately crushed the jeweled sweets between his teeth, Albus rocketed up and down, then his eyes went swirly, lastly, he foamed at the mouth, then remained motionless for several minutes. Shaking his head with his jaw slack, slobber spraying to the sides, Albus made an unintelligible noise that sounded something like "Ouuuu iiiiii." Genji watched on in horror.

Becoming aware of the fox-spirit once again, Albus grabbed

him and shadowboxed; a few of the mock hits landed for real against Genji's immaterial body. It didn't matter that they went right through him, it hurt all the same.

"Come on, man, cut it out!" Genji sheepishly chastised. "What about the sword? And the whispered word? and our quest—I mean vacation and all that?" Pausing for a moment the fox added, "What the heck are we even doing here Albus?"

Albus looked rather confused by the line of questioning as he wobbled back and forth; he steadied himself against a golden lamppost burning Dom Perignon, trying to make heads or tails of what the funny little fox man was saying. Some dim spark of realization dawned on him. "Look…Gen..Look..Ginjee. Googamel's unbeatable," he slurred. Raising a finger he added, "Esides, I'm happy here."

Genji was stunned; he couldn't believe what he was hearing. "I think Jezebel's gotten in your head man," he snapped. Albus didn't appreciate the tone his fox-subordinate was taking with him.

"Oh yeah? You think Jezebel's in my head!?" Albus spat with acid-reflux in his voice. Trying to conjure a retort that was one part witty, one part hurtful, shaken and garnished with a salt rim, he came back with, "Well guess what you...you shit fox?! You're in my head!! That's right, I made you up—when I was lonely and depressed! You're not even real!"

Genji's ears drooped. Albus was his best friend. His tail fell between his legs. *What is Albus talking about? He's lost his mind.* This was some next-level nonsense; he knew he was real, wasn't he? Genji fizzled to the ground like a helium party balloon losing buoyancy. He had memories that told him he was real. He had a fox mom that used to hum old and alluring tunes to him in their fox den. He loved to chase crickets and frogs. He had been imprisoned in a dark wooden chest in Neo Kyoto for a thousand years. These were facts. He knew these things about himself independent of Albus. He knew who he was; he was Genji, trickster extraordinaire, powerful fox-spirit of the Fukushima Daiichi Inari Shrine, and he didn't have to take this crap. Sitting on the ground, he looked up at Albus.

"Yeah, Albus? Well, you're a manic-depressive, self-righteous, egomaniac, know-it-all that thinks he's some sort of god!!" Genji fired back. Albus stood there, swaying, not saying a word. Genji immediately regretted his hurtful outburst. Before he could offer an apology, Albus bent down and clutched a fist-sized gold nugget off the street, worth more than forgiveness, and flung it as hard as he could at the fox. It whizzed right through the spirit's incorporeal body. Genji stared incredulously all the same; he wasn't going to let his best friend (*ex-best friend*) see him cry. Turning away about to run off, he paused and glanced back over his right shoulder fighting back tears, seeking one last shot at redemption.

"Get lost!" Albus shouted. "No one needs you here!" Genji turned back around, tears streaming from his eyes—and ran away, fading into the purple haze of the very early morning.

Good riddance. dumb stupid fox spirit anyways. Always yipping and shedding everywhere. Albus carried on popping more of the gems from his tasty rainbow packet into his mouth, making a drunken walk towards Jezebel's place.

....

Jezebel lived in the penthouse on the one-hundredth floor of an entirely gold skyscraper. She had adamantly insisted on not having any floors below her; so, she had them all removed, leaving just the support beams and trusses. The elevator attendant asked Albus which floor. "Hundredth, it's the only floor in the goddamn building," barked Albus. The attendant apologized and tried to explain to the man that it was just part of his job and that he had to ask; Albus shrugged. He popped another rainbow gem (a green one with a pink swirl) and rode the glass elevator in silence to the top floor; the city below, sparkling in the rays of the rising sun looked dull and commonplace.

Jezebel greeted Albus in her diamond-encrusted foyer. As he leaned in for a kiss, she put her hands on his shoulders and with the slight press of an Aikido master, redirected the momentum of his smooch, intended for her lips, to her cheeks, exposing each one in turn. "Good morning, darling," said Jezebel, noticing something was amiss. "Where is that dirty fox creature that's always hanging around you?"

"He's gone."

"Oh good. He was making you look quite juvenile anyway, like a child with his binky," chortled Jezebel.

"Yeah," agreed Albus flatly.

Jezebel led Albus to her sitting room, patting an empty section of her Venetian sofa, urging Albus to take a seat. He did. She chose a large Victorian chaise opposite him and carefully reclined on it. "Listen, darling, there's something I've been meaning to talk to you about," she began, summoning faux concern to modulate the tone of her voice with. "I'm breaking up with you." She paused, waiting for Albus to react. He didn't. She continued, "Well you see the whole, creating light from darkness thing...it's been getting a bit stale. I need to move on."

"Okay," said Albus. He wasn't totally sure he and Jezebel had even been a couple; all they ever did was go to galas where she would introduce him to every important person and give him pecks on the cheeks. He couldn't recall an actual conversation they had ever had about anything.

"Okay!?" Jezebel retorted. "Just okay? That's all you have to say for yourself? I'm breaking up with you! I'm Jezebel Kristina Lombardi of El Dorado and I'm breaking up with you!!"

"Yeah, that's fine," said Albus. Jezebel was livid by Albus' non-reaction to what she was certain would be soul-crushing news for this fanny-pack wearing cad. She chased him out of her penthouse threatening to call security if she ever saw him again. The elevator attendant asked, "What floor?"

"One's fine."

Jezebel was gone. Genji was gone. Elixabeth, his wife, was *just gone*. Albus was utterly and completely numb, but he could always get more numb. *We're all doomed anyway*. He couldn't die, but he certainly didn't have to live. Upon returning to his suite at Le Coq Hardi, he swiped his room key. A beep and a red flash, he tried again, same result. He tried a few more times before he sought out the concierge at the front desk. The manager explained to Albus that he was no longer welcome at Le Coq Hardi—Jezebel's orders—and that he would really appreciate it if Albus never looked at him or spoke to him ever again. Albus was fine with that, he didn't need nineteen golden toilets; he didn't even need one.

Albus wandered out into the golden streets and picked up a few more packets of Tasty Rainbows, washing them down with a carafe of a vintage Mad Dog 20/20. Chet's latest Cheese-O concoction for dessert. A few more (okay, a lot more) Mad Dogs later, he tried to lie down on one of the golden benches to rest, the stubby spikes making it impossible to get comfortable. Aimlessly trolling about the streets in a drunken, drug-induced stupor he finally managed to find a cozy and inviting gutter to curl up in. As he lay there waiting for the monstrous hangover to kick in, signaling that it was time to start drinking all over again, he saw them. Crawling from the grates in between the slats of the gutter were the leaf-cutter ants; they marched single file away from the city. Not having much else on his agenda for the evening, Albus began drunkenly crawling along with them, counting as he went.

....

Six point zero twenty-two times ten to the twenty-third ants later, a mole popped its head out of the dirt blinking blindly at Albus. *Well there goes the neighborhood,* she thought before going back to her important digging work. Startled by the appearance of the mole, Albus looked up from his ants; he had crawled far outside the city back into the surrounding jungles. It was then that the vicious hangover that had been stalking him like a tiger finally pounced. Albus blacked out, collapsing with a padded thump onto the piles of fallen leaves cluttering the jungle floor; the ants crawled all over him, enveloping him.

12

OUTCASTS

Albus' eyelids fluttered open against his will. He was lying on his back; no idea where he was. Above him, he spied a thatched roof bound together from spindly, dried reeds. Staring up at the vaguely familiar ceiling, for a moment, he allowed himself to fantasize that he was back at his cottage sprawled out in bed. He rolled over and saw Elixabeth next to him. Her disappearance had all just been a bad dream. They cuddled and spooned some before rousing from beneath the thick comforter of their warm bed, both of them snug as a bug. Albus jaunted down their creaking stairs, shrouded in his grey, terrycloth robe that had a minor hole developing in the armpit, to put on a pot of coffee.

Elixabeth turned the calcified shower knob and stepped into the steaming jets; she had already shampooed her long, thick hair a day or two prior so it would only be a quick rinse this morning. She squirted some goopy cleanser onto her hands, scrubbing at her porcelain face first, then lathered herself up with a slowly disintegrating orange bar of soap, fingers grazing over her areolas, her sudsy hands traveling further down her svelte tummy, getting all clean. Appearing from the alcove of the stairs with a fuzzy, pink towel wrapped tightly around her head like a Sikhs, she accepted a hot mug of coffee from his hands, while putting a stainless-steel saucepan on the stovetop to boil herself some steel-cut oatmeal; Albus usually didn't eat breakfast. They sat together in their nook, their thighs pressing up against one another, reading the paper or latest romance novel; he felt that they knew each other so well at this point, that words were nothing more than a distraction.

A sharp end of a twig poking into his backside freed Albus from his fantasy; unfortunately, none of it was remotely true. Beneath him lay not the cushioned Tempurpedic mattress he shared with his wife, but a lumpy leaf-stuffed mat resting on a dirt floor. To be honest, he was somewhat shocked that he was still here, certain he had really done himself in this time. He had to admit though, he wasn't exactly sure where *here* was.

Half expecting to see Genji hovering over him shouting some shrill nonsense while doing karate kicks in the air, he hazily recalled something about questioning the validity of the fox-spirit's very existence. *Oh...right*. He frowned.

Propping himself to his side, he found there were no walls supporting the vaguely familiar ceiling above him, only four posts crudely hewn from the trunks of palms, streaking shades of green vegetation all around. He was somewhere in the jungle still, Genji nowhere to be found. Reclining in a hammock strung between two of the trunks, an elderly man with a long white beard chewed on a shoot of young sugar cane while he swayed back and forth. Albus sat all the way up, blinking once or twice, dumbfounded that he recognized the aged man rocking in the hammock. He leaned forward rubbing his eyes and balked, "Dr. Blue!?" with some degree of confusion.

"Heya, Al," replied Dr. Blue. Adam Blue (no middle name) had been keeping watch over Albus during his most recent stint with the darkness, patiently waiting for the man to awaken. Dr. Blue knew it was only a matter of time; both men shared an inability to die.

"What are you doing here?"

"Here?" said Dr. Blue impishly, holding out both his hand's

palms upturned. "Or here?" he added, turning his palms inwards pointing his index fingers towards the dirt floor of the hut.

Albus cocked an eyebrow.

"Here...I guess?"

"Same as you I 'spose."

Dr. Blue stroked his wispy beard and shuffled over to Albus. Adam looked older than Albus remembered since last he saw him. They had worked together once a long, long time ago. Adam Blue had been something of a mentor to him; they weren't close enough that he would call the elderly man a friend, but Albus trusted and respected him. The old man was hunched pronouncedly. He had always sported a long white beard; however, it seemed much less substantial than before. A frail arm speckled with liver spots and moles sprouting their own collection of kinky hairs stretched out towards Albus, offering assistance; midway up his forearm, a square Band-Aid obscured an eggplant tinted bruise that not even Dr. Blue was sure how he had gotten.

Albus took hold of the elderly man's outstretched wrinkled hand and got to his feet, allowing Dr. Blue to think he was assisting more than he really was. "How long was I gone for?" he asked as he steadied his legs beneath him, patting off some dried and dead leaves.

"Be six days this morning," said Adam. "Come on, I'll show ya around."

Adam Blue led Albus around a picayune fishing village nestled in the lower jungles far outside El Dorado. The elderly man moseyed along with the aid of a wooden walking stick; the countenance of a poorly whittled wizard poked out from the staff's forward-facing facade, a few store-bought eagle feathers tied about the cane's top in a notch. Shabby huts and humble shacks fastened and splinted together from splintered trunks, fibrous fronds, and other flotsam culled from the jungle, spread out over a flat earthen clearing gently sloping down to a river. The same river Albus and Genji had washed up in after being flushed away by the maelstrom deep within the annals of Uruk's catacombs, (though he was much, much further downstream now).

A placid hush hung over the village; the quaint and uncomplicated abodes, a refreshing sensorial detox to the gaudy din of El Dorado. However, once you had seen one ramshackle jungle hut, you had kind of seen them all (*or have you?*); that didn't prevent Dr. Blue from describing the elaborate history of each one in glorious detail. Albus did his best to listen to his aged colleague but found himself thinking about Genji.

"And over yonder, you'll spot a stand of banana trees I planted…now was it six? Nope mighta' been seven years ago now, no definitely six, anywho, who knows. Now in a good season…" rambled on Dr. Blue to no one.

Albus couldn't recall exactly what had transpired between him and Genji that night to cause their falling out, though he was sure it was something certainly regrettable. *You called him a mental illness then threw a giant gold nugget through him,* Golgotha gleefully reminded Albus, replaying the entire scene for his edification. "Shut up," growled Albus through clenched teeth. He swatted away at his ear banishing the gloating fat man. In his defense, he built large walls around the shame and guilt uncomfortably churning inside him, securing the tops of the ramparts with reams of barbed wire.

"Everything okee dokee, Mr. Cake?" asked Dr. Blue.

"Yeah fine, just fine," said Albus regaining his composure.

"Alright then…" Adam Blue drawled, rotating his hunched frame back towards his rousing tour of the fishing village. "It just seems like you're missing something."

Overhead, isolated cottony clouds grazed through an otherwise clear sky. A chipper breeze, absent from El Dorado, coasted through the village; a few species of birds circled in the sky that Albus hadn't seen before. They must be somewhere close to the ocean, he reasoned. A modest dock, about a third the length of a stone's throw, reached out into the wide river that formed the lower bounds of the village. Three menfolk stood on the dock's edge casting out fishing nets, hauling back in empty fishing nets, over and over again. The activity piqued Albus' interest as something he would like to try.

The villagers kept to themselves mostly (more so out of shyness than rank unfriendliness), some nodding at Albus, others turning back into their huts at his approach. As they walked about, Albus searched for some common thread stitching this disparate patchwork of villagers together; as far as he could tell there was no shared creed, ethnicity, or ideology uniting them.

Sensing Albus' puzzlement Dr. Blue explained. "We're the Outcasts," he said matter-of-factly. "The ones that realized what this place *really is*. Maybe we can't never leave, but we certainly don't have to 'play ball' neither." Some residents had relocated to the fishing outpost prior to the Ascension (before everything went sideways), others were forcibly relocated by Golgotha. "As long as we don't cause too much 'a ruckus, the Big Man pays us no mind."

Resting on a fallen log outside her hut, a matronly woman with a wide frame intently observed Albus; her cheerful, chestnut-hued eyes tracked along with him as Adam led the man about the village. Her body draped in layers of purple robes, scarves, and shiny baubles made her look something like a tribal shaman. Around the woman's neck hung a braided cord of spun cotton dyed a fading asparagus-green; pulling the cord taut, resting atop her chest was a bird skull cast in bronze, the hammer of a small bell welded inside its cavity.

The trunk of the fallen log she sat on was roughly chiseled, scooping a makeshift seat into its length. Dangling from the lip of her hut's frond strewn roof, a wind chime made from wooden slats and fishing line, lazily *clacked* and *clocked* together in the underpowered breeze. Beside her crouched a shy girl, maybe only a toddler, ensconced in the protective folds of the woman's flowing robes, digging at the dirt with the broken end of a stick. Albus almost didn't notice the small girl at first.

Unable to ignore her obvious gaze any longer, Albus looked in her direction and offered a half-smile, his lips parting slightly. The matronly woman beamed back at him, flashing neat rows of pearly whites with a minuscule gap between her front two teeth.

"What's her deal?" asked Albus.

"Oh her? Never did manage to catch her name, but she's the one that found yah in tha' brush with your lights busted out. Dragged yah all the way here. Boy, you were a right mess *wooo-ee*, muttering sumthin' 'bout tasty rainbows and chasing mad dogs," he paused then added, "she's a real kind lady…lost her husband and two eldest daughters in the Ascension."

....

Adam clapped Albus on the back with his liver-spotted, withered hand, informing him he was welcome to stay in the fishing village as long as he liked; could even build a hut of his own, should he please. There were no hard or fast rules in the village, just be cool to everyone and don't cause too much 'a ruckus. Albus found an unexpected appeal to the offer. Genji had ditched him; his wife was gone, smiting Golgotha wasn't going to bring her back. Perhaps this was the change he was looking for. Maybe he would extend his vacation indefinitely, never go back to Mars. End his story here and live out the rest of his days—until the world ended—fishing and building huts, a modest life without much care or concern.

He stopped Dr. Blue as he was about to walk away, grasping the elderly man by the crook of his arm. "Did we make the right choice, Adam?" he asked, his heart seeking something, absolution maybe, from the older man.

"I stopped worrying about that kind of thing long ago, Al," answered Dr. Blue unsatisfactorily. "That kind of thinking will drive a man bonkers." Parting ways for the time being with Adam Blue, Albus meandered down to the dinky dock constructed from hand-planed wood planks, held together with ropes spun from jungle vines; he watched the quickly flowing river move beneath his feet. The other menfolk had retired for the day. He was alone. Gathering up one of the unattended fishing nets in his arms, he cast it out.

....

On his first attempt, the net wound up a tangled mess. Albus hauled it back and cast it again, this time allowing the lead weights attached to the net's edge to lead the rest of the tangle; that seemed to work better. The net spread out wide before splashing into the water. He enjoyed watching the intertwining strands of the net expand outwards as he released it through the air; like watching the birth of the universe, an infinitely dense entangled ball instantaneously exploding and spreading out into a woven structure, form from chaos, splashing down into the water, reeled back in, collapsing in on itself again, only to repeat the process forever.

He did this for days, casting out the net, hauling it back in, never catching a single fish. It didn't matter; he enjoyed the simplicity of the therapeutic motion.

"You're gettin' pretty good at that, sugar," came a voice from behind Albus mid-throw. He glanced over his shoulder to see the matronly, shaman woman. The interruption caught Albus off guard; he duffed the release of the net resulting in another entangled mess. Slightly irritated, he tugged on the rope hand-over-hand dragging the tangle through the water back to the dock's edge. She smiled warmly at him.

Albus nodded awkwardly in agreement. "I suppose so." The woman stood motionless on the dock with her hands folded in front of her, the ever-present breeze ruffling the folds of her robes. An aura of kindness radiated from her being. Albus felt self-conscious now about casting the net in front of her. "Can I help you?" he asked.

"No, but maybe I can help you?" she replied.

"I don't think so, lady," said Albus, turning his back on her, preparing to cast his net again. He could still feel her firm yet non-threatening presence behind him.

"I know what happened to Elixabeth," she said. "Come find me at the fire tonight," the Sha-mom offered cryptically before leaving the dock.

....

Most nights in the fishing village the tribe of outcasts would gather round a large bonfire sitting in silence or conversing gently with one another, sharing stories. Albus had avoided the gathering up to this point. The Sha-mom had certainly netted his interest though. *How could she possibly know what happened to Elixabeth? Elixabeth is just gone. Vanished.* Was she really gone? Was she in need of rescue? Had Golgotha absconded with her? A mob of conflicting emotions grappled and wrestled with one another within his mind; when one side had its competitor pinned to the mat, barely gaining the upper hand, the other side would rally, driving its opponent back to the brink. Part of him had resigned to living out his days in the fishing village. What if he didn't like what he found out?

Pacing back and forth eroding a small canyon into the dirt floor of his hut, the hungering void in need of answers won out in the end. That night he located the Sha-mom sitting cross-legged, back leaned against a cut log a safe distance from the roaring blaze; she wrapped herself in a rough-spun maroon blanket, a white zig-zag pattern woven into it.

"Tell me," said Albus.

"You know," she mused, "you'd probably be about the same age as my oldest daughter." This amused the man as he no longer had any idea how old he really was anymore. Time passed strangely in this world, if it passed at all. Albus didn't bite, choosing to remain silent. Recognizing his reticence, the Sha-mom didn't prod further. "Drink this," she said, palming an uneven earthenware bowl; she shoved it into Albus' hands. A foul, swirling liquid resembling perse squid ink mixing with a briny tidal pool frothing large pink bubbles, foamed over the sides of the bowl.

"What is it?"

"Jungle Juice."

"And this will show me what happened to Elixabeth?"

"Maybe," the Sha-mom shrugged.

Albus wasn't exactly sold on the idea, taking into account he had just spent an unknown quantity of time lost beneath an ocean of alcohol and rainbows. Sensing his hesitation, the Sha-mom added, "It's nothing like any of that stuff in El Dorado."

What the hell, thought Albus. In one gulp he downed the entire contents of the clay bowl, the cold and surprisingly tasteless brew washing over his palate. Pushing his back up against the log next to the Sha-mom, he tried to get comfortable as he stared listlessly into the fire, waiting for the juice to kick in. Nothing happened at first, then nothing happened for a while.

About to turn to the Sha-mom to inform her nothing was happening, the slobbering tongues of the bonfire licking at the night-air suddenly began to morph before his eyes; the flames became perfectly symmetrical then rounded out into a circle. The blazing inferno folded in on itself, interlocking and transforming into the stained glass Rose Window from the cathedral of Notre Dame.

The multi-colored glass panels illuminated from within without an external light source. Everything else in his vision fell away, leaving only the Rose Window. Like a firefly drawn to the pale-blue neon glow of an electric bug zapper, Albus was hypnotized, sucked in towards the round window. The vibrant, multi-colored cells of the glass were not static, but moving; they *glomped* and *ker-plomped* into one another, growing and shrinking in size like a Voronoi fractal. Shifting and pushing up against one another in a never-ending power struggle, some cells disappeared entirely, popping out of existence, only to spawn elsewhere in the mosaic at a later time.

As he got closer, Albus witnessed with astonishment that the individual cells of the stained glass contained stories. *All of the stories.* An unsettling number of narratives spewed forth from the window, each one a vignette into another time and place. Most belonged to other people and beings, many were foreign and strange. He caught sight of one cell that he recognized, one of his own from long, long ago. Without warning, he fell into the story like an astronaut returning to Earth from a deep space voyage, splashing down with a plop.

Albus was floating, suspended above a fluid by a sticky, rubbery, darkness. The darkness was an inflated, rubber inner tube languidly snaking its way along the surface of a lazy, spring-fed river. His backside wedged into the tube's donut hole making contact with the excessively cold, crystal-clear spring waters. Waters that welled, bubbling up from places deep within the earth, places that propriety dictated Mother Mary be ashamed of—hidden crevasses, slits, cracks, and submerged aqueous caverns with names like "The Devil's Needle" or "Satan's Butthole."

His mates and buds were all around him huddled in close, floating in matte inner tubes of their own; their round tubes tied together at the cheaply made plastic handles by knotty twine, forming a coalition that wouldn't last the summer. There was even one bloated tube reserved entirely for the gang's cheapo Styrofoam cooler, crammed into its hole, stocked with chilled aluminum beer cans and murky water. Water that had been ice moments ago; beer that would be gone before the noontime sun had crossed the sky. Oh, and his girlfriend, Marybeth, was there too.

Shuffled along the serpentine river by the apathetic current at a suitably lackadaisical pace, the rafters passed an unevenly burning blunt amongst them, a burnt offering; they joked and cajoled, not worrying about what would become of them when they grew up, which by society's standards was at the end of this summer. Concealed amongst the mossy banks of the spring, the audible buzz of cicadas reverberated off the frame of the stained glass cell, vibrating it violently, threatening to destabilize the vignette. Conclaves of six-legged, winged insects imitated the rafters, defiantly walking on the surface of the water, not belonging to the depths below nor sky above. An iridescent, turquoise dragonfly landed on Albus' drab latex float and hung out with him for a while; they became bros. He was sad when it left, only for it to land again sometime later. This was an entirely different dragonfly; but to Albus, it was a long-lost friend returning.

His girlfriend grasped at the handle of Albus' float trying to tug him in close; the inflated tubes coming into contact exerted a repelling force against one another, an equal but opposite reaction. She leaned in and whispered something in his ear. He didn't hear her; he was too busy shot-gunning another sudsy can of a Bud Light into his open mouth, much to the delight of his buds.

Along the banks of the spring, copses of stately oak trees that in times past had witnessed Conquistadors put natives to the sword, graciously extended their sturdy branches over the spring, providing shade in key places from the stern but loving sun. Their heavy reams of coiled Spanish moss descended towards the water's surface with the tension of God's finger ever reaching for Adam's, seeking so desperately to make contact with his creation. Albus playfully splashed some of the ice-cold spring water onto his girlfriend's exposed, sunbaked tummy; she didn't appreciate the heartfelt gesture as much as he thought she would.

Back on the banks, beat-up, rusted, red pickup trucks adorned with confederate flags and promises of rising again, backed up to the water's edge, bed first, with both doors of their cabs opened wide like the ears of a threatened elephant. As they floated by, Albus couldn't help but hear their souped-up audio equipment: tweeters, subwoofers, and sub-subwoofers, triumphantly trumpeting Creedence Clearwater Revival's 'Proud Mary' and Lynyrd Skynyrd's 'Simple Man.' Rolling on the river, he received a four-year college degree in classic Southern rock in a matter of moments.

Swaying from the venerable branches of the oaks, revelers of summers past had slung rope swings, hung like nooses over the innocent spring waters; hastily cut scraps of pine two-by-fours were haphazardly nailed into the bodies of the trees, making for crude ladders to reach the swinging ropes. Adults and children alike lined up at the trunks of the mighty oaks, anxiously awaiting their turn to ascend the wooden rungs and swing-out, letting go into empty space, back-flipping or belly-flopping, beer-bellies undulating like Jell-O on impact, into the clear and absolving waters below.

When Albus and his flotilla of comrades had reached the extraction point of the spring, they hauled their shoddily twined-together amalgam of tubes upstream, back along the banks; marching their rafts double-time through the dusty, loud, and grimy campsites; pebbles and rocks grated at their naked feet. Back to the eternally gushing spring-head, they tossed their craft into the waters a second time, making the journey all over again. He saw some naked boobs this time around. *Nice.*

....

Gasping for air like a newborn spanked on the bottom, Albus emerged from the vignette; he saw many others rotating and morphing in the window, some he didn't want to look at, some that he did but was pulled away from by an intangible force.

In one he saw his mother with her hand stuffed up the butt of a plush orange and white fox-puppet; she was endlessly entertaining him on his first long airplane flight. She contorted the fox-puppet making funny voices and overly exaggerated movements. He giggled uncontrollably, his brain exploding with serotonin, dopamine, and oxytocin.

Wait! Stop! In an adjacent cell of the infinitely faceted window, he had spotted Elixabeth. Already feeling the pull of the invisible current carrying him away from the scene, he strained hard to get close. Sitting at the rough, round wooden table of their breakfast nook, Elixabeth's silk robe was draped around her body. She was crying. Albus didn't recognize the scene.

It was one of his wife's stories; he must have been away at the office. He struggled to pan in closer and make sense of the vignette. Sitting in a chair opposite his wife was Golgotha—deftly feigning sympathy; the elephant's dark eyes covertly drawn to the outline of Elixabeth's nipples protruding from the fabric of her robe, potbelly wedged against the table. Albus didn't recall his wife ever mentioning Golgotha's visit. Straining and paddling against the tide with as much force as he could muster, he tried to get in close enough proximity to hear what was being said. No such luck, despite his best efforts Albus was swept away by the ebb and flow; the scene of Elixabeth and Golgotha faded from sight.

....

Another cell of the Rose Window rapidly rotated into view. Recognizing it, Albus definitely didn't want to look at this one. No choice, it accelerated towards him. He sat cross-legged on a shabby couch in a basement belonging to his highschool friend Peter; they had just ingested LSD. He loved Peter. He stopped being friends with Peter after that trip. The acceleration towards the glass cell of Peter's basement quickened; surely, he was about to crash right through it. Moments before impact, Albus had the foresight to reach behind him and toss a grappling hook, latching a shining, silver lifeline to his right shoulder back at the fishing village.

As he shattered through the pane in an explosion of glass shards, briefly, very briefly, (almost too brief to have existed) he became a silver bell. A silver bell around the neck of a cat. Albus reached up and undid the clasp of the bell from the cat's pink collar and moved with blinding alacrity, his shining lifeline whirring off its winch spanning behind him, trying to keep up.

Then Light.

Only Light. Every light Albus had ever created on his own accord became flat, two-dimensional, vanity in the presence of this ultimate Light. All that he had ever done became dull, dingy, and profane in comparison. This Light was the only thing that was real, the only thing that had ever been real, the only thing that would ever be real *and it desperately wanted to know him.* Acting on animal instinct, Albus turned away; behind him, he witnessed his own long shadow cast by the Light: his profanity, his self-righteousness, arrogance, greed, and selfishness, lain bare—exposed for all to see. Albus hated the Light for it, abhorred it; he despised it—and yet, the Light still wanted to know him. There was something there in the Light, waiting for him.

No.

An adversarial voice emanating from elsewhere lambasted him; accusing him, there was no way he could ever be worthy to stand there. Albus ripped his face away, beat his breast and thrashed. Overtaken with a madness, he broke the chains the villagers had bound him with. An inferno of red-hot, whites, yellows, and oranges incinerated him over and over again. Falling to the ground he vomited pink purulent worms; vomiting so violently that his own distended intestines turned inside out transmogrifying into a bloated, pink worm himself. Writhing on his belly, he wriggled wildly.

With a deafening bang he was ejaculated out from the presence of the Light, shot from an interstellar multi-dimensional cannon, sent sailing back through spacetime…when he caught sight of a darkness growing below him. It was nothing like the darkness that had enveloped him in the tomb tome beneath Uruk. This was a physical darkness, it had weight and dimension to it; it was a cancer and it was consuming his mother. He would do anything to stop it.

....

Albus sailed back towards the jagged and shattered hole in the Rose Window, back through the obverse side of Peter's basement, snatching hold of his silver lifeline. He gave the cable several desperate tugs and was winched back through his right shoulder, back into the jungle encampment where he sat in front of the dwindling fire, legs sprawled; his back leaned up against the mossy, cold, damp log.

The Sha-mom was still sitting next to him. Albus blinked and panned his vision around the campfire. Most of the inhabitants had retired to their huts for the night. Everything seemed large and small at the same time. Matters of scale and time felt antiquated, vestiges of a bygone era. He was everyone and no one; a part of everything—yet nothing. A child, but he was very old.

A period of silence passed punctuated with only the crackle and pop of the dying fire, until Albus began to sob uncontrollably, shaking, unable to make sense of any of it. The mother shaman draped the maroon blanket with striped zig-zags over Albus' shoulders and handed him a coconut shell of water. Albus splashed some on his face and took a sip.

In a long breath between sobs, he confessed to the Sha-mom that he felt like a total failure. That he had made all the wrong choices. His love was *gone*; he hurt or pushed people away that were just trying to help him—including his best friend; he had lost the needle, couldn't find the sword, and had no damn idea what the whispered words were, he croaked.

"There, there," she said, gently pulling him into her hefty bosom, "everything's going to be okay." Her voice the timbre of softly shushing tones, like wind coming off a lake rattling overgrown cattails, pickerel weeds, and tall grasses, she added, "sometimes it just takes a little longer than we think."

Albus was still crying some, but at least he wasn't blubbering anymore. He felt embarrassed by his emotional outburst; it was very out of character for him. Yet, strangely he did feel a little better. He looked into the Sha-mom's affirming chestnut hued eyes wanting to believe her. They sat for a little while longer before she added, "And if it's a sword you're after you should talk to our master-smith Bezosbub, in the morning," she winked. "He might have a few." They stood and hugged briefly before going their separate ways.

Albus strolled back to the hut he had been staying in, looking up at the stars as he walked. They looked quite different here.

13

ELEPHANT'S
BANE

The next morning Albus found his way to Bezosbub's shop on the outskirts of the village. A hulking, cue-ball headed man with forearms each the size of a whole Popeye hammered away at a glowing red piece of steel held tight with tongs against a brutish anvil, not looking up from his task to greet the visitor.

The Sha-mom wasn't kidding about Bezosbub's shop. "A few swords" was an understatement; there were mountains of swords and steel laid in steep piles scattered throughout the shop that was deceptively larger on the inside. Albus didn't know much about swords; in fact, he had been in favor of banning swords most his life, never thinking that he may one day need to use one.

Albus dug through the mounds of the shopkeeper's wares, somewhat relieved that the intimidating, tusk-mouthed Bezos-bub hadn't acknowledged him or launched into some hyperbolic sales pitch; telling someone you needed a sword to kill Golgotha hadn't always gone over so well. Stopping every now and then to draw a sword from one of the many piles and examine it closely, (pretending like he knew what he was doing), he pulled one blade out by the hilt that wreathed itself in bright flames as Albus raised it overhead. *A flaming sword?! Badass...but too biblical*, he thought, returning the fiery weapon to the heap.

Bezosbub, still hammering away, eyed the man between anvil strikes. He didn't like what he saw; he could recognize a first-time sword buyer anywhere. The blacksmith hated helping people: the only thing he hated more than helping people though, was someone buying the wrong sword for the job. Most novice buyers went for a sword ridiculously oversized that would break at the hilt on first contact with anything solid, or insisted on one fabricated from some fictitious, fantastical alloy concocted by Big Sword to push units. Against his better judgment, Bezosbub gruffly mumbled, "Something I can help you with?"

"Yes," replied Albus somewhat sheepishly, "I need a sword." This was why Bezosbub hated helping people; choking his irritation down his throat he put on his best salesman act.

"Well, what is it in particu-lar you're looking to kill?"

Albus hesitated a moment before saying, "I am going to kill Golgotha." He waited. No loud booming voice or exploding heads. Golgotha was away at the moment on a much-anticipated golf trip. He absolutely deplored it when people spoke in the middle of his backswing; there would be time to deal with them later.

"Hah," snarled Bezosbub, "that pompous pink prick!" He spat onto the anvil, the spittle sizzling and evaporating instantly, he added, "Why didn't you just say that!" Bezosbub had detested Golgotha ever since the Ascension had made the need for swords (and all silly things) completely moot, essentially driving Bezosbub out of business. Albus was pretty sure that he *had just said that*, but decided better to bite his tongue than argue with the burly sword-smith now keen on aiding him.

Like any shopkeeper worth his salt, Bezosbub had a back room where he kept the really good stuff, which he disappeared to, leaving Albus waiting at the counter.

The smith returned with an innocuous sword in hand, of modest size and width. A fine steel blade extended about three quarters the length of Albus' own height. The sword possessed a hilt made of scrimshawed ivory; a bronze mouse skull formed the pommel decoration. Bezosbub presented the sword to Albus, held out resting across both his open palms. Albus lifted it by the grip and gave it a few compulsory slashes through the air. Bezosbub stared on in hopeful anticipation. Albus tried to say something swordy.

"Ah yes…very nice…balance."

"Elephant's Bane," beamed Bezosbub.

"Come again?"

"Elephant's Bane," he repeated. "Elephant's Ba—it's the name of the sword."

"Ah of course. Very good. I'll take it," said Albus. Eager to come across someone who was daring (or foolish) enough to stand up to that bloated bully, Bezosbub tossed in a scintillating scabbard (from an upscale El Dorado boutique, he was sure to make Albus aware of), free of charge.

....

Elephant's Bane slung across his back, Albus lollygagged back towards the fishing village. He felt the pull of the fishing nets resting idly on the pier and wanted to cast them out just a few more times. Standing on the edge of the dilapidated dock about to toss the net, a presence he had become familiar with stood behind him. A firm hand rested on his right shoulder. He turned. "I'm not ready—"

The Sha-mom placed one finger on his lips silencing him. "No one is ever ready for the journey they are about to make," she said, "all we can do is try our best."

The Sha-mom had a rare knack for transforming what could be construed as trite platitudes into deeply profound sentiments. Comforted by her words, his resolve renewed Albus said his goodbyes to the Sha-mom, Dr. Blue, Bezosbub, and the other villagers, and marched off towards the overgrown jungle. She shouted after him, "If you see my husband or daughters on your journey, tell them I love them!" Albus nodded.

Carving a path through the dense foliage, following along the route of the river, Albus hacked and slashed the low-hanging fruits and vines in his way. With less impediment, he could have more easily walked along the river's wide-open banks, but he enjoyed pretending the vines and branches were Golgotha's trunk as he swung his sword, severing them in two. Overhead, the thick canopy began to thin out, the trees growing farther and farther apart from one another. The stifled breeze began to intensify into a light gust; in the distance, Albus heard the inter-mittent screeching of seabirds. He was approaching the ocean at the edge of the world.

As the thick vegetation transitioned to a dark coastline, a blur of movement caught Albus' attention from his left eye. From the hollow of one of the last large trees popped the snout of an orange and white blob. A fox slinked out the tree's opening followed by a foxy fox wife; three cute-as-a-button fox kits in tow. Albus halted. The amber-eyed fox crossed paths with Albus and gave the man a wink—and then a fist bump. Albus smiled. *Go get 'em*, thought Genji as he disappeared into the forest with his family.

14

APOCALYPSE
NOW

Albus Cake stood on the shore of a volcanic, black-sand beach looking out towards the unwavering horizon where charcoal sky met midnight water. Finally freed from the seemingly ceaseless morass of entangled jungle, his unproven sword resting across his back, he stood alone at this place in time. The ocean at the end of the world receded infinitely before him. Strong winds rustled and snapped at the flagging bit of loose fabric strap hanging from his tri-color fanny pack.

The time had come to make some changes around here, to hold Golgotha accountable. To confront the monstrous beast for the cost of birthing this allegedly unchanging, eternal utopia.

It was what Elixabeth would have wanted, Albus told himself. She had always lamented how unfair the Ascension had been, how Golgotha had abused his powers, promising things that were never delivered.

He bent to one knee and pinched a scoop of the clumpy, black sand between his fingers, letting individual granules slip out like the grains in an hourglass marking the passage of time; the particles fell perfectly back into place as though they had never been disturbed.

Before there existed the rebellious universe there was

only sameness, a divinely ordered, boundlessly dense crystalline edifice—utter boredom. In the absence of push and pull, everything melds to endless uniformity, flattened to sea level. Without change, without conflict, without endings, there was only stasis, stagnation, and malignant expanse—the recurse of infinite undoing. That had been Albus' folly, his downfall so long ago; in his frightened disquisition to evade his own ending, to immortalize himself, to suspend his soul amongst the clouds, he had become death.

Overhead, albatross circled in vast loops buffeted by the gale-force winds, while white gulls, sandpipers and other seabirds not quite as brave trotted about the dreary surf pecking at suffocating fish and umber sargasso washed up on the tenebrous sands. Loyalist waves did as they were bid and crashed perpetually against the shoreline locked in an endless stalemate with the land. Out of compulsion, Albus counted the frequency of the waves, *1.618 Hz.*

Enclosed tidal pools formed from solidified magma and pumice, housed blue and red crabs, among other crustaceans; crabs that would valiantly sally forth across the beachhead, sometimes battling with one another, picking the fish heads and seaweeds abandoned by the birds, clean to the bone, the white bones washing away into the sea, resetting the whole scene.

A weathered, unassuming rowboat, large enough to hold three people, bounced up and down in the waters not far offshore, moored to a buoy anchored on the sandy bottom. A painted red stripe, badly cracking and flaking, wrapped the rim of its hull, its midsection painted white. All of the wooden planks of the boat's hull had been replaced, one plank at a time, over the eons by some unknown benefactor. On its bottom lived an entire advanced civilization of intelligent barnacles, intrepid explorers of which ventured their way up the thick waterlogged rope holding the rowboat moored in place.

The man walked down the slope of the blackened beach and came to a stop at the boundary between land and sea; where solid melted into fluid. As the waves crashed, seafoam gathered about Albus' naked ankles, imploring him to turn back; do not make the same mistake they had, they begged. Shrugging off their pleas, undeterred Albus firmly planted his feet into the damp, dark sand. Cupping his hands to his mouth, he sucked in a deep breath; at the top of his lungs he bellowed, "Golgotha!!"

....

Nothing happened at first. Then nothing happened for a while. Golgotha, distracted by other matters, was running late. Puzzled, Albus prepared to summon another shout, when suddenly there came a tremor: the ground quivered and moaned. Black sand vibrated up and down, grains leaping into the air as if an underground rave had just reached its apex; Albus faltered and wobbled some but managed to remain standing.

As the ground intensely shuddered, every single squid, octopus, and nautilus inhabiting the vast, limitless seas, evacuated the entirety of their ink reservoirs in harmony, dying the tumultuous waters an inky amaranthine purple. Their thoroughly squeezed, used-up gelatinous bodies floated to the roiling surface and crashed all along the coastline. Like the lovers of Pompeii, the octopuses' multitudinous tentacles entwined around one another in one final embrace, before fulfilling their purpose.

Then came a deafening trumpet blast. *261.6 Hz.* The winds fell from the skies as the encircling albatross helplessly plummeted towards the ocean. Like faltering kites, they tail-spun, nose-diving into the thrashing amethyst-dyed sea below; the hollow bones of their delicate bodies crushed into dust upon impact from the blistering velocity. Their tail feathers, quills lost amongst an ocean of ink.

Another trumpet blasted. *349.228 Hz.* The metamorphic sanctuaries of the tidal pools cracked and fissured spilling their protected contents of crustaceans, starfish, and urchins that had made their abodes safely inside the pools, back out into the churning, uncaring seas to fend for themselves. The blue and red crabs that had been furiously sidewinding their way, scuttling as fast as their clicking legs could carry them from the convulsing beach back towards their startled families awaiting them in their pools, exploded apart, popping at the joints as if children's tinker toys dashed against a stone floor in a fit of rage.

Albus waited in anticipation for the logical third trumpet blast. It never came. The particles of black sand continued to tremble some as a colossal pink bubble of mammoth proportions, its membrane swirling with a soapy iridescence, crowned from beneath the ocean's depths and rose slowly, eclipsing the low hanging moon on the horizon. Inky streams briefly clung to its globular sides, giving way like the legs of dark red wine running down the curvature of a bulbous glass. Perfectly spherical by every measure, the soft yellowed glow of the full moon further illuminated the opalescent hues that fluidly morphed across the pink orb's sleek surface.

From the dead center of the titanic pink bubble, a sphincter dilated exposing a round unlit hole, the belly button of a fat, happy baby, or entrance to a tomb. Taunting Albus, Golgotha lowered his drawbridge. The elephant extended an arched, rainbow-hued walkway of solid light from the circular, open sphincter, forging an umbilical cord from his spherical palace to the placenta of the land, gleefully inviting the man to simply walk across and greet him. *Come.*

....

Rejecting the invite, Albus waded into the ink-dark water undaunted, waves pushing him back, fighting against his advance. The slimy bodies of deceased cephalopods ricocheted and bounced around him; the suction cups of their dead tentacles briefly latched onto him as they wafted to shore. The water deepening, Albus trod over to the anchored rowboat. Tacked into the vessel's flat stern was a thoroughly corroded copper name-plate; "Argus" it read. Albus failed to notice. As the rowboat rocked up and down, angry waves crashed against him; its slicked sides escaped Albus' grasp on his first few attempts. Finally getting a handhold, he hoisted himself out the stained water over the side, squirming into the boat's empty hull.

Looped and tied around a cleat on the boat's bow, a mind-bogglingly complex sailor's knot, frayed and crusted in salt, kept the vessel moored to a bobbing buoy. Albus struggled with the knot; a gremlin tooling about in his mind divulged the solution to him: unsheathe Elephant's Bane and merely hack apart the convoluted knot in an unbecoming fit of rage. Taking a step back from the problem for a moment, he kept his wits about him and slowly worked his way through the tangled puzzle, eventually overcoming the knotty obstacle.

The boat freed of its mooring, hand-over-hand Albus hauled the rest of the waterlogged, kelp slimed rope, coiling the remnants in the aft alongside a small three-pronged anchor. He set the oars into their posts, lowering the blades into the churning sea and began rowing, propelling himself towards his fate under his own terms.

Golgotha *knew* with the certainty of a sunrise, that he could not stop the man from reaching him, but he definitely wasn't going to make it easy on him either. As Albus anticipated, a great storm came over the ocean. *Real original,* he thought. Titan-sized clouds formed a tribunal over the small boat, harshly judging Albus, finding him wanting. Siphoning up the dark purple ocean ink, they spat it back down on Albus in torrential contempt.

He bailed the dark ink filling the hull; unlike his dream from the monorail, he did not feel any sense of panic, vestigial, visceral, or otherwise. He knew he had this; he didn't need anyone to rescue him, not the Sha-mom, not Genji, not Jezebel, not Elixabeth, not anybody. Albus rowed harder. The swells of the stormy sea became foothills as the tiny, battered craft ascended and descended each one, unerring on its trek towards infinity.

Despite the storm (or maybe because of it) Albus finally reached the edge of the glassy bubble. The dark round portal was out of reach overhead; grabbing the coiled rope, he swung the boat's small metal anchor round in circles with as much force as he could exert and lobbed it like a grappling hook, wedging its prongs against the opening's lip. Albus hoisted himself up the salt-crusted, tattered rope and crawled inside the awaiting sphincter.

15

THE TRITONE
WOMB ROAM

Albus breached the sphincter guarding the palace portal and found himself crawling along a soft, sumptuous conduit; the sides were squishy and undulating, slicked in a damp, clear mucus. Claustrophobia aside, the interior of the tube was unexpectedly inviting, serene even; the sides of the tube gently hugged Albus as he squirmed on hands and knees. After crawling for some distance, the tube dead-ended in another sphincter, this one tightly sealed; there was no turning back now. Albus pried at the ligaments of the constricted valve and forcibly squeezed his way through, plopping out onto the floor of a large, irregularly-shaped, mustard-yellow chamber. The air of the mustardy chamber felt thick, nourishing. As he got to his feet and shook off the thin coating of translucent slime, the vinyl floor wobbled beneath him as though he were standing on a water bed. Leaning back against one of the puffy, yellow walls to regain his balance, Albus ricocheted off the swollen bulkhead like a kid in a bouncy castle.

Golgotha half-heartedly monitored the man's progress. As he momentarily watched Albus squirming into the yellow room, the bombastic fat man had an idea that tickled him. He would dispatch his most inept and ineffectual henchman against Albus as a delightfully hilarious insult.

Hordes of albino rat-men came pouring out of hidden pores of the bouncy yellow room. They swarmed into the chamber intent on mutilating Albus, while Golgotha's belly trembled with laughter like a bowl full of jelly. Pallid, scurvy tails cork-screwed behind them like trolling motors as they clawed and leaped over one another eager to rend the intruder to shreds; their beady red eyes the pellets of a BB gun singularly gunning for Albus.

At first, annoyed by Golgotha's contrived inconvenience, Albus managed to reframe the massive hassle into a positive. He now had an opportunity to give Elephant's Bane a test drive before severing the pompous prick's trunk in two. With the ease of cutting through syrup-soaked pancakes served with a side of Saturday morning cartoons, Albus slashed apart the sacrificial henchmen. Bounding off the elastic walls like a WWE wrestler, Albus shot through the horde faster than a speeding bullet wielding a sword.

Wriggling tails, sharpened claws, and bloodied white ears went lopping off in every direction splatting and rebounding off the blubbery walls in a chaotic melee. Bezosbub's handiwork more than delivered on its end of the bargain.

Albus repeated his death-defying maneuver a number of more times, taking advantage of the chamber's unusual properties to trampoline off the floor and ceiling as well, becoming a blood-thirsty bouncy ball, hurtling through the throng of outmatched peons.

Golgotha, still very much enjoying the pointless game between him and the man, with an inexhaustible supply of henchmen at his disposal, flooded the bouncy castle with wave after wave of mean-spirited rodent boys.

Albus hacked away at the endless horde, never tiring, though growing quite bored of the futile exercise; he began searching for a way out of the bouncy room. Bum rushing through a cadre of rodents, his sword blithely splitting them apart, Albus stabbed at the puffy walls, ripping the vinyl apart as a blast of stale air escaped. Behind the shredded yellow tatters embedded in a solid bulkhead was yet another sealed sphincter. *Golgotha must really like sphincters.*

Prying the seal open while casually fending off assaults from the nipping rat-boys with his free hand, Albus launched himself into another sinuous, dampened duct, plumbing the depths of the self-made deva's palace.

....

Crawling along again as before through the slime slicked, constricted passageway, the conduit eventually deposited Albus into an all-stone antechamber. Albus slid out the tube on his backside landing on his feet. Similar to a medieval fortress, he found himself in a blandly utilitarian room, devoid of all decoration, nothing more than a flat, stone floor bounded by four gray stone walls. A foreboding red door painted black floated freely in space at the center of the antechamber, the only thing of significance in the stone room. Albus knew this door: this was the boss door.

In front of the double-wide, freestanding door, perhaps intending to guard it, nervously paced a short, pudgy man. The would-be guardian's thin, fair hair was balding from his forehead half-way up his cranium; his remaining greasy strands pulled back in an unflattering ponytail held in place with an elastic red scrunchy, the long ponytail hanging down to his ass. Albus immediately recognized the cretin from long, long ago by the moles, pockmarks, and acne scars striating his face.

"Mr. Molehill, why am I not surprised to see you here, you rat-fuck!" spat Albus with contempt.

The slouchy Mr. Molehill, dreading this inevitable confrontation for some time, turned to face Albus, clutching a heavy encyclopedic text against his soft belly, held tight with stubby fingers, the fingernails gnawed to nubs. The cover of the substantial volume held in the mole-man's grasp authoritatively read "The Rules" in embossed gold leaf.

In response, Mr. Molehill raised the textbook in front of his chest, donning it like paper armor. A timid child seeking succor beneath its blankie, the mole-man cowered behind the codex, relying on the book to shield him from monsters festering in the darkness.

Kevin Lorenzo Molehill had always been something of a misfit, never finding his niche in life. In the long, long ago he dreamt of becoming a famous musician. When that didn't pan out, he blamed the recording industry, his mother, and everyone else for his failings, rather than his utter lack of talent, discipline, or ambition.

To make ends meet he would do odd jobs, never sticking to one for long, working as a sandwich artist, a cold caller that specialized in relieving the elderly of their "tax burden" to the IRS, an unwitting test subject, and even a janitor at Google.

While blindly mopping his way through forgotten tunnels deep in the annals of Google's facilities, he inadvertently stumbled across the labyrinthine volume. Shocked to find his own name mentioned several times in the mammoth reams of text, he kept the volume for himself. Little did he know he had become a myopic lab rat, a rodent lost in the maze of a greater game. Sometime much later, after discovering his true gifts, his talent for being an all-around rat-fuck, Kevin Lorenzo Molehill found his way into Golgotha's service.

Mr. Molehill had never read the vast volume that he currently cowered behind, from beginning to end, though he claimed he had multiple times. He had only ever skimmed it, lightly perusing the text while searching for justifications to his own actions. Picking and choosing to promulgate those rules only when they suited his own desires. Pointing out the rules to others, exposing their own shortcomings while denying the existence of his, gave him a certain sense of righteousness, an air of superiority that had been denied to him so long, long ago.

"You betrayed us Kevin!" shouted Albus. "It was never supposed to be like this!"

"You made the wrong choices, Albus," replied the squirrelly mole through crooked teeth, tapping at the embossed title of the thick book with his index finger. Shrewdly he added, "Golgotha's unbeatable—he's a god." Albus had to stifle a laugh. As he stepped closer to Mr. Molehill, he spied a pathetic attempt at a straggly mustache growing from his crusty upper lip, feelers of sorts; this was new since their last encounter.

"You might be right, Kevin," said Albus with indifference, squaring his feet, "but I can still beat you." Without further delay Albus lunged at Kevin Molehill, his sword held prone with both hands. With an upward stroke, he slashed the mole from left hip to right shoulder, splitting the book and the creep wielding it, diagonally in two.

A surprised "EEEeee," followed by a sputtering, "pllbt unnnngugh...ggghuu," were Mr. Molehill's last words. Albus sheathed his sword as the two newly created halves of Mr. Molehill slid to the stone floor with a thud. When interviewed sometime later for the evening news about her son's tragic dismemberment, Kevin's mother asked that he be remembered by his brave final words in the face of villainy.

Striding past the mole's cooling corpse, Albus approached the wide door, two wrought-iron, round knockers hanging from its exterior. No frame nor hinges supported the door standing freely in the middle of the room, nothing behind it either.

When unlocked and pushed open, the doorway revealed a portal into Golgotha's inner sanctum, a swanky trick the lecherous elephant swore was a real panty-dropper. The glaring flaw with such a magical, floating door though, was that an intruder could easily walk around to the door's backside and undo all of its locks and deadbolts, rendering moot any of its security measures. Which Albus did. The locks and bolts undone, Albus stepped around to the front, drew Elephant's Bane from its ornate scabbard, and took a deep breath.

From the other side of the portal, the muffled sounds of slow-jams and muted giggles of a woman echoed off the sanctum walls. Preoccupied, mentally pumping himself up for the confrontation, Albus didn't register the noises. He went to grab hold of one of the large, round knockers and push when at the last minute he decided kicking in the door would be way more dramatic.

He kicked with all his might. The door burst open. Albus charged through the breach screaming, Elephant's Bane raised above his head. Golgotha was caught with his pants down, in a literal sense, writhing with a woman in his California King-sized bed, enraptured in sheets of white satin (never reaching the end) with a thread-count of one followed by one hundred zeros. The lovers shot-up, sitting upright in the bed, startled (the woman at least) by the unexpected intrusion.

The white linens slid and pulled away like an auctioneer introducing the mysterious final item up for bid, revealing Elixabeth's face—and naked body. His missing wife's perfect breasts swayed like a cow caught in the headlights. Her ebulliently flowing blonde hair, a matted and sweaty mess stuck against her cheeks.

. . . .

Albus' sword went limp, hanging ineffectually in his right hand, utterly stunned. Elixabeth stared blankly at her husband, offering no explanation, then slapped Golgotha across the face. Gathering the sheets about her naked body she fled out the back of the sanctum and disappeared, never saying a word. From his Martian monolith, Albus' cherub-like beings began doo-wopping a rendition of Del Shannon's "Runaway." Their singing was improving.

He rapidly iterated over an array of emotions: shock, pain, confusion, denial, rage, shame, disgust, betrayal, hurt, forgiveness, anger, shame, betrayal, hurt, embarrassment, disgust, denial, understanding, rage, pain, pity, disbelief. Like an emotional slot machine, he cycled round and round again, settling on rage.

Lifting Elephant's Bane above his head once more, Albus howled a guttural scream and charged at Golgotha with the fury of a man deeply wronged. Golgotha sat on the edge of the posh bed with his head hung low, not moving.

Within striking distance, Albus leapt and swung the sword with righteous wrath at the deva's tumid trunk. Nothing. His hands were empty. His sword wasn't there. It was *just gone*. The momentum of his empty and ineffectual swing, spun Albus in a circle as he crumpled to his knees at the edge of the bed and began to sob.

Lifting his heavy head some, Albus used the only weapons he had left, his words. "You fat, stupid asshole, how could you fucking do this? How could you fucking do this to me after all I've done?!" This was all the fat, stupid elephant's fault. Golgotha made her do this. He must have coerced her, forced himself on her, or enchanted her under some spell.

As the rage-fueled train of thought whistled and pulled away from the station of his mind, deep down Albus knew it wasn't true, wasn't possible. His wife had free will, just like he did. Golgotha couldn't make Elixabeth do anything she didn't want to do—any more than he could make Albus. No, Elixabeth chose this. She was a wholehearted and willing participant. Albus wanted to vomit.

Elixabeth hadn't vanished, hadn't evaporated into thin air, or been abducted by an evil wizard like some princess in need of rescue. How could he have been so dumb, so clueless, he wondered. How could he have not seen it? The love of his life was having an affair with a gaudy, boorish, morbidly obese elephant-man. That's all there was to it really...

"I didn't have a choice, Albus," said Golgotha in his own defense.

Albus seethed, staring at Golgotha in disbelief. The elephant-man sat there trying his best to mime some sense of shame, flapping his ridiculous ears, solid black eyes accumulating crusty mucus around their edges. Wrinkles and folds of his pink skin cut deeply into his face. An unexpected feeling came over Albus; sandwiched somewhere between his pain and disbelief, he almost began to pity the pink elephant. Unlike him—Golgotha couldn't make choices. Golgotha could only do what he was going to do. It was part of his contract.

Still in shock, Albus got to his feet, brushed himself off, and sat on the edge of the bed at the right hand of Golgotha. Golgotha's infinitely faceted crystal far outshone the diamond engagement ring Albus had proposed to his wife with long, long ago, which lay abandoned on the nightstand like an unwanted child.

"How long have we known each other, Albus?"

"Forever," replied the man.

Golgotha handed Albus a post-it note crafted from artisanal paper, a faux watercolor pattern of washed-out watermelons and hearts decorated the background of the square. Albus recognized the paper immediately; it was from the same stack of post-its that Elixabeth once used to write him love notes on, hidden for him about their cottage. Scribbles of purple ink lined the square; there was no mistaking Elixabeth's handwriting. The note read:

"I no longer love you, now please fuck off."

A crippling sigh eviscerated Albus slashing right through his groin and intestines as he fought the urge to sob again; bringing his hand to his forehead he pushed the tears back into his eyes. Empathy not being one of Golgotha's strengths (but he was learning), the elephant-man calculated the best course of action was to put an arm around Albus' shoulders. Albus cringed and swatted the chunky arm down as he pulled away from the backstabbing beast.

Everything Albus held dear had been stripped away. His wife no longer loved him; she was cheating on him with a disgusting creature he despised. He wasn't needed at a job he had devoted his life to. His children had relocated to places of their own and refused to speak to him. He had alienated his best friend. His vacation was at an end. He had nothing left. All he wanted to do was return to the thousandth floor of his monolith, sit in his creaky, leather chair, and think—for the rest of eternity...Except for one *small* problem. "I'll do it," Albus sighed with resignation, placing his face in his palms.

Golgotha raised his head. "You'll do what?" he asked, not wanting to get his hopes up prematurely.

"I'll go to the Low Place. I'll kill the kid. I'll save the fucking world." Albus clarified, "But not because you want me to, because I want to."

Golgotha bounced up and down, giddy as a schoolchild that

had discovered an extra Watermelon-Blast Gusher lingering at the bottom of her foil pack of fruit snacks. The elephant-man clapped his cajoling hands together sending tremors of fat jiggling all across his body as his bronze bangles clattered together singing discordant melodies.

"Excellent! Most excellent, my son!" he trumpeted. Albus hated when Golgotha called him "my son"; it felt patriarchal and condescending, besides Albus was technically older than him. Golgotha assured Albus that he was doing a great service to his country, that he would be a real hero upon his return. They would throw him a ticker-tape parade; Albus could even ride alongside Golgotha on his float at the upcoming Ascension Festival. Hell, maybe he'd even work it out with Elixabeth when he got back from his mission.

Whatever, thought Albus. Any place was better than this place at the moment.

16

UP HIGH,
DOWN LOW,
TOO SLOW

Golgotha, pleased that Albus had finally agreed to "play ball," took Albus on a tour; he led the man about his round bubble palace, down curving corridors swelling under the weight of excess, and winding hallways burdened with the trimmings of consummate success. The naked soles of the elephant-man's flabby feet left moist imprints behind on the cool white marble floor, while his puffy silk pants chafed together making alternating swishy sounds as they walked.

Not one to miss an opportunity to make a display of his stupendously splendiferous lifestyle, Golgotha nonchalantly pointed with his fat trunk, calling Albus' attention to the nearly unlimited number of priceless treasures and boundless riches he had herded into his possession over the eons. In one alcove cut into the long hallway stood the Venus Nike; a glut of fox, mink, and chinchilla fur coats sloppily hung from the marble statues outstretched wings. Passing by an opulent chamber, the Rosetta Stone leaned against the entryway serving as a doorstop. Albus begrudgingly followed along, indulging the fat stupid elephant, still in a state of shell-shock over the recent atomic bomb that had just detonated in his life.

They strolled through Golgotha's immense kitchen quarters.

Slaving away over the coal-burning iron stove, cacophonously clanging pots and pans together, Cheshire Cheato busily crafted his latest cheesy concoction, maniacally grinning at Albus all the while. *A couple handfuls of dried foreskins, a few umbilical cords, two sacks of monosodium glutamate, a few gallons of high fructose corn syrup and violá*, thought Chet as he stirred a bubbling cauldron. Behind the infernal iron stove, Golgotha had installed the Last Supper as a backsplash. The Mona Lisa, The Birth of Venus, and The Starry Night hung from the doors of stainless-steel refrigerators, held to the metallic exteriors with souvenir fridge magnets. The Mona Lisa was held in place by a magnet acquired from a gift-shop in Key West; the magnetic souvenir depicted a caricatured Rastafarian smoking a huge blunt, colorful bubble letters read, "Ass, Gas, or Grass."

As they exited the aft of the gargantuan galley, "You know Albus," preened Golgotha, "there was a time I was not much more than six colorful letters on a long lost and forgotten page. Now look at me!" How could Albus forget; Golgotha had a habit of prattling on to anyone that would listen (which was everyone) about his humble beginnings.

Albus ignored the blabberings of the elephant-man as best he could, while simultaneously trying to banish the unwanted images of the fat prick and his wife entwined together in bed. The sooner he was finished with this unpleasantness the sooner he could return to his Martian monolith in peace, catching up on some much-needed rest. Albus' thoughts meandered back to the leaf-cutter ants that had been mysteriously scurrying all over El Dorado. A slight pang of regret rattled through him; sadly, he never did figure out what the ants were up to. He didn't like it, but maybe he would have to be okay with just never knowing. Absentmindedly, he fingered the wedding band still residing in the pocket of his stylish, tri-color fanny pack with his left thumb and forefinger.

....

As they traipsed down another twisting palatial hallway, Golgotha side-eyed the shorter man walking alongside him, trying to detect any sense of deceit or treachery in Albus' intentions; he found none and was pleased. Golgotha did wonder though why Albus remained in the form that he was. Albus could be almost anything here, yet he chose to be just a man.

They turned a bend in the corridor and approached an unadorned, sleek door made entirely of silver; Golgotha halted. Albus was positive he had already seen this door; they must have passed right by it. Only a few paces farther down the corridor from where they stood, he spotted the ingress from where they had initially exited Golgotha's inner sanctum. Just as Albus suspected, there had been a much less circuitous route to this door, but the diva deva would never have allowed that. Golgotha cocked his huge head towards the silver door.

"Open it."

Albus placed his hand on the cold, smooth exterior, his fingers spread wide, and pushed; it swung open slowly on its hinges droning with a cranky creak.

"This is where I leave you," Golgotha opined. He turned his back on Albus and lumbered down the hallway, disappearing into the darkness.

....

Albus stepped across the threshold into an unimpressive darkened room, olive-green tiles covered the floor, tiled half-way up the muted drab walls before stopping. Suspended from the ceiling a single spotlight illuminated a tattered dentist's chair upholstered in green, sickly vinyl, thick leather straps bolted to its armrests; in many ways, it was the complete opposite of his office chair. Electro-mechanical gadgets that whirred and buzzed at high frequencies, tweeting their obvious importance, filled the cramped room. Arcane machines with tubes and glass cylinders full of bubbling purple fluids, billowing with bladders exhaling whistling steam, dotted the walls. Albus stumbled, almost tripping over orange extension cords running in tangled masses across the floor like invasive vines attempting to strangle the life out of an indigenous plant species.

Before entirely regaining his balance, he was assaulted from the shadows by an armada of strange men dressed in poorly fitting medical scrubs (who he surmised were not men at all). They clustered around Albus chattering to themselves, measuring him, probing him, sticking fingers into orifices without warning or introduction.

"Gentlemen, Gentlemen where are our manners?" came a vaguely familiar voice from amongst the crowd. "Why if it isn't 'The Man' himself," the voice quipped sardonically, veiling its jealousy for Albus' privileged position of power. The orderlies halted their unwelcome inspection and parted aside as a tall, thin man with receding eyes stepped forward and introduced himself to Albus as Enoch, adding with distinction that he was Golgotha's head magus. Enoch was the worst kind of man, a man acutely aware of his own importance.

The tall, slender man welcomed Albus, patting the headrest of the dental chair sending a small puff of dust into the air; without much ado, the head magus launched into his spiel, explaining the task at hand.

Like a proud new father, Enoch informed Albus that he and his underlings had accomplished what was once considered impossible. A feat of engineering marvel, they had managed to manipulate the membrane between their world and that of the Low Place, growing at its boundary a body, a new genesis. A real body made from the *very stuff* of the lower realm. Enoch's henchmen would transfer Albus into the host body that had been incubating on the edge of their world, then like a pimple on the ass of a goat, they would push and pop him, birthing him across the threshold into the infernal lower realm. Like a deep-sea explorer encased in the safety of a diving bell, Albus would be able to walk amongst the Low Place.

Enoch went on to explain that Albus' new body would be completely indistinguishable from any of the wretched denizens of the Low Place, operating exactly like theirs would, down to the letter. He ensured Albus though that he would be physically superior in construction and performance in every way. A real killing machine, Enoch promised. Albus nodded along indifferent, wanting to get the whole ordeal over with as quickly as possible. Although Enoch had begun the project at the behest of Golgotha, he had his own selfish interests vested in the success of Albus' mission; should the man's first foray into the Low Place prove a success, Enoch hoped to commercialize his down low process, selling tickets for exorbitant prices.

The details of the mission had been drawn up by Golgotha's generals, Enoch explained as he clapped his hands three times. In response one of the orderlies pushed a lit yellow button; a side door slid open. In trounced a huffing assembly of military personnel cramming into the already crowded quarters, hauling with them a collection of hexaprojectors, holo-illumineers, and large paper notepads held up by tripods.

The generals began briefing Albus on the specifics of his mission. The first lieutenant stepped forward and activated a hologram, displaying that his new body had a two-way transceiver implanted in its brain. The implant located directly behind his right eye would allow him to stream information to them, his sight and memories. Additionally, it enabled two-way communication; he would be able to communicate with Golgotha, should he have any questions or should trouble arise. Learning this information, Albus tuned out the rest of the presentation, figuring he could just query for the details once on the other side. His restless mind again turned to Elixabeth, lacerating himself needlessly with images of his beautiful wife pinned beneath the body of a sweaty, grotesque elephant-man, penetrated by his trunk. He felt sick; the unfamiliar urge to vomit washed over him yet again.

Albus reflected; he admitted he hadn't always been a perfect husband, though he had always tried his best. He realized he probably had some of his own shit to work out, though he had loved Elixabeth from the core of his being, was never unfaithful, admired her, provided for her, protected her, did everything he thought he was supposed to do to make her happy. Never would he have fathomed in two eternities, that someone he loved and trusted without question, could betray him in such a banal and clichéd manner.

The next general stepped forward and began a PowerPoint presentation; the first slide illustrated that Albus would have to assume the alias, Joshua K. Lamb, once on the other side. There was a slim chance the inhabitants of the Low Place might recognize the name Albus B. Cake. This bit of information Albus happened to grok before tuning out again; he had sat through enough meetings in his lifetime to know when to nod his head and "Mmm Hmm" at key moments to portray the illusion of rapt attention.

Other higher-ranking officers in Golgotha's service stepped forward giving presentations of their own, blathering on about many things: Albus' cover story, how best to survive in the Low Place, the name and physical description of the child prophesied to bring destruction to their world, how Albus was to locate and kill the quarry, how he was to reach the extraction point after mission completion. He would have to surrender his immortality once on the other side. Should he perish in the Low Place before reaching extraction, they would do their best to recover him (but no guarantees), so try not to die. Albus heard literally none of this. The presentations concluded, Enoch stepped forward once again. "Shall we?"

"Let's," replied Albus flatly. The head magus patted the dental chair once more, inviting Albus to take a seat and make himself comfortable, which Albus did. The vinyl surface of the chair was cool and sticky; overhead, the lone yellow spotlight flooded Albus' vision, making it nearly impossible to see what the orderlies were doing at the edges of the beam. Reaching out from the darkened borders of the circle, clammy hands grasped at him, impaling him with IVs and attaching electrodes all over; at either side of him, a pair of paws strapped him aggressively into the chair, constraining Albus with thick leather restraints. Another pair of grubby paws went to remove Albus' fanny pack. "The fanny pack stays," growled Albus as the hands slinked away beyond the perimeter of the conical beam. The malignant orderlies finishing up, they were ready to go: locked and loaded.

Enoch smiled.

"Any final questions?" asked the magus as a formality, expecting none. Albus shook his head. "Excellent. Initiate the down low process!" he screeched and gave the signal, dropping his hand. An orderly stationed against the far wall yanked down on the thick wooden handle of a hefty levered switch; its two metal prongs made contact with their junction, triggering a spray of electric sparks. The orderly then shouted over to another minion, "Commence shuffling onto the mortal coil!" Purple and green fluids from the glass cylinders began gurgling, draining from their confines coursing through the hollow plastic tubes swirling along en route to Albus. As the edges of his vision began to darken, a question did pop into his mind.

"Wait," Albus said casually, "what's the target's name again?" Looks of panic volleyed back and forth between the attendants' faces. "Shut it down! Shut it down!" one shouted. "Abort!" hollered one of the generals in alarm. Albus clearly hadn't paid attention to a single thing they had said. One of the lieutenants hastily mashed a large red button as a senior orderly frantically tried to reverse the lever; it was too late.

"Delilah!" Albus could hear Enoch shouting "Delilah!!" as he faded away into darkness. *The target is a girl?* he thought. That somehow made this unpleasant business seem all that much worse. Once more, Albus was completely devoured by darkness; he began diligently counting out the seconds. There was that number again, 3,484,000 seconds. It made no sense. An interesting thought occurred to him in that moment: maybe the number wasn't for him. Maybe the entire world didn't revolve around Albus Bartholomew Cake.

PART II

THE LOW PLACE

17

CANCER

Albus Cake lay with his face pressed against the ground; his eyes closed. He wasn't thinking; he was unconscious. An unwelcome cocktail of brimstone and burning wafted in Albus' direction, penetrating his nostrils; like infernal smelling salts, the unpleasant aroma hoisted his unconscious, melon-shaped noggin from the ground, causing the man to cough and sputter to life. *What is that awful smell?* he wondered. *What is smell!?* While contemplating the metaphysics of smell, a terrible sensation he hadn't experienced in eons radiated from his right shoulder and shot through his body: pain. The egregious pangs of angry nerve endings caused him to suck in a desperate gasp of hot air. His entire being felt heavy as if he were suffocating, drowned underneath his own gelatinous weight.

Tiny particles of matter whipped and blasted mercilessly against him; scraped at him, as he began to gain more awareness of his surroundings, each irregular granule a coarse micro-projectile grating, grinding and ripping at his unprotected, virginal skin. Lying on his belly, Albus struggled to part his eyelids: burning brightness and pain extended in every direction. It was unbearably hot.

His brain felt like runny scrambled eggs from an anti-drug

commercial, runny eggs that had been forced through a narrow feeding tube into a leaky paper sack. Thinking was slow and inefficient, his individual thoughts, hastily scrawled notes passed from cell to cell by prison inmates. He could recall the major plot-points of his life.

His name was Albus Cake. He liked counting things. He worked in a monolith. His wife had vanished into thin air. He had gone on a vacation with a fox-spirit, intent on removing Golgotha from power. Only to at the end of his journey, discover that his wife hadn't vanished; she had left him for a grotesque elephant-man. Shocked and defeated he had acquiesced; he agreed to accept his fate and descend to the Low Place to put a stop to the prophesied destroyer and save his world. His mission completed, he could return to his Martian monolith in peace and get lost in thought—for the rest of eternity.

However, specific details, minutiae, and bits of trivia he would have normally been able to recall with ease escaped him, as though they had been cached somewhere outside his person. For example, what were these tiny particles of matter blasting and grating against him called? *Sand*—his mind finally retrieved the answer he was seeking.

Sand slinked away beneath him as he pressed, pushing with his hands against the scorching, wind-torn dune; he mustered the strength to right himself onto his knees. Albus wondered for a moment if he was back on the volcanic black beach outside Golgotha's pink palace, no definitely not. This sand was bright white in color—and it hurt. There was no mistaking it, this was the Low Place.

Kneeling in the gritty, hot sand, he caught sight of his new limbs for the first time. Squinting in the overwhelming brightness, inspecting the hands and arms of his newborn body, he raised them aloft for a closer look. His splotchy, paper-pale skin felt like it was being irradiated in a microwave; skin that was so pallid he could easily see the sickly purple and green veins coursing just beneath the epidermal layer. His arms were covered in smatterings of orangish fur; freckly brown spots irregularly dotted their surface. *Is this some kind of sick joke?* Had Golgotha and his emissaries transformed him into some sort of cheetah-man? Albus lowered his arms back down, certain he was a monster (perhaps to blend in better with the Low Place inhabitants).

....

Flipping over onto his backside, trying to maintain his composure under the barrage of rasping stimuli, Albus kicked against the sand pushing himself further up the dune in shock at what he saw. Behind him, some sixty feet from his position, was a soot-black, bulging precipice, the face of which slithered and coiled, morphing with wormy, biomechanical filaments. Craning his neck upwards from his low vantage point, Albus estimated the jet-black megastructure to be maybe a thousand stories tall; clouds passed overhead.

Looking left and then right, the massive palisade ran horizontally in both directions as far as the eye could see. As he steadied himself, he was almost certain he spied a man-sized crater punctured in its dark surface (like a popped pimple) some nine or ten feet above ground level. Before he could fully process what he was looking at, lava-like tendrils snaked out of the structure sealing off the gaping indentation.

Sitting on his butt before the ominous structure that emanated a contradictory aura of being both alive and dead, Albus wasn't entirely sure what to make of it. *Am I supposed to climb up it?* Admittedly, he hadn't paid a lick of attention to the mission briefing back at Golgotha's palace; however, he was certain any mention of a monstrous jet-black edifice would have been a detail that stood out to him in bold. He was in luck though, recalling that Enoch's henchmen had implanted a transceiver in his new brain, Albus attempted to query the other side for further instruction.

*Come in, Golgotha. Come in, Golgotha.... ...*BzzzChhHZN-hhh BzzHH... Static was all he heard in response. Thinking more loudly this time he tried again, *COME IN, GOLGOTHA. COME IN, ENOCH. COME IN ANYBODY* adding an *OVER*, for good measure, since that was what one was supposed to do when communicating on that sort of thing. A hollow retort of snap, crackle, and pop resonated from within his skull. *Shit.*

The two-way transceiver's connection had been royally borked in the clusterfuck of chaos surrounding the failed abortion of the down low process. He was cut-off, stranded behind enemy lines. Albus got to his feet and cautiously moseyed towards the dark structure to investigate; palpable waves of heat intensified the closer he approached. As he walked away from the divot in the sand left behind by his body, a gold fourteen-karat wedding band lay abandoned in the impression.

Where the edge of the bulbous, black barrier met the ground, it incinerated and crystalized the granules into glass, the source of the burning sulfurous smell. All along the perimeter were bones and corpses of deceased creatures. The membrane of the blackness was oozing a viscous petroleum ointment, coating it, nearly five to six inches thick. Legions of flies, dying or on their way there, futilely fluttered their translucent wings in the throes of death, prisoners to the waxy gloop. He couldn't be totally certain, but he got the sense that the immense bulwark was advancing forward at an imperceptible pace.

Albus craned his neck skyward once more; tiny dots of creatures he recognized from his world, vultures, circled overhead. Jolting, he stumbled backwards in alarm as he watched one of the vultures fly over the perimeter of the tumorous blob; with unmitigated speed a sinew-like barb shot forth from the mass spearing the bird, pulling it back into it.

....

The sound of feet shuffled sand behind him; tiny hairs on the back of his neck levitated as if mesmerized. Something was coming over the dune. Planting one exposed heel in the hot sand, he rotated around quickly to confront his stalker.

One of the damned creatures of the Low Place was creeping towards him over the reverse side of the blistering dune. As it came into view Albus saw that it had the body of a man, but the head of a fly; covered from the neck down in tattered, canvas rags of splotchy, drab browns and olive greens. It crept closer; Albus involuntarily shuddered at the sight of the fly-man's round, glassy, expressionless eyes encased in a matte-black rubbery head. The hellish creature's distended, tubular proboscis swayed gently from side-to-side as it approached. Despite the burning pain all over his body, Albus raised his arms, clenching his palms into fists; he offset his feet contrapposto, taking a defensive posture for the inevitable conflict. The creature was almost upon him.

"I can see your penis," it said through its muffled proboscis.

"Huh?"

"Your penis," it said again, taunting him, pointing at his genitals, "I can see it."

Albus dropped his arms and looked down. The fly-man was correct; he was stark raving naked. As the capillaries in his face dilated a warm rush of blood flooded to his cheeks turning them beet red: he was blushing. Instinctively he cupped his hands over his privates like a man caught in a bad dream (or good dream depending on where one lands on the exhibitionist spectrum). Temporarily immobilized by embarrassment, he watched on in horror as the fly-man grabbed hold of its own proboscis; lifting upwards, it peeled away its insectoid face revealing under-neath—the face of a young woman.

"No need to blush," said the woman more clearly now, "not the first one I seen," (it was); resting her rubber gas mask atop her head the latex straps pushed back her curly brown hair. She examined the strange naked man in her midst that had seemingly materialized from nowhere, eyeing him up and down. He looked to be about five or six years older than her. If she had to guess, she would say he was about six feet seven inches tall, (though she would be the first to admit that she was terrible at guessing), either way, he was very tall, with large broad shoulders, chiseled chest, bicep, and back muscles to match. The stranger's face wasn't too bad to look at either with a semi-square jaw, centered pugilist's nose, and brilliant green eyes. *And look at those eyebrows,* she thought, *does this guy have hot eyebrows or what?* The woman tried to compose herself—then she noticed his hands; he had the sexiest hands she had ever seen. Whoever this new guy was, he was a total *hunk*—even for a ginger.

Clearing her throat involuntarily, she walked closer. She didn't sense any ill intentions; besides, she could take care of herself. On her key-chain hung a canister of military-grade pepper spray, not to mention her Glock 18 holstered at her side-arm. Albus took a step backwards; surprised to see a woman that looked a lot like the women from his world (and at the same time nothing like them at all). She was a black woman, but with dark brownish skin: not black skin, nor white skin, nor indigo skin. Blonde hair did not ebulliently blow in the wind; instead, the woman's tightly curled dark-brownish hair effervescently bounced up and down on top of her head. She had perfectly straight white teeth, with a slight gap right between the front two. *Wabi-sabi,* he thought.

Now standing only three feet apart, Albus took note of a shabby green patch stitched to the breast-pocket of her tattered fatigues, embroidered with faded black thread; somewhat aston-ished he was able to understand the profane symbols of the Low Place, "D. E. Fedora" it read. The two strangers inch-wormed closer, sniffing each other out for any scent of danger or malice. At an impasse, the woman decided to make the first move. "I'm Sergeant Fedora," she said, reaching her open hand towards Albus, adding, "but you can call me Delilah."

18

HEY THERE,
DELILAH

Delilah!? The name erupted through his brain like Mentos dropped into a two-liter Coca-Cola bottle; he pressed his lips together with strained effort, preventing the thought from blurting out his mouth, hopefully concealing his surprise. That name was the last thing he recalled hearing Enoch screaming as he slipped away into the darkness. *There's no way it's this easy,* he thought. What were the chances that the first being he encountered upon awakening in the Low Place would be the Destroyer of Worlds? Again, he berated himself for not following along during the mission briefing. However, he hadn't anticipated the transceiver's malfunction, and besides, it had been rather difficult to concentrate with images of his wife (*ex-wife?*) being smothered under the jelly rolls and sugar plums of a pudgy elephant-man dancing about his head.

Albus wondered if he should attack the woman anyway, just to be safe. The notion seemed rather rude; he didn't even know her. He weighed his options, looping over the pros and cons. The name could merely be a coincidence and he certainly had no intention of executing an innocent person on mistaken identity. Additionally, she wasn't a child. Though, he was well aware that time passed radically differently between that of the Low Place and his world (if it could be said to pass at all); she could have very well grown-up in the interim. However, she certainly didn't seem like the ruthless destroyer of worlds type; she actually seemed...kind of nice. He took into account the fact that he was completely naked and unarmed; who could fathom what kind of lethal Low Place weaponry she had concealed on her person. Albus decided that the best course of action was to get to know her first—and then terminate her later—when he was certain that she was the one.

....

Delilah's outstretched, expectant hand hovered in limbo; the customary amount of time had elapsed to where it was now awkward to leave it hanging any longer. About to lower her arm back down, Albus croaked, "Hey there, Delilah, I'm—err...My name is Joshua. Joshua K. Lamb," as he grabbed hold of the woman's calloused hand, shaking it far too vigorously. It had been a while since he had used his voice and it came out froggy and guttural; at least he hadn't blown the alias part of his mission, yet. Delilah wrinkled her brow as she huffed air through her nostrils; there was something a bit off about this man who seemed to have lost his way.

"Nice to meet you, Joshua," she replied, releasing her grasp. Pulling her hand away, she eyed the freckle-bedecked, red-headed man like some curiosity, a Neanderthal uncovered frozen within a glacier. The inevitable and logical next question. "Where did you come from?" she asked pragmatically. *Shit*. Like a fish trying to breathe air, Joshua's mouth hopelessly flapped open and closed. She raised an eyebrow unsure what to make of this, admittedly hunky, nude dude, wandering about the sand dunes like a stray dog. Albus was in luck though; Delilah had a soft spot for strays. "Did you just come out of cryostasis or something?" quizzed Delilah, tossing Albus a softball.

The situation in the Low Place had been deteriorating for as long as there had been a Low Place, political upheaval, wars, disease, environmental degradation, etc... As the levels of entropy and hopelessness began to approach near unbearableness, reading the emails on the walls, many of the realm's powerful and wealthiest denizens chose to either try their luck elsewhere or voluntarily freeze themselves in suspended animation, cryostasis. Kicking the can down the road, the hope being that when they were revived from their ice tombs, that future generations had solved all the problems they had so gleefully and enthusiastically created.

"Uh…yep…that's it—Cryostasis," Albus replied affirmatively, pointing a finger at Delilah. He had no idea what cryostasis was, but it certainly sounded a lot better than his explanation as to why he was here. The survival instincts drilled into Delilah by her father told her to end the interaction there, get back to her speeder, and leave the hulking nudist to fend for himself. However, most people wouldn't last long out in the wastes unclothed, and with no supplies; it felt wrong to leave the man to die. He was now a fellow survivor just like her. Albus stood there not saying anything as they eyed each other.

Huffing, "Come on," she said, "let's at least get you away from the Cancer," motioning towards the ominous, jet-black precipice behind Albus. "It emits like a metric fuck-ton of radiation." Tossing him a white pill from her pack, she instructed him to swallow it. "Potassium iodate, it will keep your thyroid from melting."

Delilah had never met someone that had been locked away in cryo. Unbeknownst to her, most cryostasis facilities had catastrophically failed after the Cancer's unanticipated and violent birth, leaving their patrons locked inside, slowly turning to dust. Although, occasionally she would hear tales of some wealthy popsicle emerging from a facility buried deep, like a newborn pharaoh clawing its way out of the sand towards the light. Other facilities had been housed in the theoretical safety of automated orbital stations and would on occasion eject their frozen residents when the time they had rented was up, sending their cryo-pods crashing to the surface like refrigerated fallen angels. Upon rousing from their dreamless, glacial sleep, only to find the situation much worse than they had left it, almost universally, these barely thawed mummies would immediately lock themselves back into stasis.

....

The sepia-skinned woman led Albus away from the amoeba-like megastructure, removing her stippled camouflage jacket as she strafed down the side of the steep sand dune, loaning it to the stranger to wrap around his waist for modesty. Beneath her jacket Delilah donned a skintight, white tank top, the cotton fabric contrasting sharply with her dark skin, revealing an athletic upper body. Her long arms blithely swaying by her sides were slender yet muscular, a side-effect of her labor-intensive lifestyle. She moved down the sandy hill with an unintentional yet appealing poise, the svelte muscles of her frame dancing with one another in confident harmony. As they trudged over the crest of the next dune, a few more sandy hills came into view leading down to a vibrant, blue ocean rolling with ivory capped waves. Incorrectly, Albus had assumed they were somewhere in an endless desert.

Traipsing down the remaining dunes towards Delilah's awaiting speeder parked along the shore's edge, from his peripheral vision a scuttle of motion sent Albus into high alert. Out the corner of his eye, he spotted a foul beast sprinting on all fours, charging right for them with a slack-jaw and slobbery pink tongue wagging like a windsock from its open mouth, revealing rows of mangled canines. Without any conscious intervention from his neocortex, the supreme reflexes of his newly-formed body kicked into overdrive, flooding his system with a potent and potentially addicting concoction of adrenaline and norepinephrine.

Albus dove headlong at the rampaging beast—the loaned jacket fluttering about his flanks like a cape—spearing it with his body, tackling it. He wrestled with the beast in the scorching hot sand, narrowly avoiding the yips and snaps of its toothy maw that sought his jugular. Somewhere behind him, over the snarls and yaps of the monster, he could hear Delilah shouting, surely cheering him on in his gladiatorial deathmatch.

Managing to get his hands between its vicious mandible and cold, snotty snout, Albus ripped outwardly with manly strength. His muscle fibers tensed like steel cables separating the animal's jaw, throat, and sternum from its body as effortlessly as one might peel a piece of string cheese. A spray of blood across his chest, then the beast was dead. Albus stood victoriously, the trophy of the monster's jawbone in hand, turning towards Delilah, expecting the woman to be wowed by his senseless bravery.

She wasn't moving; standing still, trembling in place, her eyes welled with tears. "That…that…was my dog," she stammered in shock.

"Uhhh…" Albus looked down, staring at his bulky barbarian bod splattered in blood, muscular chest still heaving from the scrap, mandible clutched in his fist, spectacularly unable to conjure a word, any word. Shamefully, he dropped the jawbone to the sand; it landed with a muffled crunch, sliding further down the dune. Placing his blood-stained hand on the back of his head, he scratched awkwardly at his shock of carrot-top hair while dragging his big-toe back and forth through sandy granules: he felt like crap. "Sorry?" he offered tepidly, "I just thought…" glancing downward at his bare feet again, at a loss for what he was supposed to offer the woman whose dog he had just ripped in two.

....

Delilah crouched over the body of her slain hound, Trudy, with her back turned towards Albus. She wasn't going to let this stranger witness a single sliver of weakness in her, as tears silently streamed down her cheeks, taking a moment to mourn the dead creature. Trudy the hound was already old in people-years when Delilah had found the stray a few years back. When they first crossed paths the cur had been wandering about the wastes, subsisting on garbage, covered in fleas, a few tumors from the radiation were already visibly protruding from beneath the canine's skin.

Out of pity she took the stubborn-stray in, fed her, and cleaned her up; for better or worse, the two had been inseparable ever since. She enjoyed the company of the uncomplicated hound on lengthy trips away from the homestead. However, she could be a royal pain-in-the-ass at times on salvage runs, choosing to bark at inopportune moments, or piddling all over the seats of the speeder during long treks when the beast's incontinent bladder got the better. Delilah wasn't sure how much time Trudy had left as the hound's tumors continued to grow, causing her pain, slowing her movements.

In truth, she had already been contemplating putting the beast out of its misery herself. Perhaps in some sense, Joshua had just done them both a kindness. Trudy got a warrior's death, and she didn't have to betray the poor thing herself, lock her in a pen, and shoot her when she wasn't even looking. Delilah thought back on the other canine companions she had had over the years. Pets didn't last all that long in the Low Place; everything she loved always left her, in one way or another.

Giving the woman her space, Albus hung back and watched as she mourned in a fashion he found to be eerily calm to an almost troubling degree, considering the fact that the person responsible for her dog's death was standing right behind her. He couldn't imagine what he would do if anyone ever hurt Argus.

Sucking in a deep, stabilizing breath, wiping a few dribbles of snot from her wind-chapped nostrils, the survival instincts imparted to her by her father whisked Delilah back to the scene around her. The loyal canine had fulfilled her purpose; there was no use letting her death go to waste. "It's okay," said Delilah turning around. "She was pretty old. Go and strap her carcass to the back of the speeder along with the rest of the meat."

Not only was he taken aback by how nonchalant she was, Albus felt revolted by the vulgar insinuation. He didn't think he could ever eat Argus, no matter how hungry he was; little did he know what hunger was. Putting his repulsion aside, he followed Delilah's bidding.

....

She fished a small dongle out of her pant's pocket and clicked a button; two beeps and the vehicle that had been resting at the shore's edge powered on. Turbines engaging, it hovered three and a half feet into the air with a roar. The shallow waves of the surf oscillated in the empty space beneath.

Albus made his way towards the back of the hovering vehicle that Delilah had called a speeder, carting the jiggly, jawless Trudy over his shoulder; he still really felt like crap for killing her dog. *I was just trying to protect her*, he thought. *And why would you want to do that?* he thought back.

He ran his free-hand along the pleasing feminine curves of Delilah's low-hovering craft. It was open-topped like a convertible, enameled in a glossy, apricot-orange finish with a considerable amount of dents and scratches scarring the paint job, exposing suggestive hints of the aluminum chassis beneath.

Mounted onto the sides of the curvaceous frame were four boisterous thruster housings, two on each side, the source of the hovercraft's levitating power. A bowed sheet of tempered glass, with a minor crack through its middle, leaned back in front of the vehicle's open cockpit, shielding its operator from the wind. Upfront were two captain-style seats upholstered in cream-colored Naugahyde, displaying their own share of wear and tear. The backseat was a single elongated bench covered in the same milky-white faux leather.

The speeder looked as though it was designed to comfortably transport a family of four (or possibly five if they crammed), if the backseat hadn't been buried in mounds of scrap metal, tubing, unidentifiable parts, and large coils of stripped copper wiring.

On the back of the vehicle, Albus located the metal carrying-rack, already loaded with the bodies of three overgrown rodent-looking things, mutated muskrats, each with a bullet hole placed squarely between its eyes. The force of the thrusters billowed around his exposed feet as he fumbled some with a mishmash of red and green bungee cords, securing the dead dog's carcass. Delilah, already impatiently waiting, hollered back for Joshua to get a move on; he ran around to the passenger-side, hopped over and flopped down into the open seat.

The dashboard of the craft blinked and booped with all sorts of gauges; in the center console, a hemispherical, smoky glass reticule striped with green grid-lines displayed a blinking red triangle. Hanging, swaying gently from the rearview mirror was a delicate gold chain, at the end of which hung a cross with the graven image of a man in great pain, surely dying. Without so much as an explanation, Delilah pulled a few levers, yanked the wheel, and stepped on the gas, darting out towards the open sea.

....

They clipped along, hovering over the face of the water a good three or four feet above the rolling waves, the downward force of the turbines generating a decent wake behind them that fanned out in a sinusoidal pattern across the ocean surface. The sun was directly overhead. Over the din of the engines and whipping winds Delilah shouted something towards Albus.

"What?!" hollered Albus in return.

"Never mind!" she yelled. Albus shrugged. A thought occurred to him; if this woman was, in fact, the destroyer, he could grab hold of the wheel and bank it hard to the right, throwing her overboard into the ocean. Then he'd really be in trouble though; he had no idea how to pilot this thing.

They continued on for several more hours as the hot sun basted them, Albus agonizingly squinting from the overwhelming sunlight and oppressive blueness engulfing him. Taking notice of the painfully scrunched expression on his face, Delilah reached over across his lap; caught off guard Albus snatched her hand with a death-grip. She shot him a stern look that meant *back off*; embarrassed he let go. Reaching past him, she popped open the speeder's glove compartment, a pair of sunglasses falling out. She pointed at them.

He put them on, shielding his eyes from the ravaging rays; much better. Albus was starting to acclimate some to the harshness of the Low Place and his new body, at least he no longer felt like he was drowning under his own weight. He turned to Delilah and gave her a thumbs-up; she shook her head and rolled her eyes.

In the distance, isolated tropical islands would occasionally crest over the horizon then disappear from view; at one point a school of flying fish sprang forth from beneath the waves, briefly gliding alongside the cruising speeder. Albus couldn't remember what they were called; out of habit he almost pinged Golgotha. That was no longer an option here and he felt some mild relief over the notion. *Red fish, blue fish, one fish, two fish,* he thought.

19

NEW DETROIT

Overhead, the sun had made its way three quarters across the sky and hung low, reduced in color from a blazing yellow to a more palatable orangish red; Ra made preparations for his battle with the underworld. Growing larger on the horizon was a big island with a single mountainous peak. Delilah tapped the hazy, glass hemisphere in her center console and plotted a course straight for it.

A good amount of the vegetation on the mountainside was burnt up, scorched, perhaps the result of a forest fire. However, it looked as though Mother Nature was making a comeback, repopulating the island in thick spans of triumphant greenery. Now less than two hundred yards out, Albus spotted half a dozen large vessels that appeared military in nature, docked in the waters offshore. The ships had been reduced to hulking wrecks, waves crashing against them, sunk into the shallow waters surrounding the island, some their bows protruding upright above the surface, others lain on their sides like slain kraken.

Delilah weaved between the wreckage; craning the wheel to the right she banked hard into a slide, skidding up the rocky shoreline sending a spray of sand and saltwater ahead of the craft, heralding their arrival. Disembarking, she hopped over the side of her speeder, cocking her head indicating for Joshua to follow.

This strip of beach was far less homogenous than the one he had awoken on, composed of rounded pebbles, shell fragments, and small stones worn smooth by the waves; he felt each one press its way into his naked, sensitive feet. Up the slope of the shore some twenty yards away, stands of tropical plants, palm trees, mangroves, and sea grapes, shielded a rocky outcropping that ran the length of the island's coastline.

. . . .

Thwap thwap thwap. Three rapid-fire gunshots rang out unexpectedly from the direction of the hammock. A sting sang out from Albus' exposed pectoral muscle like the loving kiss of a horsefly. They were under attack.

Again, his finely-engineered reflexes kicked into overdrive. Instinctively, he pulled Delilah behind him, shielding her with his body; his sharp vision scanned the rocky outcropping for the origin of the sneak attack while his hand probed at the pain in his chest. Orange and blue goo dripped down his skin. Blood was supposed to be red. *Does my new body bleed orange and blue mechanical fluid?* A mistake of that magnitude would have been a glaring oversight on Enoch's part, a dead giveaway that he didn't belong. Continuing to probe with his fingers, there were no puncture wounds to be found. *Am I bulletproof?* he wondered. *Sweet.*

Delilah shoved Joshua aside. "Get down here this instant!" she hollered, stomping her foot against the gravelly beach with a loud crunch for emphasis.

Leaning out from behind the palms, a young girl appeared, a firearm grasped in her fist with an oblong-shaped plastic tub fitted to the top. Reluctantly, the girl surrendered and trudged down the beach from her hiding place towards Delilah, concealing the weapon behind her back.

Albus wasn't falling for it; the hateful Low Place creature was obviously preparing for another sneak attack, maneuvering into proximity to finish the job. As the girl got close Albus did a double-take; he was staring at an almost identical but smaller version of Delilah.

"Fork it over!" Delilah commanded. The girl hemmed and hawed eventually relinquishing the firearm. "You shot Joshua!"

"Whatever," replied the girl with a spectacular amount of attitude. "It's just a paintball gun." Delilah continued dressing down her miniaturized doppelganger. Albus' brain, still acclimating to its slower pace of thinking, dealing with the troves of information that had been misplaced, shredded or outright deleted, strained to piece together what a paintball gun was; he knew *gun* but failed to stitch together the rest. Given that he was not dead, he filled in the blanks best he could and concluded that the girl's firearm was a non-lethal weapon. Sadly, he was not, in fact, bulletproof. *Or am I?* It was an experiment for another time.

Delilah, draping an arm over the shoulder of the girl, turned towards Joshua and said, "Meet my lovely little sister, Delilah."

Her sister's name is also Delilah? He paused, uncertain he had heard right. *Wouldn't that get confusing?* Albus continued to ponder, perhaps this new girl was his target, the alleged destroyer. She was younger, though not young enough to be considered a child, possibly a young teen. Don't forget she had just shot him completely unprovoked. *That's a checkmark in the destroyer column.*

However, he would hate to have to murder Delilah's kid sister after the woman had been so kind to him, especially if he was mistaken in his reasoning. Albus' head swam as he contemplated just how many Delilahs there could be in the Low Place. *Will I have to go on a cold-blooded rampage? Terminate every Delilah I encounter just to be certain?* He shuddered at the unsavory proposal. His quest unnecessarily confounded, a sinking feeling came over him. *What if I just never meet the right girl—to kill.*

Noting the befuddled look on Joshua's face, Delilah clarified, "But we usually just call her Dee." Adding, almost as if embarrassed, "My mom really liked the name Delilah...*like* really liked it."

Dee inspected the new arrival with suspicious disdain. Before her stood a dumb-looking giant splattered in the orange and blue splotches of her handiwork, the dye mixing with rusty streaks of blood drying on his torso, a pair of cheap women's sunglasses straining around his melon-like head. Her sister's favorite jacket knotted loosely around his waist, fashioned into some primitive loincloth, he looked like some Tarzan mother-fucker Delilah had dragged out the jungle and was attempting to civilize. Dee didn't trust the towering outsider one bit. For starters, he was a ginger, and perhaps more importantly, he was a white man showing up on a tropical island uninvited.

Delilah urged her younger sister to apologize to Joshua. "Sorry! Not sorry!" Dee hollered, as she ran off up the coarse beach kicking up small pebbles. Shouting behind her, "Papa's looking for you!" as she disappeared up the outcropping into the hammock of trees. A small white fox with cartoonishly large ears, a collar around its neck, dashed out from its hiding place within the thicket of palms; a bell dangling from its collar rattled some as it chased after Dee, nipping at her heels.

"Oh great…" groaned the elder Delilah. "Bring one of the muskrat carcasses with you. My father might like you better if you come bearing an offering."

....

Albus retrieved one of the slain mutated rodents from the back of the speeder and hefted it onto his shoulder. Its awkward and blubberous body, that he estimated to weigh around fifty or sixty pounds, jiggled uncomfortably as he followed behind Delilah; they shimmed up a nearly vertical trail in the outcropping, grabbing onto thin branches and exposed roots for stability as they climbed.

As they made their way over the ledge of the squat prom-ontory and cleared the tropical hammock guarding the coast, a sparse settlement came into view, sprawled out along a flat, hard-packed plateau. There was evidence of some past cata-clysm, some massive fire possibly. Relics of a great conflagration abounded; the ruined buildings and scorched husks of unidenti-fiable objects reminded Albus why they called it the Low Place.

What little remained of the buildings shared some of the

same drab, utilitarian characteristics of the wrecked military vessels wallowing in the shallows. Some of the structures appeared to be in various stages of rehabilitation, in the process of being rebuilt from salvaged scraps; others had been constructed de novo from concrete blocks and sheets of corrugated steel fitted in place as roofs. Closest to the edge of the outcropping, stood a sturdy tiki hut some ten feet wide by twenty feet long (reminding Albus some of the huts from the fishing village). Swaying in the breeze, three hammocks: a big one, a medium-sized one, and a small one, woven from jute and sisal fiber were strung between the hut's supporting posts.

Delilah turned to Joshua. "Welcome to—"

Albus, certain she was about to espouse some quasi-biblical, sci-fi sounding name like Neo Jericho, Babylon 2.0, or Bethlehem Minor, cut her off mid-sentence and said, "Let me guess, Calvary Prime?"

Delilah guffawed and screwed up her face.

"What? No," she said. "Welcome to New Detroit."

"Oh," Albus blushed.

Before introducing him to her pop, Delilah dumped a bucket of cold water over Joshua's head while he scrubbed the blood and gooey paint off with a sea sponge, prettying himself up. The impact from the exploded paintballs left three painful red welts on his chest. Delilah averted her eyes while the ruddy outsider scrubbed himself clean, but not before noticing, (perhaps on a more subconscious level), another strange quality of the man's body: there was not a blemish, imperfection, nor scar on him. Yes, he was dappled in regular dots of brown freckles, and smatterings of orangish-red body hair (in only the best places), but other than that, not an overgrown hairy mole, nor an overly long yellowing toenail to be found. Not a pockmark, scrape, nor minor surgery scar anywhere on the man's skin. *Maybe his scars are buried elsewhere.*

Delilah tossed Joshua a pair of her papa's old overalls; all her papa's overalls were old. The denim dungarees fit snuggly. *Her father must be a big guy*, thought Albus. All cleaned up, they walked towards one of the rehabbed cinder block buildings, large garage bay doors protecting its alcoves. In one of the open bays, the lower half of a man protruded from beneath a janky, non-operational speeder, a speeder that had been retrofitted for plow work. The rest of his body obscured by the faulty work-horse, he lay there like a mythical hybrid; the legs of a man with the torso of a burdensome beast. The sound of metal clanking on metal interspersed with mild cursing rang out from beneath the hopeless speeder. "Papa! I'm back!" called Delilah.

A large man in well-worn denim overalls stained with a myriad of mechanical fluids, reclining on a wheeled sled, hauled himself out from beneath the busted machine. "Darling!" he hollered back. "Find anything interesting—" he said, as he sat up making eye contact with the outsider. *This honky ass mutha' fuka wearing my overalls…and standing next to my daughter,* was his first impression.

"Uh-huuuh," replied Delilah somewhat sheepishly.

Standing up and wiping his greasy palms with a hole-filled rag, a stalwart, ox-like man at least as tall as Albus, plodded over to the two. Like Delilah, he was black, though his skin tone was a few shades slightly darker than hers. He had the same tightly wound, curly brown hair as his daughter, however, his was receding from his forehead, cropped much closer to his scalp. A hard-won, bushy mustache grew from his upper lip, traveling down his jowls, squarely framing the sides of his mouth. Kind, chestnut-hued eyes betrayed his gruff exterior as a trio of wrinkles creased deeply into his forehead at the sight of his daughter's discovery.

"Well…well…well," he opined like a man who had seen everything. "What have we got here?" Delilah's father took a step closer to Albus.

"Papa…this is Joshua," interjected Delilah. Her father said nothing; he continued to slowly wring the oily rag, strangling it with his strong hands. "Hmph," he snorted, as he glared at the red-headed stranger with a healthy syringe of suspicion, eyeing the man like a venomous snake his child had wrangled into a mason jar and delightfully carted home with her, begging him to keep it.

"Sweetheart, can I speak with you," said Delilah's father. "Alone." Hesitantly, she heeded her father's request, stepping over spare parts to the back of his grimy garage, leaving the stray Joshua to awkwardly stand at the bay door trying to figure out what to do with his hands. Delilah explained to her father she had found the man out in the wastes, wandering about some sand dunes like a lost baby sea turtle headed the wrong way, walking right towards the radioactive Cancer, (intentionally leaving the part about him being fully nude out of the discussion).

In hushed tones, the two argued back and forth. Delilah vouched for Joshua, swearing that he was harmless.

"Harmless?!" whispered her father a little too loudly, "the Neanderthal ripped Trudy in two!"

"It was a mistake! He was just trying to protect me!" Delilah countered. In exasperation, she asked, "What was I supposed to do? Just leave him to die?!"

"Yes! That is exactly what you were supposed to do."

Upset by her father's uncharacteristic callousness, she fought back the tears forming in her eyes for the second time that day. Through fuming whispers, she reminded her papa that hadn't *he* always been the one griping about how much *he* could use an extra hand around the homestead. If only *he* could find a trustworthy, hardworking laborer they could rebuild their little society so much faster, he would complain around the dinner table. His oldest daughter had him there; she wasn't wrong. Turning to glance back towards the able-bodied Joshua, begrudgingly he conceded to giving the outsider a shot.

They approached Joshua. With a calculated slowness the woman's father reached out his empty palm as a peace offering and said, "Hello Joshua, my name's Gellert."

Heh, that's funny, thought Albus.

"Something funny, son?" chided Gellert.

"No sir!" said Albus, grasping hold of the man's palm, shaking it firmly.

Still clasping Joshua's hand, squeezing it tightly as a reminder of who was in charge, Gellert made a mental note of how oddly uncalloused it was. He asked, "Where's about in this great wasteland did you come from?" Albus was prepared this time. He parroted Delilah's incorrect and potentially disastrous assumption; he had just come out of the cryostasis, had been frozen for decades.

Gellert narrowed his eyes as Albus told him this; it had been many, many years since he had heard any report of someone emerging from cryostasis, though the baby-smooth texture of the man's palm did make more sense in that regard.

There was something slightly off about the off-brand red-headed hulk; the older gentleman shared the same reticence as Dee, his younger daughter. Regardless, he was in desperate need of an additional pair of hands if he ever wanted to get the homestead to any state of self-sufficiency.

Joshua's strapping frame and substantial muscles looked more than capable of handling the back-breaking labor. If Gellert caught wind of any monkey business, he told himself, he could easily end the outsider. Blow his brains out with one of the many firearms he kept hidden in caches about his jungle paradise. Giving the man's hand one final squeeze, practically threatening to break it in two, Gellert released his grasp. The two stood eye to eye.

"And I have meat," said Albus, lowering the overgrown muskrat carcass off his shoulder, laying it on the dirty floor at Gellert's feet.

Gellert snorted and cracked a smile from the side of his mouth. "If you don't mind earning your keep," he said flatly, "we might be able to find a place for you around here. Follow me... and bring the meat."

Albus followed after the man, carting the carcass once again over his shoulder. Gellert walked with a slow deliberate gait, a slight limp on one side. His left leg was missing from the knee down; a prosthetic creaked along in its place.

....

The entire settlement rested on a long, curving plateau that descended like an arm reaching out from the southern side of the island's mountain; Albus estimated the narrow expanse to be about nine or ten miles long by four miles wide at its widest point. The arm of the plateau was protected on the oceanside by the stout outcropping, maybe fifteen feet in height, that he had climbed up earlier; the settlement was somewhat safely obscured from prying eyes by the thick tropical hammock growing all along the cliff's edge above the pebbly beach. Away from the ocean spray, on the island-side of the curving plateau, descended a scarped embankment that led down to a large freshwater lagoon resting in the middle of the island.

A river flowing out of the tropical, mountainous jungle dead-ended at a cliff on the northern side of the lagoon, from which a waterfall spurted forth its deliciously ice-cold, freshwater, feeding the pool. The far eastern edge of the lagoon made limited contact with the ocean, hugged by a coral atoll that almost encased the eastern lip entirely, tips of coral barely cresting through the membrane of the water's edge that fed back out into the sea, salt and fresh-water mixing in a brackish concoction at its boundary.

Running along the side of the lagoon closer to them, to the west of the base of the embankment, was a crescent of land with decent soil, an arable spit maybe three miles wide by seven miles in length, that Gellert had put to work growing life-sustaining legumes, vegetables, and grains. A half-finished irrigation project rested in its midst. Anorexic windmills, rising some twenty feet tall, welded from rusty steel beams, aluminum, and patchwork scraps of canvas, lined one of the ridges and spun diligently in the ocean breeze where they could capture the most of the mercurial, aeolian currents. Banks of repurposed solar panels sunbathing like spring breakers untroubled by melanoma, were clustered in places that Gellert had determined to be the sunniest spots on the tropical island.

Phantoms left behind by whatever had caused so much devastation haunted every inch of the settlement, with blown-out walls and hunks of rubble strewn about the flat plain. Gellert made note of some of the buildings he had reconstructed. Over yonder was the mess hall with a slanted tin roof; he and his two girls typically gathered there and cooked their meals inside on the electric stove.

On the backside of the mess sat a two-thousand-gallon cistern, mortared together from stones and debris, that captured rainwater running off the slanted roof during storms. When rainwater was scarce Gellert would pump supplemental fresh water into the cistern from the lagoon, up the steep incline. Past the cistern was their iguana pen, a few empty stone silos, and several vacant pens Gellert intended to eventually populate with more of the island's fauna.

Albus humored the older man, listening intently, though he was wondering how he was going to bring himself to murder one (or both) of his daughters. *If I just explained to him that a prescient magus foretold that she was (possibly) destined to bring ruin and destruction to my world, would he understand?* He didn't think so.

Not far past the mess hall was another nondescript, rectangular block building: their living quarters, Gellert explained. The building had a wide slab porch poured from cement, jutting out from the front. In the basement beneath, subterranean dormitories kept them cool on hot nights, though many nights when the wind was strong and the bugs were scarce, Gellert and his girls would end up sleeping in the hammocks of the tiki hut that he had constructed some few years back.

Behind the living quarters were located an open-air solar shower, and two composting toilets that smoked their feces, catalyzing their poo into viable fertilizer for his farming operation; Gellert promised to explain how the toilets worked to Joshua at a later time, (Albus wretched a little inside at the idea, but expected nothing less from denizens of the Low Place). Gellert hurried them along wanting to show Joshua their destination and his own personal pride and joy—his smokehouse.

....

Some distance past the living quarters, stood a narrow cement shed, three feet by five feet in dimension, with a locked steel door and beige brick chimney exhaling a steady stream of thin grey smoke. Albus was caught completely off guard; there was that perception of smell again, only this time, it was glorious. Particulate matter alchemically transfigured into pure joy as Albus was overtaken with sensation and memory: Thanksgiving, sweet-tobacco, corn-hole, his father.

Gellert removed the padlock and threw open the steel door, donning a pair of heat-resistant gloves. Inside the smoker hung from metal hooks were rows of skinned animal carcasses: iguanas, wild boars, and other unrecognizable hunks of flesh. Dull lead being transmuted to shining gold, the animal flesh was slowly being sanctified into irresistible morsels over the coals of a slow-burning fire. Another new but old sensation washed over Albus. His mouth involuntarily watered; saliva glands squeezed their juices onto his palate with such vehemence that his cheeks puckered in pain.

Joshua's stomach short-circuited the conscious narrative running through Albus' mind as he buckled to one knee from the stimuli of the smoked meats. *Hungry,* it vociferated with animalistic fury. Gellert chuckled at Joshua's reaction. "Being locked away in cryo for all those years I'm sure built up an appetite," he said. "Soon as we clean this critter, we'll head back to the mess. The girls will have gotten supper underway."

They removed the fatty muskrat's head, sawing away at its sinewy neck. Albus held the body aloft, cringing some as he let the blood drain out, while Gellert used a pocket knife to pop its dead eyes into an awaiting green bucket; he tossed the rest of the beasts' severed cranium into a nearby compost heap.

Wielding a pair of sharpened knives, they proceeded to shed the animal of its skin, Albus following the older man's lead. Gellert forfeited the pelt over to the outsider, instructing him to coat it in salt and hang it out to dry; they could use it later for barter. Further splitting the creature down its sternum to its anus, Gellert collected its organs and entrails in the same green bucket. Hanging the soon-to-be burnt offering from an open hook, he handed the bucket of entrails over to Joshua. Making their way towards the mess, they made the rest of the walk in silence.

20

SUPPER

The sun was disappearing behind the horizon, its once-mighty warrior rays tempered by the tranquil Neptunian ocean. Arrays of naked glass bulbs sputtered to life, illuminating the homestead as the night overtook the day. Dangling lights strung along the pathways allowed the survivors to navigate their way through the otherwise all-encompassing darkness. The energy Gellert collected during the day from his windmills and solar panels served them well, powering the lighting and other various equipment from a bank of speeder batteries sequestered in the basement beneath the living quarters.

Slipping out under the cover of darkness, droves of insects and pests such as mosquitos, biting gnats, and no-see-ums came out of the woodwork ready to party; including less pesty insects, like the familiar firefly. *Photuris,* thought Albus. In an effort to combat the pest problem, Gellert had managed to repair a busted bug-zapper; he had hung the neon-blue electrified coils from a corner of the mess hall's tin roof. Male fireflies, mistaking the alluring blue glow of the zapper for the motherlode of all babes, drifted hypnotically to their own destruction, fried to crisps like death-row inmates—their only crime—falling in love.

When Delilah the Younger was younger, each time she heard

the pop or crackle from a bug colliding with the electrified coils, she would ask her papa what would happen to all the innocent bugs that accidentally got zapped to death. Trying his best to placate her fears, Gellert would tell her, if they were innocent bugs, they went to heaven. Dee wasn't so sure she believed in heaven, and if there were bugs there, she definitely didn't want to go.

....

Inside the mess hall, the two Delilahs stood over a stainless-steel countertop, chatting discretely to one another in the patois of sisterhood, knives in hand, dicing vegetables gathered from their garden into cubic chunks. The scene was totally foreign to Albus, yet at the same time too utterly familiar. He felt split in half, un-successfully straddled between two worlds. Next to the sisters, a tall pot a foot in diameter, covered in dings, its bottom scorched soot-black, sat on the red coils of an electric stovetop, bubbling the gathered rainwater melding it together with a collection of fresh green herbs.

Again, the menagerie of interlocking aromas coiled and twisted their way up Albus' nostrils hitting his olfactory bulb, triggering an avalanche of unplaceable and abstract memories: granite countertops, home, his mother, depression.

"Hey, girls!" announced Gellert, "What's cooking?"

"Hiya, Papa!" they replied in unison.

Gellert strolled over to the boiling pot, the aromatic steam rising into the air then dissipating; he wafted some of it towards him then dumped the green bucket of muskrat organs and en-trails into the simmering liquid.

"Hey!" the Delilahs protested, "That was supposed to be a vegan stew!!"

"Don't be silly," their father laughed. Delilah the Younger playfully smacked her father on the back of his hand with a wooden spoon, which he pulled in towards his body pretend-ing as though she had wounded him gravely. She laughed and tried to bop her papa again. This time he caught the spoon and yanked it from her grasp. Dipping the wooden spoon into the pot, Gellert ladled a small helping of the steaming broth to his mouth, sampling his daughters' handiwork.

"Delish!" he exclaimed. The Delilahs smiled. Albus meandered about the mess awkwardly, an outsider to this tight-knit group. Delilah the Elder, always looking to be inclusive, hollered over to him.

"Hey, Joshua, why don't you fill the canteen."

Happy to have something to do, Albus carted a plastic orange barrel, topped with white lid, outside around to the back of the mess hall, and set it down beneath the spigot of the cistern. Turning the knob, cool rainwater gushed out into the empty container. Pausing for a moment to reflect while he waited for the container to fill, he thought about what a strange turn of events his life had taken, though he supposed his life had always been strange. He wasn't special in that regard. Life was strange in general.

He was still uncertain which Delilah he had to terminate and decided the best course of action was to observe them further before passing his final judgment. *I wish I didn't have to murder anyone*, he lamented, but he had no choice in the matter. His bare feet were getting wet; the orange water container had overflown, muddying the ground around its base. Frantically, he cranked the spigot sealing the valve, halting the flow.

Squatting down then hefting the barrel onto his shoulders, he was startled by how much water could weigh. It wasn't an issue for Joshua's Atlas-like muscles that barely strained under the load, burning mildly with lactic acid; still, it was much heavier than he had anticipated. As he carted the heavy container back into the mess, Albus glanced up into the night sky and caught sight of a shooting star streaking across the firmament—then another.

Back inside, Dee had just finished setting the table, purposely placing the forks and the knives on the incorrect side of their proper place settings, to rankle her sister. Delilah the Elder (wise to her sister's game at this point) ignored the attempted needling, denying her sister the pleasure of getting under her skin. Albus hoisted the orange barrel onto an unoccupied counter-space and began filling tin cups, setting them around the table, as the older sister ladled spoonful's of hot stew into plastic bowls. Monstrously, Joshua's stomach grumbled again; Albus felt faint.

The mess hall had a few long tables with attached metal benches, that had been pushed to the sides in disarray. The four people instead gathered around a square, wobbly card table, scorched on the edges, a gash in its vinyl cover exposing the yellowed foam beneath. As they sat down to eat, the palpable absence of someone could be felt. Albus had the sense not to ask; he didn't know these people all that well yet.

....

Gellert sat first, Albus took the white plastic chair opposite him, the two sisters sat across from each other. Soup steaming innocently in front of him, Albus, overwhelmed with desire, greedily scooped the bowl to his mouth about to drain the whole thing down his throat, when he noticed the others glaring at him, their hands joined with one another. The two sisters reached towards Joshua with open palms, waiting for him to get the clue. "Grace," the elder Delilah hissed at him.

Raising an eyebrow still not quite understanding, he made his best guess and set the steaming bowl of stew back down, joining hands with Delilah and Delilah, completing the circle. The younger Delilah held Joshua's hand rather loosely; she had another trick up her sleeve. In the hollow of her palm, she had concealed a sharp thumbtack held in position with spent chewing gum...

Gellert bowed his head and closed his eyes, his daughters did the same. Albus followed suit (only to open one eye and peek). The girls' father began speaking to no one in particular, giving thanks for their bounty among other things. Albus, peering down with his one open eye towards the scant soup bowls, recalling his time in El Dorado, didn't think it much a bounty. Gellert continued asking that this be blessed and that be blessed, even asking for Joshua to be blessed. That made Albus feel uncomfortable. He pondered, *Do they worship the Lord of the Clouds in the Low Place?* He didn't think it possible. Delilah the Younger squirmed, barely able to contain herself. Gellert's remarks concluded the three, even more strangely, then spoke in unison:

"Our Father who art in Heaven, hallowed be thy name. Thy kingdom come, thy will be done, on earth as it is in heaven. Give us this day our daily bread, and forgive us our trespasses, as we also forgive those who trespass against us. And lead us not into temptation but deliver us from evil. For thine is the kingdom and the glory and the power forever and ever. Amen."

That was Dee's cue. As they said "Amen," she squeezed Joshua's hand—hard, jamming the pointy end of the thumbtack into the exposed flesh of the man's palm. Albus, who had been silently appreciating the words just spoken by Gellert with a sense of detached amusement, emitted a loud yowl of unanticipated pain, yanking his hand away from the girl, shaking it. The youngster howled with laughter, nearly falling out of her seat. *Another checkmark in the destroyer column.* Albus held up his pricked palm, inspecting it; she had pierced the center of it with the tack, small globules of red blood leaking out. Once the shock wore off, it really didn't hurt all that bad. Albus was almost amused; he apparently did bleed, and it wasn't orange and blue.

"Delilah!" Delilah shouted, swatting Dee upside the head in anger. "Why do you have to ruin everything!"

Dee retorted, "It's only cause you think he's hot!"

The two sisters squabbled back and forth when Gellert boomed, "Enough! Delilah, you be nice to Delilah. Delilah, you be nice to Joshua—and take your dinner straight to your room, no dessert, no games."

Dee scowled, "It's all stupid Joshua's fault!"

Albus didn't like being the center of all this strife. Waving his hands, getting their attention, he said, "It's really okay!" Plucking the rogue thumbtack off the table he showed them as he pricked his other palm, laughing. For some reason, he added, "'Tis' but a scratch!" in a funny accent. He held both his pierced palms out for them to see that the wound was minor and had barely hurt.

Dee's sulking turned to unexpected giggles. "You know Monty Python?!" she asked with astonishment.

Somehow, Albus did but didn't. "Of course," he replied. The drama abated, Dee was allowed to eat her dinner at the table, though the terms of her surrender still mandated no dessert and no games for her stunt.

. . . .

Finally, the gang chowed down on their much overdue mutated muskrat stew. It was absolutely incredible, magnificent even. The rich, oily broth slipping and sliding over Albus' tongue was hot enough to scald him, but he didn't care. Tender tidbits of carrots, jungle potatoes, and celery flush with the herbaceous liquid, crushed and squished together against his molars ejecting their earthy and nourishing flavors onto his virgin taste buds; the miraculous transformation of disparate parts came together in a symphony of sensation that sent his mouth into wild applause. Masticating some salty, iron-rich, unidentified part of muskrat organ, the texture changed as he chewed, delighting him with each new act. *Ugh it's so good.*

Gellert tried to make some small talk with the outsider, get to know him, asking what he had done for work prior to going into cryo. The soup was so good Joshua almost wanted to tell him everything, right then and there, all of it—the whole story. *No!* Albus was on a mission; he had to lie. Glancing around, like a bad Kyser Söze, Albus used items from his surroundings as inspiration for his elaborate cover story; the mess hall was, unfortunately, sparsely decorated. In one corner lay a hoe and pitch-fork.

"Farmer." Yeah that was it; he had been a farmer.

Interesting, thought Gellert, asking, "You don't say...what kind of farmer?"

Stove farmer? No. Sink farmer? No. Looking out the mess hall window towards the ocean, "Kelp Farmer," said Albus, shoveling a spoonful of stew into his mouth hoping Gellert would be satisfied and stop quizzing him.

Doubly interesting, thought Gellert. He had never known a kelp farmer wealthy enough to afford cryo. When he brought the point up to the man, Albus dropped his spoon into his soup with a splash. "Big kelp farmer," said the outsider. "Biggest operation in the world. Yep. Kelp farms all over." This seemed to keep Gellert quiet, for now; Albus went back to scooping large heaps of the savory stew into Joshua's gaping mouth.

Albus followed along with the conversation as best he could, a conversation that would drop in and out at certain points without context; not saying much, he went back for fourth and fifth helpings of stew.

Delilah tried her best to not stare at Joshua's hands as he ate, but sometimes she couldn't help herself. She watched as he brought a spoonful of soup to eye level, a dark squishy ball floating in the broth. The eyeball of the muskrat was staring Albus directly in the face. Gellert saw it too and pronounced across the table, "You got the eyeball! It's good luck!" He began slowly chanting, "Eat it...eat it...eat it." Banging his fists on the table, his daughters joined in with the chant as well. Without further hesitation, Albus popped the orb into his mouth and chomped, jellified eyeball fluid flooding out. They cheered as Albus did a mock bow when he heard the jingling of a bell outside the door. The white fox with the large, floppy ears he had seen earlier on the beach, poked its head through the open door of the mess.

"Fin!" called the younger sister. The fox bolted past the threshold towards its summoner, a pink cat's collar with a tiny silver bell strapped around its neck, the origin of the tinkling sound. It leapt into Delilah the Younger's lap as she tossed him scraps of muskrat entrails which the fox gladly gobbled, scarfing them down its snout. Dee went a mile a minute. "This is Fin," she said stroking the fox's ears, "He's a fennec fox, they're desert dwellers. We found him on one of our expo-ditions. His mom was dead. He was just a pup and he was crying, so we raised him. He's transgender," squeezing the fox tight about the neck she added, "and I loooove him sooo much. He was the only thing that survived the...survived the...you know." Albus nodded along. He didn't know. "Fin protects us," she paused then smirked, adding, "and he hates white men!"

"Delilah!" shouted Delilah the Elder for the second time that evening, reprimanding her sister, turning to Joshua apologizing on her sister's behalf. She swore up and down that their fennec fox wasn't a racist nor, to her knowledge, transgender. Gellert surmised that that was just about enough out of the youngster and delivered on his promise, sending her to her room, no dessert, no games. "Just for that," sang the elder Delilah, "I'm opening our last box of Nilla Wafers for dessert." Her younger sister practically cried as she stomped off towards the living quarters.

....

Delilah put a metal coffee pot onto the glowing coils of the stove as she cleared the empty bowls from the table. Gellert tamped at a pipe and turned to Joshua, saying, "Bet the world sure looks different than when you went into cryo."

"Sure does," agreed Albus. Joshua hated lying.

"That *beast* you saw…it did this," said Gellert. The "Cancer" Delilah had called it. Albus nodded anticipating some explanation. Gellert delivered. He and his family had been out on these islands as part of a joint military-scientific expedition studying emergent psychic and telekinetic phenomena among the planet's intelligent marine life. He was the head biologist on the mission aboard their ship, The Dalmatian, a part of a civilian attaché of scientists and researchers.

They had sought to unlock the mystery behind the esoteric and perhaps, even frightening, new powers developing among the ocean's cephalopods and cetaceans, hoping to possibly employ them to solve some of the environmental crises facing their world; the military of course—hoped to weaponize them. It had been Gellert's day off and he had taken the girls on an excursion under the surface of the waves in his yellow submersible; he wanted to show them a kelp garden that a pod of psychic octopi had planted and been tending to over the last several weeks. It was quite incredible behavior; he had never seen anything like it.

That was when the Cancer erupted. It blindsided the entire

planet. Gellert would never forget the date; it was September the eleventh, the same date his great-grandfather had perished more than a century ago trying to rescue some people from a burning building. When he and his girls surfaced, all the military and research vessels that had been anchored in the shallows off the island were burning wrecks intensely huffing thick, choking clouds of black smoke, sinking to the shallow ocean bottom as they burned. As they piloted the submersible back to the beach, the intense heat from the blaze could be felt through the vessel's metallic hull. The majority of the research facility had been obliterated: leveled. A few structures still stood in ruin. Everyone they had ever known or loved was vaporized. "Just gone."

Gellert came to a stilted halt for a moment, staring past Joshua to the back of the mess hall; he swallowed with some noticeable difficulty, then continued. Within a matter of hours, the world they had known was an unrecognizable ruin, all banking and communication systems knocked out, an overwhelming majority of the population annihilated in an instant.

. . . .

There had been a paltry attempt at a counter-attack, the few supersonic jets not destroyed in the initial outburst tried to bomb the tumorous mass out of existence. However, the Cancer knew better; it had taught itself to recognize any threat to its dominance. Anything that tried to fly over it, be it jet airplane, missile, rocketeer, hang glider, hot air balloon, the black mass skewered out of the sky with pseudopod-like tentacles before it could pose any opposition. The marauding miasma of the Cancer's dark tentacles spread rapidly at first, coating and consuming most of the planet's surface within a few weeks' time. Its growth then slowed, as if it had become sated with the destruction and distracted by other matters, leaving isolated pockets of survivors completely cut off from one another, enduring the inevitable in suffocating silence.

Gellert assured Joshua that the Cancer was most definitely still growing though; he had measured it. It could take decades, maybe even longer at its current rate, but it was still only a matter of time before it reached their outpost consuming them as well. Many had their theories about what the Cancer was; some speculated that it was some kind of hybrid biomechanical nanotech supercomputer experiment gone awry, the legend of the gray goo (or in this case black goo) that had gotten wildly out of control. Others were certain it was an alien invasion, claiming to have witnessed mammoth bulbs of the Cancer liftoff into space, shortly after its growth had slowed, lending credence to their theory. Gellert had his own ideas. Joshua knew; Albus said nothing.

....

The three sat in silence. Delilah pushed herself away from the table, the audible scoot of her chair against the cement floor augmented by the hushed atmosphere. She retrieved the coffee pot that was percolating on the stovetop, passing around a box of foraged vanilla cookies for dessert.

"Dominoes anyone?" suggested Gellert. Happy to have a distraction from the morbid reality engulfing them, Albus enthusiastically seconded the idea. Gellert was pleased to have a new opponent to play; he was tired of always trouncing the girls he teased. Delilah huffed at her father's remark and laughed, reminding her papa that their current record was six-hundred and twelve to six-hundred and ten, advantage her. Of all the bits and pieces of information missing from Albus' brain, how to play dominoes wasn't one of them; he let the older gentleman give him a refresher on the rules anyway.

Gellert donned a pair of thick-rimmed reading glasses to better see the pips with. He overturned a small box fashioned of thin, mildewed wood, held together at the corners with dovetail joints, dumping the ebony and ivory tiles onto the tabletop, clinking gently as they ricocheted against one another. Doling out servings of steaming hot coffee into their tin cups, Delilah took a seat at the table adjacent to Joshua, crossing her arms on the table. The antique set of dominoes was of particular sentimental value to Gellert; it had been passed down to him, having been in the family for generations. What made it so special was that its tiles were carved from real ivory—just like they used to do in the old, old days, a barbaric practice for sure, but a priceless heirloom nonetheless.

They switched off the battery-powered generator to conserve its juice, using glass lanterns burning refined coconut oil to illuminate their game. Gellert struck a match and lit his pipe. Albus didn't care for the noxious odor of the smoldering tobacco but assumed he must be the only one and withheld complaint. Against the flickering backdrop, Delilah's father leaned back in his chair, his face obscured in shadow, only his horseshoe mustache and yellowing teeth visible in the low light, a halo of hazy smoke surrounding him.

"Weren't all that rosy before that *beast* wreaked all its havoc," Gellert grumbled to no one in particular as he slapped down a bone. As they played the game, the older man continued to grumble in lamentable fragmentary bursts. *Food shortages.* He slapped down a domino taking the round. *Political instability.* This time Delilah took the win. *War amongst the tommys.* Albus thought he had this round, but the win went to Gellert. "And the damn Cancer," Gellert sneered, aggressively exhuming large rings of tobacco smoke like a grave-digging dragon with an axe to grind. Albus shot a look of concern over to Delilah, she glanced back at Joshua and rolled her large brown eyes beneath her father's notice. *Just humor him. He gets like this sometimes,* the look said. Albus stifled a laugh, delighted by the nuance in such a small facial expression.

"What? What's funny?" asked Gellert, sliding his reading glasses down the bridge of his nose to look at his two opponents.

"Nothing, Papa."

Joshua and Delilah glanced back towards one another. Maybe it was the caffeine buzz or the late hour, or maybe it was just nothing at all; they burst out in uncontrollable laughter. Gellert just shrugged and tallied the score. The coconut oil fueling their lamps was getting low, dwindling. With the caffeinated buzz from the coffee winding down the trio of domino players yawned back and forth at one another.

Delilah wanted to win one more round to further the lead against her father, but she knew that look on her papa's face; he was bushed and would be dozing at the table in no time. Joshua could bunk with Gellert in the living quarters, in the spare bunk above his. Albus politely declined the offer, choosing to sleep in one of the hammocks strung up in the tiki hut; there was a decent breeze coming off the ocean that night. Albus walked along, a clutch of blankets and mosquito netting in his arms, gazing up at the stars. They looked strangely familiar here.

21

BEAST OF
BURDEN

Albus wiggled, precariously balancing himself into the rock-ing hammock that would scoot away from him every time he tried to plant his backside, the woven fibers of the jute matrix pressing into his flesh; spinning in place, he cocooned himself in blankets and mosquito netting. He slept.

It felt like a thousand years since he had had a deep night's sleep and for the first time since the monorail, he dreamed. The details of the dream began to sublimate as fledgling rays of the rising sun, sent like winged Valkyries to wake the world, crested over the ocean, prying at his crusty eyelids with crowbars. All he could recall of the dream was finding himself once more in a boat. Elixabeth wanted to talk to him. The multifaceted crone sat across from him; her words echoed hauntingly: a needle to pierce the heart, a sword to cut away the trunk, a whispered word once heard cannot be unheard. His eyes fully opened now; all memory of the dream slipped away like a rat diving through a hole in the wall, absconding with a jingling book.

Packets of aromas cha-cha danced their way across the airwaves, beckoning him. Momentarily vexed by his constricted state, Albus twisted and turned in the hammock; he flopped to the ground with a hard *OmpphFff.* The pain in his right shoulder returned. Pressing himself up and patting the dirt off (embarrassed by his spastic movements) he glanced around, relieved Delilah hadn't witnessed his assuredly comical display of early morning agility. The source of the smell guided him towards the mess hall. A silent pep-talk ran through his head; he reminded himself that he was here, cut-off behind enemy lines on a critical mission—to stop Delilah (A Delilah) the Destroyer of Worlds—not to eat and schmooze his way across the Low Place. The others were already hustling and bustling about the mess. They teased Joshua for his tardy arrival.

"My oh my, look what the cat dragged in," smacked Gellert.

"The worms are all gone—us early birds got 'em," joked Delilah.

"Hey stupid," her younger sister said. *Another checkmark in the destroyer column.* Gellert was on breakfast duty that morning. Unintentionally, he shook his rear-end from side to side as he sprinkled dashes of sea salt and island pepper over a heavy cast-iron skillet frying up two dozen tiny eggs collected from their iguana coop. Most of the runny yellow yolks had been inadvertently punctured, spreading out over the hot pan, solidifying.

The eggs smelled absolutely wonderful. Joshua's tummy rumbled in anticipation. Albus chastised himself for getting so chummy with these abominable Low Place creatures the previous night. He reasoned that it must have been something in the devilish food they had fed him. That had to have been what caused him to lower his guard so foolishly. That was it, he resolved then and there—no more giving in to temptation; he would stop eating until his mission was accomplished. When Gellert set a plate of iguana eggs and cup of hot coffee before him, Albus politely turned it down.

"You sure, Joshua? Got a big day ahead of us, gonna need the rocket fuel."

Again, he declined, stating that he had no appetite. Making up an excuse, Albus blamed it on a side effect of waking from cryo. "Suit yourself, more for us." Delilah the Elder gave Joshua a puzzled look; Albus avoided her gaze.

....

After breakfast Gellert handed Joshua a shovel, carrying a hoe himself, limping as he led the outsider down the sloping embankment of the flat plateau towards the freshwater lagoon. Gellert motioned, waving his hand across the curving expanse of arable land to the west, bordering the sparkling pool, stating, "This fertile crescent is our sustenance, our lifesaver."

Less than a quarter of the crescent had been put under plow. Half-finished trenches depended on frequently malfunctioning sump-pumps installed on the lagoon's edge, to force freshwater into the ditches. Amalgamations of lead, copper, and PVC pipes were strewn about; some joined sections of tubing fanned out across a few of the plots. Gellert explained how he hoped to expand his irrigation network, he would plow and plant the entire crescent one day, dramatically increasing their food supply. With their food problems solved he could invite other survivors from neighboring islands to reside at New Detroit, form a real community, some semblance of a civilization.

They passed a nearby plot; tall stalks of ripening wheat wavered in the wind. Planted in the center of the square, strapped to a wooden cross, was what looked to Albus like a chrome-plated, robotic skeleton.

"That's Cain, our scarecrow," said Gellert, "he likes to *hang out*," the man chuckled to himself. It wasn't a real robot, Gellert revealed, just some piece of rubbish, a discarded prop from an antiquated action movie lost to the sands of time.

The robotic imposter was made of hard plastic and styrofoam; demonstrating, Gellert knocked against the scarecrow's weathered hull producing a dampened hollow echo. "That stuff is immortal, it never decomposes." The faux-chrome arms of the ghastly memento were stretched out along the crossbeam of its post, held in place by rusty nails, while its false resin eyes hung downwards toward the dirt.

Dee had unearthed Cain; she had hauled the eye-catching piece of junk out of a massive landfill while on a salvage run with her sister. Pleading with her older sibling to let her keep such a treasured find, she refused to leave the landfill until they loaded it onto the speeder. Delilah the Elder eventually relented. That was the last time Dee was allowed to participate on a scrapping adventure.

Albus was on trench duty today, Gellert informed him. He instructed Joshua that he would be shoveling out one of the canals, furthering the trench in a long, evenly-spaced channel away from the lagoon. Albus regarded the macabre Cain with some misgivings, keeping his distance from the scarecrow as he set about his task.

At the onset, the work was utterly miserable. Albus toiled, slaving away under the hot tropical sun, Joshua's empty stomach protesting all the while. Within minutes he was coated in another new yet old sensation. A salty liquid dripped profusely from every pore of his body: he was sweating. Clumps of dampened ginger hair clung to his moistening brow obstructing his vision; continually he swiped the strands away with soiled hands smearing schmutz across his forehead.

He would spear the pointed tip of his shovel into the dirt, kick the spade in with his heel, then lever up a large scoop of loamy soil, tossing it aside, over and over again. As he repeated this ritual ad nauseam, unexpectedly, the work began to transform, becoming meditative, hypnotic, perhaps even enjoyable.

The sticky sweat now slicking every inch of his body evaporated in the breeze, cooling him; it felt kind of good. Thankfully, the grumbling from his stomach organ had piped down as well. Albus found himself appreciating the fibrous muscles connected to his large frame as they strained in unison, a choreographed dance enabling him to undertake his work.

His body, now convinced that this task wasn't ending anytime soon, pushed him on further with a heaping dump of endorphins. It felt euphoric to be alive, to strive, to endure. When the sun reached its mid-point in the clear sky, Delilah stepped out of the mess hall and beat a metal triangle with a mallet, a loud gong announcing that lunch was served. Gellert signaled over to Joshua who was laboring some thirty yards away.

"I'm good!" Albus hollered back. Gellert was too sweaty

and exhausted to argue with the outsider and trudged up the incline towards the mess alone. Albus worked straight through lunch, stopping only to scoop cupped handfuls of the chilly lagoon water into his mouth. When supper rolled around, again he abstained, working, tilling the land till the sun disappeared behind the horizon.

After dark, Albus stood quietly in the mess observing the Delilahs' interactions as they cleaned, silently collating data for any hints as to who was the destroyer. The sisters side-eyed him but chalked the unusual behavior up to his alleged cryo-sickness. Unceremoniously, he said his goodnights and retired to his hammock.

....

The next morning, the second day of his fast, Albus repeated the same process. Rising at dawn he went down to the crescent with a shovel in hand. He found it somewhat easier than the first day to suppress his hunger; his body had begun burning what little fat reserves it had squirreled away in its larders.

Again, he worked through the day, digging, subsisting solely on lagoon water. The chattering narrative that had been plaguing his mind, thoughts of Elixabeth, thoughts of Golgotha, anxiety about killing the right Delilah, quieted down, subsiding some (but not entirely). By the third day, his fast began to raise suspicions amongst the others. Delilah and Delilah, taking a reprieve atop the plateau, watched Joshua work the fields below, chatting with one another.

"Maybe he's some sort of robot sent from the future to kill us?" crowed the younger Delilah.

"Don't be ridiculous, Dee," chided Delilah, "this isn't some sci-fi novel. Besides, if the Cancer wanted us dead it would have done it by now." She paused then added, "Maybe he's on a hunger strike after your thumbtack stunt." Dee snickered; her sister yelled that it wasn't funny. Gellert passed by, a wooden yoke slung across his back, two metal buckets balanced on either end filled to the brim with feed for the iguana coop. "Hey, it's free labor," their father added to the conversation as he plodded past. By the sixth day of the outsider's fast they had accepted that this was just how Joshua *was*; the man would have to eat eventually, or die.

....

Albus' bulky muscles had waned noticeably; his pale, sunburnt skin stretched taut across his body, the bluish-green veins popping out from beneath. He wasn't on trench duty today; today he was tasked with harvesting the ripened wheat from the plot guarded by Cain.

An intensely hot day, hotter than others if that was possible, he swung a broad scythe back and forth, when he started to feel a bit odd. The enormous clouds hanging low in the sky lost some of their detail. Rounding out into frayed cotton balls as if from a child's diorama, they all began to look exactly the same, clones of one another, when Albus heard a familiar voice.

"Hiiiiya, Albus!" squealed Genji. Out the corner of one eye, Albus caught a glimpse of his long-lost fox-spirit! He spun wildly in Genji's direction, absentmindedly swinging the scythe along as he did, decapitating a multitude of stalks. Genji darted out of sight leaving zephyr blue trails in his wake. Albus spun back the other way eagerly trying to spot the meddlesome fox.

"Albus and Delilah sittin' in a tree, K-I-S-S-I-N-G," taunted Genji as he zipped out of Albus' view giggling, adding, "How's the quest going?"

"Shut up! Shut up!" hissed Albus. "You're going to blow my cover!" Pivoting back and forth still in search of Genji, he turned; his eyes widened in horror. Before him, Cain the scarecrow shuddered to life, its false eyes glowing a sickening, neon pink.

The scarecrow flexed its emaciated robotic arms, expelling the nails that had held it in place. It stepped down off its cross, shuffling towards Albus, dragging one leg behind through the dirt.

"The Lord of the Clouds requests an audience." Albus was certain he heard the chromatized zombie croak. Hollering feverishly, he swung his crooked scythe madly through the air, severing the plastic golem in two at the waist. Somewhere out of sight, Genji laughed hysterically.

Coming to his senses some, Albus stepped over the two halves of the possessed scarecrow, inspecting them; its shiny arms and body were still firmly restrained to the wood beams, the wooden post was split in two along with it. Its Styrofoam guts exposed, beads of white balls flaked out of the severed halves, swirling around in the dirt in tiny cyclones that blew away in the breeze.

Meekly, he glanced about his surroundings, Genji was still nowhere to be found. Again that uncomfortable feeling of straddling two realities overcame him as his vision darkened around the edges. His knees buckling, he fainted landing with a hushed thud amongst the heaps of piled grain.

....

Waking sometime later, he found himself resting on one of the canvas cots of the living quarters, a cold compress pressed to his forehead. Delilah sat over him with a bowl of room-temperature broth cupped in her hands.

"You need to eat," she said pushing a spoonful in his direction. Albus, enervated by hunger, acquiesced. Parting his cracked lips she spooned the nourishing liquid into his mouth; it felt good. "Here comes the airplane," she teased. Albus didn't get the reference but he recognized from her tone that it was a joke and laughed. The motherly, umami broth comforting his malnourished body, Albus took the bowl from Delilah's hands and guzzled the rest.

22

JOSHUA

Joshua settled into a groove, adapting to the rhythm of life around New Detroit, rising at dawn for a plate of iguana eggs or creamed oats, spending his day working diligently in the fields, breaking for a light lunch of smoked rat or boiled sea urchin, washing up before supper, joining Gellert and the girls in giving thanks, playing dominoes in the evenings; Albus harvested data all the while.

Delilah was glad that Joshua had finally started eating again. Dee was royally miffed that Joshua had 'killed' Cain, her scarecrow. When she heard the news, she swore vengeance sevenfold, threatening to pour pufferfish venom into Joshua's ear while he slept. *Another checkmark in the destroyer column.* Delilah assured Joshua her sister was only kidding and would forget about the whole incident by supper. Gellert had managed to fix Cain, joining the two halves of the gutted scarecrow back together with a few strips of very precious duct tape, planting the jangly golem back into the ground. Dee still wasn't satisfied. It wasn't the same; she continued to scowl at Joshua for the next several days.

The following morning, Gellert announced he would be away from his island paradise for the next day or two. Delilah the Elder would be in charge in his absence. Piloting his submersible from New Detroit, stocked with a few animal pelts, along with some satchels of dried tobacco, he hoped to barter the goods with a neighboring island clan for some more rolls of duct tape to replenish their dwindling supply.

With Gellert away, Albus went about his business as usual, working the fields in solitude. Soaked in sweat, his digging done for the day, he marched from the trenches late that afternoon all alone, when at a distance he witnessed the silhouette of Delilah the Elder covertly slip down an overgrown jungle trail, a blob of something in her arms. Albus' mission shrieked through his brain like screeching bats fleeing a dank cavern concealed behind a waterfall.

He still wasn't convinced she was the destroyer; she had been nothing but kind to him since his arrival. Regardless, he might not get another chance alone with her, a chance to save his world. It felt wrong. He knew it was wrong but did it anyway.

Hesitating for a moment, Albus changed headings. He silently stalked after the presumed destroyer, down the hidden jungle trail, Joshua pleading with himself all the while to turn back. The dirt path opened into a secluded clearing bordered by stands of dense palms and scrubby ferns. Arranged around the small plot, rows of twelve or so stone slabs protruded from the dirt, none more than about a foot or two in height. Delilah stood motionless, whispering to herself, facing two of the planted stones.

Other than the sound of Delilah's soft whispers and the infrequent, distant caw of a jungle parrot, it was gravely silent. Though he so desperately didn't want to, he had to strike; convincing himself that he had no other choice in the matter.

Albus crouched and mutely hefted a dense rock half the size of a speeder battery from beside the path. He felt compelled by forces outside his control as he crept into position behind the Low Place creature, hoisting the bludgeoning instrument overhead. Now only mere feet from his target, he noticed that the upright stones were engraved with words. One read "Here lies our beloved Delilah Earhart Fedora" the other "Here lies our beloved Delilah Emily Fedora."

Albus didn't understand. Joshua did.

"I'm sorry," whispered Joshua.

....

A flash of jingling lightning bolted between Joshua's legs and pranced about Delilah, alarming her. Instantly, Joshua dropped the heavy rock onto his foot, crushing his toes; he suppressed the urge to yelp in pain. Spinning around in surprise, "Joshua!" shouted Delilah, tears in her eyes. "You're not supposed to be here!"

Fin the fennec fox perched himself on top of one of the headstones, the silver bell around his neck rattling as he licked his ivory paw, his onyx eyes piercing into Albus' being. Joshua stammered and apologized profusely, feeling intense waves of shame and guilt crash into him over what he had almost done, had Fin not saved the day. Looking down at his smashed toes, Delilah asked, "What's with the rock?"

"Uhhh…" Joshua stalled. "Your dad said he needed it?" Delilah, unaware of how close she had come to death, raised an eyebrow but didn't question the outsider further; she turned back to the headstones. Crouching, she rested a bouquet of hibiscus flowers on the ground as she grazed the tips of her fingers across the inscribed names.

Delilah stood and turned back towards Joshua, wiping a few tears from her cheeks. Composing herself as she motioned towards the two grave markers, she divulged to Joshua that on the day they went under on her papa's submersible—the day the Cancer erupted, her mother and youngest sister were supposed to come along for the journey as well.

As her family of five were boarding the yellow submarine, her youngest sister, Delilah Emily Fedora, fell into a fit. The toddler threw a temper tantrum, choking out between sobs that something bad was going to happen to Fin in their absence. Dee and herself tried to reassure their little sister, but it was of no use. She cried to the point of becoming inconsolable.

Delilah's mother decided it best to stay on the island with her youngest daughter; the three of them go on without her, she urged. Gellert protested some, but she insisted. She would hang back with the toddler; they would 'look after Fin' together. Dee Dee was probably a little too young for a submarine adventure anyway.

Standing on the floating dock, her mother hoisted Dee Dee in her arms as they waved goodbye to the vessel slowly vanishing beneath the waves. When they surfaced in the submarine sometime later, her mom and baby sister were *just gone*. The tears had returned to Delilah's eyes.

....

Joshua walked with Delilah back down the jungle trail in silence. Bearing the burden of Albus' sin, he hoisted the heavy rock under the crook of his left arm, carrying the deadweight under the fiction that it was requested by Delilah's father.

As they walked, Joshua reflected; he was no stranger to loss, though death was a villain that had been vanquished in his past life. Delilah's mother and youngest sister were the source of the conspicuous absence he had felt at that first supper. The cantankerous Delilah the Younger was now Delilah the Middle in light of this new information (*another checkmark in the destroyer column*, thought Albus). Perhaps somewhat callously, he wondered if Delilah held any ill will towards her youngest sibling; if she blamed her in any way for her mother's death.

As though reading his mind, Delilah interrupted the silence. "You know I'm not mad at her or anything. I'm happy in a weird way…that they didn't have to face that terror alone. That they had each other at the end."

For reasons not quite clear to Albus, Joshua reached over and grabbed hold of Delilah's hand. She didn't pull it away; she squeezed tighter in return. They parted ways; dusk had settled over the island. The strings of guiding lights would flicker on soon along with the droves of blood-sucking mosquitos emerging from their hiding places.

Joshua carted his burden over to a rock pile, releasing it.

Gellert kept stashes of what he called 'good rocks' in scattered piles around the settlement. They could always use more good rocks to reinforce the cistern with or as a substitute for cinder blocks when repairing ruined buildings. In the fading light, as he made his way towards the mess for supper, Joshua noticed a crumbled section of bleached white wall he hadn't seen before.

A shadow was singed into the wall's surface like a lithograph; desiccated flowers laid at its base. The burned-in silhouette depicted the outline of a woman crouching beside a small child, the woman clearly trying to shield the child with her body.

23

GET YOUR ASS TO MARS

Over the following weeks, Joshua continued to prove his worth around the settlement, working without complaint, expanding irrigation canals, laying networks of pipes; a few weeks prior, he had even brought an entirely new plot of jungle potatoes online, all on his own. Joshua crouched in the freshly tilled loam, poking holes in the lumpy earth with his well-made fingers, plugging said holes with sprouted potato clippings. Albus wasn't giving much thought to Elixabeth, Golgotha, or his dastardly mission these days; neither Delilah seemed to pose much of a threat to his world. Should they ever reveal their hand, he supposed he could deal with them then.

As he tenderly covered the juvenile clippings in rich, chunky mounds of dank soil with his dirt-stained hands, a large, ominous shadow grew over him, blotting out the sun. Albus strained his neck to look over his shoulder, relieved to see it was only Delilah's father standing over him.

"Come on," said Gellert. Joshua rose from the dirt and followed after him without question, consciously having to slow his gait some to keep pace alongside the lumbering older man; his already obvious limp had worsened noticeably in recent weeks.

His confidence in Joshua growing as the outsider continued

to prove himself, Gellert felt it was about time to bring him further into the fold. He intended to increase Joshua's duties, expand the young man's understanding of what it took to keep their homestead running. Maybe impart some wisdom along the way, he could only hope.

Gellert led Joshua to a cluster of solar panels installed along a ridge above the lagoon. This particular clutch of collectors had been on the fritz of late, he explained. Fishing a wrench from the breast pocket of his denim overalls, he directed Joshua in unbolting the wires from their panel's corroded contacts. Using a rag doused in an acrid scented solution that both repulsed Joshua, yet begged him to perniciously inhale more deeply of its onerous odor, Gellert diligently scrubbed the contacts, freeing flecks of mineralized dandruff from the nuts. With learned dexterity he stripped new lengths of copper wire, twisting the ends into place.

Signaling for Joshua to lean in closer, he made a point that one must be absolutely certain to rewire the anode and cathode to their proper terminals. "Red is the anode it goes to negative, Black is the cathode, it goes to positive," instructed Gellert.

The convention of the wire's color-coding confused Joshua. *How will I ever remember that?* It seemed to him, it should be the other way around. Typically black things were negative: black holes, black cats, the growing Cancer, and whatnot.

Joshua brought this point up to the dark-skinned man. "What are you trying to say?" Gellert lightly teased in reply, roasting the pallidly light-skinned, perpetually sunburnt outsider for his miscalculated gaffe. Joshua's sunburnt cheeks bloomed with even more rosy hues and said no more on the subject.

The panels repaired, Gellert spent the rest of the sunny, brightly-lit day tutoring his redheaded pupil, passing on his accumulated knowledge about a great many things critical to their survival. Things such as how the composting toilets functioned.

"Now if the poo jams up in the collection pot, you gotta get up in there with a broom handle or big stick and knock it loose so it can flow to the burn chamber." Joshua retched as he observed Gellert demonstrate, poking and knocking loose large hunks of feces; he prayed that such a thing would never happen on his watch. "Now you try." Gellert handed him the broom handle.

The business with the composting toilets thankfully over, they came to the base of one of the tall, lanky windmills that had been underperforming its peers. Gellert shimmied up its rickety steel rungs, a crowbar in one hand, explaining how he often had to remove sea bird's nests from the appealing perches. The growing mess of twigs, sticks, and bird shit would jam the mill's gears, preventing the blades from turning.

Grasping the crowbar, he crowed back down to Joshua watching from the ground. "Before you bash the nests to pieces," he hollered, "make sure you gather any eggs! Makes for good eats!" Gellert plucked three or four brown speckled osprey eggs into the deep pockets of his denims, then proceeded to whack at the twiggy home till it was no more.

. . . .

As the sun began to set, the two made their way towards the mess, stopping at the cistern to wash away the muck and grime coating them from a hard day's work. That evening, over a sparse stew of boiled roots (and not much else), the four took their places around the rickety card table. Customarily, they bowed their heads, waiting on the older man to guide them in giving thanks.

Gellert appeared to falter some as he searched for the right words to say. "Lord...Thank you for the boiled roots..." he mumbled and trailed off. Perhaps he was just exhausted from the long, hot day. The lack of loquaciousness was not reserved solely for Gellert; Delilah and Dee were unusually withdrawn as well. Fin curled into a ball at Delilah's feet, asleep. Joshua, who was usually the strong silent type, took it upon his shoulders to carry the conversation. "So..." he asked, "how was everyone's day?"

He was met mostly with shrugs and blunted answers. As he picked at the watery gloop in his bowl, Gellert began to drone on about the status of the irrigation project, reviewing their workload for the following morning between unenthusiastic slurps of stew, when Joshua interrupted. "Do you have a plan?"

"For?" Gellert asked, somewhat confused.

"For this! For any of this. The Cancer—everything!" said Joshua exasperated.

"I thought you'd never ask," he replied, cracking a smile for the first time that night. "I'll show you."

....

After supper, he led Joshua along the paths of dangling, incandescent lights that swayed gingerly in the ocean breeze projecting animated shadows across the ground, towards a large building, the cinder block garage where the two had first met. He threw up the clanking aluminum door to one of the bays, flicking on a fluorescent light overhead; horny moths and amber-winged beetles materializing out of the darkness immediately swarmed about the unnatural light, slaves to their programming, futilely bumping and colliding against the cracked plastic covering.

The air inside the garage was hot and stunk of metal. Gellert weaved his way between engine parts, passing by the broken-down speeder making his way to the back, towards something big draped with a dusty, oil-stained canvas sheet. He halted and turned towards Joshua. With the flourish of a magician revealing his grand illusion, Gellert pulled the covering aside. Underneath the sheet was a tall, stainless-steel tube. Welded to its sides were thin metallic fins; a conical red nose was bolted on top.

Joshua narrowed his eyes, uncertain if Gellert was having a go at him.

"What...is it?"

"Come on!" Gellert beamed with pride. "It's a rocket ship!"

Just as he feared, that was it, that was Gellert's grand plan, to build a rocket...

Gellert limped over to a scientific-looking instrument resting on one of the workbenches. Twisting a few knobs, "Look at this," he said, tapping a radial display that fluctuated with monochromatic lines. "EMF signals from Mars." Gellert was convinced that there were still functional colonies on Mars. Though he had no way to communicate with them, he had faith they were there.

He explained to Joshua that if *that beast* ever found them, he would load his daughters (and Joshua too if they could make room) into his DIY spaceship. They would blast-off, straight up, avoiding the probing tentacles of the Cancer entirely. Straight on to Mars where they could join up with the colonies. Gellert had concluded that the Cancer was unbeatable, the only way out, was up. He eagerly awaited Joshua's feedback.

"Oh...awesome," said Joshua, with the enthusiasm of opening a sweater from grandma on Christmas morning. His heart sank. He didn't doubt Gellert's ambition or technical know-how, it was just that part of him knew they wouldn't find the situation on the red planet that much better off.

Albus pressed his hand to his jaw, put-off to find an uneven patch of thick stubble sprouting from his chin. Joshua wanted to tell Gellert everything but found himself incapable of speaking the words. It would jeopardize his entire purpose, the safety of Albus' world. They would probably bury him in sand up to his neck and allow the tide to drown him, should they ever discover his true nature.

As the two departed, Joshua startled some as he felt a strong hand clamp his right shoulder. "You know I had my doubts about you," said Gellert, "but you're a good guy, a real asset around here." Joshua mustered a smile; he thanked the man for his kind words as they parted ways. That night cocooned in his hammock, Albus didn't dream, only darkness in every direction.

24

SUMMERTIME AND THE LIVIN'S EASY

The near-perpetual effort required of the survivors to sustain themselves on the razor-thin edge of existence, could feel overwhelming, endless at times. However, life around the settlement was certainly not all work and no play. On Sundays they rested, taking some much-needed respite from their demanding physical duties.

Most Sundays they would gather round the inviting lagoon at the center of their island, lounging in the warm sand, sharing gathered fruits and munching on handfuls of crispy crickets that Gellert had roasted. The girls, temporarily regressed in age by the lagoon's bubbly aura, would play in the shallows, splashing back and forth at one another, or idly float on its gossamer surface. Dee would often toss a red rubber ball for Fin; the fox was brave and would galavant into the chilly waters after the object of his desires, regardless how far out of reach it had floated.

Gellert would don a floppy straw hat that drove his daughters nuts, reclining in the sand, discretely sipping from a lacerated coconut laced with his coveted moonshine that he brewed in secret. He kept the copper still and his stash of hooch hidden in an undisclosed location just beyond the border of the mountainous jungle, keeping it out of sight lest his daughters should get overly curious. *Super-secret side project*, he thought to himself as he imbibed the delicious nectar. Between booze-infused sips he would practice his banjo, regaling the others with his plucky tunes.

Joshua, never having learnt how to properly swim, did his best to doggy paddle around the rejuvenating lagoon, once eking his way a little too close to the wide, roaring waterfall. Delilah the Elder, spotting Joshua's folly, hollered at the top of her lungs for him to turn back; a strong current generated by the colliding falls would suck Joshua under, she warned sternly. Paddling away from the treacherous falls he drifted out to the pool's center; sucking in a massive breath, he attempted to sink down to the lagoon's bottom. He rocketed back up like a bubble gasping for air: it was far too deep.

When he wasn't distracted with swimming, always in need of a task to occupy Albus' tick-tocking mind, Joshua would idle by the side of the round topical pool, his butt planted into the damp, sun-warmed sand, weaving strands of coarse twine into a torn hammock, repairing its fibrous netting.

One lazy Sunday afternoon, taking his repaired hammock in hand, he knotted scraps of looted lug-nuts and metal washers around its edges. Staking out a promising spot in the shallows, he hurled the hammock into the glimmering lagoon. Striking quickly like a cuttlefish, he yanked the improvised fishing net back in by its rope. To Albus' astonishment, and the delight of those around him, the net wasn't empty; it was brimming and squirming with an entire school of flopping silver-scaled fish.

....

The next morning over a breakfast of smoked fish, Gellert had a goofy grin on his face; he teased his oldest daughter. "Someone's got a birthday coming up," he said in a sing-songy voice.

"Hush, Papa," scolded Delilah the Elder. "You know I don't like to make a big deal of it." Gellert continued to press, embarrassing his daughter in front of Joshua, asking her what she would like to do to celebrate. To quiet her papa's pestering, finally, she relented. "Well, I thought maybe we could watch a movie?" offered Delilah abashedly. Her father's eyes lit up; they hadn't done a family movie night in ages. In fact, he thought his kids might have outgrown the tradition, too cool and mature to watch a flick with their pop. Twirling her hair through her fingers, Delilah hated to burst her papa's bubble, she clarified, "Oh, I meant…just me and Joshua?" hesitating, "I mean if he wants to."

"Ooooo," crooned Dee. Her older sister pierced Delilah the Middle with an icy stare.

Joshua replied, "Yeah, sounds cool," his voice coming out a tone or semitone deeper than he would have liked.

....

On the evening of Delilah's birthday celebration, to conserve battery power for the movie, they abstained from using the electric stove. Instead of cooking, the four people (and one fennec fox) indulged in an antipasti dinner. Shaved charcuterie of Gellert's smoked meats and Joshua's fish, foraged nuts, sliced fruits plucked from the stands of banana and orange trees that the girls tended, and a savory dip made from some mashed root vegetables mixed with sea salt, and kelp, were all placed in deformed Tupperware bowls; they laid the misshapen bowls across a faded plaid blanket spread out along the cement porch of the living quarters. Everything was set for a birthday picnic.

Genteelly, they picked around the hors d'oeuvres, no one wanting to appear greedier than the others, to give the impression that they felt somehow entitled to more than their fair share by taking the last scrap of smoked iguana belly, or lonely slice of blood orange. As the evening sky dripped vibrantly in pink and blue ink, they looked out towards the horizon, snacking away in silent contentment.

Delilah tossed scraps of fish heads to Fin, the peckish fox devouring them without complaint. Gellert found himself pondering how many more sunsets he had left in him; he wouldn't be around to protect his girls forever. All he could hope, was that he had prepared them to be strong enough on their own.

Delilah the Middle, despite her acerbic attitude, was quite

the gifted gift giver; she passed to her sister something sandwiched between strips of woven green banana leaves. Delilah gently unwrapped the satchel to find a colorful bracelet braided from a mess of multi-colored threads, a tiny sun-bleached sand dollar tied to its middle with thin wire. It was a friendship bracelet Dee said. But don't for a minute think that that made them friends, she warned.

Delilah guffawed at her sister's sardonic commentary; adoring the bracelet, she slipped it over her wrist to model it for her birthday guests. Everyone cooed and nodded in approval, commenting on the craftsmanship or delightfully bright colors. Delilah thanked her sister for such a thoughtful gift, enveloping her in a hug, laughing and squeezing harder as Dee tried to squirm away.

Gellert, not as talented at giving gifts as his middle child, forked over two unwrapped, fist-sized boxes of hollow-point bullets, ammunition for Delilah's Glock, procured from his own personal stash. "Have fun," he said with a wink. Secretly, Delilah appreciated the ammo even more than the bracelet, but she would never tell her sister that, not wanting to hurt Dee's feelings. Delilah placed the two boxes to her side as the metallic projectiles within mutley rattled together.

Joshua had been dreading this moment. While hunting the recesses of his heart, he had come across the tracks of an elusive animal he once thought extinct; he had uncovered the scat of another familiar but forgotten sensation, unable to deny that some glimmer of affection was stirring within him for the effortlessly effervescent, curly-headed Delilah.

He found himself helplessly stealing glances of her over supper or wanting to impress her by carrying heavy armfuls of tools and equipment past her on his way to the crescent's trenches. A loud and vocal part of his mind railed against him, commanding him to retreat from the feelings, warning him to keep his distance should Delilah reveal herself to be in fact, the prophesied destroyer.

Furthermore, if he was being honest, he wasn't sure he was

ready; though he had stopped obsessing over it, the grievous wound inflicted by his ex-wife's infidelities still tore open its stitches and bled on occasion. He didn't think he could handle more rejection or another betrayal. Regardless, custom dictated that he must present the woman with some token, some trinket that said he cared about her (but not that he cared too much).

While strolling along the beach a few days prior meandering in and out of the surf, contemplating what he could possibly offer Delilah, purely by chance he happened across what he thought was the perfect gift. A magnificent conch shell feathered in chestnut brown hues with voluptuous pink interior, washed up on shore at his feet, bubbling in a shawl of milky sea foam.

As he plucked the curvaceous windfall from the surf, a faded scene with yellowed edges flipped through his mind; it was a scene from a book Albus had read long, long ago. Taking the conch, Joshua lopped the pointy end off with a machete. When blown through, it could now produce a resounding trumpet blast.

Joshua held his breath as he handed Delilah the gift concealed within a saucepot he had borrowed from the mess, (there wasn't exactly a Party City around to patronize for gift wrap, so he had to improvise). Delilah removed the lid, lifting the eye-catching shell out of the pot, holding it up for the others to see. A broad smile, revealing the diminutive gap between her two front teeth, spread across her face. "I love it!" she exclaimed as she fondled the conch in her hands.

"Check this out," said Joshua as he motioned for the shell, intending to demonstrate its musical capabilities, when Delilah beat him to the punch. Raising the conch to her puckered lips, she dramatically puffed her cheeks. Blowing heartily into its apex, she tooted loudly. Everyone chuckled and laughed at the boisterous report. Delilah passed the appealing chestnut-streaked conch around to the others, each taking it, in turn, to make rowdy toots of their own, uplifting a cathartic clamor, a cacophonous reminder that they were still alive.

The gifts given, the last scraps of finger foods consumed, they began setting up for movie night in the wall-to-wall carpeted rec room of the living quarters. Delilah tugged a derelict cardboard box, barely holding itself together, across the thick carpet, like a pirate uncovering a buried treasure chest. Filled to the brim of the box, angular corners of disorganized plastic bricks poked their way out, hoping to be picked.

Humbly, she revealed her stash to Joshua. The black bricks were called Vee-Ech-Ess tapes she informed him, ancient artifacts from long ago akin to vellum scrolls or clay tablets—only they had movies on them! She had unearthed the collection in the basement of a decimated building along with the tapes decoder, a device called a Vee-See-Are. To her amazement, it still functioned in lieu of its geriatric condition.

Her father dug out another fossil from a closet that must have contained a portal to the Jurassic era; he wheeled out a cathode ray tube television slapped with a vinyl sticker of poorly emulated wood grain peeling off around its sides. If the faux-wood covering was the dinosaur's attempted camouflage, it would have been the first to be eaten. Pushing the prehistoric television through the thick morass of faded mauve carpet, brushing the dust off, Gellert fussed with a number of colored cords connecting the brittle decoding device to the petrified TV set.

Joshua and Delilah poured over her treasure trove of antique tapes, debating their selection. Like their fragile husks, the movies contained within were relics as well; movies she had only ever heard her grandparents or other really old people mention. Contained in her jumbled collection were films with titles such as: *Star Wars: A New Hope*, *Terminator 2: Judgement Day*, *Toys*, *The Lord of the Rings: The Return of the King*, *Mrs. Doubtfire*, *Pocahontas*, *Dances with Wolves*, *The Chronicles of Narnia*, *Office Space*, *Monty Python and the Holy Grail*, *The Matrix*, *The Wizard of Oz*, and *Harry Potter and the Sorcerer's Stone*, just to name a few.

Delilah would pluck one of the plastic bricks from the box holding it up for Joshua to inspect. She would give him a quick synopsis of the plot; she had seen most but not all. Listening intently, Joshua would frown and shake his head. Delilah would move onto the next one. She asked him if he had ever seen *Raiders of the Lost Ark*. He couldn't recall; he didn't think so. Squirming up and down, she bubbled that he had to see it. It was one of her favorites (and Indy was so hot; she omitted that part to Joshua).

Dee, more than pleased to have some time alone, hid out in the subterranean bedroom that she shared with her older sister. She bounced Fin up and down on her lap as she gossiped with a clique of Barbie dolls that had survived the conflagration. Well mostly survived, the dolls' long blonde hair had been scorched to the scalp; the preposterous proportions of their plastic bodies had bulged and bubbled from exposure to the intense heat.

The television all set up, his usefulness waning, Gellert reluctantly excused himself from the rec room and left the kids to their movie night. In a sense, this was his little girl's first "date," but he knew better than to call attention to the notion. At twenty-six, she had finally met a boy, something he had hoped might never happen at the end of the world.

To distract himself, he aimed to get in an hour or two of banjo practice. Setting up a folding chair on the slab porch outside, he burned a foggy fire of hairy coconut husks in a hollow metal drum, the hazy, aromatic smoke intended to keep the mosquitos at bay.

Never having had a lick of formal lessons, Gellert plucked and plunked away at the taut, rusting strings of his instrument with the dexterity of an ox in a china shop, the sincere yet poorly timed notes bouncing their way through the open rec room windows; that was until Delilah leaned her head out. "Please, Papa, No banjo tonight," she kindly beseeched.

His ego wounded at first by his daughter's request, he reminded himself that it was her birthday, after all, and returned the noisemaker back to its beat-up case. Striking a match, he lit the wick of an oil lantern; the same burning match still in hand he held the rapidly dwindling fire spirit, guarding it with a cupped hand, over the mouth of his pipe, cherrying the tamped tobacco with a few large huffs.

Situating his reading glasses across the bridge of his nose, he cracked open the spine to his worn, yellowing copy of *Twenty Thousand Leagues Under the Sea*. His stinky pipe hanging loosely beneath his thick mustache, the noxious tobacco fumes mixing indiscriminately with the white fog billowing from the burning husks, he puffed away, guarding the porch as he followed along with the well-tread adventures of Captain Nemo.

....

Back in the rec room, Delilah held the cassette like the curator of a museum placing a mummy back into its sarcophagus; she delicately pushed the tape into the open tomb and pressed play, half expecting it to disintegrate. The smoky, curved tube of the neolithic television set warmed up; strafing beams of electrons whizzed at a glass screen in such rapidity as to stitch together still images into some semblance of life and narrative. Backing towards the faded seafoam couch, while simultaneously keeping one eye on the antique decoder for any sign of foul play, Delilah plopped down onto a cushion next to Joshua, their butts about two and a half feet apart.

As the movie played, Joshua did his best to get lost in the story, not wanting to disappoint Delilah. Though he found the woman sitting two and a half feet away from him far more compelling than anything transpiring on the flickering screen.

Whenever he would shift his body, contemplating reaching an arm around her, or taking hold of her hand again, as if reading his mind, the woman would preemptively counter, crossing or uncrossing her legs, or leaning away against the charred armrests of the raggedy sofa. An intense cloud of static hung in the air between the two moviegoers.

Joshua did tune in to the screen as he watched Indiana Jones tip-toe his way across a booby-trapped dungeon floor, cautiously inching his way towards the golden idol of his desires. Albus thought that perhaps the idol belonged not in a museum, but right where it was, where Jones had found it; his instincts proved correct as a massive rolling boulder thundered after the meddling archeologist, chasing him through the temple corridors.

Right at the climax, just as the Nazi henchmen were about to open the Ark of the Covenant, everything went abruptly dark: pitch-black. They couldn't see their hands in front of their face. Albus had a flashback to his time trapped inside the tomb tome beneath Uruk. "Hey!" moaned Delilah, one part annoyed, one part disappointed.

Running out of juice, the bank of batteries had petered out. No juice meant no movie, they wouldn't be able to watch the end. Joshua was pretty sure that the good guys had to win, but he couldn't fathom how. *The heroes are tied to a stake for Pete's sake!*

A couple of moments later, just as suddenly as it went dark, the light returned. The incandescent bulbs flickered back on along with the television; the movie continued to play. They glanced at one another, caught off guard by the unexpected return of the power. Joshua had tenuously slung his arm around Delilah's shoulders in the darkness. Neither one questioned the apparent miracle; he pulled her in a little closer as they watched the film's climax.

"Hands off!" huffed a gruff voice emanating from the darkness outside an open window. Without questioning the command, Joshua abashedly yanked his arm away, returning the offending appendage awkwardly pressed to the side of his body.

Unbeknownst to Joshua and Delilah at the time, when the battery juice ran dry, Gellert had retrieved the manually powered back-up generator, plugging it into the rec room's breaker located on the side of the building just beneath the open window. He selflessly cranked away at the handle of the generator, parlaying his indomitable physical will into just enough power to make it to the end.

....

Igniting a few oil lamps after the movie ended, Joshua and Delilah chatted with one another on the couch in the diffuse, twinkling light, casting misshapen shadows against the walls.

Gellert interrupted the two; his skin slicked in sweat, he

wheezed some as he paced through the rec room to say good-night, acting as though the pit-stop was on his way to his dormitory (it wasn't). He planted a fatherly kiss on Delilah's forehead, the familiarity of his walrus whiskers brushing against her skin. "Happy birthday, sweetie." Turning to Joshua, he lasered the outsider with the death-ray stare of death, practically melting the man's face. "Don't do anything I wouldn't do," he said with a wink. The timeless line of parents everywhere. Appreciative of her papa but eager for him to leave, Delilah shooed him out. "I'm going...I'm going."

Gellert gone, the two returned to chatting. Delilah wanted to know what Joshua's favorite part was. He told her it was when all the Nazi's faces melted off! Delilah enthusiastically agreed, that was her favorite part too!

They sat together conversing late into the night, beneath the shallow surface of their chit-chat and small-talk something grated at Joshua, something that had been bothering him ever since Delilah's father had revealed his big plan, his Mars-bound rocketship.

Having her alone, he tried to bring it up. "Listen," Joshua started, "about your dad's rocket..." Trailing off his eyes darted left and right as he searched for the right words; Albus found himself unable to tell her the truth, the whole truth as to why they wouldn't fare much better on Mars.

Resting a hand on his knee, "I know," interjected Delilah. She confessed to Joshua that she didn't have much faith in her papa's rocket saving them either; though if it ever came right down to it, it was better than nothing. Besides, the project, however doomed, gave her father something to work on, something to do; it gave him hope for a better tomorrow and hope was all you had in a place this low.

Hesitating for a moment, she debated playing another one of her cards. Coyly Delilah lilted, "Besides...I've got my own super-secret side project." This piqued his interest greatly. Delilah would say no more; she pantomimed sealing her lips with a zipper as the man sitting next to her practically begged, pleading with her to reveal her secret.

Delilah, reasonably certain she trusted Joshua at this point, had no qualms about telling him right then and there. However, she relished owning some tidbit of secret knowledge to lord over him. Resisting Joshua's urges, she stood from the couch, gave him a friendly peck on the cheek and said, "Get some sleep."

A rather mild-mannered storm blew in off the coast shortly after they parted ways. Albus reversed his trek from the tiki hut making it back to living quarters moments before the first acorn-sized drops fell; there would be no hammock tonight.

Carefully he clunked down the shaky metal stairs that led to the subterranean dormitories, quietly slipping into Gellert's quarters. The older man snored loudly. Sighing some, Albus pulled himself up into an empty bunk. He closed his eyes and did his best to not think about Delilah as he drifted to sleep.

Delilah cracked open the door to the room she shared with her sister, a sliver of light creeping out. Fin dashed out of the crack in a tizzy, a multitude of pink bows tied mercilessly around his big ears. Dee, still wide awake, froze in alarm as her older sister caught her in the middle of vigorously pressing two mutated, naked Barbies together—forcing them to kiss.

"I'm not even gonna ask."

25

SCRAPPY

On a morning that was unusually cool and foggy for a tropical island, Delilah the Elder walked through the mess with a leather rucksack slung over her back; she scooped two heaping spoonfuls of steaming oatmeal into her tin cup from the large aluminum pot her sister was busy strenuously stirring.

They lacked the luxury of butter made from the milk of grass-fed Irish cows to slather on top of the warm oats, but they did have something that passed for butter, from a grain-fed island boar.

A few weeks back Gellert and Joshua had managed to trap a wild boar sow, successfully wrangling the ornery beast into a pen around the side of the mess. For the first time since the destruction of the Cancer's violent birth, the survivors had access to fresh milk, if one were brave enough to try and squeeze the angry mama pig's teats.

Setting down onto the table his aged copy of *Twenty Thousand Leagues Under the Sea*, his unlit pipe hanging from his mouth, Gellert looked up at his oldest daughter. "Where do you think you're going?" he asked, already aware of the answer.

Delilah grabbed a couple chunks of hard-tack, shoveling them into her rucksack, looping a canteen around her waist, making preparations for a salvage run. Hardly paying her papa any mind, she assured him she'd only be gone for a day or two (or possibly three).

"Uh-Uh. No way," Gellert harangued. "Last time you went out scrapping...you brought a man back," her father teased as he glanced over at the outsider sitting across from him. Flecks of hot creamed oats lathered in wild boar butter landed on the table as Albus coughed, trying to stifle a laugh, mid mouthful.

Delilah—not in the mood today for her papa's commentary—chose not to engage. Kissing her pop on the cheek, she thanked Dee for the oatmeal as she headed for the door. "Take Joshua with you," her father called after her, looking back to his book.

Delilah's body stiffened, halting her in her tracks; she wanted to turn and object to her father's demand, but knew full well an argument would only delay her departure further. Once her papa had made up his mind on a matter, he could become monumentally stubborn.

Gellert never shared that every time his baby girl would venture out into the wastes, his stomach would become a tangled mess of knots. He always kept a stoic exterior, never letting on how much he worried.

His child's forays into the ruins of the world netted crucial rations, supplies, and materials key to their survival; as much as he didn't like it, he knew he had to let her go. He had offered to go with her on many occasions in the past; Delilah would always turn him down, citing how busy he already was with his litany of projects and responsibilities around the homestead. Though he suspected the real reason behind his daughter's rebuffs to be his bum leg; she didn't want her old man slowing her down.

At least with Joshua tagging along, she wouldn't be alone.

"Oh I almost forgot," said her father as he pulled a folded scrap of paper from his breast pocket. "Take this." He handed Delilah a piece of blue-lined notebook paper inked in barely legible scribbles, a lengthy grocery list of scrap he needed for some of his projects, including parts for his rocket.

....

Albus forked the dregs of runny oats into his mouth and ran out the door, catching up with Delilah. In her hand she held out her father's scrap of paper; they both read the list over as they walked across the squat plateau towards the beach. A thirty-two-gallon tank of acetylene, 555 timer, triple-axis accelerometer, and ammonium nitrate, were just a few of the items listed that Gellert hoped they would come across.

Crumpling the list into her pants pocket, Delilah retrieved a black, L-shaped object from her rucksack and pushed it into Joshua's hand. Somewhat alarmed, Albus turned the firearm over in his fist. "What do I need this for?"

"We're scrapping tommys," answered Delilah in a whisper, hushing him.

"Tommys?"

Automata, explained Delilah; semi-intelligent, artificial humanoids that had been engineered long ago by men far too smart for their own good. Servants crafted in their own image in a never-ending quest to make their already comfortable lives infinitely more comfortable.

As the pebbles crunched beneath their feet on their march towards her speeder, Delilah divulged to Joshua that prior to the Cancer's eruption the biggest story dominating the news cycle had been reports of the civil war that had broken out amongst the planet's automata. Without much explanation for the schism, the humanoid creatures of artifice had divided into two camps: one faction that desired to continue living in symbiosis and harmony with the rest of the planet's populace—and another faction that demanded total autonomy.

Most nations chose to stay out of the conflict, holding out to see which side was winning before they declared their support; while others sold weapons to both sects, turning a profit. After the Cancer's eruption, the surviving cells of automata, not obliterated by the outburst, formed settlements and outposts of their own.

On a previous run some months back, Delilah had seen a small cay. She had noticed a run-down domicile built not far from the shore as she sped past; her gut told her it might be a tommy outpost. Certain she spied movement, she had marked the location of the islet to investigate at a later time. "That's where we're heading."

Climbing into the cockpit of the hovering speeder, Delilah looked over at Joshua and asked, "You know how to use that thing?" She glanced down at the handgun he had wedged into his waistband.

"Yeah," Albus replied. He had only fired a gun once in his life, but he got the gist of it. "Point and click." Delilah shook her head. He wasn't wrong. Punching a set of coordinates into the glass reticle of the center console, she flicked a few brightly-lit toggles, rotated the wheel and throttled a lever forward, with that they were off.

For close to a day's time they sped across the vast ocean, cruising over the curvature of a glassy, blue eyeball. The turbines' loud roars made any real conversation impossible aside from garbled shouts and mostly misunderstood replies hollered in return.

Delilah, growing weary from piloting the craft for such a length of time, yelled over to Joshua, indicating for him to take the wheel. Looking at her as though she had lost her mind, he shouted back as loud he could, "I have no idea how to pilot this thing!"

"Good a time as any to learn!" She relinquished her grasp of the wheel, holding both hands in the air as if in a stickup, daring Joshua to call her bluff. The hovering speeder began to lose altitude, the nose of the craft dangerously dipping towards an oncoming wave. Delilah didn't flinch.

Wide-eyed, Albus grabbed hold of the controls, leaning his whole body over to reach, instinctively pulling up on the wheel narrowly avoiding the oncoming crash of water as it crested off the craft's belly. Joshua's white knuckles now firmly grasping the controls, Delilah wiggled out of her pilot's seat while the vehicle continued to clip along at an outlandish speed.

Albus had no choice but to take her place, awkwardly contorting his body into the captain's chair while gripping at the wheel. Delilah flopped into the passenger seat, a devilish grin sneaking across her face.

After a few more hours of trial and error, throttling various levers up, toggling certain switches, Albus found the speeder not all that difficult to manage; Delilah would slap his hand away if he reached for any button or gizmo that could cause them serious damage. However, his training would have to be cut short; the marked cay came into view not far in the distance. Pulling up on a thin sliver of shoreline, she signaled for him to cut the engines and bring the vehicle to rest.

....

Preparing to disembark, Delilah informed Joshua that they only ever scrapped the evil faction of tommys; the good ones didn't do anyone no harm and could even be bartered with in some instances. However, and this was a big caveat, there was only one way to know for sure which faction of automata you were dealing with, since they all looked identical otherwise.

When you got up close enough to one, she explained, it's lifeless, half-orb eyes would light up, revealing the automaton's loyalty. Now this was important, she locked her gaze with Joshua's to make sure he was listening. Glowering red eyes meant they were friendly. Pleasantly blue bulbs meant you needed to start blasting.

Joshua, bewildered by the color choice, questioned, "Shouldn't it be the other way around—"

"Nope," snapped Delilah, cutting him off. "That's just the way it is here." Joshua shrugged. "Look it's easy," she said. "Remember it like this: Eyes of red, it's your best friend Fred. Eyes of blue, *pew pew pew.*" Joshua didn't catch her drift.

Extending her thumb and index finger, "*Pew pew pew,*" she said again, this time pretending her hand was a gun. He got it that time and nodded. Joshua chanted the mnemonic to himself like a mantra, committing it to memory. As they walked away from the immobile speeder Delilah halted, adding almost as an afterthought, "Oh and if their eyes turn green…it's a total crapshoot."

Some fifty yards up the beach from their position stood a sorry looking shanty. Its roof sagged noticeably towards the middle; the empty windows had been done up with shreds of sackcloth serving as curtains. To the left of the hovel grew a small but dense plot of sunflowers; many of the stalks had been crushed or broken at the base, the oversized flowers trampled underfoot. An underfed rabbit poked its head out from the stand of yellow flowers, spotted the interlopers, and retreated to the safety of its burrow.

As they made their approach, the two tommy hunters rehashed their game plan; Joshua would approach from the front of the hovel and draw the automata out, while Delilah snuck into position around the side. Once Joshua had ascertained the color of their eyes, he would radio her on his walkie, "friend" or "foe," and she would take corresponding action.

Doing his best to sneak along undetected over the totally flat, open terrain by crouching some as he walked, Joshua made the advance cautiously; from inside the shanty he spotted movement through the glass-less windows.

A skeletal hominid manufactured from a pearly-white-ceramic-polymer, scuttled out the front door to greet the stranger coming up its beach. Slews of narrow acrylic tubing ran the lengths of its bony frame, bundled like pneumatic muscle fibers. The anthropomorphic technological marvel had dressed itself in faded denim overalls, a clean white-linen shirt beneath. Round, wire-rimmed spectacles, one cracked lens, the other lens missing entirely, rested over its hemispherical, unlit eyes; in its hand it held a pitchfork. Joshua would have chuckled at the incongruity if he hadn't been so nervous.

A posse of nearly identical humanoids, adorned in similarly patchwork garb, crept out the hovel's entranceway behind the one Albus assumed to be their leader. Fixating on their blank, lifeless eyes, holding his breath, he wondered just how close they had to get before their allegiance would be made manifest. Itching at the trigger of the pistol concealed behind his back, his palms exuded a deluge of sweat; at least this was an interesting respite from the backbreaking farm work he thought.

Now only ten feet away, the shambling gang of automata pivoted their bald, skull-like heads in unison to face Albus as the pitchfork toting leader began to raise his ossified hand. Their eyes flashed a menacing bright blood-red.

Shit. "Foe!" shouted Joshua into his short-wave walkie talkie, his mnemonic fleeing from his mind in fear.

Delilah dove around the side of the building twenty-feet behind the mob of mechanical creatures. Rolling into a crouched position, she leveled off her Glock 18, a stainless-steel Ruger gripped in her other hand. Poised to blow away some villainous tommy scum, she took aim, fingers on the triggers.

"Howdy friend!" the automata chieftain barked through its speaker box, its jawbone flapping up and down, goofily wagging its skeletal arm back and forth over its head.

"Friend! I mean friend!" Joshua desperately shouted the correction into his radio. "Red eyes! Best friend Freds!"

Milliseconds away from unleashing a salvo of lead, Delilah thankfully heard Joshua's correction crackle over her walkie just in time; she exhaled a tense breath as she eased her fingers away from the triggers. Lowering her firearms, she shook her head in irritation over Joshua's mix-up, her heart still beating loudly in anticipation of the conflict that didn't come.

The friendly automata pushed in closer, gathering curiously around Joshua, drinking him in with their brightly-lit crimson eyes; they did not encounter humans much these days. The overall-clad patriarch of their clan stepped forward, introducing himself. "You can call me Colonel Mustard," he said, in what unexpectedly sounded like a poorly imitated southern accent.

Delilah, her guns holstered, strode over to the crowd as they encircled Joshua, introducing herself as well, careful not to make any mention of the nearly disastrous mixup; she counted twelve red-eyed Automata, making a mental note to herself.

....

Joshua and Delilah exchanged customary handshakes with

Colonel Mustard; his articulated, fleshless palm was cool to the touch and emitted a sibilant buzz as the semi-intelligent construct seesawed its limb up and down. Delilah was anxious to get moving again; she wanted to scout the next possible tommy outpost, hoping the whole day wouldn't be a wash. When Colonel Mustard invited the pair in for supper, she courteously declined the offer. "Won't be no bother," squawked the Colonel, "fricassee rabbit and mustard greens. We don't eat none of it—just like to play this game where we make-believe we is human."

Spittle extruded from Joshua's saliva glands as he thought about the hardtack they had reserved for dinner awaiting them back at the speeder; he stared longingly at Delilah, silently begging her to stay with his green puppy-dog eyes.

"Fine," she relented.

Inside their modest hovel, Mustard's kin arranged a bevy of aluminum trays set along a counter buffet style. They patiently waited in line behind each other, taking scoops of this and steaming heaps of that onto their plates, then took their seats along a long wooden table: Delilah and Joshua sat across from one another, Mustard at the head.

Joining hands with one another, the automata bowed their heads as their patriarch led them in giving thanks, a tradition not that dissimilar to the ritual Joshua had grown accustomed to back at the homestead. They temporarily extinguished the blood-red glow in their eyes as Colonel Mustard succinctly proclaimed, "Lord, thank you for everything! Amen!"

The tommys proceeded to fork portions of piping hot rabbit flesh and lightly-seasoned, stewed mustard greens into their mechanical mouths. Their skinless jawbones smacked up and down, mashing and grinding; lacking any form of digestive system, the masticated masses fell onto the table and dirt floor in soppy splats.

Joshua barely noticed. Thankful for the hot meal, he shoveled the delicious rabbit fricassee into his mouth with as much gusto as the humanoid beings. All the while, the tommys inconspicuously observed their human dinner guests, making note of how they held their fork or cut their meat. One noticed Delilah had placed her cloth napkin in her lap; she immediately followed suit.

Delilah took the gracious meal as an opportunity to gather some intel. Probing her hosts, she wanted to know if there were any cabals of blue-eyed tommys within a day's speeder-trek. Colonel Mustard was more than happy to oblige. "Why yes," he drawled, wiping flecks of rabbit from his polymer jawbone, "There's a mean 'ol clan of nasty bluebies...other side of this here cay. Always coming over to our side and stomping on our sunflowers in the night. Calling us names. One even put a snake down poor Millicent's dress. It bit right through her tubing." As food fell through his open chin, he added, "Their leader goes by the name of, Professor Plum." Millicent shuddered.

Her anxieties abated by the news of an enclave within a short distance, Delilah relaxed and enjoyed the rest of her meal. She had to admit, the tommys were quite skilled cooks; the rabbit was prepared perfectly with just the right amount of herbs and spices. She smiled briefly in Joshua's direction; he didn't notice.

....

Mustard, always the consummate host, offered his guests his bed to sleep in for the night; wouldn't be no bother, he didn't sleep anyway. Delilah again politely declined. The sun hadn't yet set, leaving plenty of daylight left to make it to the other side of the small cay. She wanted to get the drop on the troublesome flower-stomping tommys. Examining a map, Delilah determined the fastest route was to travel overland across the long but narrow island; however, the dense, unpredictable jungle terrain would make the wide footprint of the speeder unmanageable.

Popping the trunk to the speeder, she toted two oblong, metallic objects fitted with leather straps and harnesses. "Jetpacks," she said to Joshua. *Rad*, he thought. The experimental military jetpacks were capable of propelling a person through the air for a few short miles; unfortunately, their limited fuel capacity, and tendency to explode for no apparent reason, made the jetpacks' usage untenable. As such, the military had largely abandoned the project. Though Delilah had still managed to procure a few stashed away in one of the wrecked vessels off the coast of New Detroit.

Strapping the jet-propelled rocket packs onto their backs, the pair said goodbye to their odd, but magnanimous mechanical hosts and blasted off over the jungle canopy in pursuit of their prey.

Zipping up and down, doing barrel rolls and loop-de-loops as he flew, Joshua took to rocketeering like a piglet in poo poo. He thought he might even be a better rocketeer than Delilah, who was flying along rather conservatively in his opinion. Albus reminded Joshua that back in their world, the world they belonged to, he could fly all the time, and had done so on many occasions. *Yeah but never like this.* Never had he flown with so much weight, so much gravity, never with so much risk to his life: he loved it.

Delilah could only pray that there was enough fuel in the pack to support the childish man's heavy frame, and his unnecessary showboating, to reach the blue-eyed encampment. Sure enough, a warning light, (several warning lights to be precise), began to flash on Joshua's jetpack. Delilah zipped through the air alongside him, waving her arms, making animated gestures pointing at the ground; they needed to make an emergency landing in the nearest clearing of tropical trees.

Standing in the clearing, "Fuck," she cursed, throwing up her hands as she examined the blinking lights on Joshua's pack. His flamboyant style of flying had overheated the jetpack's engine.

"It's not my fault," defended Joshua sheepishly.

"It's one hundred percent your fault."

They would have to waste valuable time while his jetpack cooled back down to an operational temperature. As they waited the sun began disappearing from the sky: it was getting dark.

As luck would have it though, Joshua and Delilah wouldn't have to traverse all the way across the cay to locate the enclave. Crashing through the dense foliage up ahead under the cover of the growing darkness, pleasantly blue orbs crackled to life.

Professor Plum, a monkey wrench grasped in his clutches, had been en route to Mustard's homestead, leading his posse of troublemakers on a flower stomping raid. The machine's blue irises zeroed in on the pair stranded in the clearing. Calculating a quick course correction, the humanoid beelined straight for Delilah and Joshua. The rest of his gang followed suit. Automata could move quickly when they wanted too; Plum rapidly closed the gap.

Delilah reacted. Engaging her jetpack, flying only a few feet above the ground, she deftly maneuvered in a wide circle around the gang; herding the bewildered tommys into a cluster, she unholstered her pistols. Professor Plum side-stepped attempting to maintain visual contact with the encircling rocketeer. Calculating, the machine made its move; the professor leapt through the air with his skeletal arms outstretched, each ossified finger sharpened into piercing talons.

Delilah fired. *Bang*! She hit Plum mid-leap, boring a smoking hole right between his baby blues that went instantaneously dark. She then unloaded the rest of her clip into the mob, nailing every single one; Joshua didn't even get a chance to take a shot.

Decelerating as she somersaulted to the ground before her jets had entirely cut out, she shouted, "We've got to do this quickly!" Delilah raised a power-drill that had been clipped to her tool belt and gave the drill a few quick clicks of its trigger, throttling the spinning head with a *Bzzchhz Bzzz.*

....

Hunched over the animatronic corpse closest to her, drill in hand, almost frantically she began working on the chest cavity of the carcass. Joshua followed Delilah's instruction. Working in tandem, they removed large rubberized sacks from the chest of each downed automaton. Air pumps, Delilah explained, that acted like hearts for the machines, circulating compressed helium gas through their pneumatic tubing, breathing life into them.

The bulbous rubber organs, with arteries of transparent tubing dangling from them, still spasmed some as they were cut free from their hosts' bodies. Delilah showed Joshua how to cap the valves, trapping the compressed helium within.

Collecting the gas-filled sacks into a mesh bag, playfully Joshua sucked in a deep breath from one, intending to tease Delilah. "Nice shootin', Tex," he squeaked in a high-pitched voice.

"Hey! Don't waste any of that!" she snapped, snatching the heart out of his hands with a dirty look. Taken aback by her harsh rebuff, he reviewed Gellert's list as he hooked a full bag onto his belt.

"I don't see these on your dad's list."

"Super-secret side project," she whistled back at him, tauntingly.

Joshua mumbled childishly under his breath; she still hadn't revealed her secret to him. Albus used the opportunity to mentally lacerate himself, plaintively complaining to Joshua that the bold, capable, exotically beautiful Delilah didn't trust him and never would; he would always be an outsider. Even though he had unearthed zero evidence, she probably was the destroyer; he should just kill her now and be done with it.

"You okay?"

Delilah had already engaged the engine of her jetpack, three heart-packed mesh bags dangling from her own belt.

"Huh? Yeah! Fine."

Firing up their jetpacks they launched into the night sky, making a straight shot back towards the waiting speeder, no antics from Joshua this time. Loading their impressive haul into the vehicle, Delilah set a course for home.

The luminous, voluminous moon in the sky hit Delilah's eye like a big pizza pie that evening as the pair sped back over a flat, calm ocean. The usually strong briny breeze was taking a breather, combined with the sweltering humidity, making the clammy night that much stickier. The big island growing in size on the horizon, offering no explanation, Delilah shut-off the turbines and pulled a toggle on the dash. Large air bladders inflated beneath the vehicle as it drifted to rest, bobbing on the barely rocking ocean. She turned to Joshua.

"Thanks for the help."

"I didn't even get to shoot one."

"No," she said, "I mean, thank you for everything."

Without saying anything more, she stood on the cream-colored faux-leather seat of her vehicle, backside turned towards Joshua; she shimmied out of her baggy camouflage work pants, pulling her white tank-top off overhead as it ruffled her bouncy curls, her nude silhouette illuminated by the reflected light of the full moon.

Joshua felt powerless not to gawk at her narrow waist, and wide hips that curved into a strong and round backside. As if overcome with madness, Delilah dove off the side of the vessel, head first, into the dark unknown waters; bioluminescent bacteria minding their own business sparkled to life all around her at the perturbation.

"What are you doing?!" shouted Joshua over the side of the craft.

"What's it look like?"

She coerced Joshua, imploring him to join her; he balked that it didn't seem like a good idea. She taunted in return, "It's not like I haven't seen you naked before!" Delilah wasn't wrong about that; out of excuses, he stood with his back to her and stripped from his sweaty, unwashed dungarees, cannonballing into the cool ocean depths.

As his head breached the surface, Joshua found himself giggling ecstatically, even though no one had told a funny joke. Doggy paddling over to where Delilah was treading, they splashed saltwater back and forth at one another, escalating in intensity, in bigger and bigger waves, laughing all the while.

In retrospect, Joshua wasn't sure who struck first, neither was Delilah. They embraced in the buoyant, salty fluid; their naked bodies pressed together underneath the moonlight, kicking and intertwining their legs beneath them, their inexperienced lips making contact for the very first time.

An old sensation, a very old sensation—perhaps one of the oldest, the creative forces of the universe coursed through Joshua's body, begging and pleading to be brought into existence, carousing and mingling with physiological stimuli, heart rate quickening, blood vessels dilating: Joshua—had a boner.

Feeling him pushing against her, Delilah reacted with stuttered ambivalence; she was twenty-six and still a virgin for obvious reasons (like the world ending), and some not so obvious ones as well. Somewhat flattered and admittedly aroused by the response elicited in the man, she found herself at the same time terrified in a way she couldn't quite accurately convey. Terrified by the responsibility, by the piercing vulnerability; terrified by something potentially bigger than herself.

Coughing unnecessarily, she cleared her throat, awkwardly shoving Joshua backwards through the water. Hurriedly, she backstroked away, back to the safety of her speeder, the vessel floating like a discarded champagne cork on the ocean surface.

She pulled herself up the metal rack; Joshua couldn't help but stare at the mercurial beads of saltwater capturing droplets of milky-white moonbeam as they rolled and dripped off Delilah's round backside. Toweling off, acting as if nothing had happened, Delilah called over the side of the craft to Joshua still treading water.

"Let's go, you big goof."

"Yep. Just give me a minute."

26

THE ADAM BOMB
TABERNACLE

Over the course of the next few days Delilah and Joshua developed a strange new habit of bumping and bungling into one another around the camp, sliding past one another in the mess, neither one sure which direction they should turn as they scooted by. They would bumble on in obvious small talk as they did: "Hot day were having," "Sure is." Avoiding each other's gaze as they passed in the corridors of the living quarters, an unspoken and implicit pact existed between the two, to not mention or address their midnight skinny-dipping escapade or the events that followed.

Luckily, Gellert seemed oblivious to their awkward new habit. However, Dee was most definitely not. "Did you trip on a rock and accidentally kiss Joshua or something?" she pestered her sister, not that far off. Delilah the Elder responded in kind, swatting her sister on the bum.

Dee gave chase around the scorched couch seeking retaliation, intending to mash a mushy, overripe banana into her sister's plaid pajamas. Joshua, (sometimes guilty of being a walking cliché), attempting to avoid the quarreling siblings, inadvertently stepped on the discarded banana peel as his foot slid out beneath him. He grabbed hold of the back of a chair to steady himself, when they all heard the early warning sirens of Gellert's approach. The shifty metal stairs leading up from the dormitories clanked loudly, alerting them, as Gellert trudged up the steps.

"Hope everyone's showered this morning!" he hollered out as his head crested above the alcove of the staircase; he turned to see his two children frozen solid, Delilah standing on the coffee table, a bruised banana in Dee's outstretched hand, Joshua splayed out grasping onto a chair for balance, all posing motionlessly as if the subjects of a renaissance still life. Gellert clenched his jaw and shook his head.

"Do we really have to?" complained Delilah the Middle.

"You bet your butts," her father reprimanded, further flabbergasted by the fact that none of them were even dressed yet. Gellert had on his best pair of dress-overalls, not a stain on them, well besides that one (and that one). He had even gussied himself up with a faded, red cotton tee, his mustache freshly trimmed and waxed.

Scrambling towards their room, the two sisters made haste to ready themselves. Both were fully aware they had shirked long enough and risked summoning the full ire of their father should they try to cash in on any more borrowed time.

Perplexed, Joshua asked, "What's going on?"

"It's Easter, stupid!" replied Delilah the Guess Who.

"And?"

The elder Delilah scoffed as well, a bit weary, in too much of a hurry to explain everything to this toddlering hulk; she wondered if maybe he had hit his head when he fell from outer space. An image of the red-headed Joshua bucked off a Pegasus that had been stung by a horsefly, flashed in her mind and she chuckled to herself.

She reminded herself that all those years locked away in cryo must have really done a number on his brain. The rational side of her brain blared loudly, hoisting red banners up tiny flag poles, yelling that she hadn't witnessed the man she was intensely crushing on—actually come out of cryostasis. She had just assumed, and he had never denied it.

When she found him, there was no hard evidence: no deflated stasis pod, no cryo-caul, not even a discarded feeding tube; for all she knew, he coasted to that island on the back of a half-shell fully formed.

So, she thought, *maybe he came out of cryo on another island and swam over to that one.* Another image flashed in her mind, this time of Joshua doggy paddling in the ocean around the side of her floating speeder, barely keeping his head above water. Waving her hand she banished the incongruous images away; she wasn't going to entertain these nay-sayers on Easter.

The gang, now all cleaned up, dressed, and in attendance, made their way towards Gellert's submarine docked in the lagoon; as they were about to board, Dee called out for Fin.

Lazing about in the jungle some mile and a half away, the fox with the gargantuan ears could easily hear the girl calling out for him. Shaking his head, Fin was certain he had informed Dee he wouldn't be attending; he had a full agenda that day of playing, frolicking, and leaping about the jungle. Gellert reassured his middle child that the fox was fine; it was a wild creature and could take care of care of itself for a few days in their absence.

"All aboard!" Gellert hollered, which he got way more of a kick out of than his children. Sealing the hatch, they descended beneath the waves and were off. The sisters played cat's cradle to pass the time; Gellert intermittently conversed with Joshua as he piloted the sub, informing the carrot-topped man that their destination was not another island, like he might have assumed. They were headed to a peninsula that had been part of the mainland. Not that it mattered much these days since the protruding landmass had been cut-off, most of it covered by the black mass, leaving only the southern tip of the peninsula exposed.

Gellert slowed the submerged vessel at one point as they passed by one of the few surviving coral reefs, bringing it to rest on the sandy ocean bottom; he pointed out a pod of telekinetic octopi hard at work. Dee rushed over to the porthole, squeezing her sister out of the way. Huddled up, their faces glued to the convex windows, they watched with rapturous amusement as the fuchsia and turquoise colored octopi used their otherworldly abilities to float and stack blocks of coral into place.

The cephalopods were busy erecting a prison to incarcerate the bad octopi of the reef, using only the power of their minds. Joshua pressed his face up against the glass; when one of his fingers accidentally brushed across Delilah's hand, she abruptly yanked it away.

Pausing momentarily from its task, one octopus turned towards the submarine and made direct eye contact with Albus. Waving a friendly tentacle, it looked through the porthole with alien eyes and beamed a salutation right into Ablus's head. "*BlluruuuBburuBllurb*," it said. Their curiosity temporarily sated, Gellert yanked on some levers and pulled the yellow submersible away from the reef, picking up steam again.

....

The crew of New Detroiters traveled on for many hours more, eventually emerging from beneath the waves off the coast of a long sandy beach lined with waving palms. Beyond the coast were what was left of a razed city, the majority of the city's former buildings leveled completely to the ground.

The Venn diagram of surviving faithful had begun arriving off the coastline for the Easter service in various vessels of their own: sailboats and catamarans outfitted to survive an indefinite amount of time at sea, kitted with solar panels, urine-to-water converters, small gardens, and key lime trees planted on the decks, veritable ecosystems in their own right; others turned up in speeders similar to Delilah's, submarines, or aquatic seaplanes, their pilots careful to not fly anywhere near the watchful Cancer.

As Gellert inflated the rubber dinghy from atop the deck of the lolling submersible, an obnoxiously loud fog horn blurted out from over the horizon. Coming into view was a massive ship, a cruise liner. "Ugh, the Andersons..." moaned Delilah the Middle.

The Andersons were the wealthiest of the surviving faithful; the family of eight, Dough Anderson, his wife Jane Anderson, and their six perfect, towheaded children, traveled the remnants of the world in their looted cruise ship.

They gathered on the poop deck of their ostentatious craft preparing for muster. Dough, decked in a solid white suit, his blow-dried hair coiffed in a gold-trimmed captain's hat, blew into a shrill, shiny whistle corralling his brood of children into a line in height order, while Jane precariously balanced her wobbly green Jell-O mold resting in her upturned arms. Each Anderson child, blonde hair perfectly parted, sported their mandatory bright orange life vests, as their automata man-servant ferried the family to shore.

Arriving last to the Easter gathering, an elderly man with a long alabaster beard, his skin cured to cracking brown leather by the baking sun, paddled an ocean-faring kayak, alone, through the shallow surf. As the old man tugged the small craft up the beach, at first blush, Albus thought he saw someone he recognized. However, it wasn't him.

An adventurous type, this man's name was Dr. Charles Diggity (no middle name), but you could call him Chuck. Embarking in his bright-orange vessel made-for-one from his floating island, an island that he had cobbled together himself, constructed of wooden pallets and buoyant rubbish (Styrofoam coolers mostly), Chuck Diggity had spent the better part of three months kayaking solo across the vast oceans to reach the gathering, preaching the "good word" as he called it, to pods of telepathic porpoises as he went, whose language he had taken the time to learn along the way.

A milieu of survivors congealed on the sandy beach meandering towards the Easter service, greeting one another, chatting and exchanging news as they did. Most made small talk about current events, which mainly consisted of concerned whispers about the black mass slowly consuming their world. Chuck Diggity gave Gellert a hearty clap on the back as they navigated their way through the piles of rubble towards one of the few buildings still standing, a large edifice where the service was to be held. Gellert smiled. He didn't exactly *get* Chuck, but was fond of the aged man nonetheless.

The site hosting the Easter gathering had the trimmings of a religious building, though it certainly didn't resemble a church to Joshua, no steeples, no bell towers, no ornate stained-glass windows. It was large and had imposing steps leading up to its double wooden doors, an impressive vaulted dome sat on top, but the semblance stopped there.

Two of the building's adjacent walls had been blown clean off, leaving the interior of the holy place exposed to the elements. Against all odds, the rotunda had not collapsed; it remained intact precariously resting atop the two remaining walls. Despite the obvious damage, the edifice was in far better condition than the decimated structures surrounding it, which were nothing more than glorified rubble.

Entering through the building's double doors, which Joshua found unnecessary, he glanced up at the interior of the rotunda; tiled into the domed ceiling was a monochrome mosaic of a triangular six-pointed star. *A Star of David*, a little tidbit of trivia Albus managed to pull up. Towards the back of the temple the only thing that remained standing was the charred remnants of some ornamented wooden cabinetry. Out the shattered windows of the temple, many miles in the distance across the flat terrain, one could see the tenebrous tumor of the looming Cancer; the heat from its surface caused the air to shimmer like an unwelcome mirage.

....

Some forty or so surviving faithful had turned up from the surrounding lands and islands; they filtered into the place of worship and took their seats, waiting for the service to start. Their parish had no ordained priests or preachers, instead the faithful were invited to come up and speak whenever they felt the Spirit move them.

Dough Anderson took the stage first, strutting down the aisle in his pristine, all-white suit, taking a spot at the pulpit as if he lived there; he talked a lot about a man named *JAY-ZUS* and his coming day of judgment, as his captain's hat bobbled along to his overwrought gesticulations. Joshua, glancing around at the missing walls of the temple, staring towards the leering black mass in the distance, thought that day of judgment may have already come and gone.

Dough Anderson concluded his time on stage by saying that he and his family were still fully committed to the temple rebuilding project, once they had more time and resources. The massive fuel demands of their cruise liner required that they sail from abandoned oil-rig to abandoned oil-rig, looting fuel reserves, coasting into the next one on fumes, leaving time for little else. The Andersons were nice people and they meant well; they were just a bit clueless.

Gellert limped down the aisle and spoke next; he said some beautiful words about a man that spoke a lot on loving your neighbor, forgiveness, salvation, and resurrection. Joshua heard none of it; he was too busy thinking about Delilah. Had it been a mistake to kiss her, he wondered; things had been so awkward between them lately. When he thought she wasn't looking his way, he would glance in her direction trying to sneak a peek. Delilah was doing the same.

Joshua was caught like a frog in a flashlight beam, as Gellert said, "...Speaking of coming back from the dead, let me introduce Joshua." A man, Gellert explained, who his eldest daughter had found wandering around a deserted island after being frozen unconscious in cryostasis for many decades.

Delilah's father waved, beckoning to Joshua, urging him to come up to the pulpit and say a few words. Joshua fidgeted, that innocuous cryostasis fib was taking on a life of its own. Standing on stage, his mind completely blank, he recalled the words of Colonel Mustard's blessing. Asking those gathered to bow their heads Joshua said, "Lord, Thank you for everything. Amen." That seemed to cover all his bases and Joshua took his seat back amongst the congregants as Gellert began to wrap up his sermon.

In years past, Gellert would spend four or five weeks away from his island enclave doing stints at the holy site, cutting stones and hewing crossbeams, volunteering his time and effort with fellow survivors to rebuild the temple. Although, with the growing discomfort in his amputated stump and his endlessly multiplying unfinished projects demanding his attention at home, those four or five weeks had dwindled to one or two, if he went at all.

When his daughters were younger, he would bring them along, making a retreat out of it, a chance to socialize with other survivors their own age. Older now, the girls often opted to remain behind.

Gellert looked out over the congregation; exhaling heavily, he closed his time at the pulpit by also vowing to contribute more of an effort to rebuild the temple, as soon as some of his projects, like his irrigation canals (and his rocketship, which he surreptitiously failed to mention), were finished.

Chuck Diggity, something of a real iconoclast, spoke last. Coming down the aisle of the temple with a spritely gait, he moved easily and gracefully for a man of his advanced age, pausing here and there along the way to shake a hand or dole out a hug to a friend he hadn't seen in ages. Chuck was mostly well-liked amongst the other survivors, though some in the congregation eyed him, as he passed, with a certain degree of suspicion for his often unconventional, and in their opinion— downright silly ideas.

As he jaunted up the steps to the pulpit, he threw his long white beard over his shoulder and began to deliver a lively homily. Chuck argued that rebuilding the temple was utterly irrelevant, a fool's errand, stupid even; the encroaching Cancer would consume the temple (and all of them) one day anyway.

"What really matters," said Chuck, "is to face the unknowable with integrity and zealous bravery, to have faith that everything is going to be okay in the end." He paused and looked directly at Albus for a moment. Looking back over the congregation he continued, "And most importantly, we must stay focused on supporting each other in our struggles, this tapestry of survivors, this mosaic of diverse individuals united in common fellowship." Chuck concluded his remarks and held for applause. This was a very unpopular opinion and he was booed off the stage.

....

After the service, the congregants supped together in a pot-luck fashion, sharing dishes they had brought from their homes arranged amongst the rubble outside the temple. Gellert chatted with the Hams, a husband and wife who resided on a neighboring island not that far from New Detroit. While the couple's son Abram, a teenaged boy a year or two older than Dee, tried to impress Delilah the Middle.

Abram scaled a pile of rubble, climbing to its highest point some six feet above the ground. He called over to Dee and leapt off, clicking his heels together in the air as he did. Abram landed with a dull thud. Delilah the Middle rolled her eyes; though secretly, she was very impressed.

Joshua stabbed at a green gelatinous blob, Jane Anderson's Jell-O, avoiding Delilah's gaze, while Delilah side-eyed him a few feet away, neither saying a word. Even Gellert was now getting suspicious of the way the two were acting; something had changed, he just wasn't sure what. Joshing his daughter, he turned to her and asked, "Did you trip on a rock and accidentally kiss Joshua or something?"

Huffing an exasperated breath through her nostrils, tiring of the elementary school awkwardness, Delilah extended an olive branch, reaching towards Joshua's hand. "Come on, I want to show you something," she said as she tugged him away from the pot-luck.

Sneaking away from the crowd, Delilah led Joshua around the side of the temple to a cellar door, taking him down two flights of stairs to the temple's sub-basement. She lit two oil lamps, one for each of them, to light their way through the darkness. Joshua pushed aside cobwebs and collapsed support beams as they crept; Albus hoped that there weren't any kobolds or gibberlings concealing themselves in these subterranean chambers, waiting to pounce on the intruders.

Entering a dusty, tomb-like room towards the far end of the temple's sub-basement, a highly ornate chest that looked like it belonged in one of Joshua's favorite movies, sat quietly, undisturbed, radiating a palpable authority.

The chest was gilded in gold filigree, figurines of two bird-like beings with wings outstretched towards one another guarded the top, wooden poles meant for carrying the box flanked each long side. Delilah approached the ark with hallowed stillness, hooking her hollow oil lamp to a chain overhead as she glanced at Joshua. Like a child about to reveal her parent's stash of paraphernalia and other inexplicable *adult* things, she slowly pushed and slid the lid of the chest. Subatomic particles of dust orbited in the dim lantern light. Joshua caught the other end of the hefty lid with an *umph*, easing it downward, preventing it from crashing against the ground.

The two hung their heads over the gold-plated sides of the sacred chest, peering at the contents contained within as prostrating rays of lamp-light bounced off a glossy, walrus-sized egg; upon making contact with the metallic object, the enervated rays wisely turned away and fled in abject terror. Joshua and Delilah bore witness with hushed reverence. "It's an Adam bomb..." whispered Delilah, puncturing the numinous reprieve.

Joshua whimpered back, "...I think you mean an atom bomb..." his voice ninety-three million miles away; he knew exactly what it was.

"Yeah, that's what I said."

Joshua didn't hear her; his eyes had widened into two flying saucers as he contemplated the all-consuming, destructive force cached inside the ark. In the span of a moment Albus' head finally caught up to what Joshua's heart had known for some time now: he was falling in love with Delilah the Firstborn, Destroyer of Worlds. Kali, the Dark Mother. Albus' mission, his purpose for being in the Low Place came loudly trumpeting back to him.

Desperately hoping it couldn't be true, Albus' head swam as Delilah rhapsodized about her omnipotent discovery. She had found the Adam bomb buried deep in a submerged wreck, a voice had been calling to her; to her knowledge, it was the only one still in existence not detonated by the Cancer. She had stashed it here, hidden in the crypts of the temple for safekeeping. Delilah mused, with a maniacal gleam in her eye, that if she could just get the Adam bomb over the origin of the Cancer and drop the payload, like shoving lit dynamite into the hollow of a tree, she could blast the whole thing to kingdom come—trunk, branch, stem, and leaf collapsing in on itself, freeing their world from its tyranny.

That was some good news at least, thought Albus. The Destroyer didn't yet possess a way to deliver her precious world-killer. However, he knew now, beyond the shadow of a doubt, there was no way he could ever bring himself to terminate Delilah. Like a dog leaping about the floor of an electrified cage, his mind howled, cranking away on its axis, looking for a way, any way, out of this mess.

He had an idea; some semblance of a plan was formulating in his head. Maybe...just maybe, if she felt the same way about him—he could marry Delilah, distracting her from her mission just long enough to grow old and die together. It was crazy enough that it just might work.

27

IT'S MY PARTY

On the quiet and uneventful submarine ride back to New Detroit, Delilah the Middle took the opportunity to remind everyone that her birthday was coming up in a month and a half. Turning to her father she begged him to invite the other families of survivors to their homestead for a party; she wanted to have a dance with a Cleopatra theme, her idol. When Gellert hedged some, she pleaded that it was only fair; her older sister got to have a movie night.

Saying that he would think about it, Gellert deflected and changed the subject. Dee knew that this was code for her father; if she just pestered and badgered enough, he would break. Truly, she didn't care all that much about the party or the other survivors; using her birthday as an excuse, as a guise for her ulterior motive—she wanted to dance with the boy Abram from the Easter gathering.

Over the next few days Dee was on her best behavior: abstaining from complaint while carrying out her chores, handing tools to her father while he puttered away on his rocket, offering to braid Delilah's hair without a trade; she was even kind to Joshua, only calling him stupid when he did something truly dumb. Over supper one evening she broached the topic again, this time catching her father well sated and in a good mood; he was amenable and agreed to the idea. Gellert would get on the ill-tempered, refurbished ham radio (which always carried a risk of attracting unwanted attention) and send word out to the neighboring settlements; they were having a Cleopatra themed dance party.

....

The day of the party had arrived; the New Detroiters tidied and decorated the mess hall as best they could. Sweeping up the floors and scooting some of the long tables back into position, Gellert laid down slabs of warped plywood in the center of the hall; using spare nail and screw, he assembled a passable dance floor. Situated in front of the dance floor he placed the card table on a raised platform for "Cleopatra's dais" (Dee's idea).

They lit every coconut oil lamp they owned and laid palm fronds around to accentuate the Egyptian theme, while Delilah the Elder crafted ceremonial headdresses from their limited supplies. She asked Joshua if it would be alright to use the conch shell he had gifted her as the centerpiece for Dee's crown. "Of course," he said. He had given it to her; it was hers do with it as she pleased. Joshua pitched in with the festivities as well, wrapping the fidgeting Fin with strips of palm frond; his best attempt at a mummy, which the fox quickly shook off. As Albus tried to recall exactly how birthdays worked, this would be the second one he had celebrated in New Detroit, he wondered if that meant he had been here two years; no that wasn't quite right.

A spread of appetizers were set along one long table: roasted crickets, deviled iguana eggs, the obligatory dried pieces of fruits and foraged nuts, slices of boar cheese, and something that passed for sushi—raw slices of grouper and boiled root vegetables wrapped in kelp. A delectable punch sat at the end of the table, mixed from coconut water and a scoop of a very special reserve of orange Tang found years ago among one of the wrecked military vessels, which Gellert made even more special by adding a cup or two of his own coveted moonshine; they were ready.

As the guests began arriving offshore and anchoring their crafts, Dee stood amongst the tropical hammock anxiously scouting for any sign of Abrams family's sailboat. When she spotted the mast of one ship flying the Ham's family crest she practically squealed and ran back to the decorated mess hall to take her position.

....

Of the twenty or so people invited, fourteen had made their way to New Detroit, not a bad turn out for a party at the end of the world. The guests mingled about the hall, complimenting Gellert and company on what an incredible job they had done. Most were happy to have an activity, any activity, to punctuate the otherwise drab routine of their existence.

The guests craned their necks towards the entryway as Delilah the Middle made her grand entrance. Walking through the door, a headdress made of woven fibers, brightly colored parrot feathers, and the exquisite conch shell as its centerpiece, rested atop Dee's head like a crown. Gellert, Delilah, and Joshua fanned 'Cleopatra' with palm fronds as she waltzed to her dais, politely waving to her adoring subjects.

Even Chuck Diggity managed to make the soiree! Arriving late, Chuck hauled his neon-orange ocean-faring kayak through the shallows and up onto the coarse beach as the sun began to set behind him. A telepathic porpoise, leaping above the waves offshore, flipped and splashed its tail in Chuck's direction, then swam off.

Making his way to the festivities, Chuck approached Dee's dais. Bowing before his queen, he handed her a message in a bottle. Hermetically sealed inside a green beer bottle worn completely smooth by the sea, a dainty bell knotted around the bottle's neck, was a tightly wound papyrus scroll. Dr. Diggity instructed Dee to only break the seal when she felt the darkness had truly won; Dee thanked her loyal subject.

The guests noshed on yummy morsels, loosening up a bit after a glass or two of the spiked punch. Gellert broke out his banjo and pulled up a seat next to Abram's father, Mr. Ham, an overturned steel oil drum in front of him. They began to play, Gellert plucking away on his Banjo while Mr. Ham beat at the steel drum with a stick he had whittled, doing their best to provide the partygoers with music to dance along with.

Surprisingly, Ms. Matilda, a perennially barefooted and aged survivor that chose to live alone on a nearby cay, began crooning in a husky and haunting voice. Chuck Diggity joined in with the trio as well; hamboning, he slapped his open palms and wrists against his thighs, chest, and cheeks as his long beard flopped wildly, adding another welcome percussive layer to the island jam.

Couples that had been together forever unabashedly took to the dance floor and swayed side to side in each other's arms, as the warped sheets of plywood rocked along beneath them like the sea. Joshua and Delilah looked at each other; Delilah turned away and began clearing some of the plates from the tables.

....

Abram stood against a far wall of the mess, palling around with another boy his age, glancing over at Dee who was staring into his soul from on top her dais. The other boy snorted and pointed over at Dee with as much discretion as a teenager can manage, whispering something into Abram's ear. Deep into his second cup of punch, as Abram finally found the courage to approach Dee and ask her to dance—a loud roar, multiple roars actually, like the death throes of a dying hydra, emerged from the direction of the beach.

"Oh great..." said Delilah the Elder, exiting the dance, making her way towards the shore. Joshua chased after her. Gellert trotted over to the living quarters to retrieve something he hadn't had to use in a long time.

A gang of teenagers and young men pulled up onto the beach, piloting looted mag-bikes, throttling the narrow, hovering vehicles onto their hindquarters, while racing in donuts sending pebbles and rocks flying.

The gang called themselves the Beastie Boys. They had

been part of an elite glee club on their first international flight to the Worldwide Glee Championships, when the black mass ruptured. Their jet was forced to crash land onto a deserted island; miraculously all the boys survived. When their own island was eventually consumed by the encroaching mass they took to looting and causing general mayhem.

Their leader, Jacques, bringing his bike to rest parallel to the shore, swung his legs round to the side of the saddle as his bike drifted to a halt; leaning against it he shouted in the direction of the party.

"Red rover! Red rover! Send Delilah on over!!"

Delilah the Elder, steaming mad, cussed down the side of the outcropping, storming down the beach; Joshua followed not far behind.

"Hey there, Delilah," sneered Jacques, "We're actually looking for your sister." He hocked a loogie into the sand. "You're a little too old for our tastes."

Joshua stepped in front of Delilah; his fists clenched into bludgeons. Delilah held out her arm, pushing him back, telling Joshua that they were nothing but a bunch of drunk hooligans and weren't worth a damn. She shot back at Jacques yelling, "Figures at the end of the world, only the cockroaches would be left!"

The rest of the Beastie Boys hooted and hollered, revving the engines to their mag-bikes, drowning Delilah out. The electric engines of their levitating bikes operated in complete silence by design. That didn't stop the Beastie Boys from kitting them out with stolen lawnmower and weed-wacker engines welded on to the backs, hooked up to a cacophonous array of metal tubing and pipes to produce the maddeningly loud, obnoxious revving noises. A bumper sticker slapped to the back of one of the bikes read: "Loud pipes are just really badass."

....

From the anonymity of the gang one of the Beastie Boys whizzed an empty beer bottle in Delilah's direction, not intending to hit her, only to give her a good fright. It crashed against the gravelly ground a few feet in front of her sending shrapnel of green glass flying. Again, Joshua stepped forward, this time as Gellert joined the scene, trudging down the beach with a Louisville slugger in hand, studded in nine-inch nails.

"Well if it isn't Gellert the Gimp and the Jolly Red Giant," taunted Jacques.

Gellert stood stoically, brandishing the studded bat. "There a problem, son?" he asked, unperturbed.

"Yeah! You raised a brood of stuck up lil' piggies!" Jacques shrieked.

With that, Gellert and Joshua marched into the melee. The Beastie Boys swarmed like flies, Gellert indiscriminately swinging his vicious weapon at the contorting gang, catching one by his leather jacket shredding three long tatters into it.

A ringing sensation exploded in Joshua's left ear; one of the beasties had sucker-punched him. Mostly unfazed, he turned towards his attacker who was dawning brass knuckles. Joshua couldn't help but chuckle, the beastie had leapt two-feet into the air just to land the blow against his temple. Joshua brought his clenched fists together with commanding force on either side of the scrawny beastie's cranium, knocking his lights out, nearly popping his head.

He slugged his way easily through another three or four savages. Two ambushed Joshua from behind, grappling the Goliath about the waist; Joshua clasped his fists together into a hammer and mashed the swine's skulls in turn, knocking them into the dirt. As his bruised knuckles thumped with ache, knocking another two to the ground, an animalistic animus within Joshua found some perverse pleasure in the senseless violence; as long as he was winning, the banal beating was kind of *fun?*

....

A hooligan howled, Gellert had caught another one in the leg with his spiked club, extricating his weapon in a spray of blood. The two men beat the beasts back; the Beastie Boys began to bunch up towards their mag-bikes, preparing to flee the rout.

Then *BANG!* Jacques stood motionless, his eyes widening in

shock, a slithering wisp of white smoke flicking its forked tongue in front of his face. Gellert stumbled backwards. He dropped his bat, clutching at his stomach where the blood was beginning to pool. The next few moments happened very fast and very slow.

Jacques hollered waving his smoking gun overhead commanding his boys to mount up and get the hell out of dodge. Delilah screamed and ran towards her injured papa. Joshua, his bloodlust evaporating, came to his senses and sprang into action. They kept a first-aid kit in the living quarters; using his powerful legs he galloped gazelle-like, bounding over obstacles to retrieve the lifesaving kit.

Gellert sank to his knees, looking down at the hole in his chest as his life force spurted out. It didn't hurt nearly as bad as he had always imagined it would. Watching as Jacques shouted and fled in slow-motion with his cretins, Gellert craned his neck turning to see his eldest daughter, Delilah—unharmed—sprinting in his direction.

He smiled, overjoyed. He felt guilty he was going to have to leave her like this, but he had taught his children everything he knew; there wasn't much else he could do. Hoping to see Dee one last time before he had to go (and even that silly fox Fin), he thought about his wife, Delilah Sr., and youngest daughter, Dee Dee, again feelings of overwhelming joy permeated his being from his leaking heart.

Thinking back through the choices of his life, he regretted nothing. His only sadness was that he wouldn't stick around long enough to see the birth of his first grandchild. When a soothing voice assured him that he would see her one day, he felt at peace and laid back on the pebbly beach that he loved so much, staring up at the stars, making his preparations to leave.

The rest of the partygoers, hearing the commotion, piled out onto the beach. Dee, screaming in utter horror, threw her conch headpiece to the ground, the comely shell cracking in two on impact; she ran to join her sister kneeling at their father's side, Fin bolting behind her. Joshua, returning with the first-aid kit, crashed through the tropical hammock and leapt off the outcropping onto the hard, uneven beach, spraining his ankle; he didn't even notice. Unraveling medical bandages between his hands, he pushed through the crowd towards Gellert's body. It was too late; the man was dying.

Delilah and Delilah huddled by their father's side wailing, begging their father not to die, as Gellert tried to reassure them that everything was going to be okay. Joshua desperately tried to dress the bullet wound in the man's torso, wrapping bandages to stymie the bleeding; Gellert pushed Albus' futile efforts aside. Grabbing hold of the outsider's thickly calloused, trembling hand, grasping it tightly, Gellert pulled Albus in close to him. With dwindling breath he whispered into Joshua's ear, "It was a good scrap, son," and died.

28

MOURNING
SICKNESS

Delilah and Delilah inconsolably howled, throwing their bodies over their dead father, refusing to leave his side. Delilah the Elder wrapped her arms around her papa's head, rocking it, sobbing, while Dee futilely pushed against his chest, screaming into her father's face not to leave her, to no avail. Fin licked the man's forehead—twice; one precious long lick upwards, then a gentle swipe across, saying goodbye. The fox sat back to observe Gellert's passage through his glimmering onyx eyes.

Joshua sat a while longer, grasping the dead man's rough hand, surprised by how quickly the flesh was beginning to cool. For a moment, he thought back to the loss of his own father, contemplating the man, Jimmy Cake, from some past life of which Albus valiantly tried to preserve the fading images of.

From what he recalled, his father had been something of a complicated man. On some level, Albus understood his father had tried his best, but was often distant or busy spelunking his way down to the bottom of a bottle.

A genius artist in his own right (though never recognized), sometime after Albus' parents divorced, Jimmy Cake threw himself in front of a speeding car, committing suicide. He was an alcoholic and your clichéd troubled artist anyway, so why not.

Joshua never forgave his father for his final act of cowardice, ironic in a sense.

What Jimmy and Jimmy's soul alone witnessed on that day, was an adorable, pigtailed African American girl, six years in age, pedaling her second-hand, red bicycle, still outfitted with wobbly training wheels, along a congested street. The unattended girl pedaled quickly, riding blissfully unaware towards a busy intersection.

Standing there at the intersection, impatiently waiting to cross to the other side, the entire scene unlocked itself before Jimmy's eyes like peering through a stained glass window. Glimpses of time and space pierced through him, incomprehensibly revealing a tangled web of events that would reverberate far into the future.

A distracted driver on her cellphone, yelling at her two bickering kids in the back seat, barreled up the blind hill in a black Cadillac, about to blow through the four-way stop, cruelly introducing the adolescent girl to her fate.

Without hesitation, Jimmy Cake threw himself in front of the ill-fated automobile, his shoulder-length red hair flapping behind him as his body collided with the windshield, successfully diverting the vehicle from careening into the bicycling child.

Before the driver of the Cadillac could recover from the horrific shock of hitting a pedestrian, the little girl had already ridden on, disappearing from view, wholly innocent to the events that had just transpired behind her. Jimmy caught a glimpse of the girl safely vanishing around a corner; he died on the hood of the car.

It wasn't until Albus eventually released his grasp from Gellert's cold, stiffening fingers, that he realized he had lost his father for a second time that day. He made a bargain with himself to cry later, needing to remain strong in this moment.

. . . .

Looking up at those standing around, the crowd of gathered guests that had been celebrating the remembrance of a birth only moments ago, stood in shocked silence at the senseless and sudden death of a good man; a man that had been a dependable, resilient paragon of their broken world. Some began to cry quietly to themselves as they pulled each other in close.

Delilah, snapping back to the scene around her, stood with the blinding rage of a woman deeply wronged; she grabbed her Glock and vaulted off towards her speeder intending to give chase, intent on mercilessly slaughtering the whole gang of beasties. Joshua ran after her, grabbing her by the arm. He tried convincing her it was no use. There were too many of them; they would kill her too. It wasn't what her father would have wanted. The Beastie Boys would get theirs in the end.

As she tried to escape his grasp, he pulled her in tight, enveloping her in a bear hug flush against his body. She beat at Joshua's ruddy, hairy chest with her fists, crying and screaming, calling him a good for nothing coward. It didn't faze him; he only held tighter until Delilah's outbursts abated, replaced with salty, unintelligible sobs that ran down his chest.

Delilah the Middle sat with her arms hugged in around her knees, sucking in silent sobs, rocking herself back and forth as Fin licked at her limp hand. She blamed herself for her father's death, and would for the rest of her life. She pulled what remained of her Egyptian headdress down over her tearful eyes like a cowl.

As the reality of the situation set in, Joshua and Mr. Ham soberly carried Gellert's heavy body back to the mess hall and laid it lengthwise along one of the long tables, the festive accoutrements an unwelcome juxtaposition to the gruesome scene. A number of lamps and candles placed around it, Abram's mother cleaned and dressed the body while other guests attempted to console the two grieving sisters.

They all agreed to stay the night in New Detroit so that they could pay their respects to a good man in the morning light. The night that felt like it would never end had worn thin, most of the oil lamps running out of fuel, snuffing themselves out; there was not much else they could do besides try to get some sleep, if they could.

The guests retired to their vessels to rest, while Delilah and Dee chose to stay in the mess hall beside their slain father. Joshua stopped at the cistern and cleansed the blood from his hands with a spray of rainwater from the spigot; exhausted, he trod towards the tiki hut.

He laid in one of the limp hammocks blankly staring up at the thatched ceiling of the primitive hut; the strong ocean winds had died down as if also saddened by Gellert's passing. Unfortunately, the parasitic insects of the island did not show the same respect. Shifting from side-to-side as he swatted away mosquitos that penetrated his netting, some archaic memory of Albus'—of trying to conqueror death—drifted through his liminal state. It had all been hubris: vanity.

Startled from the murky dregs of his pensive reflections, he heard the shuffling of gravel behind him; footsteps approached.

Wobbling to his side, he sat upright in the rickety sling; Albus watched Delilah approach out of the darkness. They stared at each other with forlorn eyes, neither one needing to say a word. Delilah squeezed her way into Joshua's hammock as the rocking swing pushed back against her. Laying on top of the man, she pressed her plump lips against his.

That ancient feeling once again reviving Joshua, he pressed back against her as red blood cells flooded to his sun-chapped lips, his tongue sneaking out of his mouth to meet hers in a secret liaison. As they tore and grasped at one another, Delilah's wrist slipped through one of the gaps in the woven jute becoming entangled, as Joshua's foot did the same. Nervously laughing at the situation, they struggled in the hammock a bit longer, groping at one another, before giving up on the swaying swing entirely, untangling themselves, plopping out onto the gravel-covered ground of the hut.

The two embraced, Joshua sitting upright, Delilah on his lap. She pushed the man back as she pulled his stained cotton shirt over his plumage of blazing red hair that had grown long and unkempt during his time in residence on the island. Joshua following suit, removed Delilah's top as her breasts made their presence known. She clawed and grabbed at the curly fur adorning his full chest, sliding her hands around his wide back, running her fingertips, each spread wide, up into his thick scalp as she pulled the man into her. Delilah yearned to fill the void inside her, to thaw the shock of her father's passing. She hungered to feel a connection to something, to anything.

Under the direction of forces outside their control, lost to time and space the two disappeared into one another as they oscillated, vibrating like superstrings in the tenth dimension, giving heat and weight to the universe. Electromagnetism and gravity, energy and mass, meeting each other for the very first time, an unstoppable force pressed into an immovable object.

The energetic instability of their union of opposites caused an infinitely dense point to abruptly erupt in a fountain of endless potential. The exploding globules of the fountainhead's cosmic energy morphed and evolved under the guidance of gravity, taking on every imaginable shape and form possible: living, telling stories, dying.

"We shouldn't have done that," said Delilah, as she reached for her discarded button-up shirt, covering her exposed breasts; black and white checks striped the fabric. As she rushed to clothe herself, she felt overcome with a pre-installed sense of shame over her dalliance with Joshua. Her father's body wasn't even cold in the ground; what would the nuns from her Catholic parochial school have said to her. Without another word, she hurried back towards her dormitory while still struggling to get one leg through her now inexplicably ill-fitting pants; they were Joshua's pants.

Joshua sat there, on the ground, unable to move as he watched the woman he was falling in love with disappear into the darkness. His tummy rumbled some; Albus was hungry. Albus Joshua Cake laid back in the hammock wrapping some more blankets around himself and adjusted his mosquito netting; he slept that night, having many, many dreams, none of which he recalled upon waking.

29

X-CALIBER

The sun rose the next morning, as it had a habit of doing; those staying on the island anticipated its arrival by several hours, lying awake in the cots or bunks of their various vessels in the bewildering stillness of the pre-dawn. Sure enough, the abrading sunbeams exposed that they had not experienced a collective nightmare; Gellert's lifeless body still lay across one of the long tables, draped in the blossoms of early-morning light. Dee lifted her head from the table, roused from her state of half-sleep by the footsteps of her older sister creeping through the backdoor of the hall. "Where'd you go last night?" Dee asked with a degree of suspicion.

"What do you mean?" Delilah answered with a question.

"I looked around and you weren't here."

"Oh, I must have gone to the dorms to sleep."

"No. I checked down there too."

Rescued from her sister's inquisition as a few of the menfolk entered the mess, Delilah escaped her sister's probing line of questioning; she rushed to put a pot of coffee on the electric stove.

Some of the men hauled their meager collections of rusty handsaws, hammers, and nails, from their vessels along with them. Without speaking to one another, they began sawing, cutting apart the plywood dance floor that had been a source of such revelry only so many hours prior.

One man would hold a ripped plank in place as another hammered silently, cobbling together a ramshackle coffin large enough to house the Ox of New Detroit. A bleak task, to say the least, the men longed for a more respectable material to work with, some nicely planed mahogany, walnut, or oak, not the warped and waterlogged scraps available to them. Truly though, Gellert didn't mind.

Gellert's inert husk laid in the coffin, they all shuffled past offering their goodbyes, some placing their hands on the slain man's chest. A gut-wrenching sob leaked from Delilah's lips as she kissed her papa's brow one last time. Gellert had always gently kissed her square on the forehead each night before tucking her into bed; that was until she reached an age where she had forbidden her papa from continuing to do so, chiding him that she wasn't some "little kid" anymore. What she wouldn't give to feel his kiss against her brow in that moment.

Joshua, like the others, had been up before dawn. While the menfolk wrapped up their wood-working project he had gone to the palm cloistered cemetery. Doing what he did best, he dug a trench into the loose, shifty dirt six-feet in-depth, parallel to Delilah Earhart Fedora's headstone, certain Gellert would have been satisfied by his exacting dimensions.

A few of the more able-bodied hoisted the heavy wooden box onto their shoulders, solemnly walking it down the hidden jungle trail. Delilah, Dee, and the others followed after, Fin jingling behind the procession, darting in and out of the foliage creeping across the path.

Gellert, being the old ox that he was, had prepared for this day's inevitable arrival rather pragmatically during his waking life. Some years prior, he had taken it upon himself to carve his own headstone. The thought of leaving such grim, unfinished business to his children filled him with more dread than dying.

Joshua carted the man's headstone down from the workshop. Gellert's final project complete, they positioned the marker squarely at the head of the grave, wedging it into the dirt.

Delilah and Delilah held hands as they leaned a braided wreath of hibiscus, birds of paradise, and heliconia against the stone monument.

Chuck Diggity stepped forward and spoke a few words. He began to recite a well-known poem. "No man is an island, entire of itself; every man is a piece of the continent, apart of the main."

As Chuck spoke, a kaleidoscopic blur buzzed about the wreath; a tiny, colorful hummingbird zealously beat its wings against its breast, supping on the cut flowers of the wreath, garnering life-giving glucose from the dying stems. "And therefore never send to know for whom the bell tolls; it tolls for thee," Chuck concluded.

As they shoveled clods of earth over the coffin, Delilah tossed in a bird skull cast of bronze strung on a pale-green cord, it rattled some before hitting the dirt. Hugging the girls and saying their goodbyes, the guests left, sailing away in their airy vessels.

....

With the last of the guests gone, disappearing over the horizon, the settlement began to feel unsettlingly empty. The following weeks were shrouded in a dour and gloomy cloud as those left behind struggled to go about their lives with a huge, Gellert-sized hole punched prematurely through the middle. Gellert hadn't just been the girls' father, he was the chief, the progenitor of New Detroit; his absence left an unwanted power vacuum.

Joshua attempted to fill Gellert's very large shoes (quite literally, his own raggedy boots had disintegrated); he wholly committed himself to finish the irrigation networks, continue to plow and plant new plots, bring the Fertile Crescent up to the full potential of its fecundity. Though his new role certainly left him with no real power, no authority to make salvage requests of Delilah, or admonish Dee when she acted out, who had been spending a great deal of time locked away in her dorm, eating her lunch and dinners in solitude.

Following their late-night liaison on the night of her father's death, Delilah the Elder had reverted back to the awkward habit she had developed after she and Joshua had first kissed while bobbing up and down in the ocean. She took to mostly avoiding him, acting as if the whole thing never happened.

In the evenings after the quiet suppers, Albus would tinker away on Gellert's unfinished rocket. Although he had no faith in the project, he wanted to honor the man's legacy as he cussed through perplexing schematics and puzzling shorthand left behind by the father of New Detroit. Incorrectly soldering the anode and cathode wires to a tiny circuit board, Albus found himself thinking about Delilah, almost obsessively. Unlike Delilah, Albus couldn't pretend this time. He kept wondering if their midnight union was just some fluke, a one-time thing. *Did I do a bad job?*

In his heart he could no longer suppress the strong feelings growing for the captivating, curly-haired woman; he began to despair that she must not feel the same about him. Perhaps his devious plan to one day marry the Destroyer, then spend the rest of their lives together blissfully not destroying things, was failing.

Albus and Joshua grieved over gruesome, unwelcome fantasies propagated by his unsettled mind in which he would ultimately be forced to kill Delilah the Firstborn, Destroyer of Worlds, in some final showdown, before she could put an end to his precious world.

Unable to suffer in silence any longer, he approached Delilah the Elder one afternoon as she tended to a stand of semi-domesticated banana trees growing at the jungle's border. As she hacksawed bushels of the dwarfed, starchy fruits into a wicker basket, Joshua approached from behind her and said, "Hey, can we talk?"

Dreading this inevitable moment, Delilah turned, a bunch of yellow-green bananas grasped in her clenched fist. He hemmed and hawed at first, clumsily trying to convey his feelings for her. Tugging her in close, Albus whispered something into the woman's ear. She didn't whisper back in return. Offering only half-answers and couched explanations, claiming she needed some time still to process her father's death. Joshua felt his heart squeezed in a vice within his chest cavity. Despite being a perfectly reasonable response, it was not the answer he had hoped for; Albus dropped the issue, quietly replying that he understood.

In truth, Delilah cared a great deal for the man. She had very much fancied the closeness of their intimacy and wanted to do it again, many times again, to be exact. *I just can't.* The risk of getting close to him roused sleeping bugaboos that she had been forced to put down many years ago, just to survive. Outside of Dee and her father, everyone she had ever known or loved, had vanished on her in an instant; now her papa was gone too. She wept, but just barely, as she sawed away the last bushel. Again, she felt that sense of piecing vulnerability mixed with abstract notions of responsibility, of something potentially greater than herself.

Albus turned about to walk away from the banana stand; something that had been eating at him ever since his arrival in the Low Place vomited up. "There's something else I have to tell you..."

His dark secret, his real identity, his own cancer that had been festering inside needed to be purged, brought to the light and sanitized in the all-revealing rays of the sun. Delilah looked at him, waiting impatiently, eager to get back to harvesting the rest of her fruits. Struggling to come up with the words, he delayed hesitating further. *Maybe this isn't the best time.* The woman had just lost her father, after all.

"Out with it?"

"Those are some nice-looking bananas," Albus said, pivoting away. "Keep up the good work." He walked off, offering a clumsy and unnecessary thumbs up.

The specter of Gellert's passing haunted them less and less as time crawled, though his absence could always be felt if one looked for it. The three had begun supping together again, giving thanks; however, they did not converse as freely or jovially as in the past. One might turn away from the table and briefly release a sob into their napkin, returning to their bowl of creamed oats or pickled jungle potato.

On one very average morning, Albus sat on a stool in an animal pen behind the mess; he milked the teats of the wild boar sow, that they had named Megan. Between squirts of warm boar's milk, he was thinking about nothing in particular when Delilah entered the enclosure behind him. Albus spun in place on his milking stool; a few moments of silence passed interrupted only by the heavy breathing and snorts of Megan, before Delilah said, "It's time I show you something."

Judging by her tone, Albus didn't question further. He set his pail down as a few sloshes of milk were lost over the sides and followed after Delilah the Elder. She led the man down the scarped incline towards the placid lagoon. As they sidewinded down the embankment the shuffling of their feet kicked loose a few small rocks. Stones and pebbles tumbled down the steep sides, creating dry, dusty trails in their wake as they rolled, the ephemeral trails temporal testaments of the stone's actions, before they were hastily erased, blown away by the gentle breeze.

From the embankment, they headed west along the beach of the wide, circular pool, coming up on the Fertile Crescent, still in a state of disarray. Cain the scarecrow eyed them sorrowfully as they passed. Walking along the curving shore of the lagoon past the crescent a few miles north, they made their way towards the base of the large waterfall pouring out the jungle over the cliff's edge.

Approaching the bottom of the cascade that fell fifty or sixty-feet through empty space before splashing down into the crisp coolness of the lagoon, Delilah crept carefully along some slicked rocks hugging the base of the sheer cliff face. Joshua inched along behind her; she disappeared behind the roar.

....

The wide torrent of rushing water concealed a hidden pocket, a cavern that receded some forty-feet into the rock of the cliff face. A sparse collection of nubby stalactites growing thirty-feet overhead dripped onto the cavern's smooth, flat floor, dampening it, forming small puddles in some spots. Strewn about the cave in the haphazard fashion of a teenage girl's bedroom were toolboxes, welding torches, and various piles of scrap.

In the poor lighting, Joshua craned his neck side-to-side, trying to make sense of what exactly he was looking at, and more importantly why it could possibly be so significant to Delilah. "This...is my super-secret side project," she said with a sense of pride. Parked on a pair of wooden beams in the center of the hidden crevasse, sat the hull of a threadbare, mastless sailboat about thirty-three feet in length. The sailboat, if restored to a seaworthy state, looked as though it could house three people in cramped quarters.

Joshua approached the vessel with some skepticism, unsure where Delilah was going with this. Abandoned half-junked sailboats weren't all that hard to come by in the wastes; furthermore, they had a functional speeder and a mini-sub at their disposal. Standing next to the boat's stripped-down hull, grinning like a newborn mother, Delilah beamed, "I call her the X-Caliber. She's named after—"

"After the sword of Arthurian legend bestowed upon the rightful king by the Lady of the Lake," Albus interjected.

"What? No, you nerd! Mansplain much?" Delilah teased and continued, "No. After my favorite show, X-Caliber."

Joshua went on to protest that mansplaining wasn't just when a man explained something to a woman, it was when a man explained something to a woman—in a condescending way. "Oh..." he said in sheepish realization, and shut his mouth.

"You done?" X-Caliber, Delilah continued, was a TV show, a smash-hit crime drama that would air every Monday night. The show was about a sentient, talking pistol (yes, an intelligent firearm), that was also a hard-bitten, ace detective. And who could forget X-Caliber's partner, the lovable but simple Ralph Mandu. The duo were tasked with solving the most heinous and vicious crimes. She had seen every episode and was practically obsessed. The X-Caliber series finale had been slated to air the night the Cancer erupted; she never got to see the end.

Walking around the craft inspecting it further, he spied a number of steel cables attached to the rim of the hull with pieces of tack and metal hardware; the cables ran up and over the port side, their ends hooked into large deflated bladders resting like soggy flapjacks draped around the side of the hull. The boat was further retrofitted with two airplane propellers sticking out the stern, amongst other puzzling modifications, *Is that an exercise bike on deck?* Coming up at a loss, "But what is it?" asked Joshua.

"It's a dirigible!" exclaimed Delilah, no look of recognition dawning on Joshua's face "...a Zeppelin?" she clarified. Still nothing. "...like in the Indiana Jones movies," she said flatly. That time he got it.

Delilah divulged her purpose behind harvesting the gas-filled hearts of blue-eyed automata; she had been saving the helium contained within to one day inflate the craft's air bladder. She already had hundreds of the gassy sacks trapped in mesh bags around her cavernous workshop. Once she had sequestered a sufficient amount of helium, she would simply float through the air; sailing right over the Cancer's origin, she could drop her devastating Adam bomb, blowing it to kingdom come. She claimed the idea had come to her in a daydream one afternoon as she lay on a deserted beach watching the clouds.

Albus momentarily panicked over the revelation—the De-stroyer did have a plan to deliver her world-ending payload after all. Then a wave of relief, he recalled that the black mass could recognize any threat to its existence that attempted to fly over it. Her resistance was futile. The Cancer would simply skewer the X-Caliber, and Delilah along with it, right out of the air. *It will kill her.*

Then once again more panic, somehow, he had to persuade Delilah, the woman he was in love with, not to undertake such a doomed, foolhardy suicide mission; he needed to convince her to give up on her dreams. Albus opened his mouth, intending to remind Delilah of the Cancer's always watchful, ever-searching, air defenses.

As if reading his mind, Delilah silenced Joshua, placing one finger to his parted lips. She beamed more broadly than before. With a flourish, she climbed aboard the X-Caliber's deck; somewhere near the ship's wheel, she began flipping banks of toggle switches. Metal nozzles studded innocuously across the exterior of the vessel's hull, began to hiss, emitting a misty vapor. Flipping more switches, the rest of the nozzles began to sputter as well, filling the cavern with white mist.

Delilah and her airship faded from view, consumed by the growing fog. Slowly, realization began to dawn on Albus' face. He experienced a brief flashback; he has awoken in the Low Place on the side of the dune, smothered in confusion and suffering, his neck craned up the coiling biomechanical edifice in front of him, only clouds passing overhead.

"It's a cloud!" shouted Delilah with jubilation, completely concealed behind her incredibly convincing cumulus camouflage. "The Cancer doesn't recognize clouds as threats! It doesn't attack them!" It was genius. It was brilliant. Why had he ever doubted this beautiful, brilliant woman?

Clenching his fist, a vein tensed in his forehead; Albus' mission flashed before him yet again in bright-red neon lights, on and off again: kill the destroyer, save his world. The impetus and specifics of which had gotten a bit hazy with the passage of time, confusing himself further he questioned, *Or was it to find my wife, or kill Golgotha, or retrieve a needle at the end of a book, or eat a bowl of udon soup with a fox?* It was ambitious—but maybe there was some way he could accomplish all of the above.

Delilah further explained that she had been working on the airship in total secrecy over the last few years, not even daring to whisper mention of its existence to Fin the fox. Had her father ever caught wind of what she intended to do, he would have never allowed her to pursue it. Possibly even going so far as to destroy the X-Caliber in an attempt to protect his baby girl; therefore, Dee definitely couldn't know either.

She had come across the deserted hull out in the wastes, laying on its side, castaway on the shore of an uninhabited island. A spitting image of the boat from her daydream, it was the perfect vessel to become her X-Caliber. While her father was away from the homestead, attending to rebuilding the temple, she had returned for the shell. Towing the busted-up husk with her speeder through the lagoon, she tucked it away into her hidden alcove. Clandestinely converting the junked boat into a flying weapon of war underneath the shroud of the cataracts, she would slip out from her dorm at nights, her sister snoring loudly, to covertly haul surplus canvas, cables, and parts from their salvage heaps to her cavernous berth.

···········

Albus and Joshua wrestled with himself, perhaps he could destroy the airship. *No*, he was the only one that knew about it, besides that would be like really, really mean. As he pondered, Delilah stepped down from the vessel emerging from the halo of her nimbus. The triumphant expression faded from her face, turning more serious; her full, upturned lips relaxed, pressing together some.

Approaching Joshua, "There's something else I have to tell you," she said. This newly somber Delilah filled Albus with dread; he could feel the time skeins reverberating with some information of importance. He could only assume what she would say next would be consequential, world changing even. Pulling the man she was falling in love with close into her, she whispered into his ear, "I'm pregnant…"

A baseball bat studded in nine-inch nails bashed him in the stomach, at least that was how he felt. Enoch wasn't kidding about his new body working down to the letter. Joshua took a few steps backwards and involuntarily sank onto the closed lid of a rusted, red toolbox, sitting on it while he processed Delilah's revelation; his head hung low covering his mouth with his palms. This wasn't part of the plan. Joshua wasn't sure he was ready to be a father, though he was certainly a willing participant in its conception; the choice was now largely out of his hands. To bring a child into such a broken, crumbling world seemed irresponsible, cruel even.

Delilah did not share the same dismay. To her knowledge,

there hadn't been a child born, let alone conceived, to their abandoned and dying world since the Cancer took over. Crouching alongside the father of her unborn child, she placed a warm, affirming hand on Albus' shoulder and said, "Don't you get it?" This was something bigger than her, bigger than him, bigger than either of them, this was hope.

30

LABOR

Joshua took the news of the pregnancy in stride; Albus reasoned that there was some small silver lining. With Delilah expecting it would at least slow down the progress some on her world-destroying airship anointed with sword sobriquet; perhaps foolishly, he hoped after the baby was born, she would give up on the silly notion entirely. He decided it best to stick his hands in the sand and continue about his back-breaking labor.

The digging of trenches and laying of pipes, which had already been an arduous and slow-going endeavor with two people, had slowed to a three-toed tanuki's pace with Gellert *just gone*. He yanked up a cluster of potatoes, their leaves a limp yellow color; Albus stared disappointingly at the underdeveloped, wrinkled bulbs dangling before him. *How am I supposed to provide for another when I can barely provide for myself?* Frustrated by his progress (or lack thereof), toiling under the exceedingly hot mid-day sun that afternoon, Albus had a stroke of genius, or possibly just a stroke; it was hard to tell.

"No way. They can't be trusted," Delilah argued.

"We need the help," countered Joshua.

In exasperation, she yelled, "What would my father think!"

"Gellert's gone, Delilah!" Joshua regrettably rebutted.

Delilah burst into tears and fled from the mess hall. Joshua hollered behind her, chasing after her towards the living quarters, down the clanking metal stairs to the basement dormitories. She slammed the door to her room in his face. Joshua, well aware that he had royally fucked up, pounded at Delilah's door with his brawny fist. Leaning up against the locked steel door, "Look...I'm..." he muttered, "It's just something I have to do." No response.

In a huff Joshua gathered a rucksack, hastily cramming it with a few days supplies and made for the pebble-strewn shoreline. Absconding with Delilah's apricot speeder, he kicked the hovercraft into gear as he scrolled through the vehicle's logs, querying for the coordinates of his quarry. Punching in the latitude and longitude of the small cay from their last adventure, he set a course for Colonel Mustard's clan and sped out over the open seas.

Thankfully, the journey to the Colonel's cay was an uneventful affair, nothing but smooth sailing. The inclement weather of the previous few weeks had subsided, taking its deluge of rain and wind elsewhere; only clear skies and bloated cumulus clouds floated overhead. Had Joshua pushed straight through, he could have covered the distance in a day's time. His eyelids growing heavy, eclipsing green irises, his mortal body was awash with sleepiness as his distracted and overtaxed brain endeavored to stay on course; he chose to inflate the speeder's ventral air-bladders and allow the craft to gently rock him up and down on the ocean waves while he caught a few hours of shuteye.

As he dozed, he thought a lot about Delilah; their heated exchange had been their first real fight, he reckoned. Joshua wished he had conducted himself differently, better; he vowed to offer her a real apology upon his return, hoping the fruits of his venture would vindicate him some in Delilah's eyes. Feeling rested he started out again moments before the sun peeked from behind the perfectly flat horizon, arriving sometime around mid-morning at the narrow islet. The scene was comfortably unchanged; the automaton Colonel's dilapidated hovel still stood some fifty yards up the slivered strand of beach, though the plot of sunflowers looked to be much healthier, thriving in fact, not a trampled or broken stalk in sight.

Bright red eyes stared at him through the glass-less windows as Colonel Mustard sallied forth to greet the familiar face approaching from the direction of the shoreline. Still wielding his rusty pitchfork, the Colonel once again spastically waved his skeletal arm, welcoming Joshua, inviting the man in, this time for brunch. Fricassee rabbit and mustard greens—yet again, he had a sneaking suspicion that it was always rabbit and stewed greens at the Colonel's house. No complaints from Joshua, he was not one to ever turn down a hot meal to calorically placate his unceasing hunger.

Over brunch, Albus laid out his proposal to Mustard and kin. He wanted to recruit the humanoids, relocate them to New Detroit to assist in farming and various construction projects. In exchange for their labor, the clan of automata would have unparalleled access to the settlement's human inhabitants. They would be allowed to observe them at all times: learn their ways. It was a creepy bargain to say the least, but one that Joshua hoped would prove to be well worth it.

The automaton patriarch mulled over the offer, turning to other members of his clan, his red eyes flashing in rapid bursts. The other skeletal humanoids looked back and forth at one another; their glowing eyes began flashing alarmingly, as well. Joshua grew momentarily anxious; he hadn't thought to bring his loaned pistol and was starting to feel that may have been a short-sighted decision. Eventually, the pulsating half-orbs of the man-made creatures began to sync up, all strobing in unison with one another as beads of sweat formed on Joshua's brow.

Mustard slowly looked over to his guest. "Why we'd be delighted to aid your kinfolk in their time of desperate need," he crowed, in his now familiar artificial accent. Relieved, Joshua shook Mustard's bony hand, sealing the deal. They hammered out the specifics of the agreement; over the following week Joshua would return, transporting the automata three-by-three, back to the island of New Detroit.

Initially, Delilah was not pleased with the growing presence of the supposedly friendly machines, though she could not deny that the additional labor they provided had its benefits. Joshua had written her a lengthy, heartfelt apology for how he had conducted himself prior; she felt she would be able to forgive the red-headed jerk, eventually. Though she still chose to not speak to him for the next few days to drive her point home.

....

The automata set to work on the irrigation project with glee, digging trenches through the fertile soil and fitting pipes into place without an iota of complaint. Chores requiring a more delicate touch, like collecting the iguana eggs from their coops or milking their captured boar sow were still left to the human inhabitants. One hot, steamy morning as Joshua relieved himself in the stall of the composting toilet, a pair of glowing, red orbs burst unannounced through the privy porthole. "What are you doing, Joshua?" blabbered Mustard through his speaker box.

"For the hundredth time, Colonel...I'm pooping," replied the man, unamused as his cheeks turned red as the machine's eyes.

"Pooping," said the automata patriarch as though he had just plucked some valuable lost wedding band out of the surf. Later that morning Joshua observed the artificial creature in the field, squatting in front of his compatriots, bobbing and swaying slightly; the machine elicited a series of evenly spaced grunts through its vocoder. The rest of his cohorts chuckled mechanically, shrugging their pneumatic shoulders up and down in rhythmic succession with one another. Minor humiliation was a small price to pay for the much-needed help.

....

Colonel Mustard's kin were most tickled when they learned of Delilah's pregnancy. At night the automata would stand over her as she slept, their pervading, red eyes twinkling a dubious signal to decipher, a child's night-light fashioned in the likeness of the boogeyman. When the machines thought no one was looking, they would sneak pats and rubs of Delilah's continually ripening belly with their calcified, gaunt hands.

However, the ghoulish agreement struck by Joshua and Mustard was proving to be worthwhile. The ceaseless labor of the artificial humanoids made short work of the irrigation project; what had taken Gellert and Joshua months to accomplish, the tireless automata completed in a matter of weeks.

In a relatively short time, their crops now properly hydrated, fertilized, and attended to, the clan of human survivors found that they had more vegetables and grains than they knew what to do with. For the first instance in its history, New Detroit had a surplus, some might even say a cornucopia, of food. If only Gellert could see them now.

They pickled and canned what they could, eventually running out of pickling jars and cans. The squat stone silos that Gellert had erected in anticipation of this fortuitous day, that had stood empty for so long, were brimming to their edges with potatoes, soybeans, wheat, and corn; and yet the twelve machines still showed no signs of slowing, dumping bucket after bucket of harvested crops into the overflowing repositories.

....

As it so often goes, solving old problems only creates new problems; it was quickly becoming clear that they had harvested more foodstuffs than Joshua, Dee, and Delilah could possibly consume before it all began to spoil. Even when factoring in the pregnant woman's avid appetite and the impending arrival of a new mouth to feed, there was still more than enough to go around.

Without a doubt, it was a good problem to have. However, it felt like a reprehensible sin to let so much highly coveted caloric gold potentially go to rot. Debating what to do with their ever-growing supply, Delilah the Elder called an emergency meeting. Gathering around a table in the mess, Joshua suggested that they establish trade routes with survivors on other islands. Delilah pointed out, rather astutely, if word spread too far and wide that they possessed such an abundance, New Detroit would become an instant target. They didn't have the numbers to defend themselves against marauders and looters looking for easy prey. Dee agreed with her older sister. Besides, what could their neighbors, like the old hermit Ms. Matilda, possibly trade that they didn't already have. It wasn't worth the risks involved.

Dee proposed that they continue to realize her late father's vision, starting by extending an invitation to Abram's family, the Hams: come join them at New Detroit. The Hams could contribute to the rebuilding of society, safety in numbers, that sort of thing. Hadn't that always been her father's dream, she asked rhetorically. Perhaps rather deviously, Delilah the Middle didn't give a crap about rebuilding society or any of that; selfishly, she just wanted an excuse to spend more time with Abram.

Joshua and the pregnant Delilah began to nod as they mulled the proposal over; it wasn't a bad idea. Delilah voiced some mild concern. With a child on the way, she was hesitant about upsetting their delicate ecosystem by introducing new people. Though, she thought highly of the Hams; she had only ever had positive interactions with them. Additionally, she recalled Mrs. Ham mentioning she had worked as a nurse in the time before. Deciding that the pros outweighed the cons, she voted in favor of the proposal. The issue was settled; voting unanimously, they would extend a formal offer of citizenship to their island neighbors, the Hams.

....

Over breakfast the following morning, they decided the best way to go about the offer would be to send a formal ambassador. There weren't a lot of options for the open position. Delilah, plagued by a bout of morning sickness, felt too ill to go; that only left Dee or Joshua to fill the role. Dee was too young and irresponsible to be trusted with the speeder, therefore, the de facto choice was Joshua. Dee complained loudly; Joshua was too big and dumb for such an important diplomatic liaison. Crossing her arms, she stomped her foot, demanding to be part of the delegation as well.

Delilah, who had been up before dawn vomiting into a

bucket, was far too exhausted to deal with her little sister's bullshit and looked over to Joshua. He shrugged; he wasn't opposed, though not entirely keen on leaving his ailing pregnant partner unattended for a long stretch of time. Delilah assured Joshua she would be fine. The Ham's island was only a few hundred miles away; they could be there and back in the speeder before sundown. Joshua hadn't spent any real quality time alone with Dee, perhaps it would be beneficial to get to know the soon-to-be auntie of his unborn child. That was that then; New Detroit's first two ambassadors struck out on their inaugural mission.

"So…" said Joshua spinning his gears, trying to conjure some common ground to discuss with the teenager.

"Silence," commanded the former Cleopatra. Joshua was more than fine with that.

Some hours later they arrived on the Ham's island, a smallish, flat belch of land encompassed by a wide white sand beach, a fetid jungle occupying the middle, the Ham's sailboat moored nearby offshore. The Hams had built three modest arboreal huts high off the ground, treehouses essentially, perched in a grouping of sturdy Banyan trees at the edge of the marshy jungle, connected together by swaying rope bridges. During monsoons, the low-lying brackish swamps of their island would overflow, making the elevated lifestyle much more preferable.

The Hams were in far more dire straits than they had ever let on at any of the gatherings, not wishing to burden their fellow survivors with their troubles. The only freshwater aquifer on their flat island had run dry almost a year back; ever since then they had been dependent on capricious rain gods for the majority of their potable water. Additionally, their island lacked any decent-sized tracts of arable soil, constraining them to only grow small gardens scattered about their homestead, foraging and trapping the rest of their sustenance from the wilds of the scraggly jungle.

Mr. and Mrs. Ham were elated to spot Joshua and Dee pull up in Delilah's recognizable apricot speeder and strode down the beach to greet them. Abram was off in the jungle at the moment, busy throwing a stone knife into the pulpy trunk of a banana tree.

The Hams invited the two would-be diplomats into their humble home; Dee and Joshua climbed up a rope ladder, entering the couple's living room through a hatch in the floor. Mrs. Ham passed around split coconut shells for refreshment, offering again her condolences for Gellert's passing, asking how they had been getting on in the recent months. This was Dee's moment to shine. She blurted out that her sister was pregnant, Fin was recovering some from her father's loss, and that Joshua had done something smart for once; he had enslaved a bunch of automata to do their bidding.

Joshua spat the coconut water from his mouth; interrupting Dee, he clarified that the automata were not, in fact, enslaved, but that he had struck a deal with them. In exchange for their labor the humanoids could observe them and learn their human ways, something the artificial creatures seemed to hold in high regard for inexplicable reasons. The automata had been an undeniable boon for New Detroit, allowing them to grow and harvest a huge surplus of food, which led them to the purpose of their visit.

"We'd like you to come live with us," said Joshua.

"Become our new city-zens," added Delilah the Younger.

....

Mrs. Ham looked over at her rugged, hard-working husband. She hugged the man around the neck, tears beginning to stream down her cheeks as she did. Mr. Ham remained stoic, though was certainly moved by the godsend. He and his family had been struggling a great deal on their island in recent months. The malaria he had contracted a number of years back had relapsed recently, causing him to cough and hack while undertaking any strenuous activity, severely limiting him around his homestead. Truth be told, he wasn't sure how much longer they would last; especially after their sailboat had been so brazenly broken into and looted of crucial supplies. Mr. Ham swore the amount of looting and marauding had been worsening, growing bolder, ever since the terrible news of Gellert's passing had begun to spread.

Exiting their treehouse, Mr. Ham hollered towards the jungle calling out for his son. Abram came trudging from behind a few palms several moments later; Dee's lips entwined in a devious smile. The Hams could not thank New Detroit's ambassadors enough for the magnanimous offer. Abram, shielded by his parents as to just how dire their situation was, complained some at first, saying that he would only leave if he could bring his pet parrot, Tooty, along as well. Joshua saw no issue with the boy's request; gladly, he granted the wish. As they nailed down a time table for the migration, Dee, ever boy-crazy for the lanky teenager, suggested, "Why not just leave today?" Mr. and Mrs. Ham looked back and forth at one another, failing to invoke any sound reason why that couldn't be done; they were more than ready to set sail for greener pastures.

Joshua looked down at his shortened shadow. The sun had just barely scraped past its midpoint overhead; there was still plenty enough daylight left to make it back to his awaiting Delilah before dark. He turned to Dee suggesting, that in the spirit of their newly formed alliance, they hang back and help the Hams prepare to relocate. Shockingly, Dee gladly agreed with him; even going so far as to claim that if he hadn't proposed it, she was going to. The two volunteered, assisting the Hams with packing what meager possessions and valuables they owned into milk crates, plastic industrial drums, washtubs, and any other kind of container that had washed up on shore over the years, carting the packed containers onto the moored sailboat. Mrs. Ham held up a silver hairbrush that had been passed down from her grandmother and showed it to Dee; the teenager politely feigned interest.

Dee aided Mrs. Ham in uprooting a couple types of herbs and fruiting plants from her garden, delicately wrapping their clumpy roots in dampened sackcloth. Though they were preparing to embark for a settlement that had an abundance of food crops, the Hams possessed a few species absent from New

Detroit's ecosystem: cucumbers, hot peppers, tomatoes, beets, dwarf key limes, and an adolescent avocado tree that would start bearing its fatty fruits in a few years' time.

....

Joshua hugged Tooty's birdcage into his chest as he carried the cloth draped enclosure towards the lolling sailboat, when he heard a piercing, otherworldly screech. "Albus Cake did nine eleven!" Startled out of his boots for more reasons than one, he unintentionally dropped the birdcage into the sand as the aquamarine blanket slid quickly off its side, revealing a very angry, all-grey parrot clutching and biting at the rungs of its confinement. Abram, who had been walking alongside Joshua, arms loaded with several sacks of DIY parrot feed, dropped his load as well, as he rushed over towards his agitated, highly-intelligent bird. "Albus Cake did nine eleven!!" the African Grey parrot loudly squawked again. Abram, crouching beside his pet bird's cage, attempted to soothe the distressed creature, placating it with chunks of carrot he slipped between the bars into its clacking beak.

Joshua still hadn't moved. The voice of an aged and mystical man, a voice belonging to a character in a movie he had watched many moons ago with Delilah, drifted through the confines of his mind, *Now that's a name I've not heard in a long time...* Albus rushed to his own defense *What?! What is that imbecile bird yammering?!...I...I didn't 'do' nine eleven.* Joshua's heart raced; it beat rapidly as his mouth went dry. *...it was ...it was that dirty rat... We were betrayed!* Albus' eyes darted around the beach, glancing at the others, frantically attempting to ascertain if his cover had been finally blown.

"Bet she startled you," offered Abram as the salty bird eventually piped down.

Joshua snapped back to the beach. "Huh? Uh yeah," said Albus nervously laughing. "Gave me a good scare."

"It's just some nonsense," said Abram. "No one know what it means. Some phrase she picked up before I found her. An earworm, my mom calls it."

Abram suggested he swap with Joshua; the boy covered his parrot's cage with the calming scrap of cloth and awkwardly carried the enclosure (that was far too large for him to adequately get his arms around) the rest of the way to the boat. Albus scooped the sacks of bird feed out of the sand, loading them into the vessel as well.

Their sailboat packed to the gills, Mr. Ham and his son rigged the sails, hoisting the main sheet up its mast, flying their family's distinguished crest, a spiral ham with a two-pronged fork pressed into its flesh. Standing on deck, the family of three enthusiastically waved towards their literal saviors, shouting that they would see them again in a few days' time as Joshua and Dee embarked on the hovercraft, speeding ahead of the antiquated, slow-going dreadnought.

....

Albus stared blankly towards the horizon as he piloted the speeder, mutually ignoring Delilah the Middle who was scribbling some drivel with pink and purple ink in a partially singed notebook; he was still shaken by the shrieking Tooty's accusatory revelation. *Does someone, somewhere really think I did nine eleven? That I'm solely responsible for all this?*

He continued to stew over such a notion the entirety of the short ride back to their homestead. Parking the speeder, making their way for supper, Albus found himself unable to derive any joy from the success of their first diplomatic mission, when a familiar and comfortable odor snuck up on him, grappling its way ninja-like up Joshua's nostrils. Delilah was preparing his favorite, muskrat and veggie stew.

Joshua entered the mess to spot Delilah standing at the stove, sprinkling the finishing touches into the large aluminum pot, her back turned. He waltzed over to the pregnant woman, gently wrapping her about her expanding tummy with his strong, fur-smattered arms, pulling Delilah away from the electric stove into him. Delilah giggled. Before she could extricate herself from his embrace, Joshua buried his face into her bouncy dark-brown curls, his pugilist's nose rooting about her tangled mess, inhaling deeply: salt, safety, joy, orange tang.

....

Four days later, Dee, who was currently on beastie watch, spotted the Ham's hammy crest cresting over the horizon. It was about time. Delayed by a day or two on their way by inclement weather, the Hams had finally arrived at the growing island sanctuary of New Detroit. The elder Delilah welcomed their newest residents with the unintentional grace of a reluctant queen. Her pregnant belly swelled to about six months now; Mrs. Ham patted it tenderly, swearing it was a boy by how Delilah was carrying.

Delilah directed Mr. Ham to sail their tall ship around to the Eastern side of the island, bring it between the narrow gap in the coral atoll where the lagoon's edge met the sea. Mooring the easy-to-spot schooner hidden in the lagoon would maintain some of their anonymity from the prying eyes of looters. The haggard dreadnaught docked, they all pitched in, helping the Hams unpack, doing their best to make them feel welcome. After showing them to their quarters, Dee eagerly gave the recent arrivals a tour of their new home, adroitly explaining that she was the one really in charge here; they just let her know should they have any questions or need anything.

....

The next few months proceeded as smoothly and uneventfully as a pregnancy can in a post-apocalyptic hell-scape. New Detroit now had a population of six people, twelve automata, Abram's petulant pet parrot, Tooty, and one fennec fox, Fin. The new transplants meshed well, pulling their weight, supping together, idyllically idling by the lagoon on Sundays. Dee was perhaps the most thrilled by the Ham's recent relocation; Abram and her were dating now as evidenced by the myriad of braided, multi-colored bracelets the boy was now required to wear around his wrist at all times.

Delilah shook an empty box. "We're out of Nilla Wafers," she hummed, irritated at everything and everyone for things they had done to aggravate her, but she couldn't recall exactly what their crimes were at the moment. Using her eyes, she bore a hole through the back of Joshua's skull, prompting him to take action as the eight-and-a-half-month pregnant woman rattled the empty box again; this time aimed directly at the man sitting a few paces away, minding his own business.

At the moment, Joshua was playing dominoes with Reginald Beauregard Esq., an automaton he had taken weeks to teach the game. Delilah was silently furious that their child was inches away from B-day and Joshua still hadn't had the wherewithal or insight to ask for her hand in marriage. Though she was certain to make no mention of it, often scoffing at ideas like marriage; she would call such things unneeded and outdated institutions. Maybe he was waiting a few more days, making sure everything was perfect for the proposal that she was convinced he was planning.

"I hear yah," Joshua replied, straining diligently to abate any snappiness from his voice. "I'll make a run." This would be the third run in four weeks. In truth, he was relieved to have an excuse to get away from camp for a few days, get some time to himself. He needed to clear his head; tempers had been getting tense as the impending birth approached.

Each inhabitant of New Detroit had to come to grips with the reality of it, that there would be a new reality living amongst them in a few short weeks. Delilah would be a mom. Dee would become an aunt, a duty she anticipated with relish; she was certain the title would provide her with some new levels of authority to lord over others. Abram would remain exactly as he was, unchanged, a teenage boy. Abram's parents suspected they would become surrogate grandparents and welcomed the exciting transformation best they could. The settlement hummed along, poised to welcome a new being into its midst; yet in the secluded privacy of their thoughts anxieties danced on sun-baked sand. What was to become of the babe—become of them all? One day the end would come, even for New Detroit.

....

Albus slapped his last domino down, rose from his wooden stool, and shrouded himself in goggles and a dark-grey duster, a looted overcoat he had taken to wearing recently, with zero sense of irony. Hoisting his rucksack over his shoulder, a black rubber gas mask hooked with a carabiner into the straps, he made his way towards the door. Tooty cocked her gray head and squawked from her palm frond and shit-lined cage. "Albus Cake did nine eleven!" "RRRwAAH." "Albus Cake did nine ElevEn!!"

Shut up, you stupid bird! he thought, as he quickly strode past the metal cage, steeling any twitches of his facial expressions against the annoyance, and one might even say *guilt?* that he felt inside, over the avian accusation. The phrase meant absolutely nothing to the others, some forgotten syllogism the bird had latched onto long before Abram had begged his parents to let him keep the motley fool. Albus knew he didn't "*do nine eleven.*" *Well not like that anyway.* Regardless, the insinuation unsettled him all the same.

His mood soured by the parrot's off-handed heckle, Albus became increasingly irritated by the notion that the dumb bird, with the vocabulary of a speak-n-spell, had no understanding— no concept—behind the meaning of the words it so delighted in parroting. *Or did it?* he wondered absently.

....

He looked about blankly for a moment at his all-blue surroundings; having no recollection of how he had gotten there, Albus found himself zipping along behind the controls of the speeder over open-ocean, the homestead shrinking in size behind him to a pea-sized point in space.

Accelerating away at two-hundred miles per hour, Joshua reclined his seat; he activated the vehicle's cruise-control while he loosely steered with his feet propped on the wheel. The warm sun beating down on his now permanently freckled and sun-burnt cheeks banished all thoughts of the mimicking macaw from his mind. Parting the water behind him, the downforce of his thrusters cut undulating waves across the otherwise calm surface. It wasn't a beautiful day by any measure, but it was a day nonetheless and it was most beautiful. He thought, in all honesty, it was something of a paradise, this Low Place.

It didn't really matter in which direction he went. As long as he stayed away from the black mass, he would eventually intersect some razed city, some ruins partially reclaimed by nature, most they had already combed over many dozens of times by now. The chances of finding unopened, still edible Nilla Wafers was slimmer than a Slim Jim. Still, Joshua took the time to stop off at an old stomping ground and have a look. Traipsing around, he kicked empty cans about a civilization past its prime; coming up empty-handed, he sped on.

....

The indicator lights on the craft's dash began to blink at him; in his absentminded rush to get away from the settlement, he had not checked the speeder's charge level before taking off. The battery was dying. Currently over the open ocean in the middle of nowhere, he had to act quickly. As the craft's last will and testament, Albus funneled the remaining battery juice into inflating the ventral air-sacs. The thrusters cutting out, the speeder came to a skid on top of the waves, spraying Albus with a cold saltwater bath that whooshed over the sides.

Not the end of the world, all he had to do was set up the emergency solar-array; the photovoltaic panels would slowly charge the craft's aging battery while he endured some time "helplessly" stranded at sea. He retrieved the solar-array out of the speeder's trunk from where he had also conveniently stashed a fishing rod, along with a quart or two of Gellert's infamous moonshine; the location of the brown jugs' hidden coordinates left behind in one of Gellert's many notebooks, Albus had "mysteriously uncovered" them concealed within the jungle brush some weeks prior. Two shiny jetpacks secured in the trunk laid near the jugs. *I might just fire you up, later,* thought Joshua.

Albus propped an off-white pup-tent around the edges of the open-topped cockpit, providing some refuge; the midday sun was hot. He dangled the corked jugs of moonshine tethered tightly with twine to the sides of the floating craft, the ocean keeping them cool. Lazily, he cast out a line with the fishing rod while casually knocking back burning gulps of the uncut caustic spirits. Not expecting to catch anything, he didn't. Getting more boozed up than he intended, he couldn't help but think for a moment about he and Elixabeth on that beach so long ago; he was saddened by how the way things had ended—even though they had to end.

He knew he wasn't supposed to think these thoughts anymore. He was in love with Delilah; he was going to be a dad soon—but he did. He no longer felt any longing for Elixabeth from within that deep, scarred-over chamber inside his heart. He only wished that it all hadn't had to end so stupidly, in such a flaming turd fireball. He didn't like these thoughts. Backsliding onto an old, wobbly crutch, Albus imbibed swig after swig of the acrid shine (that one could scour corroded battery terminals with, in a pinch). His fishing pole flagging, he eventually blacked out.

As the loose flaps of his pup-tent waved in the wind, beating against one another, the bobbing hovercraft continued to drift, passively recharging its battery-cells in the presumably indifferent sunbeams, no one at the helm.

31

AND ENOCH
WALKED
WITH GOD

Back at Golgotha's palace, the bombastic fat man sat with his bloated mainframe wedged into his favorite La-Z-Boy, reclining in the lower depths of his entertainment wing; his thick eyelids hung halfway down. For an all-knowing entity he had a terrible concept of time and space. Damp, poorly-chewed flecks of puffed-corn smacked from his lax lips in an orange-tinted miasma as his trunk shoveled troves of the vaguely peanut-shaped Cheese-Os into his open mouth between snorting breaths. Finishing off his sixth bag of Chet's latest recipe, his free hands were already ripping into the foil of bag number seven.

Sitting next to him, his body sprawled out across a black corduroy beanbag chair mushrooming across the floor, was Golgotha's good friend Cheshire Cheato. Golgotha detested Chet, but for reasons different than Albus. The lazy, speckled cheetah rolled to his side atop his mushy, toadstool-like throne that squished and crinkled beneath his unambitious movements, grasping for his opulent crystal bong resting in front of him on the thick rug. His stoned, oversized paws knocked the tall water-pipe over spilling rancid, ash-rich bong water out onto Golgotha's plush Afghan rugs and Oriental floor coverings. The cheetah-man shot to attention, fumbling to right the fetid, leaking bong before his boss took notice.

Of course, Golgotha being all-knowing, already knew. When the elephantine tyrant elicited no response to Chet's graceless gaffe, the cheetah incorrectly assumed he had gotten away with the incident free of recourse; little did he know, Golgotha had already charged his infinitely growing tab with the cost to completely re-carpet the entire wing.

The two were idly eyeing a rebroadcast of an NHL hockey game, the New Jersey Devils versus the Los Angeles Kings, on Golgotha's collection of Jumbotrons. Cheshire Cheato putzed with his wobbly, ostentatious water-pipe composed of a useless number of interlocking crystalline bulbs and clear glass chambers, pinching-off and sprinkling into the bowl of the smoking apparatus a questionable witch's brew of shredded flower power, crushed gemstones from a Tasty Rainbow's packet, and his secret ingredient—some ground unicorn horn Chet had pilfered from one of El Dorado's monorail depots.

Leaning back onto his fungal footstool the orange and black cheetah-man ignited the volatile mishmash and inhaled deeply of the bubbling Delphian vapors. Incinerated particles of pink smoke and electric ash came alive momentarily, dancing like trained elephants in a circus through the many rungs and rings of a crystalline carnival tent.

Leaning back farther, he spasmed out stampeding clouds of calamitous pink smoke that sent the Herald of Hype into an uncontrollable coughing fit, sputtering out herds of pink plague between hacks and desperate gasps for air. Golgotha smiled some. Recovering from his fit, Chet turned towards Golgotha and asked, "How's that monkey-man's mission going?" as he began to cough some more.

"Huh?"

That was rare for Golgotha to forget anything; Chet assumed he must not have heard him and clarified between coughs, "The whole Albus, Low Place, kill that kid, save the world thing?"

"Oh that?!" said Golgotha bursting out into a raucous belly laugh. The mammoth elephant-headed man leaned forward continuing to ruckus, flapping his ears and pounding his trunk into his thigh in loud slaps. Something was clearly very funny; Chet however, was in the dark and begged to be let in on the secret. Golgotha laughed even harder at the fact that he was the only one that knew, his eyes tearing up. He wiped a tear away from his eye with the sensitive, nubby tip of his trunk. Still trying to calm himself, he turned to Chet; his sides about to burst he said, "I made it all up!"

Chet raised his new pair of sharp-edged, quadrahedral sunglasses that Golgotha had gifted him in his most recent redesign. "Yeah." Golgotha explained; he had made the whole thing up, the prophecy, the destroyer, everything. Still somewhat beside himself, he went on to confess that he just needed to get Albus out of the picture for a few, while he seduced (*boned*) Albus' babe of a wife, Elixabeth. *Do my tusks make you horny? Yeah Baby!* It didn't go exactly how he had planned due to a few of Albus' choices, but he still had gotten what he wanted in the end.

"You know what would be really funny?" said Cheshire Cheato devilishly.

"If we go and tell Albus right now?"

"Exactly." Chet smiled; his huge saber-toothed incisors dripped with saliva.

....

Golgotha and Chet got to their feet making their way towards the silver door where Albus had undergone the down low process. Golgotha stopped in front. "Open it." Chet reached out his four-fingered white paw and pushed open the silver door, behind which stood chaos.

Inside the down low room, slews of scribes and myriads of Enoch's underlings were pouring over pages of dense three-ring binders, manuals, and textbooks. From the various terminals and formerly whizzing gizmos of the chamber, many multi-colored wires were sticking out and re-wired into other things. The scene didn't look good for Enoch.

"We'd like to speak with Albus," Golgotha requested nonchalantly leaning against the entryway, as he examined a chip in one of his polish-caked nails. The tall, slender man stepped forward in front of his boss, attempting to obscure the frantic scurrying occurring behind him. He had dreaded this moment, the day this silly side project would pique the despot's desires again. As Enoch raised his hands about to offer an explanation that would stall for more time, an unhelpful lackey with a squeaky voice yelled from the back, "You can't right now!"

Enoch was well aware that the transceiver's connection had been royally borked since day one; he had been pushing his underlings around the clock since looking for a fix, a solution to the bug. He had desperately hoped they'd have it all resolved before Golgotha came calling again; they didn't.

"Walk with me, Enoch," said Golgotha, raising a heavy arm, holding it aloft intending to rest it around the magus' thin shoulders. Enoch slinked away, ducking underneath the looming arm. "Uh uh, not so fast." In a difficult to mentally imagine maneuver, Golgotha walked backwards through himself, his outstretched arm still coming to rest on the fleeing Enoch's avoidant shoulder. He walked his loyal servant towards the back of the poorly-lit down low room, pushing him up against a few of the cylinder-lined machines along the curving walls.

Towering over Enoch, the bestial tyrant violently thrashed his elephantine head, his prodigious ivory tusks impaling and skewering the man, mercilessly goring the magus for his failure. As the jackhammering tusks pierced through Enoch, fiery sparks and shards of glass exploded into the air from the machines directly behind him. He shrieked in pain, howling for it to stop; his underlings ignored the incident, pretending to have never met the man before. Golgotha continued to pulverize the poor magus till there was nothing left but a thin mist of blood in the air; a liquefied puddle of guts pooled on the floor, running down a drain-hole situated beneath the green dental chair.

Carelessly turning away from the gruesome scene, Golgotha stretched out an arm towards Chet. The cheetah-man, anticipating this outcome, had a clean cloth at the ready for his boss to wipe down his blood-stained, soiled face. Golgotha swatted the cloth away, instead grasping for the foiled bag of Cheese-Os in Chet's other paw. Popping a few into his mouth, he turned towards Enoch's second in command, Lamech. "You're in charge until Enoch recovers." Addressing the rest of the room, Golgotha commanded, "And get this goddamn thing working!" Informing his lackeys to notify him immediately upon completion, he exited the down low room with his cheetah valet in tow.

32

BIRTH

Albus awoke from his blackout, his mouth achingly dry and head spinning; he was still a bit drunk from his wanton overindulgence of Gellert's formidable spirits. The sagging flaps of the off-white pup-tent were damper than usual; it had stormed, but just barely. He reckoned it must have been a windy one at best; the floating apricot craft had washed up on the shore of a sandy, nondescript coastline. In his absence, the speeder's ventral floats had lost some of their air pressure, losing a bit of buoyancy as the rocking craft was bullied up the shore by the ceaseless tyranny of the waves.

Groggily, he poked at a few dials on the hovercraft's dashboard, relieved to see that the emergency solar-array had done its job, fully recharging the battery while he had snored off his drunken stupor. As he broke down the pup-tent, unhooking the pliable plastic rods that kept the covering tethered around the open-cockpit, Albus startled momentarily by what he witnessed, thinking he must have been far more intoxicated still, than he had first assumed. Past several rolling dunes rising up away from the coastline was what he first mistook for a solid obsidian horizon.

The grotesque, bulging perimeter of the Cancer loomed not

far in the distance. This was the closest Albus had been to the jet-black megastructure since arriving in the Low Place in what felt like eons ago. As he was about to engage the speeder's thrusters and begin his return voyage to New Detroit, he paused. Delilah would probably be worried about him by now; he wasn't sure exactly how long he had been gone. However, he found himself unable to resist; call it foolishness, call it morbid curiosity, but for whatever reason Albus removed his finger from the speeder's ignition and hopped over the side into the surf. Donning a gas mask and a protective overcoat, he had to get a closer look, to see it for what it really was.

He trudged up the wind-torn dunes, the scorching sand ineffectively ripping at his body sheathed in protective clothing. He came to a stop some twenty-yards out, gazing at the black mass like a man staring out from behind a mirror. Deep down he knew how it all worked; his deathless paradise running indefinitely on the out-of-control, ever-wanting, dark substrata of it all. The only real currencies left were time and space.

Impossibly, a glimmer of gold caught his eye. Peeking preposterously through the grains of white-hot sand, a fourteen-karat wedding band glinted meekly in the sunlight. Exhaling heavily through his mask's respirator, he bent down and plucked it from the sand, feeling sickened by the reappearance of something he was quite certain by this point had only ever existed in the hallucinatory prose of a slowly dying mind, the amaranthine requiem of cherub-like beings and metamorphic blobs. Turning the band over in his hand, the inscription on its interior read, "Albus and Elixabeth Forever." Albus scoffed. Against his better judgment, he chucked the worthless ring as hard as he could at *that beast*.

The ring landed with an audible suck into the layer of viscous gloop oozing from the Cancer's exterior. He watched with some detached enjoyment as the powerless golden band began to sink into the goopy epidermis of the calculating monstrosity, a wooly mammoth that had just taken a critical misstep into a bubbling tar pit, the intense heat causing the wedding band to deform.

Satisfied with his act of juvenile defiance, he turned away.

Shuffling back down the dunes to head home, he unexpectedly heard an unfamiliar voice emanate from inside his head.

"...I think it's working now, your Grace," said Lamech. Albus jolted in surprise, turning and glancing all around, up to the sky, searching for the source of the voice, when he began to witness a deluge of images rapidly flickering through his mind's eye, like a flipbook revving up. *Fuck. The transceiver!* The images started with scenes of him awakening on this very dune, progressing to his first meeting of Delilah. Now he was killing Trudy. Now they were heading down the beach together about to set off for New Detroit for the first time.

Golgotha's minions, managing to repair the connection with Albus' brain, had begun transmitting his memories, downloading his adventures in the Low Place, back to their despotic deity. *Fuck, fuck, fuck,* thought Albus. He couldn't let them find New Detroit, or Delilah, or maybe even more importantly what she planned to do with her airship. He sprinted down the dunes as fast as Joshua's expertly-engineered legs could carry him, kicking up swirling specters of sand behind him.

As the scene of him and Delilah cruising along over the open ocean, flying fish leaping about in the background, played on in his mind, Albus leapt for the speeder, still a good couple of feet from the vehicle. His left foot snagged on one of the sides, sending him sprawling out into the open cockpit. Desperately, he grasped about for the only thing he could think of, one of the emptied jugs of Gellert's moonshine. His hands fumbling beneath the backseat, Albus grabbed hold of one of the hardened clay containers and began mercilessly beating it against his right temple. *Stop hitting yourself. Stop hitting yourself.*

As he bludgeoned the bottle against the side of his head, intending to intentionally concuss himself, he heard a *tap tap tap* echo throughout the cavern of his cranium, bouncing loudly off the interior walls of his skull; followed by Golgotha's booming voice. "This thing on!?" The scene of Albus and Delilah weaving through the wreckage, approaching New Detroit's shell-fragment and pebble-strewn beach began to play.

"Albus! How the *hell* are you? Been awhile—" he heard Golgotha say, as he madly hammered the brown jug as hard as he could against his head; twinkling rainbow-hued blooms of stars and violet comets exploded into being at the edges of his vision. Shattering into one thousand six hundred and eighteen pieces, the jug broke apart against his temple, cutting Golgotha off, halting the transmission in one final blow. The voices and images stopped; for now, at least, Delilah's secret was safe.

It wasn't all copesetic though, he was pretty sure they had seen the location of New Detroit. As he rubbed the side of his bruised and battered skull, some droplets of blood forming from a gash in his skin, he placed his hand on the side of the speeder to steady himself. Panting some, the stinging waves of pain intensifying as the adrenaline receded from his bloodstream, he glanced back at the Cancer behind him; his mouth went completely dry once more.

The oppressive bulwark bulged, separating at a seam, spreading open like the legs of a pregnant woman. Fissuring vertically, it split with groaning pops, pushing more of its wormy flagellating self forth through the gash, an ouroboros shedding its skin, only to reveal more blackened skin beneath. Laboring to push trunks of its dark line forward, the mammoth megastructure lumbered, transmuting the silicon-rich sand into processing power as it sluggishly lurched forth.

....

Coming to his senses, Albus hurtled over the pilot-side of the speeder; he fled from the ensuing black mass, throttling the hovercraft's engines to maximum overdrive, threatening to burn out the vehicle's turbines. The thrusters whined and protested under their overseers taxing demands as opposing Aeolian forces and sea-spray whipped at Albus' unprotected face. If the engines blew, he would be stranded at sea, a sitting duck, easy prey for the gluttonous Cancer's consummate consumption. He didn't care; he had to warn his family of the impending doom.

Like an arrow unleashed from Artemis' divine quiver, Albus careened the speeder towards New Detroit. He blasted up the beachhead nearly crashing the skidding vehicle into the outcropping. Leaping over the side, turbines still running, he bounded up the rocks and exposed roots of the protective cliff as though they weren't there. He sprinted towards the mess.

Albus burst through the door. "It's coming!" he shouted. He was too late; something was already here—almost.

Crowded in a semi-circle around Delilah, stood Dee, Mrs. Ham, and the automata that identified as female. They were taking it in turn to coach Delilah, cooing at her to take deep breaths. Mrs. Ham wrapped her soft, plump hand tightly around Delilah's increasingly damp palm, wiping sweat from the young woman's brow as Delilah exhaled and cursed loudly.

Delilah had gone into labor in Joshua's absence: like it or not, the baby was coming. Its timing was a few weeks early, though not early enough for cause of major concern. Abram, Mr. Ham, and the rest of the automata had been excommunicated, banished to wait outside, forbidden from entering the mess until further notice.

....

Laying eyes on the man that had put her in this position waltz through the door, Delilah commanded Joshua to her side. She grabbed hold of his hand and squeezed with the force of a thousand suns. Delilah was adamantly opposed to becoming an unwed, single mother, a terrible sin the nuns had impressed upon her as being tantamount to murder. "Marry me," she demanded of the man whose finger bones she was compressing into tiny diamonds.

"What?"

"You heard me," she bawled between pangs of pain, "Marry me. Now!"

"I…I don't have a ring," Joshua stammered. Delilah pierced her beau with swords. Joshua had been intending to marry Delilah for some time, but had never managed to find the right moment. Knowing better than to cross her further, he bent to one knee and asked the woman he loved, now more than ever, if she would be his wife.

Dee, witness to the whole exchange, mimed a barf. Mrs. Ham fetched Colonel Mustard from outside, whose military rank vested him with the power to perform the rites of matrimony. In between Delilah's contractions and bouts of expletives, the mechanical man guided the couple through their impromptu vows. The Colonel affirmed that they forsook all others; there weren't many others so that was an easy one. They promised to care for each other in sickness and in health; Joshua had never been sick so that seemed like another no brainer. Delilah's free hand, not currently pulverizing Joshua's finger bones to dust, twirled through the air, attempting to speed Colonel Mustard along.

"Do you take this woman to be your lawfully wedded wife?"

"I do."

"It's crowning!" shouted Mrs. Ham.

Delilah glowered at the Colonel imploring him to expedite his rambling as the baby's mushy head, then right shoulder entered the world. The semi-intelligent creature, not quite grasping the need for such a rush, craned his ceramic polymer skull towards Delilah who was propped on one of the mess hall's long tables with her legs straddled between two leather straps. Looking upon her with his vermilion eyes, he droned through his speaker box, "And do you, Delilah E. Fedora, take this man to be your lawfully wedded husband?"

"I do," rasped Delilah through gritted teeth. The worst was over.

"It's a girl!" shouted Mrs. Ham, holding the crying, perfect, pinkish little girl up to the light for all to see. Mrs. Ham snipped the umbilical cord, formally welcoming the newborn into their broken world; she gently placed the infant to Delilah's breast to get to know her mother better. As the baby girl began to suckle a sublime sphere of silence temporarily ensconced those in the hall; there was no need for words.

Dee approached her infant niece with a sense of responsibility she had never felt before. Its pinkish skin already beginning to darken some, gently she placed the tips of her fingers on the babes back; it was alive alright. Mrs. Ham beamed, holding her clasped hands up to her chest as tears rolled from her eyes. To her knowledge, a child had not been born alive and healthy to their world since that *thing* had ended it.

The six female automata stood motionless, scanning the scene with their ocular-orbs dimmed to half capacity, so as to not theoretically startle the newborn spawn. While their leader, the Colonel, his matrimonial duties completed, shuffled himself into a corner and extinguished his eyes.

Delilah cupped her infant daughter to her chest with an overwhelming sense of relief and peace, as their hearts began a dialogue that would last for the rest of their lives.

Joshua, though an integral part of the story, was still an outsider in some sense, his body remaining physically unchanged by the ordeal; which in no way staved off the sundering upheaval of his being, his entire world.

The hubris of his half measure, his foolhardy, selfish plan, his half-baked compromise to greedily grasp the best of both worlds, had laughably failed. Even if he and Delilah had grown old and died together, recusing him from being forced to murder the woman he loved, while still lovingly preserving his world— his world, would still one day end this one.

Albus stared deeply into his newborn daughter's whole, innocent eyes. As he continued to fall into the babe's infinite orbs, his mission, his purpose, his dharma for incarnating in the Low Place stood resolutely before him: Kill the destroyer. Save his world. He asked that the others leave the mess hall as he turned towards his wife. Dee and Mrs. Ham exchanged a troubled glance as they exited.

....

The mess emptied, "It's coming," Albus said again. "The Cancer." The fierce mother did not shrink or shudder at the revelation; part of her had always known this day might come. Albus explained to Delilah what he had witnessed. The Cancer was on the move again and it was coming for them; lumbering along at its current pace he wasn't sure how long they had, a couple of weeks, maybe a month or two at best. That was some small silver lining to the otherwise apocalyptic news; they at least had a window of opportunity, a chance to strike.

Delilah wasted no time; wrapping her infant babe in swaddling cloth, suspending her snuggly in a mesh-shawl slung from her shoulder around her waist, the warrior woman retrieved a myriad of charts and notebooks from her dormitory. Spreading them out across the long tables of the mess, she looked them over with Joshua.

Inheriting the mathematical gifts of her father, Delilah began scrawling scads of figures across blue-gridded graph paper while meticulously examining unfurled maps that had been largely scribbled over, blackened out with dark magic-marker. As she crunched the numbers, she began to hang her head, propping it with her hand.

"Shit."

"What is it?"

"We don't have enough."

There wasn't enough helium sequestered, Delilah explained, to make it over the origin of the Cancer, the only place the Adam bomb could be effectively utilized. Their dirigible, the X-Caliber, would begin losing buoyancy many miles before the drop zone, fizzling in a death-spiral to the devilish surface of the ravenous tumor. It was a wash. Their only hope for survival was to flee their island paradise; they would have to make a run for it, settle somewhere on another uninhabited island. Delilah stood, preparing to alert the others.

"We'll just go get more," said Albus.

"There isn't enough time."

Albus felt a chilly tapping on his right shoulder that sent shivers down his spine, a mechanical hiss whistling behind him. He turned, coming eye to eye with the blood-red orbs of Colonel Mustard. The mechanical man perched in the corner of the mess had been silently observing Joshua and Delilah's exchange.

Mustard drawled, "Perhaps, me and my kin can be of assistance." Albus and Delilah looked at one another, their pupils widening in realization. "Use our hearts," the Colonel solemnly offered, his eyes dimming some.

"You can't," countered Delilah. "It will kill you." The new mother had become quite fond of the automata over the last several months, considering them just as much a part of her family as the others; she had already factored Mustard and his clan into her headcount as she was formulating their evacuation plan.

"It won't be no bother," said the Colonel. "We have completed our mission." The automaton's southern accent had improved considerably, even his speech cadence had become more natural. Hesitating slightly Mustard added, "We have learned what it means to be human."

Albus was taken aback. In all the time he had spent thinking, philosophizing, pondering, pontificating—in all his unlimited time—he had never been able to adequately arrive at a conclusion to that quandary.

"And what is that then, exactly, the meaning of being human?"

"Sacrifice," replied the Colonel.

Shivers ran down Albus' spine once more. Delilah continued to push back against Mustard's suicidal offer. When the mechanical man resisted, insisting that he would remove his own heart and throw it down on the table if she wouldn't, Delilah acknowledged the fearless gift and consented.

....

The others caught wind that something was amiss as the automata dropped what they were doing and began marching towards the mess hall in lockstep. Mr. Ham poked his head through the doorway attempting to gather some intel. "Everything alright in here?" he asked. Delilah assured him that the baby was perfectly fine.

"Go let Mrs. Ham know as much," she implored, promising to provide answers just as soon as they could. She urged that Mr. Ham and everyone else should go about their business for the time being.

With measured gravitas the Colonel informed his compatriots that they would need a number of them, including himself, to give their lives, making it crystal-clear that their participation was voluntary. No one would think less of them for objecting. One by one they each stepped forward. Unanimously, all eleven elected to sacrifice their lives for the cause. They wouldn't take "No" for an answer, adamantly insisting that any additional helium would be needed for the X-Caliber's return journey. With a heavy-heart Delilah gathered the tools necessary to extract the selfless simulacra's hearts in the most respectful and humane way possible. The Colonel, in a show of quintessential courage, volunteered himself to go first.

As Colonel Mustard lay across the table, awaiting his turn to meet his maker with zealous bravery, the infant babe hanging from Delilah's papoose began to cry. The Colonel, turning his head towards the newborn, blinked his red eyes in a wild array of color palettes neither Albus nor Delilah had ever witnessed. The impenetrable pattern soothed the infant back to a state of quiet tranquility. Delilah leaned over a tray, readying the instruments to put the Colonel under. The mechanical man craned his cranium towards Joshua who was standing over him, grasping his chilly hand.

"What's her name?" asked the Colonel.

An intense flush of embarrassment came over Albus; it dawned on him he had never discussed with Delilah what the child's name should be. He had just always assumed the obvious; should the child had been born a boy, *Gellert, no question,* and if it was a girl, *obviously Delilah Jr.*

"Hope," said Delilah plainly, rescuing her husband from a potentially awkward moment. She turned from the tray back to the table with a long needle in her hand.

"For Hope," said the Colonel.

Delilah nodded. Inserting the needle into a port on the Colonel's acrylic tubing, the mechanical man's glowing red eyes dimmed to dark-gray orbs one final time. Delilah tried to remain composed as she performed the sacred task, fighting back the tears welling in her large brown eyes. Joshua lost his battle almost immediately, practically blubbering as he held tightly onto the inanimate objects hand. The rest of the eleven automata patiently waited, showing no sign of fear or regret; each gently touched the newborn baby's soft head as they laid down their lives on the improvised operating table. The somber deed completed, they now possessed enough of the precious gas for their buoyant, world-saving mission.

....

The time had come to break the bleak news to the others; gathering them in the mess, Delilah and Joshua calmly informed the rest of New Detroit's citizens of the dire situation. Delilah, nursing Hope at her breast, reassured them though, they had a plan. If anyone felt panicked by the news of the Cancer's spread, they certainly didn't show it; remaining stoic, they all implored, wanting to know how they could be of aid. Delilah took charge, instructing Mr. Ham to first dig graves for the valiant automata; lay their bodies to rest in their cemetery plot hidden within the jungle. "Start by placing Colonel Mustard next to my father."

Momentarily leaving Hope safely in the arms of Mrs. Ham, Delilah piloted her creamsicle-colored speeder from the eastern edge of the island across the surface of the glittering lagoon heading towards her secret alcove obscured behind the waterfall. Securing a thick steel-cable from her hovercraft's winch to the vessel's bow, she revved the engines and yanked the X-Caliber from its berth, tugging the ship out from its cavernous concealment.

The ship protested some at first as it lurched forward with a creak, stumbling off of its support beams making a loud crash against the floor of the cavern drowned out by the sound of the roaring water; Delilah pushed one of the speeder's many levers forward, funneling more juice to the turbines. She was unconcerned with any potential damage to the integrity of the sailboat's hull, it wouldn't matter much once they had inflated its helium bladders and were airborne.

As the bow crowned through the falls, rushing water battered and splashed off the airship's wobbling deck, christening the X-Caliber. For the first time, the light of day caressed the weapon, muted by the matte-gray hull slathered in several generous coatings of radar-absorbing paint.

The craft's hull bobbled across the surface of the lagoon; the steel cable attaching it to Delilah's speeder pulled taut as she towed the vessel behind, its deflated air sacks a crumpled and slightly damp mess bunched on the deck. She tugged it up onto the lagoon's beach closest to the embankment leading down from the settlement.

Standing at the head of the steep incline overlooking the lagoon, Dee watched the odd-looking, retrofitted sailboat waddle up on shore behind the speeder, somewhat dumbfounded that her sister had kept such a massive secret from her. She had thought Delilah confided everything in her. Choosing to act like the mature auntie she now was, she let the issue go without harassing her older sister about the betrayal.

. . . .

The new mother summoned Dee, Joshua, and Abram over to the beached airship. First ensuring she had released the anchor into the sand and tossed the long rope ladder over the side of its hull, Delilah directed them in utilizing the pressurized hearts to begin inflating the craft's air-bladders with the sacrosanct gas. Perched from atop the edge of the plateau, Mrs. Ham watched, gently rocking and soothing newborn Hope in her arms.

Like the growing belly of a pregnant woman, slowly the airship's baggy bladders swelled, beginning to crinkle some at their seams under the pressure. Delilah sighed with relief as the vessel began to levitate, the lighter-than-air sacks lifting the hull of the craft off of the sand. She had faith in her calculations, but up to this point it had all remained purely theoretical.

The X-Caliber confidently floated into the air, hanging over the lagoon shimmering in the noonday sun, a triumphant parade float proclaiming that they would not go quietly into the dark. The buoyant vessel continued its upward climb until the thickly coiled chain attached to its anchor grew taut and strained under the tension, preventing the craft from floating away into the stratosphere. The bottom rung of the rope ladder dragged in the damp sand, leaving sidewinding trails in its place. Albus, a look of earnest determination on his face, marched over to the swaying ladder preparing to ascend. He turned to Delilah and said, "Okay how do I pilot this thing?"

"What do you mean? We're doing this together," she replied matter-of-factly.

Another flawed assumption on Albus' part. He had been certain that this mission was his burden and his alone to bear, to stop the destroyer and save his world. He knew there was a slim chance he wouldn't return; there was absolutely no way he would allow the love of his life, the mother of his newborn daughter, to take such a risk.

He pulled his newlywed to the side and put his foot down. Delilah stomped on his toes. It was Delilah's mission just as much as Albus'. She was the X-Caliber's captain and knew how to operate it better than anyone. More pragmatically though, it was a two-person job. That was the unfortunate reality of it.

Delilah explained that she had built the X-Caliber intentionally devoid of any thrusters, motors, or engines. It was far too great a risk to generate a noticeable heat signature coming from a "Cloud." The shrouded craft was intended to be sailed through the skies pushed forward by two aft-mounted airplane propellers. The propellers were spun manually by pedaling a stationary exercise bike that she had retrofitted with, (what was in her opinion), an ingenious gearbox that greatly amplified the force output by its rider.

Such a means of propulsion created an obvious short-coming though. Assuming their cloudy disguise was convincing enough and they weren't immediately skewered out of the sky, the airship would have to be continuously pedaled around the clock to reach the Cancer's epicenter in time, which was still a fortnights ride from the tumorous mass' perimeter. Should anyone stop cycling for any reason, they risked being blown hundreds of miles off course like a helpless balloon, carried away by uncooperative winds. Not even a man of Joshua's herculean fortitude could so demandingly exert himself day and night without rest for several weeks straight. They would have to take it in shifts to manually power the craft. They both had to go.

"You can't. Hope needs you," said Albus, unsure why he had begun to weep. Albus pulled his wife in, hugging her into his body and whispered into her ear, "I can't lose you."

"It's not up to me, my love. I don't have a choice."

"You always have a choice."

"Then I choose this."

Albus wracked his brain, there had to be another way, a way out of this predicament. He looked over towards Dee and Abram, the young paramours frolicking in the shallows of the lagoon underneath the shadow cast by the X-Caliber as it floated in front of the sun, even in the face of annihilation they still had each other. Abram snatched a starfish out of the lagoon and chased after Dee with it. Abram was only a boy. He looked up the embankment spotting the worrisome Mrs. Ham with a mother's look on her face overseeing the scene below, still rocking the newborn in her arms. Mr. Ham approached from behind her, a dirt-stained shovel slung over his shoulder, coughing and heinously wheezing from his efforts in burying the deceased automata.

"I can do it. I'm strong enough to do it alone," said Joshua.

"Then we'll all die," replied his wife.

Albus hung his head; his fearless, brilliant, gorgeous partner was right. It would take them both to kill the destroyer.

....

Delilah gathered her clan around the base of the awaiting dirigible, holding Hope tightly against her chest. She reassured the others that herself and Joshua would be back in a few weeks' time after they bombed that wretched Cancer to kingdom come; she effortlessly laughed with a wink. Mrs. Ham insisted they pray over their mission; they joined hands, asking the Lord to watch over Delilah and Joshua. Bring them home safe and sound she implored.

Delilah the Elder pulled Delilah the Middle aside. If they saw the black mass approaching over the horizon they needed to run, get everyone into her speeder and papa's submersible; make for another island as far away and fast as they could, Delilah told her younger sister. "And if I don't make it back, take care of Hope for me."

"Don't say that!" Dee whimpered as she began to sob, hugging her older sister in tight, her best friend, while wiping runny snot dripping from her nose. Delilah embraced her, pointing to the colorful friendship bracelet Dee had gifted her; the braided band was still tightly secured around her wrist, its ends beginning to fray some with wear. Dee wiped her eyes with the back of her palms and nodded; she was stronger than even she knew. The sisters released their grasp on one another.

Delilah the Middle ran up to Joshua wrapping her arms around the big, red-headed galoot's waist. Startled by the first, she let go before Albus could return the hug. "I'll see you again soon."

Delilah and Albus held their wonderful creation, their infant daughter cradled between the two of them. Some pangs of sadness clutched at Albus' wide chest as he contemplated. Should things not go according to plan, should he not make it back, Hope wouldn't even remember his face. As if reading his mind, his infant daughter's aimlessly circling arms reached out, a little clenched baby fist crash-landed onto his mouth; Hope pressed a tiny finger across his lips, silencing him. Albus pressed his nose gently on the top of his newborn's head, inhaling deeply, making a memory.

Delilah kissed Hope's fat cheeks as much as she possibly could, bouncing the babe in her arms, tears understandably rolling down her cheeks. An impulse magnetically drew her into the child, unable to ever let go. Hypnotized, she found herself about to turn to Joshua, telling him to go on without her. She knew such a decision would only destroy the thing she loved more than love itself; she had faith that they would see their daughter again. Agonizingly, she draped Hope into Dee's strong but spindly arms, shredding her heart in two as she did.

Joshua and Delilah climbed the rungs of the swaying rope ladder upwards towards their destiny, rucksacks protruding with rolled maps and nautical charts slung across their back. They would be navigating using the stars, just like the ancient mariners had. When she glanced back at her husband coming up the ladder behind her, she caught sight of two oblong metallic objects slung across his shoulders with leather straps; he was lugging along the jetpacks. *I just don't know what I'm gonna do with that man.* Delilah scowled.

"What!? Just in case," said Joshua.

Stashing the jetpacks out of the way under some canvas flaps, Albus went to winch up the anchor, its heavy chain rattling as he turned a crank hoisting the iron weight off the ground. Delilah instructed her husband to finish rigging-up the airship. He shuffled around the deck tying and untying many sailors' knots, slinging ropes into place, while Delilah did a quick test of the X-Caliber's camouflage system. The orchestra of pipes, pumps, and metallic nozzles steamed with the sibilant din of innovation; the system appeared to be working swimmingly.

They rigged some more ropes into their pulleys, winding the lengthy cords around hand-cranked spindles used for steering the airship as Delilah gave her husband a crash-course in piloting. Whoever was at the helm would sit in a narrow cockpit situated some feet in front of the stationary bike, cranking ropes, pulling flaps up-and-down, left-or-right to direct the airship's movements through the sky. Thankfully, piloting the craft didn't require the same around-the-clock effort as powering it did; one could plot a course and rig the ropes in place for a while without readjustment, perhaps catching some shut-eye in the interim.

Mustering on deck for the maiden voyage of the levitating X-Caliber, Albus (or was he Joshua?) and Delilah leaned over the sides waving to the others gathered on the ground beneath, blowing kisses, shouting that they would see them again real soon.

Delilah leaned against the saddle of the vessel's bicycle-powered dynamo poised to take the first shift, as Albus made his way towards the piloting cockpit, stopping he turned towards his wife, hesitating. He wasn't sure if now was the best time and place to bring it up. Lambasting himself, he had castled behind that same defense so many other times he had wanted to come clean about his true identity, about where he was really from. This might be his last chance to absolve himself; he could no longer shirk in the shadows in fear of Delilah's reprisal over his veiled betrayal. If he didn't make it back, he figured it didn't matter all that much. And if he did make it back, well then he'd have to deal with the fallout like an adult.

"There's something I need to tell you," he said, taking a deep breath, staring into his wife's trusting brown eyes. His last chance to turn back; he didn't know how to say it so he just said it. "Delilah...It's...Look. I'm not exactly from *here*. My name's not Joshua. It's really—"

Delilah approached her husband, placing her index finger across the man's stammering lips before he could say anymore. "I know," she said, silencing him. "And I don't care." A rockslide of shame and guilt tumbled from Albus' shoulders as his tensed muscles relaxed, free of their heavy burden. He was momentarily stunned, unaccustomed to the undeserved grace of such a forgiving person, a person that was truly his partner.

Albus tried to mumble something; gently, she only pressed her finger harder into his chapped lips, quieting him further. It didn't matter to Delilah where someone was from, what their name was, or what empty words they said; all that mattered to her was their actions, their choices. "And I couldn't care less what your name is. It could be Lord Voldemort for all I care."

Albus chuckled. Delilah laughed; together they broke out in snorts. He leaned in for a kiss. Delilah only pushed him away lightly laughing some more as she mounted the frame of the red stationary bike and began to pedal. The X-Caliber scooted forward.

....

They planned to first sail the airship to the temple's peninsula, where the Adam bomb rested still safely cached in its ark. Delilah figured they would need to pedal for three days straight to reach their first pit-stop, getting a feel for their wings in the process. As agreed, they would take shifts, cycling for a twelve-hour period while the other piloted, ate, or slept. In a pinch, whoever was cycling could also steer the airship by grabbing hold of the reins from the cockpit. Delilah demonstrated briefly; though it was a less than ideal situation, the strenuous demand of powering the craft further compounded by yanking and pulling on the thick ropes.

They arrived at the temple on the morning of the third day, slightly earlier than Delilah had estimated, a fortuitous tail-wind speeding their progress. The rays of the rising sun illuminated the dome precariously balancing atop the half-ruined edifice, the site of the Easter gathering that felt like another lifetime ago. Maneuvering the airship into position nearest to the cellar doors, Albus pushed on a lever intending to release the anchor. Befuddled by the absence of the recognizable metallic rattle of an iron chain whirring off its winch, he glanced over the side of the hull, the anchor still held tight in place. *The winch must have jammed, not the end of the world.* Albus informed Delilah as much and made his way below deck to investigate the problem. As he tugged and strained at a mess of ornery links that had become entangled with one another, preventing the anchor's descent, he heard a familiar jingle behind him. *Oh crap.*

Albus reappeared from below deck, walking over to his partner, a fidgeting stowaway wriggling in his arms. Delilah was just as surprised to see Fin as Albus had been. "This is a problem," she said. The troublesome fennec fox was a loose variable, an unaccounted-for parameter in her plan. Packed aboard the ship they had barely just enough water and rations stowed for themselves to make it to the origin and back. Having a hungry fox onboard their voyage wasn't an option. They couldn't risk an inopportune barking fit, or worse; the slimmest possibility of which could alert the adversary to their presence.

Delilah looked down at the white, cottony puff-ball of a

fox; his stupidly cute ears flopping as he played around her feet, gently nipping at her ankles. "We have to leave him behind," she said. "Release him back into the wild." Albus agreed. It saddened him some, but he knew she was right; they had no other option.

The X-Caliber now anchored in place, they climbed down the rope ladder, Fin secured in a sack slung across Albus' back. Walking to a location some hundred yards from the temple, they set the confused fennec fox down amongst a thicket of trees and vines that had begun reclaiming piles of rubble and rebar. Crouching over Fin, hating to say goodbye, Delilah and Albus did their best to incomprehensibly explain to the little guy that this was his new home now. It didn't help that Fin was staring back up with them with his cherubic onyx eyes, a look that passed for bewilderment on his fox face.

They turned to head back towards the temple; Fin chased after. Albus turned and shouted, trying to shoo the fennec fox off, some pangs of his treatment over Genji gnawing at him. As he attempted to get Fin to flee, he heard someone speak, coming from amongst the thicket. "Is this the Fin?" asked a kindly and familiar voice. An elderly man with a long white beard emerged from the stand. Chuck Diggity was on vacation and had been lounging not far off in a hammock strung between two palms when he had heard Delilah and Albus approaching with Fin.

Delighted to see an old friend, the three embraced and explained to Dr. Diggity the situation at hand. "Well, why don't I take the little critter," Chuck offered. Relieved, Delilah and Albus thanked Chuck, gladly leaving Fin under his watchful wardenship. They made their way back to the temple's cellar doors. With some assistance from Dr. Diggity, they retrieved the ark from the building's sub-basement, hoisting up the Adam bomb with a number of ropes and pulleys between the bomb-bay doors built into the X-Caliber's belly, securely harboring the world-ending weapon within. The easy leg of their journey completed, saying their goodbyes to Fin and Chuck one last time, they boarded their flying warship and set their sights on the origin.

They sailed on from the temple pedaling for close to another day's time, the tenebrous precipice of the malignant beast glowering and growing always larger in the distance. Now only some few miles out, Delilah reasoned it was time to put her theory to the real test. Flipping some toggles, she crossed her fingers as the multitude of metallic emitters she had painstakingly installed across the craft's hull began to hiss, once again concealing the X-Caliber in a halcyon mist. They both held their breath as the dirigible creaked across the border of the Cancer, some several thousand feet beneath them. No lacerating tentacles racing for them; no booming voice or exploding heads, at least not yet.

33

MISSION

Albus and Delilah took it in turn, pushing the X-Caliber onward—sheathed in a very convincing cloud. The unchanging days and nights began to blur together as they monotonously pedaled non-stop through the chilly, oxygen-depleted atmosphere. Delilah's ingenious intuitions had proven correct; the marvel of her artificial cloud kept them safely concealed from the probing purview of the ever-watchful Cancer below. They didn't speak much to one another, reserving their energy for the task at hand; not that there was much to talk about anyway.

Growing ambient light lifted the dark dome of the night sky, shifting its hues to a lighter gradient of midnight blue as the sun slowly crept up behind them. Delilah neared the eleventh hour of a twelve-hour cycling shift, glancing at the hash-marks she had scratched into the red paint of the stationary bike's handlebars, they had entered day seventeen of their journey. The lumbering tentacles of the pillaging Cancer would lurch into view off the coast of New Detroit any day now. Delilah pedaled harder. Thanks be to God, the finish line of their pilgrimage was nearly in sight; according to her various maps and charts, by her estimations, they were only another seven hours from the drop-site, the Cancer's origin.

Her tired thighs ached as she strenuously pushed her blistered feet against the stirrups, turning the crank, powering their propellers. Discomfort blabbered from her left ankle as she pressed; she had sprained it a day or two prior while making an unintentionally awkward dismount from the dynamo's saddle. She had kept the injury to herself, choosing instead to work through the pain. They were so close, then it would all be over.

Albus, napping in the bow, caught some fitful shuteye before his next shift. Rousing from his groggy siesta, he offered his partner a meager smile; she didn't see it. Delilah stared at the horizon as if in a trance, cycling furiously.

Preparing for his shift, he made his way below deck to the head, relieving himself into a device that filtered their waste into drinking water, stretching their thin supplies. As he whizzed inside the vessel's head, it was at that moment that their fortuitous winds, which had blown mostly in their favor, shifted, turning against them to blow in the other camp's direction. An unexpected cross-gust hammered the X-Caliber off its port side, causing the light craft to bobble to and fro. Albus banged his head against the head of the head as he was involuntarily jolted into the air from the turbulence. A *snap crackle pop* faintly echoed around inside Albus' head. Ignoring the interference, he raced above deck to check on his wife.

Outside his head, they both heard an unusual pop followed by a stuttering crackle. Embedded somewhere towards the bow of the airship's hull, a handful of the metallic nozzles responsible for producing their cloudy facade began to sputter and malfunction. The glitch immediately caught both their attention; sharing a worried glance, Delilah kept cycling as she motioned for Joshua to go fix it, find the source of the malfunction, repair it, do something!

He hooked his feet into the railing of the airship, dangling his body over the side; he reached for the dying nozzles. A troubling sliver of the X-Caliber's bow started to marginally protrude from beneath its vaporous camouflage. Albus twisted and torqued the misbehaving emitters with a wrench, resorting to banging against them with his clenched fists, occasionally glancing down towards the endless, nightmarish plateau of the Cancer a few thousand feet beneath them as he worked.

A couple of the nozzles sprang back to life; however, it was just the start of their troubles. More clusters of the cloud-emitters disastrously began to fizzle and fail on the vessel's starboard side. Albus hauled himself back up and dashed over, again hanging precariously over the edge risking life and limb to repair their failing systems. *This can't be happening,* thought Delilah, *We're so close.* She pedaled harder.

Dangling upside-down, their protective camouflage billowing some as more emitters started to peter out, Albus looked down in alarm as the black mass below their airship began to rumble. From its surface, fibrous bundles of stygian muscles retracted, splitting apart like two halves of a monstrous jet-black clam revealing a lightless aperture. An enormous, glistening blue pearl pushed its way into the vacant gash; five smaller blue orbs tore their way through the flesh of the Cancer, ripping, opening in a pentagram around the gargantuan sphere. The watery blue eyes began aggressively rotating, rapidly strafing side-to-side in their sockets, scanning the skies. The Cancer was looking for them. It was a small miracle that it hadn't spotted them already, but it was only a matter of time if their cloud cover continued to falter.

Delilah grabbed hold of the airship's reins while continuing to pedal her heart out; she yanked them hard to the left, veering slightly off course to hug the perimeter of a rolling herd of cumulonimbus heading in their general direction.

....

Back at Golgotha's palace, deep inside the annals of his war room, the imposing elephant-man leaned over a henchman stationed in front of a matte gray console with a rectangular green screen, demanding to know if they had gotten a location on Albus yet.

"Where is he? I will not ask again!!"

The underling shrunk under the weight of the pushy elephant as he submissively tapped the green screen, cringing in fear of his boss's inevitable outrage over the sheer impossibility of what he was about to say.

"It looks like it says…he's somewhere right over us?"

"Not possible!" boomed Golgotha, clutching the expendable flunkey's head with his large palms, bursting his unfortunate skull like a piñata.

Close by, a couple of lackeys lackadaisically leering at a lit circular display of clouds passing overhead were engaged in deep conversation. "That one looks like an octopus," said one and chuckled.

"And that one looks like a boat," said the other laughing.

"That one really kinda looks like a boat."

"Uh boss…we've got kinda like a…strange cloud…overhead."

Golgotha trampled over, toppling several grey terminals and green office chairs aside as he trounced towards the two cloud-struck lackeys. Glancing at the monitors, "Well! Do something about it!" shouted Golgotha, as colorful beads of electricity hotly shot about his veins underneath his pink epidermis.

"You mean, like attack the cloud sir?"

"Yes. Attack the clouds!" his voice quaked.

He jiggled over to another station, forcing a headset and microphone over his boulderish head, jamming his flapping ears between the strained headband, getting on his end of the transceiver that had just been repaired for a second time.

··········

Albus, still dangling dangerously upside-down wrenching on a nozzle as more continued to fail, again heard a voice. Unfortunately, this time it was an all too familiar voice. Golgotha commanded from inside his skull, "Albus, whatever it is…you think…you are doing—don't."

Below them, the scanning blue eyeballs searched the skies more fervently for their partially concealed airship; their cloud cover may have been faltering, but it was still causing enough confusion to throw the enemy off their game. Regardless the glassy peepers were beginning to zero in over their quadrant of the sky, seeking to identify any threat to Golgotha's ascendancy.

Beneath Albus a portion of the churning black mass quickly coalesced into a blistering pimple, bunching up in a mound, like some trillions of ants swarming in lockstep. Without warning the mound surged forth; it stretched into an ichorous tendril whipping through the sky at several hundred miles per hour, causing the air to crackle with false thunder. Albus dropped his wrench in shock. The spurious tentacle jetted past their airship, skewering a neighboring cloud, missing them by only a few hundred yards or less.

Albus took stock of their dire situation; he knew it was only a matter of time before their camouflage completely failed. They were so desperately close. He had one choice left. With resolute determination he hauled himself up, back over the sides of the hull. Throwing off the canvas sheet to his stashed jetpacks, he hoisted one of the personal rockets onto his broad back and began strapping into its leather harness.

Delilah, equally startled by the attacking protuberance, shouted at Albus, "What the hell are you doing?!" Another dark tentacle cracked like a titan's whip some fifty yards off the X-Caliber's port side, straight through another nearby cloud. "Making a choice," Albus shouted back.

Delilah understood perfectly. Albus climbed up to the side of the stationary dynamo where his strong, beautiful, brave wife still hadn't stopped cycling under all this. He leaned in welcomingly kissing her sweaty, delicious face. She whispered into his ear, "I love you." Albus whispered back, "Remember me…after all this."

They were only another three miles from the epicenter, the origin, the monstrosities metaphorical belly button. Albus could only hope to provide a distraction; he would try to buy Delilah enough time to drop the Adam bomb, then rocket back to the safety of the X-Caliber's decks with what little fuel he had left in his jetpack.

Albus Joshua Cake perched on the stern of the X-Caliber, the ship named after a talking gun, not a sword; he whispered a small prayer known only to him and stepped off the side of the boat into empty space, momentarily walking across a cloud as he ignited the rockets of his jetpack.

"Albus, don't do anything you're going to regret. Now just wait a minute. We have Genji here, you don't want to kill Genji now do you?"

Somewhere from the back of his mind he could hear his fox-spirit biting and struggling out of constraints. Barking loudly, Genji shouted, "Give 'em hell, Albus!"

"Red rover, red rover, send Golgotha on over!" Albus roared, launching into the air as he began to rocketeer wildly, his flashy, fiery maneuvers captivating the blue marble seekers. Golgotha, enraged, bashed wildly at consoles, commanding his lackeys to focus all their attention on the rocketing Albus. The formerly placid surface of the dark mass beneath him churned like a storm-tossed sea as more and more of the wormy dark spears formed from the substrate and launched into the air after him.

Pushing his screaming jetpack to its absolute limits, Albus dodged the streaking tentacles of the acrimonious mass by the skin of his teeth as they whizzed past him. As he jetted between two of the javelins he looked hopefully into the distance. For now at least, his diversion was proving successful; the X-Caliber, its hull almost completely exposed now, continued to sail towards the origin.

....

Delilah the Firstborn, Destroyer of Worlds, was nearly spent; she had been powering the craft for close to fifteen hours straight. Her muscles bathed in pools of lactic acid; nearly every last molecule of adenosine triphosphate had been cashed-in as her mitochondria worked overtime to replenish the demand like a Walmart on Black Friday. Only two more miles and it would all be done, unfortunately, her body, along with her ship, was failing. Her muscles, pushed to the absolute zenith of their physical limits, began to mutiny, refusing to respond any further to her impossible demands. The airship began to slow.

Albus, just barely out-maneuvering the increasing barrage

of heaving tendrils, glanced back towards the horizon with concern as he watched the airship falter some. Returning his attention back to his death-defying diversion, he looked down. Mr. Cake's jaw flapped open in awe. Thousands of feet beneath him the mercurial mass had reorganized itself into the undulating likeness of an enormous elephant's head. From its center it hurled its gargantuan trunk through the air at an incredible speed, monstrously grasping for Albus; the end of its ichorous appendage stretching, thinning into a viciously sharp point as it reached for the man.

Time slowed as Albus watched the hateful trunk accelerate unavoidably towards him; in that moment it all made sense, he was overcome with more clarity than the infinitely faceted crystal sitting on the center of Golgotha's head. Looking through the Rose Window one last time, Albus finally understood his entire life: the needle, the sword, the whispered words.

Delilah, her body seizing, thought of the hope of her new-born daughter, of the love between her and her husband, of the indomitable will of her father, of all of the other survivors depending on her, of the entire family of humankind depending on her. In front of her shone the face of her mother and youngest sister, beckoning her onward.

Floating above her physical body, commanding it with divine authority, she pedaled onward. Pushing forward, her muscles ripped apart at their seams like the velveteen rabbit, the cottony stuffing escaping back out into the wild. Depleting the last vestiges of her physical will, she levitated directly over the origin. Albus could hear his cherub-like beings singing mightily in jubilant exaltation as he watched Delilah reach the drop-site. She pulled the lever; the Adam bomb entered freefall.

In that exact moment, the rampaging trunk of the Cancer, its end sharpened into a needle, pierced Albus directly through the heart, skewering him. His jetpack cut out as he coughed up blood. The pointed needle of Golgotha's trunk impaled him from front to back. Mr. Cake was shocked he was not instantly dead at that moment.

Harpooned through the heart by the molten tusk, Albus' body slid further down the spike. The frame rate of his vision slowed dramatically: a flipbook revving down, slowing, coming to an end. *60hz, 24hz, to one hertz*. He watched, laboring his last few breaths as the scene before him became still images.

Click.

The bomb fell.

Click.

A tendril reached for the airship.

Click.

The bomb fell farther.

Click.

Albus exhaled his last breath; Carla the air-bubble waved goodbye to him as they both began to dissolve.

Click.

Darkness.

AFTERMATH, AFTERWARDS... JUST AFTER

Albus Cake sat in his brown leather-bound office chair. His eyes were closed. It was all a dream; he used to read *Word Up!* magazine, Salt-n-Pepa and Heavy D up in the limousine. Certain that he was back on the thousandth story of his monolith, seated behind the ancient desk of his office chambers, he grasped at the worn-out armrests for anchoring, about to part his eyelids. He braced for the inevitable; without a doubt, he would see an overweight pink elephant-man sauntering in his direction. He didn't.

To his surprise, his dog Argus was bounding in his direction, the mutt's floppy brown ears streaking behind him as he ran to welcome his long-lost master home. Albus stood from his chair overjoyed at the unexpected sight; he fell to the ground embracing his loyal companion about the scruff. Argus licked and lapped at his face, coating the man in a generous film of smelly dog slobber. Albus didn't care.

"Hey, boy!" Albus cooed. "Who's da good boy? Who's da dood boy?!"

As he rolled around on the floor playing with Argus, he glanced around at his surroundings; he realized he wasn't in his office at all. He hadn't the vaguest notion of where he was, though it felt whole, like coming home.

When he stood from the ground to get his bearings, he spotted a man in the distance with long shaggy hair and a beard. Albus almost didn't recognize him at first without a bottle in his hands. His father, Jimmy Cake, stood with outstretched arms, open palms turned outwards, awaiting a big hug from his son. Behind Jimmy stood his own father, and his father's father, and his father's father's father, and so on, for all the generations of man. Standing next to his dad was his mom Maria, holding large round needles in her hands knitting a baby blanket some thousands of miles long. Tears of joy streamed down her cheeks at the sight of her son. Behind her stood her mother, and her mother's mother, and all her mothers, for all the generations of woman.

Albus ran to embrace his parents. Glancing upwards he spotted his cherub-like beings flitting about the vaults overhead! Only, they were all grown-up now. They had blossomed into full adult cherubim, six wings, and all! His cherubim sang gloriously, joined by a chorus of sea angels, foxes, and frogs. Dog piling in with his family in a huge hug, he embraced all of humanity, from beginning to end, Argus barking triumphantly and leaping about the pile. Albus couldn't help but weep over the beauty, and the wonder, and the mystery.

All around him he was bathed in comforting light, rolling green hills, their overgrown grasses shushing and rattling in a confident breeze. Brilliant cherry blossom trees shed their pink petals that swirled all around on the sublime wind. Albus snatched hold of a petal and rubbed it between his fingers, tearing it apart, appreciating its supple texture and pleasing aroma; it was real alright, wherever he was.

There was someone still missing though. Albus searched (and this time, not endlessly) for his missing wife. Immediately behind him, he spotted Gellert, a huge grin across his face, his arm clamped across Delilah's shoulders. Delilah smiled at her husband, radiating beams of pure joy. He ran to his wife and scooped her off her feet, twirling her all around. Delilah giggled ecstatically.

Coming out of a spin he spotted someone else he unexpectedly recognized; the Sha-mom from the fishing village was standing next to Gellert. Delilah took Albus' hand and introduced him to her mother, Delilah Earhart Fedora. She cracked a smile, the slight fissure between her front two teeth appearing. Delighted and somewhat shocked, Albus embraced the Sha-mom, his mother-in-law, squeezing tightly. A toddler poked out from the folds of her robes, Delilah Emily Fedora; he tousled her bouncy curls.

Together they looked over the scene below. Dee cradled Hope in her arms. Abram plowed and harvested the fields. Mr. Ham wed Dee and Abram. Dee gave birth to a child of her own, another girl. Mrs. Ham sewed dresses for the girls. More survivors joined them at New Detroit. Mr. Ham died, they buried him alongside the automata. Hope grew up. She met a boy named Abel. Albus and Delilah watched a little while longer.

"We did it, Albus," said Delilah, grabbing hold of her partner.

They clasped hands and together they walked into the Light.

FIN.

Made in the USA
Columbia, SC
16 July 2020

14051554R00202